W9-BXC-354

LIE FOR ME

**Center Point
Large Print**

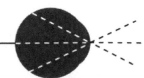

**This Large Print Book carries the
Seal of Approval of N.A.V.H.**

LIE FOR ME

KAREN YOUNG

CENTER POINT PUBLISHING
THORNDIKE, MAINE

The text of this Large Print edition is unabridged.
In other aspects, this book may vary
from the original edition.
Printed in the United States of America
on permanent paper.
Set in 16-point Times New Roman type.

ISBN: 978-1-61173-207-8

Library of Congress Cataloging-in-Publication Data

Young, Karen.
Lie for me / Karen Young.
p. cm.
ISBN 978-1-61173-207-8 (library binding : alk. paper)
1. Truthfulness and falsehood—Fiction. 2. Murder—Investigation—Fiction.
 3. Large type books. I. Title.
PS3575.O7975L54 2011b
813'.54—dc22
                                        2011023934

DE '11

For my family.
You bring me joy. You make me proud.

LIE FOR ME

PART ONE

1

The golden retriever was agitated from the moment Tucker Kane let him out of the company truck, dashing up to the old house and back, whining and carrying on. But as Tucker was busy maneuvering the cart up onto the porch, he didn't pay much attention. Besides, the weather was deteriorating. Intermittent flashes of lightning meant rain any minute. He wanted to be done before it started.

A porch light would have helped. He thought he'd left it on when he dropped off his tools earlier that day, but he'd been intent on making a meeting with a city building inspector at another site, one who hadn't shown up, to his disgust. Had the man forgotten it?

The heavy metal contraption was awkward to handle, but he finally managed to get it up the steps using a couple of old planks as a ramp. He needed the cart to transfer the wood paneling from the house to the truck. Bracing against the bars of the cart, he took his keys from his pocket.

Suddenly, fierce lightning flashed and thunder boomed. Wincing, he squinted in the dark, trying to find the right key. At his feet, Buddy crowded him, frantically pacing and whining. Some dogs were nervous in a storm, but Buddy wasn't . . .

usually. Still, he was clearly agitated over something, but Tucker didn't have time to do anything about it now.

"Buddy! Calm down," he commanded. "Sit."

The dog instantly did as he was told, but every nerve quivered. Watching Tucker jangling keys, he literally vibrated with anxiety.

"What's the problem, Buddy? You think we'll find a ghost inside this old house?"

The dog's tail swished, acknowledging his master's voice with a hopeful look and a plaintive whine. With the correct key finally in hand, Tucker aimed it at the lock. But, to his surprise, he found he didn't need it after all. He frowned, distinctly remembering that he'd locked the house when he'd left earlier. First the light, now the door. A little wary now, he pushed it open as lightning flashed again and, on the heels of that, loud thunder. All too close.

"Okay, Buddy, we're in." Normally he wasn't leery of weather, but he was glad to get inside. Taking the wood out in a rainstorm might be a little tricky, but he had a tarp to protect it. He had to do it tonight. The house was to be demolished the next morning. And he was in a hurry. Lauren was waiting. He didn't want a late job and a little rain ruining his date with his fiancée.

Thinking of his beautiful bride-to-be, his irritation faded. He'd been soured on women after the disaster of his first marriage, but finding

Lauren changed that. Thank God, she was nothing like Margot.

Buddy startled him by leaping over the threshold and instantly disappearing into pitch blackness. Tucker muttered to himself at having left his flashlight in his tool kit somewhere in the back of the house. Despite streaks of lightning, the dark interior felt out-and-out creepy. But he finally found the light switch and flipped it on. Relieved, he took a minute to get his bearings and quickly closed the door as another flash of lightning lit the room. Houston was in for a gully washer of a storm.

He saw nothing different from when he'd left earlier. Any thief intent on burglarizing the place had been out of luck. The house's treasures had been removed earlier in the week—hand-blown windowpanes, vintage gas light fixtures, heart pine floors—most everything dating from the nineteenth century. Like Tucker, some people valued age-old relics.

Sad that the place couldn't be preserved in its entirety. But Tucker had been lucky to win the bid on the rare paneling in the library. He had a contract to use the mahogany to outfit an office in a newer house in River Oaks. Earlier today he'd carefully pulled it off the walls, marked it, and stacked it so that now he could quickly load it into his pickup. Just then, Buddy dashed back after his foray to the interior. Obviously distressed, the dog whined and circled around Tucker. "Okay, boy, what's got you so worked up?" Tucker moved past the stairs and down the hall pulling the cumbersome cart behind him. He glanced at his watch. Five after eight. He guessed he had just enough time to load up and leave and still meet Lauren as planned. He'd heard excitement in her voice when she'd called to tell him she had a surprise.

So, upon reaching the old library, he was still smiling as he turned on the lights and saw the body.

For a long moment, he simply froze, eyes wide in shock. He struggled to process the grisly sight before him. A woman lay sprawled on the floor, both arms flung out. Her hands seemed ghostly white, nails tipped in blood-red polish. Taking it in, he felt dizzy and disoriented. Bile rose in the back of his throat. It was only when he felt Buddy's nose nudging his slack hand that he pulled himself together enough to take a hesitant step forward.

The woman's hair was in a wild tangle, partially obscuring her face. What was she doing here? She didn't appear to be homeless. He could see the sparkle of a ring on her finger. And that dress . . . No, not a homeless person. Then who?

With his heart hammering in his chest, he was now close enough to lean over and see her face.

"Oh!" He jerked back, giving out a shocked

sound as if he'd been punched in the belly. He stared in horror. He knew that face. He knew that hand, those red, red nails. Holy crap! It was Margot!

For an instant, he could not move. He felt nailed to the floor. He swallowed hard. Shaking his head as if denying the evidence before his own eyes, he wiped a hand over his face and drew in a deep breath, trying to steady himself.

"Margot . . ."

He dropped to his knees beside her. Bracing himself, he put out a shaky hand and gingerly brushed her dark hair aside. With his heart slamming in his chest, he looked into her blue eyes—familiar blue eyes—now wide and fixed. He looked quickly away, then saw the blood pooled beneath her . . . a lot of blood.

He shook his head to clear his thinking. He would have to touch her to be sure. He shuddered with revulsion, tempted to run out of the room, to get out of the old house. He desperately wanted to escape this nightmare. Margot was dead. No getting around that.

Another colossal crash of thunder rattled the very foundation of the house. Taking a fortifying breath, he forced himself to press two fingers to her carotid. He felt nothing. Moving his fingers and holding his breath, he tried again. Still, he felt nothing. But she was not cold. How could that be?

Withdrawing his hand, he grimaced at the blood

on his fingers. Saw they were trembling. He took out his handkerchief and wiped them. His stomach rolled sickeningly. He had to stop and take a few deep breaths. Buddy leaned against him, whining . . . but in a different way now, sniffing at blood on the knees of Tucker's jeans from kneeling beside her.

He stood up abruptly, backing away from the body and scrabbling at his belt for his cell phone. Tearing his eyes from his ex-wife's body, he turned away and managed to dial 911.

"Hello," he said, clearing his throat when his voice came out as a croak. "I need—" He stopped. He didn't need an ambulance, which was what he'd been about to say. He tried again. "I'm calling to report a . . . a death."

"What is your name?"

"Tucker Kane. You need to send the police right away."

"Do you need an ambulance?"

He turned, his gaze coming to rest again on Margot's ghostly pale, still face. "It's too late for that."

He gave the dispatcher the address, hung up, and stood for a second, dazed, struggling to wrap his head around the horror of Margot's murder. The authorities would be here in a minute or two. He turned away, avoiding looking at the body again. But the image was already emblazoned in his memory. She had been bludgeoned beyond overkill. Whoever did this had to have been enraged. Someone who knew her? *Had to be,* he thought. *But who? Who? And why?*

His gaze fell on his tools. He'd left them here earlier, intending to load them up tonight after he'd taken the paneling. He should do it now, before the police came. No doubt they would want to talk to him. Who knew when he'd have a chance to gather them once this was a declared crime scene. Taking a wide berth around Margot's body, he went over to the canvas satchel. He found it gaping open. He stopped as a sick feeling came over him; he knew he'd closed it. Using both hands, he reached inside, checking to see that everything was there. But even before he was half done, he knew.

His hammer was missing.

Lauren Holloway stood smiling as she surveyed the table set for three. It was Tucker's weekend to have Kristy, his little girl, so she'd set a place for the toddler using her favorite Dora the Explorer plate and bowl alongside two china place settings that sparkled in soft candlelight. The silver gleamed. Yellow roses added the perfect touch. They'd been an impulsive buy in the supermarket as she was on her way to the checkout with rib-eye steaks and the trimmings for this special dinner.

She had such thrilling news. She'd been

promoted to assistant principal at St. Paul Academy with the promise of running the school as soon as the aging incumbent retired. That was most certainly within the next year. And with her wedding to Tucker Kane in June, it was a wonderful start to their future together.

She couldn't wait to tell him, but not on the phone. She wanted to see his face. Hear his ecstatic congratulations. Get from him a big hug and a kiss. She expected him to lift her right off her feet in his enthusiasm and swing her around as if she were no bigger than one of the tiny kindergartners at St. Paul. He was that kind of man.

She was so in love with him.

She twitched at the linen tablecloth so that it hung just right and plucked at a napkin artfully arranged in crystal stemware. Was it too much? No. Her promotion was the result of hard work and a sincere desire to make a difference to children. She wanted to celebrate that and it was all the more meaningful to celebrate it with Tucker and Kristy.

She glanced at her watch. What was keeping him? She went to the kitchen to tinker with the plans for their dream house. She'd been doing this for several weeks—looking at magazines for design ideas, consulting with flooring suppliers, deciding on lighting fixtures. It would be a wonderful house. They were going to be so happy.

She transferred a stack of brides' magazines and a large catalog of samples for wedding invitations from the island to the kitchen counter and perched herself on a stool alongside the blueprints. Pencil in hand, she soon lost track of time.

But an hour later when Tucker still had not arrived, she blamed it on the weather. A thunderstorm had moved in and she knew that in Houston, traffic snarled in a mere shower. Heavy rain produced havoc. Now, with the sound of every car outside, she looked out at the wet street, hoping to see Tucker's SUV. She'd tried calling him, but his cell went straight to voice mail.

Moving from the window, she went into the kitchen and put the now wilting salad in the fridge. She stood frowning at nothing in particular . . . and hoping Margot wasn't the reason Tucker was detained. Lately, his ex-wife had been more vindictive than ever in fighting him for custody of Kristy. Why, Lauren couldn't begin to fathom— Margot hardly spent any time with the child.

As she stood thinking, her cell phone rang. Seeing Tucker's name on the screen, she breathed a sigh of relief. Traffic or the weather, it was one or the other, she guessed. Her voice was joyful when she answered. "Hello! It's about time. Where are you?"

"In the Heights," he said in a somber tone.

"What's wrong?"

"It's Margot," he said.

She thought she heard a catch in his voice. "What about her?"

"She's dead, Lauren. She's been murdered."

Lauren sat down on the nearest chair. She stared unseeing at the yellow roses. "What on earth are you talking about?" she whispered.

He drew in a shaky breath. "She's been murdered. The police are here. I . . . I'll be pretty late. But I'll be there. Just . . . well, just hold on, will you? I'll tell you when I get there."

"Wait, Tucker. You can't—"

"Sorry, sweetheart. They're headed this way again. I've got to go."

He hung up. She looked blankly at her phone while her thoughts raced with a thousand questions. Margot murdered? How? Why? It was a horrible thing. And almost impossible to believe. Murder happened to people in books, on TV shows, not to anybody she knew. Although Margot was thoughtless and spoiled, she was young and beautiful, a Houston socialite. How could she be dead? How could she be murdered?

She was pacing when the doorbell rang at midnight. She quickly stepped up to the peephole, saw Tucker, flipped the lock, and opened the door.

He was wet from head to toe, his jacket dripping, boots caked with mud. Seeing the blood on his jeans, her eyes widened. If Margot's murder had felt unreal, bloodstains on Tucker's

20

jeans changed all that. And his face! He looked shattered. Heedless of his wet clothes, she threw her arms around him. "Oh, Tucker. This is terrible."

For a long, mute moment, he held her close. "How can I tell Kristy that her mother is dead?" She felt his desperation in their embrace. His breathing was uneven. He was trembling. Her tall, stalwart man trembling? How could that be? "Come inside and tell me what happened."

He took his baseball cap off and ran a rough hand through his dark hair. "There's not much to tell. She . . . Margot's dead."

Lauren was shaking her head. "I'm having a hard time believing it. How . . . ? What . . . ?"

"I don't know how or what or even when," Tucker said. "I just know she's dead." Suddenly he looked down as if he'd just realized he was dripping water on the floor. "Could I have a towel, please?"

A towel? She gazed blankly at him before the words registered. "Oh. Oh, yes. Just . . ." She put out a hand as if to hold him in place. "Let me just go . . . uh . . . I'll be right back."

She headed to her laundry room in a daze. She'd taken towels from the dryer just a few minutes before he arrived. She took two from the basket, holding their warmth close for a minute. When she headed back, she found Tucker sitting on a bench in the foyer, removing his wet boots.

"I'm putting these outside," he told her, holding them up. "I don't want to track mud on your floor."

"It's okay. Don't bother."

But he opened the door and set them outside anyway. She watched as he shed his drenched jacket and reached for the towel she handed over. A dozen questions swirled madly in her head as he mopped his face and hands. Finished, he draped the towel around his neck, seemingly unaware of the streaks of blood now on the towel.

"Let's go in the den to talk, Tucker. Would you like some coffee?"

"No, I'm okay." He sat down on the couch and when she was beside him, he sighed wearily. "I'm sorry to drag you into this, Lauren. It's bad enough that she's dead, but a thousand times worse that she was murdered."

"Her poor parents," Lauren murmured, thinking of Evelyn and Martin Houseman. They'd often been the ones to bring Kristy to Tucker's or pick her up from his weekends with his daughter. Martin was Tucker's business partner, and they were active members of their church. "They'll be devastated—" She stopped as another thought struck. "Where is Kristy? You're supposed to have her this weekend."

"She's with her nanny," he said, adding bitterly, "Where else?"

Sarah. Of course, Lauren thought. "Should we go and get her?"

"No. It's late. After talking to the police Martin offered to pick her up and keep her there. She'll stay with him and Evelyn until I can make arrangements." He looked at Lauren with despair in his eyes. "How can I tell her about this?"

"The blood . . . how did you find out about it?"

He rubbed his hands over his face before looking up at her. "I found her."

"Where? At her town house?"

He shook his head. "You remember I told you I'd won the bid on that paneling?" Seeing her nod, he went on. "The wood was in this old house in the Heights scheduled for demolition tomorrow morning. I'd dismantled it earlier, but I had to leave to meet a city inspector at another job site. I waited over an hour, but he didn't show. Anyway, I knew I'd be late picking up Kristy, so I went over to tell Margot. Her phone was off or something. She was not happy when I told her."

He glanced beyond her, noticing for the first time the pretty table with flowers and candles, long since snuffed out. He turned to her. "That looks like a special occasion."

"It's nothing," she said. The joy she felt over her promotion had evaporated in the face of Margot's death. "Is there anything we can do?"

Tucker shook his head. "I was thinking about that on the drive home. I wonder if Kristy should stay with Evelyn and Martin," he said.

Lauren frowned, not understanding. "She should be with you, especially now."

"I don't think it's possible. . . . She'll need to be with her nanny—Sarah's the one Kristy is most attached to. I can't rip her away from Kristy, too. I just don't have room for Sarah. Martin and Evelyn do."

The deep furrows in his forehead stopped her. "What is it, Tucker?"

"Will you be with me when I tell her?"

Her heart ached in sympathy for him . . . and for Kristy. "Yes, of course I'll go with you. Just tell me when."

"Sometime tomorrow, I think."

But he still looked distracted, his lips pulled in a tight line, his brow furrowed. "What else is bothering you, Tucker?"

He was shaking his head. "She was murdered at that house where I was supposed to pick up the wood. It's deserted, derelict. I keep wondering what the heck she was doing there. It would be the last place I'd expect Margot to ever go."

"The police will probably be asking a lot of questions."

"Yeah." Tucker sighed and raked a hand through his hair. Lauren guessed that he was reliving the events of the night.

"Tell me," she prompted.

His eyes met hers and he reached to hold her hand, intertwining his fingers with hers. "She looked . . ." He closed his eyes. "She had already bled so much, I knew . . ." He shook his head. "I knew she was gone."

"That's how you got blood on your jeans."

He glanced down as if noticing for the first time. "I guess so. I had to check her . . . for a pulse. Just to be sure."

She touched his arm, giving him a deeply sympathetic look. "It must have been terrible."

"Worse than terrible," he said with a shudder. He got up from the couch as if he couldn't sit still. "She was bludgeoned. Her head . . ." He looked pale and sick. "An official showed up—I guess the medical examiner. He didn't need to say death was from a blunt object. It was obvious. I don't know how long she'd been—" He scrubbed both hands over his face. "I guess the autopsy will tell us a lot."

Lauren pressed fingers to her lips. She could almost see the scene as he told it.

"He hit her," Tucker said in a tone that was flat and lifeless. "Whoever did it hit her over and over again."

"Did they find it, the murder weapon, I mean?"

"I don't know. They wouldn't tell me anything." He rubbed the back of his neck wearily before looking at her. "They asked me a lot of questions. I expected that, especially since I found her. And I had blood all over me."

"Not all over you, Tucker. Just on your jeans and with a reasonable explanation."

"My hands, too." He held them out as if to show her even though the blood was now gone.

"Because you checked for a pulse."

He almost smiled at the way she defended him. "I hope the cops are as trusting as you, babe. Everybody knows Margot and I were going at each over custody of Kristy. She'd told anybody who would listen what a jerk I was and how she just couldn't take it anymore."

"She was lying."

"Who'll believe that now?"

Lauren went to him and put a gentle hand on his arm. "There are always two sides to every story in a divorce, Tucker."

"I said some pretty nasty things to her today." He stared down at his feet.

Her heart turned over. "People say things they don't mean when they're angry."

"Yeah, but I did mean it. So now she's gone and the last words we had were mean." He drew a strong breath. "I was so ticked off at her, Lauren. She didn't want Kristy. She never did. She just wanted to torment me."

Lauren put her arms around him. He was so tense. It hurt her to see Tucker brought low like this. He was usually so strong, so confident. With her heart overflowing, she kissed him softly.

He made a sound, something between a wince and a moan, and wrapped his arms around her, holding her close. "I need you, Lauren. I need you to help me get through this."

"And I'm here, Tucker. Don't worry, we'll get through it together."

After a minute, he leaned back with his hands on her forearms to look at her. "The police always look at the person closest to the victim, you know." A sad glimmer filled his eyes. "That's me."

"But you're innocent, Tucker. That's a fact. Besides, God will see us through."

"God can't give me an alibi. She was murdered while I was waiting for an inspector at another site. And I was alone when I found her body at the Heights house. Nobody saw me at either place."

"You had a reason to be there," she reminded him. "You came for the wood. That's your alibi."

"That's not an alibi; that's part of the problem."

"What?"

"The wood I came to pick up was gone, disappeared without a trace." He looked at her. "The detective who questioned me asked if it ever existed."

"That's ridiculous."

Tucker was shaking his head. "So you see . . . I have no alibi."

The killer sat in a car outside Lauren's condo. It had been an impulse to follow Kane to see where he went after leaving the Heights house. If the plan was

27

to work, every move Kane made had to be watched. Every opportunity to implicate him had to be seized. Made the most of. The fiancée would probably be a useful pawn. How and when to use her would depend on the course of the investigation. Kane probably had an excess of southern chivalry where she was concerned. A threat to her might prove very effective. The kid, too.

It had been dicey there for a minute with Margot dead and the possibility that Kane might appear before it was decided what to do. Very dicey. He could have gotten there before the wood was removed or, worse yet, while the wood was being loaded. Or, there was always a chance that he could have spotted the pickup leaving. But none of that happened. The plan—once it was conceived—went like a well-choreographed performance.

No question it was brilliant, but risky. It was always a challenge when dealing with idiots. But in the words of that old sixties rock classic, you can't always get what you want. And in a perfect world, the whole situation would never have existed in the first place. Thank Margot for that. Nothing would have happened to her if she hadn't intruded into territory where she did not belong. But the selfish little witch had no boundaries. That had been obvious from day one. And she couldn't say she hadn't been warned.

But there was no future in dwelling on the whys

and wherefores. What was done was done. What was important now was that suspicion had to be focused on Kane. And focused with such undeniable force that he was quickly seen as the prime suspect.

Putting the car into gear and smiling with macabre satisfaction, the killer eased away from the curb and drove off into the night.

2

Tucker was bone tired the next morning when he got to the home of his ex-in-laws. It was early and unseasonably chilly. Hardly anybody stirred in the posh neighborhood except a few hardy joggers. But he knew the Housemans would not be sleeping, not with their daughter lying cold in the city morgue. He shuddered at the possibility that Kristy could have been with her and that he could have lost his baby girl as well.

He saw movement inside. Not wanting to rouse anyone who might be sleeping, he refrained from ringing the doorbell, but knocked quietly and stood where he'd be seen through the leaded glass. In a moment, a woman made her way to the door and opened it. Not his ex-mother-in-law, but Evelyn's close friend and Margot's godmother, Juliana Brumfield.

"Tucker." She managed a small, sad smile. "Come in."

29

In her early fifties, Juliana was petite and attractive. Her white hair was cut in a stylish bob, her makeup flawless. She wore a purple sweater and immaculate white pants. Married to Carter Brumfield, Houston's district attorney, she was the quintessential politician's wife—smart and politically savvy. She'd be ready when Brumfield made his run for governor of Texas next year. Juliana stepped back to let him inside. "You almost look sad," she said, eyeing him.

"My daughter's mother was killed, Juliana. Of course I'm sad."

She crossed her arms over her chest and stood like a guard dog.

"I'm here to see Evelyn and Martin."

"They are devastated, of course."

Tucker made no reply. "Juliana, what do you want me to say?"

"Do you have something to say?" She leaned toward him threateningly despite the fact that Tucker was a full foot taller.

"Can you just tell them I'm here? I need to talk to them about Kristy."

"Fine." She turned to go. Juliana had always been cordial to Tucker in the past, before the divorce. But since then he'd known where she stood with him, not that she was best friends with her goddaughter either.

Nodding mutely, he looked toward the stairs. "Is Kristy awake?"

"No, not yet. Sarah's with her. I'm sure when she wakes up, she'll bring her down for breakfast."

"Does . . ." He cleared his throat. "She doesn't know anything, does she?"

"Of course not."

"Good. That's good."

"Have you seen today's paper?"

"No, not yet."

She raised a thin eyebrow. "Then I'd advise you to look at it. And don't let Evelyn and Martin see it. No sense upsetting them." She handed the paper to him.

He frowned. "Why? What's in it?"

"A very disturbing report about Margot's murder." She paused with a look of regret as she pointed to the front page. "It's Jordan's byline, I'm sorry to say. I would have cautioned him if I'd known he was going to write such an unflattering piece." Her eyes met his. "He almost indicts you."

Jordan Raines was Juliana's nephew. He and Margot had been close through the years. There had been times when Tucker thought they'd been a little too close, so he wasn't surprised that Raines was all over the story of her murder.

"Jordan was apparently on the scene last night shortly after the police arrived," Juliana said. "I know he has connections at HPD. Most reporters do."

"What did he say?"

31

"Nothing good, I'm afraid," she said.

She paused while he scanned the article. Tucker's face flamed in indignation at the inference that "the ex-husband was ironically the one to find her bludgeoned body."

He crumpled the paper and looked for a place to toss it. Finding none, he tucked it inside his jacket, then turned back to Juliana, who studied him with accusing eyes.

After a long moment, she cleared her throat. "Martin and Evelyn are in the breakfast room having coffee. I'll tell them you're here."

He'd rather see Kristy first. He wanted to pick her up whether she was sleeping or not and just hold her. He was so glad that she was safe. So glad that she hadn't been with her mother last night.

"Coming, Tucker?" Juliana stood with a hand on her hip.

He moved reluctantly, nodding.

"Have you eaten?"

"No. I don't think I could."

There would be funeral arrangements, a sad duty he wished to be able to relieve Martin of, but he knew as an ex-son-in-law, it probably wasn't possible. It was troubling. Not only were he and Martin co-owners of H & K Contractors, he was also the closest thing to a father Tucker had. Sometimes he wondered if marrying Margot had been a subconscious way for him to get inside the Houseman family circle. He'd fancied himself in love with Margot, yes, but he'd soon realized his perception of the Housemans as an ideal family was mostly illusion. And marriage to Margot had been a big mistake. She had only cared about herself and what to wear to the next party. Fortunately when they split, Martin had made it clear that nothing had changed in his relationship with Tucker. They'd been best friends before he married Margot and, in some ways, their relationship was stronger after the divorce. Both men had been victim to her selfish disregard of their feelings and her erratic mood swings.

Martin started to rise as Tucker and Juliana approached, but Tucker put out a hand to keep him in his chair. His partner looked as if he'd aged ten years overnight, since seeing his daughter's battered body at the Heights house the night before. But Evelyn looked worse. Pale as milk, she appeared ready to collapse.

What could he say to a woman who'd lost her only child? Especially knowing he'd been the one to find her body? Evelyn was aware that the relationship between him and Margot had been stormy and she'd always taken Margot's side, ever the loyal mother. But upon seeing him, Evelyn's eyes filled. She reached out her arms to him. He went to her and, taking her hand, he squeezed it gently. Her lips trembled and she gave out a broken sob as she turned her cheek for his kiss.

"Thank you for coming, Tucker."

"Have a seat, Tuck," Martin said in a grave tone.

He felt too uptight to sit. But he took the coffee Juliana offered. "I'm okay. I came to check on Kristy. I wanted to be sure she was okay."

"I hope you aren't thinking of taking her," Evelyn said, blotting her tears. "I don't think that would be wise, Tucker."

"No, Evelyn, not today," he said gently. Naturally she'd want to cling to Kristy now that Margot was gone. He understood that. He felt the same way. "But she'll need to come live with me soon."

"Well, of course . . . eventually," Evelyn said, "but not just yet." She took in a stuttering breath. "What about her nanny?"

"I'll talk to Sarah about staying on," Tucker said.

"There's no room in your town house." Two spots of color stood out on her pale cheeks. "It has three levels, Tucker. It's totally unsuitable for a child long term. Plus you're a workaholic. Are you planning to cut back your hours?"

She had a point. He'd had the same argument with Margot. He cursed himself for not having started building the house he and Lauren planned before now.

"Kristy staying here temporarily does make more sense," Juliana said, offering Evelyn a fresh tissue. "Once you and Lauren are married, of course, you'll be able to make a real home for Kristy."

They made it sound reasonable, but he couldn't shake a feeling that he shouldn't put off taking Kristy right away. Staying too long with Martin and Evelyn might be the first step to Evelyn's coming up with some argument to keep her. But that was unlikely . . . wasn't it? He was her father. She would have to find something truly rotten to make a case against his having full custody.

He set his cup on the counter and turned to Martin. "I'm thinking you'll want to stay close to home for a while," he said. "Funeral arrangements and all that . . . I can handle things at the office for as long as you need."

Martin nodded. "I appreciate that, Tuck."

"I don't think a funeral can be set for a few days," Juliana said. "An autopsy will be required."

"Oh, no-o-o-o," Evelyn said, looking stricken.

"It's the law, Evie," Juliana said, gently patting her shoulder. "Besides, maybe an autopsy will turn something up."

Juliana stood behind Evelyn's chair as if ready to prop her up. Like Tucker, she appeared too antsy to sit. "Tell us how you happened to find Margot in that old house," she said to him. "What in the world were you doing there?"

He glanced at Evelyn, thinking she didn't need to hear anything more than Martin had chosen to tell her last night.

Seeing his hesitation, Evelyn said brokenly, "It's

all right, Tucker. Whatever you say won't change the fact that my girl is gone forever."

"I'm sure Martin told you everything last night," he said. "I went to the Heights to pick up some special paneling. The house was open, which should have alerted me that something was wrong. I had locked it when I left earlier. I found Margot, but the wood had disappeared."

"Disappeared?" Juliana repeated, arched eyebrows rising. "How could that be?"

"Good question." He took his coffee to the sink on the far side of the kitchen counter and emptied it. "I wish I knew the answer."

"Well," Juliana said, "if this wood you say you came to pick up wasn't there, the police will probably wonder if you're telling the truth."

"I'm afraid you're right," he told her in a wry tone. "I'm hoping to figure out what happened to it."

Grabbing at a chance to end Juliana's questions, he said, "About Kristy. I wish she didn't have to know what happened to her mother, but she does."

"We can say Mommy's in heaven," Martin said, adding after a pause, "if she asks."

"Of course she'll ask!" Evelyn said, giving him an accusing look. "I know what you're thinking, Martin. You were always critical of Margot's mothering. But she was very active in some worthy organizations. You can't do that kind of thing without having a full social calendar."

Martin sighed. "Let's talk about it later, Evie."

But Evelyn was unwilling to let it go. "What did you want her to do? Stay inside the house with Kristy and watch *Sesame Street* all day?"

"We don't need to discuss this right now, darling," he said quietly. "We'll all be very careful not to say anything to upset Kristy."

"I don't think that'll work, Martin," Tucker said. "Kristy's pretty sharp. We don't want her finding out about her mother from one of the kids she plays with at the park. That's why I want to tell her myself. Lauren will help me."

"Oh, I can't believe this is happening," Evelyn wailed. "How can you tell a three-year-old that her mother has been murdered?"

"I wouldn't tell her that," Tucker said dryly. "After Lauren's done at school today I'll call to let you know we're coming to get her."

"But you won't take her away just yet, will you, Tucker? You'll finish your house first?" she insisted. "And you'll keep Sarah?"

He knew when to fold. It was probably best to go along with their plan anyway. Too many changes in Kristy's life could be overwhelming. "I'll be around a lot more. And Lauren, too. Are you okay with that?"

Evelyn sighed and pressed a fresh tissue to her eyes. "I suppose I have to be, don't I?"

Martin stood up. "Take a walk with me, Tuck?"

Tucker gladly left with him, going out the

French doors to the patio. He stood looking about. The sun had taken away some of the morning chill. The leaves on an ancient live oak, still wet from last night's rain, glistened. There was a freshness to everything, to the air, to the lush landscaping, to the whole world, it seemed. If only . . .

"Have you learned anything since last night?" Martin asked.

"No. I was about to ask you the same thing."

"That detective was pretty rough on you, Tuck."

"Sherman. Yeah, but don't they always look at people close to the victim?"

"If you believe what you see on TV," Martin said dryly.

"They won't find anything." Tucker turned and looked directly into Martin's eyes. "I swear to you, Martin. I did not kill Margot."

Martin gave his shoulder a squeeze. "I know that, son. But that detective's gunning for you, so you'll want to watch your step."

For a few long moments, he stood looking out over the immaculate lawn. "You might think this sounds a little paranoid, but I'm thinking somebody could have lured Margot to that house, somebody who knew I was going to be there. So they removed the paneling and left me with no good reason to be there. Does that sound crazy?"

"No, because I know you. But I'm not a homicide detective."

Tucker looked again into Martin's eyes. "This is a hard question, but I have to ask. Can you think of anyone who might want to kill Margot? Was she involved in something that could have endangered her?"

"Could be. I don't know." Martin sighed. It was his turn to send a thoughtful gaze into the distance. "She had a capricious personality, Tuck. You'd know that better than anyone. Even as a teenager, she was unpredictable, out-and-out reckless at times." He shook his head wearily. "I dread what the authorities might dig up in the search for the person who killed her." He swung his gaze back to Tucker. "But you have to put that aside and think about yourself and the future. You have Kristy to consider."

"I know." Tucker realized he knew very little of Margot's personal life in the two years since their divorce. He'd been glad to be free of her and, once he started seeing Lauren, was uninterested in what Margot did or where she went. He was thinking now that he should have paid more attention.

"Did you talk to her or see her yesterday?" he asked.

Martin shook his head. "No. Margot and I haven't said anything that mattered to each other in years, Tuck." He looked sad. "Fact was she and I were strangers. You'd know about that, living with her. She had torn down too many bridges between us. . . . Now that she's gone, I feel guilty that I didn't try harder to fix what was wrong. Seemed like every time we had a chance, we ended up in a shouting match. I'd list everything she did wrong and she'd react like a wildcat."

His confession was old news to Tucker. Many times he'd been tempted to shake some sense into Margot. Tell her how lucky she was to have a dad like Martin. She'd always shoot back saying he could have Martin. That Tucker and Martin probably wished she was out of their lives anyway.

He pushed the ugly memories aside to ask, "Do you think Evelyn talked to her yesterday?"

"I asked her last night. She said no."

Tucker sighed. "This is a nightmare. I'm going to try to trace her steps to see what I can find. I owe her that much as Kristy's mother."

Wordless, Martin finally clapped him on the shoulder. "Good, that's good."

Tucker nodded. "But right now I want to see my little girl. I don't care if she's awake or not. I just want to hold her."

"Then do it, son. Me, I need to get back to Evie."

Later, back in his SUV, Tucker's stomach was in a knot. Who would have wanted to kill Margot? And why? How had the killer come to do it at that house in the Heights? What happened to the wood? Head spinning, he drove off. Too many questions and no answers. But one thing he knew: Since he didn't murder his ex-wife, there was a killer out there somewhere. And he meant to find him.

3

Lauren hoped to slip into her office without being seen, but before she reached the door, Eileen Warren, current principal at St. Paul, intercepted her in the hall. She took one look at Lauren. "Oh, my, Lauren, you look terrible!"

Lauren slipped her sunglasses back into place. "Does this help?"

Eileen had the grace to wince. "I'm sorry! Of course, you could never look terrible." She gave Lauren a closer inspection. "Just a little . . . rattled, I guess."

"And don't I have good reason?" Lauren said dryly.

"I heard about Margot. It's all over the TV."

"And the newspaper." Lauren had been shocked to read Jordan Raines's lurid report of the crime in the *Chronicle*. He'd single-handedly indicted Tucker. She wondered about Juliana Brumfield's reaction. She'd have thought that as her nephew, Raines would have been more considerate of Juliana's feelings as well as the Housemans'.

"I don't get the *Chronicle* anymore," Eileen said.

"Cutting back, don't you know? I read it online." She frowned, looking puzzled. "What in the world was he doing at that old house anyway?"

"He went to pick up some paneling. The house was to be demolished this morning. I don't suppose it will be now since it's a crime scene."

Eileen made a dismayed sound.

Lauren continued. "I hope they find the killer soon, Eileen. Otherwise, between Jordan Raines's articles and television's ghoulish coverage, Tucker's reputation is going to suffer massively."

"What about your wedding plans?" Eileen said.

"We haven't talked about it, though I'd feel a little guilty looking at *Bride* magazine and picking out china and crystal and silver with Tucker's ex-wife just murdered."

"Life goes on," Eileen said, patting her arm.

Maybe so, Lauren thought, but it still didn't feel . . . well, right. It would break her heart to postpone the wedding, but it might come to that. The murder was too close to ignore.

"Uh-oh," Eileen said, sending a look over Lauren's shoulder. "Here comes Mr. Personality. Can a day go by when we don't have a visit from this guy?"

Lauren turned to see Craig Rawls, school board chairman, striding toward them. She almost groaned out loud. From the frown on his face, she guessed he was on a tear. She hoped Eileen was his quarry and not her.

"Good morning, Craig," Eileen said. "You're out early today."

He gave her a curt nod before turning to Lauren. "We need to talk."

She took a second to reply. "Of course."

"In your office."

"All right. Would you like coffee? I was just about to—"

"I've had mine," he said brusquely. "I'll wait until you get it . . . if you need it."

She managed a smile. "I don't need it, Craig." She turned, meeting Eileen's eyes briefly, and walked ahead of the chairman to her office. Pausing at the door, she quickly unlocked it and stepped aside to let him enter.

"Give me a minute to unload these files," she told him, placing a stack she'd taken home the night before on the credenza. That done, she sat down. With her hands clasped on the desktop, she said, "Now, what's on your mind so early today?"

He gave her a stern look. "Is that a joke?"

She sighed. "You've read the morning paper."

"Yes. And I've watched our local TV channels complete with graphic details. It's shocking. We don't want it tainting our school."

Puzzled, she asked, "How do you think it taints our school?"

"You're engaged to Tucker Kane. By what the news is saying, the police are already acting like he's a suspect in his ex-wife's murder."

"Why do you say that?" Lauren wasn't willing to admit that the investigation had come to that overnight.

"It was implied in every piece I saw on television . . . and in the article in the *Chronicle*, Lauren. You must have seen it."

"It was over the top. And it did not name Tucker as a suspect." She allowed her outrage to show. "It was a cheap effort to stir up suspicion without first having facts."

"Lauren." He paused to give her a pitying look. "Can you be that naïve? If you want to talk about facts, how about the fact that Kane was at the scene, and that the victim is his ex-wife? Do you think he was detained for questioning by the police for no reason?"

"Of course they'd question him, Craig," she said, striving for patience. "He found her body. That's exactly what I'd expect them to do."

He waved her words away with an impatient hand. "Nevertheless, it looks very suspicious. And because you're engaged to him and you're soon to be named principal here at St. Paul, we of the board are concerned."

"Did you call everyone in the middle of the night? Or are you speaking for yourself, Craig?"

He ignored the barb. "Maybe you should consider distancing yourself a bit."

"And how do I do that? He's my fiancé," she said. "We're getting married in June."

"Maybe you should consider postponing that."

Stiffening her shoulders, she put a firm note in her voice. "I don't see how the murder of a woman who has no connection to our school will, as you say, taint St. Paul Academy, Craig," she said. "You're overreacting . . . with all due respect."

"What if your fiancé killed her?"

She stared at him. "Are you serious?"

He leaned forward in his chair. "Lauren, you may choose to dismiss murder lightly, but I don't think the parents of our children will."

"I don't dismiss murder. That's an appalling thing for you to say. And I won't let an obviously slanted media make me forget that we have a justice system in this country." She removed her trembling hands from the desktop and placed them in her lap. "I'm convinced that the police will find the person who committed this crime."

Rawls gave her a keen look. "And it's not Kane?"

"Why are you convinced it is? I know Tucker. You know him, Craig. He isn't capable of murder." Seeing the skeptical look on his face, she added in a desperate tone, "He's an active member of this church. He has a reputation for honor and integrity. Should you be casting judgment before knowing the facts?"

To her intense relief, she saw that her words seemed to give him pause. "Well . . . I don't want

45

to be guilty of judging . . ." He held up a finger, adding piously, ". . . lest I be judged. But this is very disturbing, Lauren. Very disturbing."

"I can agree with you there," she said quietly. More than he knew. "It's disturbing when anyone dies, especially by murder. But I saw Tucker last night. He was as shocked as everyone else. Margot is the mother of his little girl. And the unjust way he's being characterized is hurtful." She paused, giving him time to consider her words. "Do you really want to add to that, Craig?"

"Well . . ." He got slowly to his feet. "Naturally, you'll want to defend him, Lauren. You're in love with him."

"I don't have to be in love with him to want to see justice done," she said.

Shaking his head, he moved toward the door. But once there, he turned for a parting shot. "I just hope you know what you're doing."

Tucker didn't go to his office after leaving the Housemans'. The company was working on several jobs, and with Martin not expected for who knew how long, he swung by each site to reassure the crews that it would be business as usual. Most had heard about Margot's death and they all said they were sticking by Tucker and sad for Martin's loss. Heartened by the loyalty of his men, he left feeling somewhat optimistic. He'd asked around about the paneling, but no one seemed to know a thing. That troubled him. Someone had to know something.

Arriving at his office, his mood took a nosedive when a police car pulled in at the same time. Resigned that he would have to talk to them again, he waited on the steps while Detective Sherman, the officer he'd talked to the night before, took his time ambling over. "So what can I do for you this morning, Detective?"

"You can answer a few more questions." Sherman took from his back pocket a small notebook. "You want to do it out here or inside?" He hitched his chin toward the front door.

"Inside," Tucker said.

Janice Inman, H & K Contractors' girl Friday, was at the front desk. Judging by her expression, she knew who Sherman was, as she knew almost everything that happened relating to Tucker or Martin and the business. How she managed to be so informed was a company mystery. She gave Sherman a frosty look when he passed her desk with Tucker.

Once in his office, Tucker waited until Sherman took a seat before doing the same. The detective took his time studying his notes. It was a tactic used to stampede a person into talking, Tucker guessed. But he'd been raised by an abusive, unloving grandfather so he knew how to handle such manipulation. When he was a kid, he'd visualize a peaceful place, usually a stretch of beach with white sand and blue water and seagulls in flight, since he'd never seen such a thing on his grandfather's hardscrabble farm in Oklahoma. But today he pictured Lauren barefoot in the sand walking toward him with that smile that never failed to enchant him.

"Something funny?"

He realized he must have been smiling. Glancing at his watch, he said, "Not to rush you, Detective, but I've got work to do. You have more questions?"

Sherman's pen was poised to write. "What time did you arrive at the crime scene?"

"I told you. Eight P.M. Just as the weather broke."

"And you went to an empty house in a questionable neighborhood in the dark for what reason?"

"I told you that, too. To pick up some rare mahogany."

"Which you claim had mysteriously disappeared." Sherman leaned back in his chair, resting an ankle on his knee, and gave Tucker an openly skeptical look. "Let me hear you explain that."

"I wish I could. Someone had to have removed it."

Sherman licked a finger and turned the page of his notebook after writing something. "You said you were at the house earlier."

"To take down the paneling, yes."

"One of your employees couldn't do that?"

"I didn't want to chance it being damaged. It's fragile and rare."

"Rare, yeah. What time was this?"

"A little before two o'clock. It took me about two hours, so it was close to four when I left."

"Why didn't you take this rare wood then?"

"No time. I got a call from Janice that an inspector was headed to another job site. I had to leave to meet him. You don't miss a city inspector when he calls."

"What's this inspector's name?" Again Sherman had his pen ready to write.

"I don't know." Tucker started to rub at pain beginning to throb at his temple, but caught himself. Sherman would get satisfaction from knowing he had a headache. "I was never given his name," he told him.

"I guess I could get it from—" Sherman glanced at his notes. "Janice Inman, right? She the lady out front?"

"She's the lady, but no, you can't. She wasn't told who it was either. I asked. The message was that an inspector would meet me at the job site and I was to get over there ASAP. City inspectors do that sometimes."

"But he never showed up." Spoken deadpan.

"That's right. As I told you last night."

Sherman simply looked at Tucker in silence for

a long minute. He made no effort to conceal the fact that he didn't believe a word. Tucker had a bad feeling. In Sherman's place, he thought, he'd probably be skeptical, too. The wood had vanished; he had no reason for being at the house and no name for the phantom inspector. He told himself not to panic. These questions were routine. This cop had a job to do.

"How about a witness?" Sherman said. "Anybody at that job site where you claim you had a date with an inspector?"

"No. I'd pulled the crew earlier and sent them to another project. But Janice can verify the phone call."

"But she can't verify that you actually went there, or who the mystery inspector is."

"No, sir," Tucker admitted.

Sherman sighed with exaggerated patience. "You don't have a lot going for you, do you, Mr. Kane?"

"I know it looks . . ." Tucker paused, searching for a word that didn't sound too incriminating.

"Fishy?" Sherman supplied helpfully.

"Whatever. But I'm telling the truth." He wanted to shift in his chair, but forced himself to be still.

Sherman grunted, flipping through his notebook. "The medical examiner estimates that your ex-wife had been dead about an hour and a half when you called nine-one-one at eight-ten

P.M." Tucker had not yet been told the time of death, though he'd guessed as much given when he'd left and returned. Sherman seemed to be studying him, as if gauging his reaction to this information. "He says it was about six-thirty. So, where were you at six-thirty, Mr. Kane?"

"I told you last night. When the inspector didn't show, I tried calling. That office closes at four-thirty. I gave up waiting and left around five to tell Margot I'd be late getting Kristy. That's the last time I saw her. I went back to wait for the inspector."

Tucker felt an overwhelming need to move, to get up and pace off some of the nervousness building inside him. But he knew that was what Sherman's technique was intended to do—rattle him so that he'd say something to incriminate himself. But he hadn't killed Margot, so he felt confident he could handle whatever Sherman dished out. Still, he sent up a prayer.

"I was to pick up my little girl at Margot's place," he repeated, his tone going low and tight. "I was to have her for a four-day weekend. But because I needed to get that wood before the house was demolished, I told Margot I would pick her up later."

"And all hell broke loose then, didn't it?"

Tucker gave him a startled look. "What?"

"I talked to the nanny this morning, Mr. Kane." Another glance at his notes. "Sarah. She says you

51

and Margot had words over that. Real nasty words."

"We . . . we did argue, yes." Tucker waited, warily braced for whatever Sherman had up his sleeve.

"Just a minute here," Sherman said, letting a sly smile play at the corners of his mouth while flipping pages. "Ah, yes, here it is. And I quote, 'You'd like to see me dead, wouldn't you, Tucker? That way, you wouldn't have Kristy every other weekend. You'd have her forever.'" He looked up at Tucker. "Do you deny she said that to you about an hour before she was murdered?"

"She said it," Tucker replied shortly. "But I don't know how long it was before she died."

"The nanny said the two of you fought just about every time you came to pick up the kid."

His heart was now beating hard and he realized it had been a mistake to talk to Sherman without a lawyer, but it was too late now. "Margot liked giving me grief."

"Well, she won't be giving you grief anymore, will she?"

Tucker stood up. "If you have any other questions for me, it'll have to be in my lawyer's office."

"I retract the question."

Tucker said nothing, but simply looked at him.

"I know you killed that woman. And if I have to move a mountain I'm gonna prove you did it."

Tucker walked around his desk and jerked the door open. "Like I said, I've got work to do."

Sherman stood up. "Me, too, Mr. Kane. Me, too."

Lauren was ready to break for lunch when Tucker appeared. She stood up as he closed her office door and walked to her. Without a word, he took her in his arms and brought his mouth down to hers for a searing kiss. It was not the quick, friendly greeting she usually got when he came to her office. It was a deep and passionate plundering. He didn't have to say anything for her to sense the chaotic emotion in him. He literally vibrated with it. And as always with Tucker, she gave herself up to the sheer sensuality that was so rich and real between them. Her pulse pounded. Everything female in her responded to the blatant masculinity of this man she loved. And for a few delicious moments, she was awash in sensation. The immediate threat to her happiness became—briefly—distant and unreal.

But then Tucker ended the kiss. "Thanks, I needed that," he said with a crooked smile, still holding her close.

With her head nestled beneath his chin, she could hear his heartbeat, steady and strong. "Me, too," she said, smiling with him.

They stood together swaying a little, savoring the blessing of love while hearing the joyous cries of students released from the classroom through the windows. She reluctantly stepped back from Tucker to get a look at his face. "Let me guess. It's been a horrendous morning."

"Yeah."

"So, tell me."

"Detective Sherman was waiting when I got to the office. He asked me the same questions he put to me last night. The police think I did it, Lauren."

"That's ridiculous! How can they think that?"

"The same way the rest of the world will think it," he said grimly. "Ex-husband involved in custody fight finds ex-wife's body in deserted house. Claims he knows nothing about how she got there. I could write the headlines myself."

"This is a nightmare!" She moved away, pacing in the tiny space. "It's innuendo and suspicion, nothing else. And it's burgeoning like a mushroom cloud." After a beat, she gave a tired sigh. "Craig Rawls came to see me this morning. He's worried that the school will be 'tainted,' his word, not mine, since I'm engaged to a murder suspect. He actually suggested that I consider postponing our wedding."

"That's just great!" He threw himself into a chair. "That's all I need, for this to affect your job."

She moved to his side and put a calming hand on his shoulder. "I can handle it, Tucker. It's just that

I find it so frustrating that we can't do anything to make it all go away."

"I would do anything to keep you from being tarred by the same brush they're using on me, Lauren." He paused, looking up at her. "Craig's right about one thing. People are going to talk. He's the first, but he won't be the last to urge you to rethink your decision to marry me."

"They can try," she said, smiling.

He stood as if he was too worked up to stay in the chair. "And yet, I don't know if you realize yet how big a scandal this is."

She studied his face, trying to decide if he truly meant what she thought he was saying. "The date is set, Tucker," she said. "I only waited to order the invitations because I wanted your opinion on which ones to get."

"Nobody would blame you for backing out," he said, pacing now and not looking at her.

"Tucker." There was a sigh in her voice. "If you want to call off our wedding, just say so straight out."

"No! Lord, no." With a groan, he hauled her into his arms and buried his face in her hair. "I love you. I don't want to lose you, but I have to think of what this could mean for you . . . personally and in your career."

As she stroked the back of his neck, she felt the tension in him. She was at once touched and dismayed that he felt so concerned for her when he was the one in trouble. "You won't lose me over this," she told him, adding with a smile, "unless you jilt me at the altar."

"Never."

"So stop talking about putting off our wedding."

She felt him relax a little as he drew away reluctantly. "I just want you to know we probably haven't seen how ugly this can get."

"Don't you believe we can handle whatever comes?" She paused with a hand on his arm and smiled. "With God's help we'll get through. I'm praying pretty hard over this."

"Me, too."

Her smile faded as she asked, "When are we going to tell Kristy?"

He glanced around her office. "Could you get away around five?"

"Absolutely. Let me drive home and you can pick me up there. Is that okay?"

"It's fine." Still restless, he paced the small room. "There's something else. . . ."

She frowned. "What else?"

He stopped in front of her. "The house we were going to build? I know you were looking forward to it and I want to give it to you, Lauren, but what's happened to Margot changes everything."

She held up one hand. "I can guess where you're going. You need to get a house, an existing house, and right away . . . because of Kristy."

"Yeah. Something with more bedrooms plus a nice yard. I want her to have a yard with a jungle gym, a pool, and a sandbox, and neighborhood kids to play with."

She touched his cheek. "I think that's a great idea," she said lovingly. "Do it."

He took her hand and brought it to his lips. "I promise I'll make it up to you. I'll—"

He stopped at a tapping on the door. Eileen Warren cracked it enough to look in. Her expression told Lauren something was up.

"Lauren, the police are here." She made a face, something between dismay and irritation. "A Detective Sherman. I told him we'd prefer not to have the police around when the children are outside, but he won't leave. He wants to talk to you."

Lauren's heart skipped a beat. "Me? He wants to talk to me?"

"That's right, Ms. Holloway," Sherman said, pushing his way past Eileen, who backed away rolling her eyes.

"Well, looky here," Sherman said when he saw Tucker. "We meet again. You get around, Mr. Kane."

"What's this about, Detective?" Tucker asked stonily.

"It's about murder, Mr. Kane." He turned to Lauren. "I have a few questions, Ms. Holloway. Can you talk?"

"Yes, of course, but could it be elsewhere? Say at lunch?" She glanced at her watch. "I'm ready to leave now."

He smiled. "We don't do lunch, ma'am. I need to get this behind me. I promise to be brief."

"What difference will one hour make?" Tucker demanded in a gruff voice. "This is a school, Sherman. Talking to her here is inappropriate. In fact, talking to her at all is inappropriate. This doesn't concern Lauren."

Sherman looked at Lauren. "You have a problem with me asking a few questions, Ms. Holloway?"

"I have a problem with it, Detective," Tucker said.

Sherman shrugged his massive shoulders. "You want to come down to police headquarters instead, Ms. Holloway?" he said, ignoring Tucker. "Me, I don't have a preference. One place is as good as another so long as we get started now. This is a murder investigation. We don't work around anybody's schedule."

"It's okay, Tucker." Lauren touched his arm to stop him from making matters worse. She reached for her purse from a desk drawer. "I'll meet you downtown, Detective. The children don't need to be scared by your presence. I assume I can drive myself?"

"I'll drive her," Tucker said with a hard look at Sherman. "Otherwise, we'll wait for her lawyer, and I don't think you want him complicating things, do you?"

Lauren didn't have a lawyer. Besides, what could they possibly ask her that would implicate Tucker? With her purse in hand, she moved past both men. "That won't be necessary."

At the door, the detective waited, politely indicating that she should precede him. "You can follow me."

"She'll ride with me," Tucker said.

Again, Sherman shrugged. "Suit yourself, Mr. Kane. But when we get to HPD, I will be talking to Ms. Holloway alone."

Tucker fumed on the way to his SUV. "This is harassment, Lauren. He has no reason to drag you into this." He stalked to the passenger side and opened the door for her. "It's just a ham-handed way of letting me know who's got the power here."

Lauren said nothing, just buckled up and waited until he was behind the wheel. "Sherman does have the power, Tucker," she finally said. "But you're innocent. We have to trust that the truth will come through. I'm okay if he wants to ask me a few questions. I can handle that."

"Maybe. But if it gets sticky, I want you to walk out. And the next time he wants to talk, you be sure you have a lawyer."

"You really think I need a lawyer?"

"He's after me, Lauren. And he'll try to use

anything you say to build his case. A lawyer knows how to cope with that."

Frustrated, he backed out of Lauren's reserved slot and, to his credit, Lauren noted, did not exceed the school zone's fifteen mph speed limit. Sherman waited on the street in his police car. The students who'd been playing on the soccer field now stared wide-eyed, all activity in the game forgotten.

"Can you believe this?" Tucker ground out.

"All we need are lights and a siren," she said, wanting to sink down in her seat and hide.

"I wouldn't put it past him," Tucker said through gritted teeth. "But coming here and throwing his weight around at the school, it's out-and-out harassment."

"Let's just get going," Lauren said in a subdued tone. She dreaded having to explain this to Craig Rawls. But she knew she would have to.

4

Lauren had never been to police headquarters in Houston. She knew it was downtown, but she had no clue where or on which street. But today it wasn't necessary to know with Sherman leading the way. The detective pulled into a reserved slot and Tucker stopped beside him. Lauren quickly opened the door and got out of the SUV, knowing Sherman wouldn't allow Tucker the privilege of parking in a reserved area while he waited for her.

Sure enough, Sherman knocked on the driver's side window. "Public parking is in the garage, Mr. Kane." He pointed.

Before Tucker could reply, Lauren leaned in and said to him, "I'll call you when I'm done. You should go back to your office. There's no point in hanging around here."

"I'll wait," he said grimly.

She could see by the scowl on his face that there was no point in trying to change his mind. Closing the door, she walked toward Sherman, who stood waiting, arms crossed over his chest. Yes, she thought, he was definitely in control. Without looking at him, she zoomed past and entered the building.

"We'll take the elevator up to Homicide," he told her, easily keeping step with her.

"Whatever you say."

"How long have you known that guy?" he asked as they waited for the elevator.

"That guy?" She gave him a look that usually quelled an impudent student.

"Yeah, Kane."

"Why do you need to know that, Detective? I can't see that it has any relevance to Margot's murder."

"That wasn't a question relating to the murder, Ms. Holloway. Just curiosity on my part." He punched a button for the appropriate floor.

"Maybe I need to make something clear. When I do begin questioning you, it's not up to you to find relevance. I've been doing this a long time. Like I said to Kane, this is a murder investigation. You never can tell what little scrap of information might turn out to be the key to solving a case. So I ask a lot of questions."

Lauren was beginning to feel distinctly uneasy. She wished now that she hadn't agreed to let him question her on his territory.

"Maybe I should call my lawyer after all, Detective Sherman," she said.

He released a heavy sigh as the elevator stopped. "Look, there's no reason to panic. You're Kane's fiancée. The more people I talk to, the better fix I'll get on him. Who knows, you may convince me I'm on the wrong track."

Lauren said nothing, thinking she should probably walk out now. But Sherman's tone gentled. "How about I ask a few questions and if you think you need a lawyer, you're free to call one. I don't think you'll need to, is what I'm saying."

"You won't get any little gems from me," she said, watching the floor numbers flash over the number panel. "I promise you, I don't know anything useful."

"Sometimes people don't know what they know."

The elevator opened to an area of multiple offices located down a long hall. Gray walls and floor tile in the same dreary shade made it seem like an underground tunnel. She felt almost claustrophobic. A person would have to be part mole to work comfortably here. But . . . maybe homicide detectives didn't need to feel comfortable.

Sherman's office surprised her. The walls were painted a soft cream—nothing like the hall. A green plant—real, not fake, and well cared for—stood in the corner. His oak desk was mostly clear except for a laptop computer, a yellow legal pad, and two framed photos. One picture was of a young boy in a Little League uniform grinning big and the other was of a pretty teenage girl. Grandchildren? Apparently, even homicide detectives had personal lives, though it was hard to see Sherman as a doting grandpa.

"Take a seat," he said. "You want some coffee? It's not too bad, but it's not Starbucks."

"No, thank you."

"We got bottled water."

"I'm fine, Detective." Still standing, she turned as he closed the door. A bulletin board covered most of the wall directly in front of him. Pinned on it were crime scene photos, grisly pictures of murdered persons. For a minute, she gazed at them in horrified fascination. Murder was ugly. Dying violently took all humanness from someone who'd once been a unique individual. She dropped her gaze, guiltily aware that staring at the victims felt somehow like a violation.

"Is a photo of Margot on that board?" she asked.

"No. I just got the pics back from the crime lab." He pulled a couple from a folder and placed them right side up on the desk. Margot's body, ghostly white in death. This, she thought, was what Tucker had seen inside the Heights house. Feeling queasy, she sat down suddenly.

"You okay?" Sherman said, watching her.

"Yes, I'm okay."

She was determined not to give him the satisfaction of knowing how shocked and horrified she felt. Margot had been beautiful and vivacious in life. The . . . the . . . thing that lay sprawled on the floor in that old house was not Margot.

"Not a pretty sight, is it?"

"No, it isn't." She managed to keep her voice steady. "It makes me wonder how anybody could choose this line of work."

He went to his desk and sat down. "Well, I'll tell you, sometimes I wonder that myself. But when I build a case against an animal who's murdered another human being and it's my work that puts him behind bars, I know why."

Did he consider Tucker an animal? She shifted uneasily in the chair, wondering whether he had any real evidence or if he was just fishing. "I need to get back to school, Detective Sherman, so if you're ready with those questions . . ."

"Right." At that, he flipped open a small notebook he'd taken from his back pocket. "You saw Kane yesterday?"

She knew Tucker had answered that. "Yes."

"What time was it?"

"Around midnight, I think. He came straight over after leaving the Heights. You can verify that. He told me you were there when he left."

"What I'm asking is whether you saw him before then."

"No, I did not."

"So you couldn't say where he was around six-thirty P.M.?"

"He told me he was at his office."

He studied her for a moment in silence. "You believe him?"

"Absolutely."

"Hmmm, interesting. Because he told me he was at a job site at six-thirty waiting for a building inspector . . . who never showed."

"I knew about him waiting for the inspector," she said, feeling a blip of unease. What had Tucker told her? She couldn't remember exactly.

He looked at her face as if judging whether she was lying or not. Lauren felt an urge to squirm in her chair. She fought it and forced herself to hold his gaze. After a beat or two, he looked down at his notebook again. "Tell me about Kane's relationship with his ex-wife."

"What I know would only be secondhand," she

said cautiously. "I'm not sure it would be helpful."

"Tell me anyway. You're engaged to Kane. You had to be curious. He would have talked, no?"

"Tucker and Margot divorced on grounds of incompatibility," she said. "Their child, Kristy, is three years old. Both wanted custody, so I guess you could say their relationship was strained."

"Some folks might think that gives Kane a strong motive to kill Margot."

"Tucker could never kill anyone. He's not that kind of person."

"In fact, he *is* that kind of person, Ms. Holloway," he said, making a play of studying a page in his little notebook.

"I'm not following you," she said, frowning.

"I guess he didn't tell you about his grandfather." Seeing her confusion, he added, "I ran a background search. When he was fifteen, he was deer hunting with his grandfather." He paused then said, "You know he was raised by his grandparents in Oklahoma?"

"Yes . . . ," she replied, wary now. After being tripped up over the time a few minutes ago, she sensed another trap. She cleared her throat. "Yes," she repeated in a stronger voice. "His parents were killed in a car accident when he was twelve so they took him in."

"Well, like I said, he and his grandfather were deer hunting and somehow the old guy caught a blast in the chest from Kane's rifle. The current sheriff was a deputy then. He remembers it well. He told me that if it hadn't been for a couple other Okies hunting nearby who heard the ruckus, Gramps would have died. Luckily, one was a doctor."

"It sounds like an accident," Lauren said, shocked, but trying not to show it. Tucker never talked much about his upbringing in Oklahoma. He occasionally mentioned his grandmother, but never his grandfather.

"Yeah, well, that's what Kane claimed, and when the old geezer was able to talk, that was his story, too. But the sheriff said he always had doubts." He gave her a shrewd look. "He never told you about it, did he?"

"Do you have other questions regarding what happened to Margot?"

He paused for a long moment, but she stayed stubbornly silent. "When did you last see Margot?"

"Me?" She put a hand to her chest. "Am I now a suspect?"

"These are just routine questions."

She settled back in her chair to think, but found it difficult to concentrate. "I saw her two weekends ago," she told him.

"Alone?"

"No."

"You want to share the circumstances of this meeting?"

"It was hardly a meeting. I went with Tucker to pick up Kristy. Margot met us at the door. She told us she was already late for a fund-raiser at the museum. I remember because I saw a picture of her at the event in the paper later."

"What was her attitude toward Kane at that meeting?"

"Not friendly or unfriendly. She seemed distracted, if anything. She just shoved Kristy at Tucker and went back inside. We realized after we left that we hadn't asked if Kristy had been fed and she hadn't told us."

"What was Kane's attitude?"

"Tucker was always careful never to say anything negative about Margot in front of Kristy."

"Hmm . . ."

"It's true, Detective."

"How about you? Did he vent to you that night? After the kid was asleep?"

"Naturally he was frustrated, but he knew there was nothing he could do about the situation but be the best dad he could to Kristy."

"Because she had such a bad mommy."

"I didn't say that, Detective Sherman."

He was nodding slowly, visibly skeptical. "The guy must be a saint."

She realized he wouldn't believe anything positive she might say. She had to hope, when all was said and done, that truth would win out.

"I'm wondering why she'd put up such a fight for custody of the kid if what you say is true."

"Tucker often wondered the same thing. It seemed obvious that she didn't really want the bother of a child."

"That's your opinion?"

Lauren sighed. "I truly don't know. Maybe it's just that divorce is painful. And when people are in pain, they react."

"Did you get along with Margot?"

"I barely knew her. With Margot . . ." She hesitated, thinking of the best way to express her thought. "It wasn't about me or the fact that I was going to marry her ex-husband. It was about Tucker. For some reason, she liked tormenting him."

"Because of the way he treated her before she divorced him?" Again, he thumbed a few pages of his notebook. "I've talked to a few people," he went on. "She told anybody who'd listen what an SOB he was. That she was lucky to get away from him."

"I know you won't believe me, but that's just not true." In her zeal to convince him, she leaned forward in her chair. "You can ask Martin. Her father. He respects Tucker. Actually, he loves Tucker. He treats him as a son. They're in business together. Wouldn't he be the first to break all ties with Tucker if he believed Margot?"

"Does the business make money?"

She gave him a long look. "I see where you're going. Yes, it makes money, but Martin is a wealthy man. He could buy Tucker out twice over and it wouldn't make a blip on his bottom line."

"Her own daddy taking the ex's side," Sherman said, closing his notebook. "That must have ticked Margot off."

"I don't know. Maybe you could talk to her mother or the nanny. Or Juliana Brumfield, her godmother. They were close. Maybe they talked." Lauren stood up. "But if you continue to focus on Tucker and no one else, the real killer will go scot-free."

Tucker was waiting when she got outside. He reached for her arm to escort her across the street to public parking, but she shifted slightly out of his reach. A quick glance at her face gave him an uneasy feeling. He waited until they were in the garage elevator to say something. "You look pale," he said. "Was it bad?"

"When we get to the car," she said, eyes straight ahead, "you can tell me about your grandfather."

"My grandfather?" He'd felt anxious waiting, wondering and worrying about what Sherman was putting her through. But he hadn't expected this. He should have told her long ago, but he hadn't been able to bring himself to tell her about that sorry slice out of his life.

They left the elevator at the third level, the

silence between them dark and heavy. She waved Tucker away when he reached to open the passenger door of his SUV for her. So he got behind the wheel with a tight feeling in the pit of his stomach. He didn't back out, only watched as she buckled up and turned her face from him, going somewhere a thousand miles away.

"Let's go," she said distantly. "I have a lot of work to catch up."

"It was an accident, Lauren." He waited for her to look at him, but she wouldn't. "Did he tell you it wasn't?"

"Sherman? No." She turned then and simply looked at him with a world of hurt in her eyes. "I need to get back to the school."

"I was a thirteen-year-old kid," he said, needing her to understand. "Until I lost my parents, I'd never seen a deer except in the St. Louis zoo. I didn't know anything about hunting, but my grandfather said every self-respecting male in Oklahoma hunted. Killing a deer was a rite of passage and I was expected to measure up."

"Sherman said you were fifteen."

"I was thirteen. My parents had been dead less than a year. You can check."

She looked at her watch. "Are you going to drive me back or not?"

He waited a beat, studying her stony profile. When she stayed silent, he had no choice but to back out and drive down the circular exit. The rush hour had not yet begun, so he was able to get quickly to the interstate.

"I know why you're upset," he said, merging into traffic. "And you're right. Just let me try to explain. Will you listen?"

She finally looked at him. "You think you know why I'm upset? We're on the brink of marriage, Tucker. We're supposed to trust each other, but trust means we don't keep deep, dark secrets from each other."

"I didn't mean to keep it a secret." He felt like a jerk. But telling it meant going back to a time that he'd spent years trying to forget. "It was a miserable thing," he said, ". . . shooting my own grandfather."

"Then it wasn't an accident?"

"It was the first day of hunting season. A fun thing to my grandfather, but not to me." He frowned, dragging up the memory. "Mostly I just felt cold and miserable. We'd tramped through the woods since daybreak. My feet were numb, my ears felt frozen and ready to fall off. My teeth chattered, but my grandfather didn't notice. Then suddenly this big buck appeared. He had an unbelievable rack—eighteen points, my grandfather said. He was elated. Couldn't believe our good luck. He whispered how great that rack would look mounted in the den. Then he ordered me to take the safety off my rifle and get ready to shoot."

Tucker signaled to exit the interstate and came to a stop at a traffic light. He turned to look at Lauren. "I remember how stunned I felt that he thought it was okay to kill that magnificent animal. I told him I didn't want to do it. He cursed and grabbed the rifle and took the safety off. Then he shoved it back to me and ordered me to shoot."

Tucker's voice dropped in the telling of the moment that changed his life as dramatically as the sudden loss of his parents. "I was shaking and crying, but all that did was enrage him. *Sniveling,* he called it. Even if I'd wanted to, I couldn't hold the rifle steady enough to take a bead on that buck. He saw that it was going to get away, so he made a grab for my rifle. I wouldn't let go because I knew he would kill it. So I held on in a sort of tug-of-war."

"It's no surprise the gun went off," Lauren said in a shocked tone. "What was he thinking?"

He heard her, but a part of him was still in that forest, cold and scared. He felt again the explosion, the kick of recoil, and the stunning pain when the stock slammed into his cheek. And terror when his grandfather fell to the ground. With a shake of his head, he brought Lauren's face into focus. She didn't look so distant now.

"The bullet struck him in his shoulder," Tucker said in a low tone. "He would have bled to death right there, but a doctor who was hunting nearby heard me screaming. Later we learned it missed his heart by a whisker."

"Sherman said the deputy who told him about it also told him that the sheriff had doubts that it was an accident."

"Maybe he did, but it *was* an accident. I didn't try to kill my grandfather, if that's what Sherman implied. But what has always bothered me is that I knew I caused the rifle to fire. And I think my grandfather knew and maybe wondered if it was accidental. But he swore to the sheriff that it was his fault." He looked at her. "He lied to protect me."

A driver behind them honked his horn. Tucker pressed the accelerator. "My grandfather never wanted the responsibility of a kid dropped on his doorstep just when he was looking to enjoy retirement. And I was a handful." He turned onto the tree-lined street near the school. "I was grieving over losing my parents. I was mad at the world—at my mom and dad for abandoning me, silly as that sounds, and at God for doing it, and at a mean world that I had no choice but to live in." He managed a short laugh. "I was a mess."

Lauren studied him for a long moment. "How do you know he never wanted the responsibility of a child?"

"He never said it, but I knew. He was a mean old cuss. I remember my mother telling how she escaped his tyranny by eloping on the day she graduated from high school. We didn't visit them more than three times before I had to go live with them."

"What was your grandmother like? Why didn't she intervene?"

He parked next to Lauren's reserved slot at the school and faced her with his left arm propped on the steering wheel. "Have you ever noticed that men like that often have sweet-natured, passive wives? My grandmother was like that. She would slip into my room after dark and bring me something to eat when he sent me to bed without supper. Or she'd take the blame for something I did so he wouldn't beat me. She'd make up excuses for me when I acted out."

"She'd lie for you, too," Lauren said.

He shrugged. "I guess so."

With a sigh, she opened the car door.

"Are you still angry?" he said.

Lauren shook her head. "No, Tucker. I'm not angry. I just wish I'd been prepared. As it was, I felt blindsided."

"I'm sorry."

Resignation was in her eyes, though something he couldn't pinpoint remained. She said, "I need to get back to my office. As it is, I'll be working late to catch up."

Meaning she didn't want to see him tonight. "Does that mean you've changed your mind about going with me to tell Kristy?"

Half out of the car, she paused and drew a deep breath, looking as if she wished to be a thousand miles away from him and the problems that came with him. "No, I'll go. Let me take care of anything urgent on my desk. Where should I meet you?"

"I thought we were going together," he said.

She waved her hand as if just remembering their agreement.

He watched her, guessing she wanted to tell him to go to blazes, but in the end she shrugged and gave in. "I appreciate you doing this."

"I'm doing it for Kristy."

Deep regret filled him. She was still hurt, and there was nothing he could do now to change that. Tucker got out and waited until she came around, intending to walk her to the entrance. "I know Sherman blindsided you, Lauren. I should have told you a long time ago."

Staying put, she pulled her coat more closely around herself. "Stuff like that undermines trust in a relationship, Tucker. Would you have waited until after we were married to tell me something so . . . so significant in your life?"

"It must seem like that," he said, finding it hard to look her in the eye.

She studied him a long minute, her expression so cool she seemed almost a stranger. "This makes me wonder what other secrets you're keeping."

"There are no more secrets," he told her.

She waited a little too long to nod. He could see that she wasn't sure she could believe him. He was suddenly struck with fear that he might lose Lauren and he was helpless to do anything about it. He'd known what it was to feel helpless. He'd felt it often enough when he lost his parents and then with his overbearing grandfather. But not with Lauren. Never with Lauren.

They picked Kristy up at the Housemans', then took her to get ice cream. They would take her to Tucker's condo later. Lauren set aside her feelings for the sake of the little girl, but she was still upset and angry.

"I'll have bubblegum with sprinkles," Kristy said, finally settling on the bright blue flavor. Because Kristy rattled on about her day with Sarah as she ate, it was easy for Lauren to ignore Tucker.

"Maybe you could try strawberry next time," Lauren said, once they were in the bathroom in Tucker's condo cleaning her up.

"Does strawberry make my tongue pink?" Kristy asked.

"Probably not."

"Then I don't want it," she said, turning her face up for Lauren to wash. "The best thing about bubblegum is that it makes my tongue all blue." She stuck it out. "See?"

"It also turns your face, your hands, and your clothes all blue," Lauren said dryly.

Tucker tapped on the door. "You ladies coming out any time soon? I'm getting lonely out here."

Kristy yanked the door open and grinned up at him. "See, I'm all clean, Daddy."

He smiled at her. "Let me check." He bent down and made a big show of looking behind her ears, at her tummy, and behind her neck. "By golly, you sure are."

"Can we play Candy Land now?"

He touched her dark curls gently. "Not tonight, lovebug. Tonight you and me and Lolly are going to have a talk."

"Is it about my birthday?"

"Uh . . . no . . ." Tucker was suddenly at a loss. He gave Lauren an imploring look.

She took Kristy's hand. "Let's go to the couch, okay? You sit in the middle and Daddy can be on one side of you and I'll be on the other."

As Kristy scrambled up on the couch, Lauren closed her eyes and prayed a silent prayer that they'd find the right words to tell this child the awful truth in a way that would not cause lasting harm. Kristy was a precocious three-year-old, but still too young to truly comprehend the concept of death.

"Kristy," she said, "do you remember a few weeks ago when your friend Carey had to take her kitty cat to the animal doctor because he got sick?"

"Yes. I wish I could have a kitty cat." She turned

and looked at Tucker. "Daddy, where do you buy kitty cats? Let's go there and get one for me."

He patted her hand. "We'll think about it, lovebug."

She wrinkled her tiny nose. "When Mommy says that it always means no."

"Kristy." Lauren touched her shoulder to get her attention. "Carey's cat was so sick the doctor couldn't do much to help him. So he isn't coming home again. He's somewhere in heaven now."

"Oh." Kristy's eyes got big, not quite understanding.

"That means Carey doesn't see her kitty anymore," Lauren explained.

Kristy cocked her head, thinking. "Never, ever again, no more?"

"That's right."

"I bet she's sad."

"Yes, she's sad." Lauren took a deep breath. "So, Kristy, something like that has happened to your mommy."

"Did she get sick, too?"

"Yes, in a way." Lauren glanced at Tucker. "She got very sick."

"Did she go to the animal doctor?"

"No. But like Carey's cat, there wasn't anything they could do to help her, Kristy. So your mommy is now with the angels in heaven."

"How long is she going to be there? 'Cause I'd like to stay with you until she comes back, Lolly."

Lauren caught the little girl's face between her hands. "Listen to me, Kristy. Your mommy is with the angels in heaven forever. Your mommy won't be coming back, darling."

For a minute, Kristy didn't seem to understand. "She has gone somewhere far away from me forever?"

"Yes, she has, sweetie."

Kristy's chin quivered and her eyes filled with tears. "Why?"

"It was not because she wanted to leave you, Kristy. She loves you very much."

Kristy began to cry. "I'm n-never going to s-see Mommy again?"

"I'm so sorry, honey." Lauren gathered her into her lap and wrapped her arms around her. Sobbing brokenly, Kristy buried her face in Lauren's breast. With her heart aching, Lauren simply rocked her, stroking her and murmuring, wishing she could take the little girl's grief into herself.

Lauren met Tucker's eyes over the child's head. His were wet, his face ravaged. She could see that it tore at his heart to see his child hurt and grieving and yet be unable to do anything to prevent it.

"Listen, Kristy," she said when the sobbing eased. "You can always remember your mommy. You can talk to her in heaven every night when you say your prayers."

Kristy lifted her head, her little fists rubbing away her tears, and looked at Tucker with some anxiety. "You aren't going away, are you, Daddy?"

"No, sweetheart. I won't ever leave you."

Kristy turned her gaze up to Lauren. "Lolly, can I come and live with you now?"

"Not right now, sweetie." Lauren managed a smile. "Right now, you'll be staying with Grammy and Papa. Sarah will be there, too. You'll like that, won't you?"

"And I'll come see you every day," Tucker said.

"Can I have ice cream every day?"

"No way." He laughed and tweaked her nose. "Nice try, lovebug." He stood up. "So go to the closet and get Candy Land. We still have time for one game."

He watched her dash away down the hall, his smile fading. "She doesn't have a clue, does she?"

"No," Lauren said. "It'll take a while before she realizes she really won't ever see her mother again."

"Thank you for what you did," he said, "and for how you said it. I could never have done that."

"I love her."

He could hear what she left out loud and clear—she was doubting her love for him.

The next day, Tucker got the key to Margot's house from Martin. His efforts to trace her steps on that last day of her life made him realize how much he didn't know about his ex-wife. He didn't know where she went, or who she spent time with. How she filled the hours in her days. Questions to Evelyn got him nowhere. As for Juliana, she could barely be civil to him, so having a conversation with her about Margot wasn't even possible.

An hour later, he stood in the center of her living room and slowly turned a full circle, hoping he'd see something—anything!—that might tell him who his ex-wife really had been. He had not wanted the divorce, mostly because he feared losing touch with Kristy. But once it was a done deal, he had felt overwhelming relief. Finding Lauren had almost wiped the pain of his life with Margot from his memory.

In the kitchen he spotted a note stuck on the fridge. "Drinks, 7:00." Drinks with whom? he wondered. Where? Had that person tried to call when she hadn't showed . . . because, for some reason, she'd detoured to the Heights house? Was that person the very one who'd persuaded her to go to the derelict house in the run-down neighborhood?

He studied the note, wondering what, if anything, the police made of it when they saw it. As of now, nobody had come forward saying he had a date with Margot on the night she was murdered. Why hadn't the person come forward?

He felt a familiar wave of disgust. Being married to Margot had been a roller-coaster ride of horrendous arguments and rock-bottom disappointments. He never knew what to expect. She was up one day and down the next. And always on the go, often neglecting Kristy. When he'd complained, she'd ignored him. She had about as much conscience as a flea.

With so much turmoil in their marriage, he suspected she might have been having an affair. Which she'd hotly denied. But if it had happened, she and her lover had managed to hide it. After the divorce, he didn't care . . . except where her behavior affected their custody battle for Kristy.

Still holding the note, he stuffed it in his pocket.

Seeing the landline telephone, he picked it up and dialed star 69. If he was lucky, it should ring the last number Margot dialed. A call went through . . . four, five rings and then his own voice mail. Disappointed, he hung up. Margot's last call before she died had been to him, demanding to know why he was late picking up Kristy.

Another dead end.

Upstairs, he opened drawers and rifled through her closet. In the bathroom, he found birth control pills. Holding them in his hand, he frowned and thought of the date to meet someone at seven. Did she take the pills to be prepared for whatever transpired? More than he wanted to know, he thought, closing the cabinet.

Giving up, he went back downstairs. Everywhere he looked was a dead end. He had not found anybody who'd seen her that last day. What she'd done to fill those hours before meeting her killer was still a mystery. That alone was mystifying. Margot was outgoing and social to a fault, but in death she was turning out to be far more secretive than he'd ever suspected. But somebody, somewhere knew. He just had to find that person.

5

"He wrote the F word on Melissa's backpack!"

While Carol Sanchez rattled off details of Rickey Armstrong's latest transgression, Lauren prayed for patience. Handling discipline was the most tiresome aspect of her job. And Rickey was an all-too-frequent visitor to her office.

"Well, Rickey?" she said.

He gave a careless shrug. "I thought it was my backpack. They're both the same color."

"And you would want to write that on your own backpack?" Lauren asked, to which Rickey shrugged.

"He used black permanent marker," Carol said. "It's ruined."

"My dad will buy her a new one," he said, unfazed.

Carol speared Rickey with her fiercest look. "I will not tolerate vulgarity in my classroom, Rickey."

"It was an accident!"

"Be quiet, Rickey." Lauren rose to her feet. "I'll take care of this, Miss Sanchez. You can go back to your class."

With a last venomous look at Rickey, Carol departed, stiff with outrage. Lauren pointed to a spot in front of her desk. "Over here, Rickey. Now."

The fourteen-year-old slouched up from his chair . . . taking his time. She felt a wave of helplessness. How to reach this boy? Because his father poured tons of money into St. Paul Academy, Rickey thought he didn't have to obey the rules.

"Whether it was your backpack or Melissa's, writing that word was wrong, Rickey."

"Why? Everybody says it."

Not everybody, she thought sadly, *but too many.* "We don't say it here and we don't write it. Not only because this is a Christian school, but in any context that word is evil."

"It's just a word, Miss Holloway."

She sighed. "I'm taking you back to class and you will apologize to Melissa."

"In front of everybody?" He rolled his eyes.

"In front of everybody," she said, moving toward the door. "And after that, I'm calling your father."

"You can try, sure." Another careless shrug. "But he's traveling."

"Is your mother at home?" She drummed her fingers on the desk.

"Who knows?"

Lauren fought an urge to shake him until his teeth rattled. "I'm calling her to pick you up, or failing that, the housekeeper. It's Friday. I don't want to see you back here until Monday."

"Cool," he said. "I've got a new game for my Xbox."

"Come with me," she ordered.

He followed as she left her office, moving at a good clip. When her promotion came through, she looked forward to someone else having the sticky job of handling discipline problems. And Rickey Armstrong was definitely a problem.

"Can we come in, Lauren?"

Evelyn Houseman stood at the door with Kristy, holding her hand.

"Hi, Lolly, we are visitin' you!" The three-year-old beamed.

Lauren rose and quickly rounded her desk. "What a nice surprise," she said, meaning it. She swept the little girl up and hugged her. After Rickey, Kristy's sweet face and wide smile were balm to her frazzled nerves.

"Can I stay with you?" Kristy begged. "Please, please . . ."

"No, honeybun, I'm sorry. I'm working."

"I wish I could go to your school and I could be with you every day. Can I play with the tea set?"

"Yes, you can make tea for Grammy and me."

"I can tell that she's been here before," Evelyn said, watching Kristy settle in at the tiny table and chairs in the corner of her office.

"Yes." Tucker brought her often. "How are you, Evelyn?" An unnecessary question. Lauren thought she looked like any mother who'd lost her daughter just two days ago. Grief had carved deep lines on her face and she wore sadness like a cloak.

"I'm sad and I'm mad and I'm frustrated that they won't tell me anything," Evelyn said.

"You mean the police?"

"Yes. Do they have any leads? Do they have any suspects? What's happening? They won't tell me." She sighed, crossing her thin arms.

"It must be frustrating. Here . . ." Lauren pulled a chair around so that they faced each other. "Sit down. What can I do to help?"

Evelyn dropped into the chair. "There's nothing anyone can do. All they'll say is that the investigation is ongoing. They'll call if there's something I need to know. I have to accept that and be patient." She managed a smile. "I've never been a very patient person."

"I'm thinking nobody in your shoes would be patient," Lauren said sympathetically.

"It's maddening. I've read that if a murder case is not solved within forty-eight hours, it's likely never to be solved. It will be forty-eight hours tonight."

"I'm sure they're doing what they can." She wondered if Evelyn knew that Sherman had questioned her and Tucker. And what she would make of that. Would it affect her willingness to let Kristy see her? Or had they questioned her as well?

"Well . . ." Evelyn's tone changed, becoming almost brisk. "I'm not here to cry on your shoulder. Lord knows that won't help find Margot's killer." The last words were a whisper as her gaze moved to Kristy, who was happily playing at the little table. "But there is something you can do that would be very helpful, Lauren."

"Oh?" She waited for a moment, curious.

"I want to put Kristy in daycare here."

It was the last thing Lauren expected. She was thrilled. She also felt a bit guilty. Tucker had tried several times to call her today, but she'd been too upset with him to pick up. No doubt this was the reason. "Have you discussed this with Tucker?"

"Yes. And he's all for it. We agree it's the best thing. She's been to Sunday school here since she was an infant. She's familiar with a lot of the children here . . . and you, of course."

"I think it's a great idea," Lauren said. "Do you want to enroll her for half a day, all day, or what? You still have Sarah, don't you?"

"That's just it. Sarah has asked for a leave of absence. I don't know if it's because of Margot or something more personal going on in her life. And to be honest, Lauren, I feel that taking care of a small child full-time just now is more than I can handle." Again, her gaze strayed to the little girl. "We could get a new nanny, but I don't think Kristy needs any more changes in her life. Coming here every day—seeing you—will make the transition easier."

"That does make sense," Lauren said, her heart beating with joy. "How about bringing her at nine and picking her up around two? She'll play and learn with other kids her age, have lunch and a nap. That way, you'll have a chunk of your old life back and she'll have fun."

"I'm glad you understand, Lauren."

"Then it's settled. There are forms, but they'll have to be signed by Tucker. I'll see that he gets them. Kristy can start Monday." Lauren started to rise from her chair thinking they were done, but something in Evelyn's expression stopped her. "Was there something else?"

Hesitating, Evelyn's gaze dropped to her hands. "I had a very distressing phone call today. From Juliana." She got up and closed the door. "I don't want anybody else to hear this."

Lauren braced herself. "What is it?"

Evelyn glanced toward her granddaughter, then, as if reassuring herself that the child wasn't listening, she said very softly, "Margot's death has been horrible. How she died . . . well, you know it's all over the TV and Jordan Raines's dreadful article in the *Chronicle* made it even worse. You'd think since Juliana is his aunt that he'd be more respectful, wouldn't you?"

"He's probably trying to impress his editors."

"Well, it's very thoughtless of him." She clicked her tongue and shook her head. "But I'm not here to discuss Jordan. Martin and I are trying to arrange the funeral, yet they're not releasing Margot's body. It's bad enough that my daughter was murdered, but I just wasn't prepared for how awful people can be."

"What do you mean? You can't be saying that Juliana—"

"No, no. She would never say anything to intentionally hurt me. But someone—a vicious person—called Juliana claiming to be a nurse. She said she'd seen Margot's pictures on the news and had a feeling that something she saw might have been connected to her murder."

"So, why would she call Juliana and not the authorities?"

"I don't know. Maybe she recognized Juliana from some of the pictures they've splashed out there on the Internet." She seemed annoyed at the question. "Anyway, she'd been at this clinic when Margot came in pregnant and bleeding. She had a miscarriage."

Margot pregnant? "When was this? I'm assuming it was after the divorce."

"No, of course not. She was still married to

Tucker. She wouldn't have been pregnant otherwise."

In a perfect world, no, Lauren thought. But it happened. Often. Still, Tucker had never mentioned Margot's suffering a miscarriage. "Where is this clinic, Evelyn?"

"Not in Houston. Somewhere in the Woodlands."

Conveniently far enough away that Margot could have done it and kept it a secret.

Evelyn glanced at Kristy and, keeping her voice low, said, "This nurse said that Tucker caused the miscarriage."

"In what way?"

"Margot . . ." Evelyn's voice caught, but she managed to gather herself after a bit. "Margot said they had argued and that Tucker became violent. She said he lost his temper and threw her against the wall." Evelyn's eyes filled and she put a shaky hand to her cheek. "That can't be true, can it, Lauren? He would never do anything like that, would he?"

"No, never," she murmured. She would know, wouldn't she? But after what she'd discovered yesterday, she couldn't be absolutely certain, could she? "It sounds suspicious, Evelyn. Tucker was thrilled when Kristy was born. In fact, he told me Margot wanted to abort, but he objected so strongly that she gave in. I can't see him not wanting a second baby. More likely he would have welcomed it."

"That's what I thought."

"I assume you called this clinic," Lauren said.

"Yes, of course. But they wouldn't tell me anything because of privacy laws."

"I'm not surprised. They could get in big trouble giving out information like that."

"But Juliana seems convinced that it's true and not just someone wanting to add to our misery," Evelyn said. "And what's to keep that person from calling the media?" She almost shuddered. "It's getting to where I'm afraid to look at the paper or turn on the TV."

"I know what you mean," Lauren said. "But medical professionals are supposedly paranoid about lawsuits. I'm surprised she even called Juliana."

But she had a sinking feeling. Not about the possibility that the story would turn up on TV or in the *Chronicle*, but about what would happen if Detective Sherman got wind of it.

A few minutes later, as she walked Evelyn and Kristy out of the building, she wondered how long it would be before the rest of the world agreed with him. Evelyn and Martin included.

On her way back to her office, she texted Tucker asking him to stop by her place when he was done for the day. She'd defended him to Evelyn and she believed the miscarriage thing was a lie, but she needed to ask him about it. She was still upset that he hadn't told her about his grandfather.

She knew all about teenage loneliness and isolation. Her parents, who were missionaries in China, had sent her away to live with an elderly aunt so she could go to middle school in Texas. Not only had she found herself in a new world—having spent her childhood in China—but her aunt had no concept of teenage culture. In many ways, she had been as elderly as her aunt all the way through college. Which probably explained why she was so late in having a serious relationship. Falling in love with Tucker had been a joyous surprise.

For once, she managed to leave the school at five. When she turned onto the street where she lived, she saw Tucker's SUV parked at the curb. He got out as she pulled into the garage. By the time she'd collected a stack of files and her purse, he was beside her.

He looked good in a classic leather bomber jacket, faded jeans, and boots. She could tell he'd worked outside today, mainly because he brought the scent of the outdoors with him along with the wood shavings that clung to his boots.

"Do I get a hello kiss or are you still punishing me?" It was an attempt at humor, but she saw in his dark eyes a wary watchfulness. When she hesitated, he said, "Can't make up your mind?"

She rose on her tiptoes and gave him a quick peck.

He smiled a little crookedly and took the files from her. "Still mad, I guess."

"I'm not mad, Tucker. I'm just . . . I'm having some trouble dealing with everything." She edged by him and made her way to the door. "And worried that more of the secrets you claim you don't have will pop up and bite me."

"How many times have I told you to lock this door?" he grumbled as she went inside. "If somebody managed to get in your garage, they could walk right in your kitchen."

"I know, I know," she said. "I was in a hurry when I left this morning." Taking the files from him, she headed to the breakfast nook, intending to place them on the glass table. But she stopped short in her tracks when she saw a stunning flower arrangement sitting in the center of the table.

"Omigosh!" She bent and sniffed gorgeous stargazer lilies, closing her eyes as she savored their scent. "Oh, Tucker, these are just beautiful."

He leaned against the doorframe, smiling as she examined the flowers in the mix. "The lady at the florist told me they will last ten days if you use that little pack of stuff in there."

"They're wonderful. And it's so cold and rainy right now that they'll make it seem like spring is around the corner." She tenderly touched a purple iris. "You shouldn't have."

"I had to do something to get back in your good graces."

She turned and tried for a stern look. "Bribing me with flowers is so unoriginal."

"I didn't think you'd accept a diamond bracelet."

She was smiling as she went over to him. She put her hands on his chest and, rising to her toes, gave him a soft, sweet kiss. "Thank you."

But when she tried to step back, he caught her up against him and, with a sound that was utterly male, brought his mouth down to hers, taking the kiss to another dimension. When he pulled his head back, she rocked on her heels, her head spinning.

"I guess that'll show me," she murmured when she was able to speak.

"I wish we were married," he said fervently, still holding her close.

She smiled, twining her fingers through his hair. "At times like this, I do, too."

Pushing back, she led the way to the kitchen. "Do you want something to drink? Check the fridge. I need to take off these heels and change. I'll be right back."

Instead of staying in the kitchen, he followed her, stopping at the door as she went into her bedroom. When she went into her walk-in closet, he said, "Did Evelyn get in touch with you today about Kristy?"

"Yes." She put her shoes away and began to undress. "I brought the forms you need to sign to admit her on Monday. They're in that stack of stuff I brought home with me."

"You're okay with this?"

She pulled a sweatshirt on and leaned around the door to look at him to see if he was serious. "Of course. You know I am."

"Good. That's good," he said, nodding and looking relieved.

Dressed now, she headed down the hall and stopped at her living room. Settling on the couch, she patted a space beside her and said seriously, "There's something I need to ask you."

Tucker sat looking wary.

"When Evelyn came today, she was upset over an anonymous call that Juliana got."

"What kind of anonymous call?"

"A woman said she was a nurse and that Margot had been treated for a miscarriage at the clinic where she worked."

He was frowning. "When was this?"

"It was before the divorce, Tucker. Margot told them that you had thrown her against a wall in a fit of temper and that was what brought on the miscarriage."

Lauren wasn't sure what reaction she expected. Outrage maybe. Flat-out denial? Maybe he'd be upset with her for passing along vicious gossip. But she saw none of that. His expression was unreadable as he simply looked at her . . . for a long, long minute.

"Well, don't you have anything to say?"

At that, he began to slowly, sadly shake his head. "I'm wondering what else can crop up to make you doubt me." He reached for her left hand and studied the engagement ring he'd given her on Christmas Eve. "I felt like I had it all the night I gave you this ring, did you know that? I was free of Margot. I could rebuild my life with you and Kristy. Now I feel like it's all slipping away."

"It's not slipping away, Tucker, unless it was built on lies and deception to begin with." She freed her hand. "I told Evelyn that what that nurse said could not be true. Now you need to tell me I was right."

He made a frustrated sound and surged up from the couch. "I don't want you to have to ask! I want you to trust me."

"And I would have . . . until yesterday," she said quietly. "I'm only human, Tucker."

He moved to the window and stared out. It was dark now. And a chill had settled inside the room. She realized she hadn't adjusted the thermostat. She reached for a cushion and wrapped her arms around it. And waited.

Still at the window, his back to her, he spoke in a low tone. "If Margot had a miscarriage, I never knew about it. I don't see how it could have happened without me knowing. But we slept in separate rooms for several months before we got the divorce."

She was surprised by that.

"And, just so you know, I've never struck a woman in my life." He turned to look at her from eyes that burned. "There. Does that satisfy you?"

It should have. She wanted to believe him, utterly and completely. But there was an ache in her heart. He was right when he worried that something they had together was somehow slipping away. And it would take a miracle to get it back.

Not only did the day of Margot's funeral dawn cold and rainy, but the newspaper chose that day to run another hit piece. "SUSPECT IN SOCIALITE MURDER HAS VIOLENT PAST," Lauren read with equal parts dismay, shock, and disgust. The reporter—again it was Jordan Raines—quoted "an unnamed source at HPD" that a teenage Tucker was responsible for the near-fatal shooting of his grandfather in a hunting accident.

Her heart sank. Who was feeding Raines this sensitive information? Next, she expected to read about Margot's miscarriage on the front page or see it on the nightly news, whether it was true or not. When her doorbell rang, she knew it would be Tucker and that he would have seen the paper. On her way to the front door, she wondered what she could say to make him feel better. After a look through the peephole, she let him in.

He was soaked from the rain. It dripped from the bill of his baseball cap to the shoulders of his leather jacket. And his expression was as miserable as the dark and dreary day.

He glanced at the newspaper in her hand. "You've seen it."

"Yes. You look terrible. Come in." She stepped back while he removed the cap and shrugged out of his jacket. He raked a hand over his hair and wiped his wet palm on the side of his jeans.

"I'm dead in the water if this keeps up, Lauren."

She reached up and kissed him, but when he didn't kiss her back, she said, "You need coffee." Taking his hand, she led him to the kitchen.

He gave a short laugh. "You think coffee will help?"

"It can't hurt."

He followed her into the kitchen and watched her fill a mug. "My phone started ringing at dawn and hasn't quit."

She handed over the coffee. "Do you think Sherman leaked this?"

He was thoughtful, gazing into the mug. "I don't think so. Not because he isn't enjoying the fallout—I bet he is. But he wouldn't want the hassle of defending himself if I accused him." He made a face. "Not that I could prove anything."

It made sense, Lauren thought. Leaking investigative details would jeopardize Sherman's job. He wouldn't want to chance being taken off the case. He wanted to take the credit if and when Tucker was arrested.

Tucker leaned against the kitchen counter. "You know that old saying, A secret shared is a secret bared? Well, Sherman found out easy enough. Jordan Raines could have looked into my background same as Sherman. He's definitely going after me hard."

"This must be so difficult for Martin and Evelyn," she said.

"Evelyn especially," he said. "Martin showed up at my place an hour ago. He was afraid I'd skip the funeral."

"I wondered about that. It could get . . . awkward."

He looked at her. "Would you blame me?"

"Not really. . . . Some people may be downright hostile if you're there." She knew it would take courage to face that. "I guess it depends. What did Martin say?"

"He told me to suck it up and come anyway. Look folks straight in the eye. Kristy needs me." He was shaking his head, eyes on his feet. "If I want people to believe I'm innocent, I need to act like it."

"He loves you, Tucker," she said.

"Yeah. He's amazing." He paused a beat. "I don't know what I'd do without him."

She studied his face. "A lot different from your grandfather, isn't he?"

"Light-years."

"Did you tell him the shooting incident involving your grandfather was true?"

"Yeah, but turns out he'd known for years," he said, fixing his eyes on her. "I don't know what amazed me more—the fact that he knew or that he never let on. Never asked me about it."

"That's because you build up these walls, Tucker," she said, gently chiding him. "Not even the people closest to you can break through."

"I've apologized for not telling you about my grandfather." His voice grew defensive. "I don't have any more secrets."

"I wasn't implying that you did." She took her mug to the sink and rinsed it. "So, are you going to the funeral?"

"Yeah. Even if Martin hadn't pushed it, I was going. I was hoping you'd go with me."

"You aren't taking Kristy, are you?"

"No. She's too young. I'll drop her at daycare, like always. She loves being there."

Lauren smiled, knowing it was true.

Tucker placed his mug in the sink. "So, will you?"

"Go with you? Of course."

At the same time, in another house, the killer drank coffee while reading Raines's latest hit piece. And laughed softly. Amazingly, it looked as if everything might turn out all right in spite of a few panicked minutes. Killing Margot in a blind rage had been stupid. No getting around that. But it was the witch's own fault. From the day she was born, she'd led a charmed life. She'd been mistaken in assuming it would always be that way, the silly twit. Thinking she was free to savage other people's lives and pay no price. The cup rattled as it touched the saucer. Coffee splashed. Well, she'd paid. And paid good.

A grab for the napkin. Mopping up. Thinking. Fingers drumming on the table. The next step now . . . that was something to be carefully executed. It was like building a complex puzzle, choosing each piece and fitting it with precision. Until eventually Kane found himself caught in a web of deceit and intrigue from which there would be no escape. Hmm. More finger drumming. Exactly how Lauren and the kid could be used was not yet clear. But it would come.

Pouring fresh coffee. Planning the next move. Another chuckle. What could have meant real disaster was turning out to be rather fascinating. What was that phrase the kids used—*Who knew?*

6

The funeral was every bit as awkward as Lauren thought it would be. She'd hoped rain and cold would keep attendance down, but whether out of respect for Margot and the Housemans or just from curiosity, the place was packed. Martin and Evelyn had elected not to have a formal wake. Instead, an hour had been set aside before the service to receive condolences. They stood near the closed casket, flanked by Juliana and Carter Brumfield.

From the moment Lauren and Tucker arrived, he had endured looks ranging from suspicion to cool disapproval to downright hostility, some extending to her simply because she was with him. But if it was awkward for her, it was much worse for Tucker. She breathed a fervent prayer for him.

When they finally reached their turn in line, Tucker's mouth was tight, his face pale and set. If there had been a way to escape, she knew he would have . . . gladly.

Juliana was first. She smiled at Lauren and offered her cheek for a peck and murmured, "Thank you for being so sweet to Kristy." But her smile slipped when she looked at Tucker. She was polite . . . barely.

Evelyn was next. She nodded tearfully when Lauren expressed sympathy for her loss and echoed Juliana's thanks about Kristy. Because Lauren knew Martin better than anyone else in the receiving line, she moved gratefully to him and got a lump in her throat when she was warmly enveloped in a bear hug. Consequently, she missed the moment when Tucker greeted Evelyn.

Last was Carter Brumfield, who was like any politician at a public gathering. His smile was tempered with the proper restraint for the occasion as he took her hand in both of his. "Good to see you, Ms. Holloway," he said.

That done, she turned and would have headed for the small chapel where the service was to begin soon. Tucker hustled her from the room and toward the exit. When he reached to open it, she balked. "What are you doing? We can't leave, Tucker. The service is starting in ten minutes. We need to get a seat now, otherwise we'll have to stand."

"That'll be our excuse."

She gave him a stern look. "We are not leaving. You got through the worst. Think of Martin. Of Evelyn. We're going in there and sitting down and paying our respects to the mother of your child."

The resistance went out of him like air from a balloon. His disconsolate gaze clung to her. "I don't know if I can handle any more," he said. "People are looking at me as if I'm Jack the Ripper."

Slipping an arm around his waist, she leaned in to him. "It'll be over soon. We'll take Kristy back to your place. You should keep her with you tonight."

Something in his expression made her pause. "What is it?"

"Evelyn may have something to say about that."

"Did she say something?"

"It wasn't so much what she said. It's what I saw in her eyes." He turned his face to the window where rain streamed down the glass panes like cold tears. "She's beginning to think I killed Margot."

The day after the funeral, Evelyn stopped by Lauren's office after dropping Kristy off at daycare. "I'm closing the door," she said. "I don't want anyone to hear this."

"That sounds serious, Evelyn." Lauren lifted her gaze from some paperwork and sat back.

"It is." Evelyn perched on the edge of the chair, her expression fixed on Lauren. "I don't quite know how to say this . . . and I know you'll want to defend him."

"Who?" But she knew.

"Tucker. I don't like saying it, but I think he knows more about Margot's death than he's telling us. Or the police."

"Why would you think that, Evelyn?" She knew to tread gently, so she kept her voice even and reasonable-sounding.

"When it first happened, I didn't question Tucker's story. But now . . ." She trailed off, her gaze straying to the window. After a minute, she took a deep breath. "I've had some conversations with Sarah. She thinks Margot and Tucker often forgot she was there. But she was there and she heard things."

Confused, Lauren said, "I thought Sarah was gone. Has she returned?"

"No. She and her sister are still in Massachusetts visiting relatives. We've been communicating by email."

"So what did she say?"

"She heard Margot telling someone that she was afraid of Tucker." She looked directly at Lauren and added meaningfully, "Of how far he'd go to get custody of Kristy."

It was no secret to Lauren that Tucker and Margot argued over Kristy. She'd seen firsthand how frustrated he was after their blow-ups. She understood his frustration. Margot could be unreasonable and petty. But in thinking about it now, Lauren realized she hadn't been around Margot enough to actually witness her being unreasonable and petty. An uneasy silence filled the room. What could she say to reassure this woman that Tucker had not murdered her daughter?

Realizing she had no strong argument, she said, "I know when you put all these things together—the articles in the paper, the nurse's phone call to Juliana, and now Sarah's words—it puts Tucker in a bad light. But it's all circumstantial, Evelyn. I wish you'd step back and give the police time to sort all this out. You've known Tucker longer than

I have. You know the kind of man he is. You know he isn't capable of murder."

Evelyn was shaking her head before Lauren finished. "No, I don't know that at all, Lauren. And one of the reasons I'm telling you is to caution you. Oh, I know Tucker seems head over heels about you, but he was head over heels about Margot, too. And look how that turned out. I think you should postpone your wedding."

For a minute or two, Lauren was at a loss. Evelyn was grieving, she understood that. Clearly, she was letting herself be influenced by people who meant well—Sarah, Juliana, Jordan Raines—but that did not give her the right to suggest that Lauren rethink her decision to marry Tucker. And yet she didn't want to argue with Evelyn. There was Kristy to consider.

"I know you mean well, Evelyn," she said gently, "but until I see some hard evidence, I'm sticking by Tucker. What does Martin say about all this?"

She waved her hand impatiently. "Oh, like always, he's blinded by Tucker's personality and their friendship. He's a great business partner and he's active in the church. All that. Well, I know he's charming, but Ted Bundy was charming."

"Evelyn!"

"I see I've shocked you, and I don't mean to," Evelyn said, rising from her chair. "But I just don't know what to think. You know that old saying: Where there's smoke, there's fire. He did shoot his grandfather; he admitted that. And Margot said often enough how difficult he was to live with. She—"

"When did she say that?" Lauren asked, frowning. "And to whom?"

"Oh, here and there." Another dismissive wave of her hand. "After she died, people couldn't wait to tell me. Juliana, too."

"A lot of people criticize their ex when they're divorcing, Evelyn. I would just ask that you remember that."

Evelyn stood with both hands gripping the back of the chair and gave Lauren a concerned look. "Doesn't the fact that all this is piling up bother you a tiny bit?"

"I'm trying not to be caught up in the hysteria. It's unfair to let gossip and innuendo influence us, Evelyn." Suddenly she remembered something she'd promised Tucker. "Evelyn, Tucker saw a note on Margot's refrigerator. She had a date for drinks at seven on the night she died. Do you have any idea who it was?"

Evelyn frowned. "No."

Lauren sighed. "I was hoping you'd know. But don't you think it's odd that person hasn't come forward? I mean, at the funeral, you'd think someone would have said, 'I feel so sad. We were to meet for a drink at . . . wherever.'"

Evelyn seemed to consider the new evidence,

her brow furrowing. Finally she said, "You'd think so, yes."

"We need to find that person, Evelyn. And it's not Tucker."

But after Evelyn left, she had a sick feeling in the pit of her stomach. She wanted to see Tucker. Touch him. Feel the strength and comfort of his embrace. This whole thing was getting very scary.

The following week was hectic. When Friday rolled around, she was determined to clear her desk so that she could enjoy the weekend. Eileen was gradually shifting work to her, easing her into her new role. But it meant she was still doing her current job while training for her new role as principal.

It was dark when she stepped outside and began walking against the icy wind. It had been an unusual January, wet and cold. She was more than ready for the return of Houston's warm and humid weather. Huddled up in the fur collar of her coat, she almost collided with Tucker a few feet from her car.

"Tucker! I didn't see you."

"The way you were walking, you couldn't have seen anybody. What in blazes do you think you're doing?"

Startled, she dangled her purse in front of his nose. "I'm walking to my car. What does it look like I'm doing?"

Grim-faced, he took her arm and steered her toward her reserved space. "You shouldn't be here this time of night. The building is deserted."

"I don't usually stay so late, but I got busy and lost track of the time." She made a quick survey of the parking lot, frowning. "Actually, the cleaning crew is supposed to be here until seven." She glanced at her watch. "Heavens! I didn't realize the time. I guess they've left."

"I saw them drive off in that dilapidated van twenty minutes ago."

She blinked in surprise. "You've been out here that long?"

"Yeah."

"Why didn't you come inside?"

"I was on my cell." He paused. "Talking to Martin."

"Oh. Business?"

"No." He sighed and lifted his gaze toward the school. "It was about Kristy. Evelyn wants custody of her."

"Oh, no, Tucker . . ."

"C'mon, you need to get out of this wind."

She didn't wait. Her teeth were chattering from the cold. She punched in the code that unlocked her car and tossed a stack of files onto the passenger seat.

"I'll follow you home," he told her when she was behind the wheel. "We can talk about it there."

"I saw Evelyn a few days ago. She didn't say anything about this."

"Because she didn't want you interfering before she saw a lawyer."

Lauren released a sigh. "She's actually seen a lawyer?"

"Yeah." He stepped back. "Let's go. It's cold out here."

Tucker was close behind in his SUV when she pulled into her garage. She waited beside her car until he was inside before pushing the remote to lower the door. "Oh, wait. I need to get my house key. It's in here somewhere." She opened her purse and began digging. "You'll note I've mended my careless ways," she said, flashing a smile. "I now lock that door."

"Glad to hear it." But as she searched for the key, he reached around her and tried the door . . . which opened easily. "Looks like you'll have to do a little more mending of your ways," he said.

"I know I locked that—"

She gasped and staggered back against Tucker. Her kitchen was a war zone. Once-white cabinet doors were smeared with food. Cans had been opened and dumped. The pantry had been raided, the contents tossed on the floor. Food from the refrigerator was strewn about everywhere.

"Oh, my gosh, Tucker! What in the world?"

"Wait," he ordered when she tried to go around

him. He firmly moved her away from the door. "Open the garage. Go out that way." He gave her a little push. "Now."

"No! I need to—"

"Do it! Somebody could still be inside." He reached in and pulled the kitchen door shut. "We're calling the police."

She stood frozen in shock, trying to take it in.

"Go, Lauren!" He hit the wall remote that raised the garage door.

Lauren turned and ran out of the garage to Tucker's SUV parked in the driveway. Chilled and stunned, she drew her coat close. Grim-faced, Tucker helped her onto the seat. Standing in the open door, he took out his cell phone and punched in 911.

"Who would do this?" Lauren's voice rose in distress. "Why?"

"I don't know." Tucker held up one hand to give his name and the address to the dispatcher, then reported the break-in. Reaction was beginning to set in. She was in his SUV, which was still warm, and she was wearing her coat, but she was trembling, chilled to the bone. And terrified.

Finally, he hung up. "What if someone's still inside, Tucker?" Lauren asked, looking fearfully at her house.

"No way we can know, but if he was, we surprised him. If he's got any sense at all, he'll leave by the back door." He reached over and cupped her face in his hand. "It'll be okay, sweetheart. Just hang on until the cops get here."

"I'm afraid to look at the rest of my house, Tucker. What if—"

"I know. We'll check it out as soon as we can." Looking over the top of the SUV, he spotted a police cruiser turning the corner. And behind it, a second one. "They're here now," he said.

"Oh, thank heaven."

"You stay here," he told her. "I'll tell them what happened. After they check it out and give us an all clear, I'll come back and get you."

"You aren't going in there, Tucker!"

"No, they wouldn't let me anyway."

She got out of the SUV. "Then I'm staying with you."

He gave her an impatient look, which she met with a mulish one of her own. "I'm staying," she repeated.

They headed to the street to meet the two cruisers pulling up at the curb. Four policemen got out. They made an impressive sight. Before addressing Tucker or her, they focused on her home, surveying the grounds, the open garage, and the adjacent buildings. Finally, one of them spoke. "Tucker Kane?"

"Yeah, that's me."

"You made the call?"

"I did. This is my fiancée, Lauren Holloway. It's her home. There's been a break-in."

"We didn't go inside," Lauren informed him. "Once we saw the horrible mess in my kitchen, we left. We were afraid he could still be in there."

"We'll check." The spokesman, whose name tag read LOGAN, signaled to the three officers, who peeled away with weapons drawn. Two of them headed into the darkness on each side of the building. The third stationed himself just outside the garage, but stayed in the shadows. Logan studied the lighted interior. "You have another outside door in the rear?"

"Yes."

Logan unsheathed his weapon and said to Tucker, "Sir, stay here until we give you the all clear." And without waiting for a reply, he moved away from the SUV and headed toward his partner at the garage. "Let's do it."

When Logan and his partner reached the door, one stood to the side with his weapon at the ready as Logan pushed it open and called out, "Police!"

Lauren shuddered and moved closer to Tucker. He slipped an arm around her. "Let's get back in the car. We shouldn't stand out here in case something happens."

She didn't argue. As they headed to the truck, she could see her neighbors watching, agog with curiosity. Some were at their windows, others were bunched up on the opposite side of the street a safe distance away, murmuring among themselves.

"Rubbernecking," Tucker said, his mouth twisting with distaste. "A favorite Houston pastime."

Lauren let Tucker help her into the passenger side of the SUV and waited as he climbed in behind the wheel. "How long do you think it will be before they know if he's in there or if he's gone?"

"Not long." Then about ten minutes later: "Here he comes." Officer Logan made his way toward them, wiping his hands on a paper towel. When he reached the SUV, Tucker lowered the window.

Logan looked beyond Tucker to Lauren. "There's nobody inside, Ms. Holloway. But your kitchen is a mess. Did you say you didn't go inside and look around before calling us?"

"No, we closed the door as soon as we saw the . . . the carnage."

"It is that," he agreed. "So you didn't see the words written on the glass tabletop in your breakfast room?"

Lauren gave him a bewildered look. "No. What words?"

"I took a picture," Logan said, flashing his iPhone. "You can't go in. I've called a fingerprint specialist. He should be here in a few minutes. But I'd be surprised if we get anything . . . prints or DNA."

"You want to share that?" Tucker opened the door and got out, looking as if his patience had

115

reached its limit. Without a word, Logan passed his iPhone over. Tucker read it in one quick glance. With a tired sigh, he handed it to Lauren, then turned and gazed out into the night while she read it.

First he killed Margot. Are you next?

7

Lauren stared at the words in shock. Her first reaction was to dismiss it as a mean-spirited prank. At school she'd had to severely reprimand a couple of teenage boys before the Christmas holidays. This could be their way of getting back at her.

But the message had an evil feel to it. Those boys were mischievous, not evil. Still behind the wheel of Tucker's car, she sat gazing at her house, at the police activity. She felt chilled. And not because of the weather. What was happening to her nice, safe world?

"Ms. Holloway?"

"What?" She'd almost forgotten Officer Logan. She returned his iPhone. "I'm sorry, I was just trying to think of who might have done this."

"Somebody who doesn't like you very much. The rest of your house is pretty much okay, at least from what my partner and I could see. The two officers checked outside but didn't find anything either. So after we get fingerprints, you'll want to check your house for yourself . . .

see if your jewelry is all there. But this seems to me more like somebody with a personal grudge." He paused, giving Tucker a measured look. "You have any ideas, Mr. Kane?"

"No," Tucker said.

"I don't either," Lauren said. If it turned out to be the boys at St. Paul Academy, she didn't want the police involved until she had a chance to check it out for herself.

"You'll need a copy of the police report to file your insurance," he said, taking out a card. "The number to call is on the card."

As she took it, a van stopped at the curb and two men in white jumpsuits got out.

"These guys will get the prints," Logan said. Strolling over, he spoke briefly to the two technicians. Both shot quick glances at Tucker and Lauren. Tucker had been stonily silent since reading the note. She guessed Logan was sharing the information about the message. They wouldn't be the only ones Logan would tell, she suspected. Detective Sherman would be next.

"You take care now, Ms. Holloway," Logan said, as the two technicians passed on their way to the garage entrance. "Our guys will be inside a while, but if you'll take a word of advice, I wouldn't spend the night alone until you can get someone to change your locks."

Hearing that, Tucker spoke up. "You don't think the lock was forced?"

117

"No. Looks like somebody got in with a key. Since the garage was closed, he probably came in by the back door. We found it unlocked."

"Are you sure?" Lauren was stunned.

"Yes, ma'am . . . unless you unlocked it before we got here tonight."

"No," Tucker said. "She didn't."

"Anybody else got a key?" Logan asked.

"Only—" She stopped. Tucker had a key, but she didn't want that fact entered on the police report. Not until she and Tucker had a chance to talk about what happened.

Officer Logan waited a moment, but when both remained silent, he touched his hat politely. "As soon as the techs are done, you'll want to check to see if anything of value is missing. If so, they'll add it to the police report."

"I'll do that," she said.

"And if you think of anything that might be helpful, give us a call."

"Thank you," she murmured, "I will."

As the police cars turned around and left, she got out of the SUV, knowing she had to go inside. But the thought of it, knowing some evil person had desecrated her home, was abhorrent. Who would do such a thing? Who would try to scare her this way? Who would write those words?

First he killed Margot. Are you next?

She trusted Tucker with all her heart. No message from a crazed person could change that.

She realized Tucker was looking at her, his dark eyes hooded.

"I'm sorry about this, Lauren," he said.

She put her arms around him, resting her head on his chest. She could feel his heartbeat. For a long minute, she allowed herself the comfort of being in his embrace. So much of her world was being threatened, but at least she still had Tucker and their love, their plans. She would soon be his wife, but in her heart the joy was slipping away.

"It's not your fault," she said, almost sadly. When he didn't say anything for what seemed a little too long, she stirred and looked up at him. His gaze was fixed somewhere beyond her, his expression bleak.

"I'm not so sure about that."

She gave him a confused look. "Why?"

"It just strikes me that with Margot's murder and my name in the paper and on TV and you being my fiancée, having your house trashed is a little too much coincidence."

"But why would anybody do that?"

"I don't know. To harass you? To get to me through you?" His gaze roamed her face as if memorizing it. "The worst part is I bet this is going to get a lot meaner and nastier."

"But you don't know that, Tucker," she said in a gentle voice. "This could be just some druggie looking for something to pawn."

"I hope you're right, but this is personal. First,

we have the message. No common thief would write that. And whoever did this took time to trash your kitchen, opening cans and tossing food around. They must have been here in broad daylight. Which tells me it was someone who wasn't worried about being noticed by the neighbors. There's no doubt they wanted to give you a message." He paused, then added dryly, "And me."

He took her hand, his thumb moving over the engagement ring he'd given her. "You didn't tell Logan that I was the only other person with a key to your house. Why?"

"Why should I? You didn't do this. I don't know who did, but I don't want Sherman climbing all over you, which is what would happen if I'd told . . ." Her words faltered.

"The truth?"

"I didn't lie, Tucker. I just didn't choose to share the fact that you have the only other key."

"And it's right here." He took his keys from his pocket and singled out her house key. "Where it's been all day," he said, "in case you're wondering."

"I wasn't wondering any such thing. So stop it!" She pressed a hand to her heart. "You're upsetting me by talking that way."

"I'm sorry," he said, shaking his head. "It's just that—"

"What? Just what, Tucker?"

"I just have a really bad feeling about all this."

"You're letting it get to you. I can understand that, but we have to keep believing that right will prevail. We've got to hang on to our faith here, Tucker."

He released a heavy sigh. Then, taking her arm, he walked her back to the house. "You never found your key when you were digging in your purse, did you?"

"Didn't I?" She frowned, realizing she couldn't remember. "I was so shocked I think I dropped my purse. I couldn't tell you whether I had them or not."

They spotted the purse on the garage floor a few feet from the door. Tucker waited while she rooted around inside looking for the key. "I usually keep it in this pocket," she muttered.

"That thing's as big as a suitcase," Tucker said, watching her. "I don't know how a woman your size manages to haul around so much weight."

"Everything in here is a necessity," she told him. But when she couldn't find the key, she carried the purse to a utility shelf and dumped everything out.

"A tape measure is necessary?" he asked, holding up a retractable model.

"Yes, to measure things." She sorted through the motley contents, setting aside her wallet and iPhone. She found pens—several pens—bulldog clips, a comb, a brush, a zippered bag containing her makeup, a small notebook, a bottle of ibuprofen, a nail file kit, a tube of medicated lip balm, a powder compact that should have been in the makeup kit, a balled-up pair of socks, but no key.

Tucker reached for the socks, but she rapped his knuckles and made him drop them. "My feet get cold when I'm sitting at my desk," she told him.

"I could take care of that for you," he said with a gleam in his dark eyes.

She stood looking at the items, frowning. "It's not here. How could someone have taken my key out of my purse?"

"Good question," he said. "Tomorrow, first thing, you're getting a good security system. I blame myself for not pushing it before."

"But I had it this morning," she said, still puzzling over it. "It must have been taken at school."

"By any one of twenty people, right?"

"Well . . . I guess so." She gave him a stunned look. "I can't believe this."

"But for tonight, you need a locksmith. I'll call the man we use at H & K. I'll also call our cleaning service. Hopefully he'll get someone out here as soon as the fingerprint guys are done."

"We're done now, Ms. Holloway." The taller of the two appeared at the open kitchen door. "It's an unholy mess in there, but it doesn't look as if the rest of the house has been disturbed." Setting his case down, he balanced on one leg to strip the booties from his shoes, one after the other. "We'll wait while you check your jewelry and to see if it looks like anything else is gone, okay? Watch your step, though. We laid down some paper to make a path, but it's still slippery."

Rather than going through the kitchen, she went around to her front door to get upstairs. She saw quickly that her jewelry was untouched, then stood looking around at the room. It did not appear that anything was disturbed. Whoever did this had desecrated her kitchen just to write that note.

But why? Was it meant to put a wedge between her and Tucker? For what purpose? Why would someone want her to begin doubting Tucker? She pressed her fingers to a spot that was beginning to throb between her eyes. She felt as if she were being bombarded with one shock after another. What would be next? She closed her eyes and breathed a prayer. And in a minute, she felt a gentle calm steal over her.

"Thank you, Lord," she said. And headed downstairs.

When the technicians left half an hour later, she followed Tucker, picking her way through globs of goop on the floor to get to the breakfast nook. She wanted to see the message for herself.

It was more ugly scrawled on the glass table than it had been on Logan's iPhone. She stared at it a long moment before moving her gaze to Tucker. She forgot what she'd intended to say.

Something about how he looked caught at her. A part of him was here, she realized, but another part was far away. Somewhere he didn't want her to follow.

"If you're thinking that I'm one bit influenced by this sick message, Tucker, you're wrong," she said. "I'm not."

He looked at her with a deep sadness in his eyes. "Not yet, maybe, but for how long?"

"For however long it takes!" she said in a stern tone. She moved closer and put her arms around him, holding on to him fiercely. "I love you. I'll stand by you, no matter what." She looked up at him. "You've got to be strong. How many times do I have to say it? You've got to have faith."

"Mr. Kane?"

Lauren stepped back quickly as a man appeared at the door to the garage.

"Orly Tipton, you got here fast," Tucker said, then, turning to Lauren: "He's here with the cleanup crew."

While Tucker gave Tipton instructions, Lauren inspected the living room and her office, but found nothing missing or even out of place.

"Did you check the powder room?" Tucker asked a minute later.

"Yes, but I didn't see anything."

Tucker opened the door to the tiny space. "Whoever did this had to have cleaned himself up before he left," he said.

She hadn't thought of that. "If he did, he was very neat," she said, looking over his shoulder. The room was as pristine as ever.

"Maybe . . . maybe not . . ." He reached for a trash basket in the corner. Using his pen, he poked around inside it.

Still peering around him, Lauren said, "What is it? Do you see something?"

"A used paper towel."

"I don't keep paper towels in here. . . . You're thinking maybe he washed his hands, but didn't want to leave traces of his DNA on the fabric towel?"

"Are you thinking his DNA wouldn't get on paper?" He arched an eyebrow.

"It was just a thought," she said defensively.

"Uh-huh . . ." he said, smiling.

"What?"

"Perhaps one of the technicians left it," he said thoughtfully. "I don't think they'd overlook something so obvious."

"Oh. You're probably right," she said. But when Tucker bent down to set it in place, something rattled in the trash basket.

"There's something under the liner," Lauren said, her voice bubbling with anticipation.

Tucker removed the bag and looked inside. Seeing what it was, he made a short surprised sound.

"What is it?"

He held up her keys.

・ ・ ・

After a thorough search of the house, they found nothing missing or out of place beyond the kitchen and adjoining nook. The intruder had done his damage, scrawled the note, and apparently left the way he got in . . . through the French doors that opened onto the patio.

When they were done, Lauren turned to Tucker. "I guess I should call the police and tell them about finding the key," she said.

He shrugged. "It's up to you."

She looked at him a long moment and, without comment, picked up her cell phone to call.

Tucker left Lauren with the locksmith and the cleanup crew to canvass the neighborhood asking if anybody had seen anyone near her town house. Even though the police had questioned the neighbors, he wanted to personally check. It was a vibrant area, alive with activity during the day. He'd seen the traffic on her street—people coming and going, nannies strolling their young charges, delivery trucks going in and out, yardmen working from daylight to dusk. It was no surprise no one had noticed anything out of the ordinary.

"How would anybody know if the intruder was a stranger who didn't belong?" Lauren said after he came back.

"They wouldn't," he said shortly. "Which is

probably how he managed to get inside without suspicion."

For a minute, he watched one of the men mopping the floor, then turned to her. "All this—the trashing of your kitchen, the key—it has to be Margot's killer. You realize that, don't you? For some reason, he wants to shake your trust in me."

"But why, Tucker? I can't think of anybody who'd want to do that."

"Beats me, too, babe." He shook his head despondently. "But we've got to figure it out . . . and soon."

They left to get something to eat while the cleanup crew worked. Most of the evening crowd had thinned by the time they got to the bistro. They ordered at the main counter, then Lauren found a table while Tucker collected sugar and cream for their coffee at the condiment bar across the room. When he returned, she fixed her gaze on his hands as he stirred sugar into his coffee. He had square, strong hands. Capable hands. He used them with a natural male grace that was captivating to Lauren. But then, most everything about Tucker was captivating to her. Still, she couldn't quite quell a feeling of unease . . . that something unseen threatened her fragile chance at happiness.

"Tell me about Evelyn wanting custody of Kristy," she said. "Why would she do that?"

He studied the contents of his coffee cup. "She's

influenced by everything she sees and hears. In a way, I can't blame her. The media already has me tried and convicted." He drew in a deep breath and let it out, then raised his eyes to hers. "What happened tonight at your place is going to make her even more determined."

"What about Martin?"

"When it comes right down to it, he'll support Evelyn. And maybe I should just back off and let them have Kristy temporarily. I'd get her back when this is over . . . when we find who killed Margot. No court in the land would refuse me custody of my daughter then."

But what if we don't ever find who killed Margot?

She didn't say it out loud, but she could see that Tucker had thought the same thing. If Margot's killer was never found, he'd live under a cloud of suspicion for the rest of his life.

She took a sip of coffee and found it strong and bitter. The unease that had been lurking was growing. She loved Tucker. She wanted to be his wife. But was she willing to live forever with that sword hanging over their heads?

What would that mean? She would have a husband who was believed to be a killer. It was a daunting thought. She'd spent the time since Margot was murdered believing that the real killer would be quickly found. If that didn't happen, Tucker would be focused on proving his innocence. She would be faced with defending him. Day in, day out.

Her heart heavy, she gazed into the dark coffee. She couldn't deny reality any longer. Maybe the wedding should be postponed.

8

Lauren spent Saturday putting her house back in order with Tucker's help. On Sunday, they took Kristy to church. She'd hoped that people who'd known Tucker as a strong Christian and an active church member would give him the benefit of the doubt in spite of the media hype. He needed their prayers and encouragement. To her dismay, they seemed every bit as suspicious as if he were a stranger. She wondered if they'd forgotten that a man was innocent until proven guilty.

She was actually glad to get up Monday morning and dress for work. Unfortunately, she was not quick enough in leaving her house to avoid Detective Sherman at her front door. But it was probably just as well, she decided, letting him inside. She'd rather deal with him here than at school. If Craig Rawls had heard what happened—and she knew somehow he would— he would be waiting when she got there.

Sherman handed her the newspaper, still in its plastic sleeve. She took it and held it unopened, choosing to keep him in the foyer area.

"Just a couple questions, Ms. Holloway," he said, taking out his little notebook. "What happened the other night was a nasty way for somebody to give you a message."

Things will get meaner, nastier.

Tucker's words coming full circle, she thought. "Yes," she said, "and I hope you can tell me who did it."

"That wouldn't be my department, but you can bet they're working on it. I doubt they've processed everything. They'll see if they can get fingerprints or DNA. It's doubtful. So you may never know."

"I was afraid of that," she said, unsurprised.

"Are you afraid of anything else?"

"Like what?"

Finding the right page in his notebook, he adjusted his bifocals and read, " *'First he killed Margot. Are you next?'* That's pretty scary, Ms. Holloway."

"It's scary only if I believe what that horrible person wants me to believe."

"That would be that your fiancé killed his ex-wife?"

"Tucker is innocent." She met his eye. "In spite of what you might think."

He waited a beat, then clicked his pen and held it poised over the notebook. "So, who besides yourself has a key to this house?"

"Detective Sherman, why are you here? What

happened is not a homicide. It's a simple case of breaking and entering, isn't it?"

"I'm surprised you consider it simple if those photos I saw in the police report are anything to judge by."

Lauren remained silent.

"Okay—" He consulted his notebook again. "Because of that message, we consider this matter part of Margot Kane's murder investigation." He raised his eyes to hers. "Let me be frank, Ms. Holloway. Tucker Kane is our prime suspect. It's my job to follow up on anything that links a prime suspect to the case. That's why we'd like to know who else has a key to your house."

"It's irrelevant now," she said, keeping her voice calm. But she had a sick feeling in the pit of her stomach. "Whoever it was took it from my purse while I was at school, used it to get into my house, then left it here. It was just a fluke that we found it last night. It could have been there for days before I finally stumbled on it."

"How did you find it?"

If she told the truth—that Tucker found it—what would he make of it? Would he think Tucker planted it? If so, for what reason? He'd probably scoff at what she believed: that it was planted by the real killer, meant to add to the growing suspicion that Tucker was the killer.

"It was in the powder room. In the trash." A

half-truth. She had to work to meet his eye. "It was under the plastic liner."

Sherman didn't quite roll his eyes, but his look was openly skeptical. "I understand from Logan that Kane was here with you last night when he responded to the nine-one-one call."

"Yes."

He closed his notebook and tucked it into the inner pocket of his jacket. "Ms. Holloway, you'll forgive me for saying this, but your loyalty to a man like Tucker Kane could be dangerous." Then he added with a shrug. "I'm just saying . . ."

"Thank you." She opened the door to show him out. "If you want to talk to me again, Detective Sherman, please call first."

"I'll do that." He indicated with a nod to the newspaper she held in her hands. "You might want to look at that before you leave."

The article was on the front page, but fortunately below the fold.

"GRIM SCENE GREETS BRIDE-TO-BE." And in a smaller font: "Possible Link to Socialite Murder."

Swamped by an overwhelming sense of dread, she sat down. Her heart sank when she saw Jordan Raines's byline. Of course. She braced herself to read what was sure to be another damning piece.

"Police responded to a nine-one-one call reporting a break-in last night at 8:10 P.M., at the residence of

Lauren Holloway." She closed her eyes, feeling every bit as much a victim of this reporter's invasion of privacy now as Tucker. Would this ever end? "According to the police report, food from Holloway's pantry and refrigerator was strewn about on the kitchen floor and other surfaces. Holloway is engaged to Tucker Kane, whose ex-wife, Margot Kane, was found murdered in an abandoned house in the Heights almost two weeks ago." Closing her eyes, Lauren lowered the paper. Margot's name and the word *murder* in one sentence still had the power to shock her. It still seemed unreal . . . like a very bad movie where she found herself an unwilling player. Shaking, she quickly scanned the rest of the article. "An unnamed source claimed Kane was with Holloway when she entered her home and discovered the break-in. Kane is presently a person of interest in the investigation of his ex-wife's murder."

Lauren tossed the newspaper aside. She moved to a window and stood looking out. A rare overnight frost was on the ground. The lone tree in her backyard was stripped of leaves, its limbs naked against a gray sky. She felt like that—naked, exposed, cold. She was living a nightmare. Each day something worse happened.

How had it come to this?

Tucker turned his iPhone off and tossed it on the dash. He'd had no fewer than ten calls from various media and it was only 9:00 A.M. How they'd found his cell number was a mystery. He chalked it up to the string of mystifying things that had been happening. He longed to have his life back, but until Margot's killer was found, he was doomed to take each day as it came.

He pulled into the Housemans' driveway. He'd decided last night to try to get Evelyn to talk to him about Margot. Maybe he'd get some scrap of information from her, something she didn't know she knew that could lead to her killer. It was worth a try. God knew, nothing else had come to light.

He rang the doorbell and waited to be let inside. He'd told Martin what he was doing, even though he thought nothing would come of talking to his wife. He said Evelyn had been taking tranquilizers to excess since Margot's death and who knew what she could recall with any level of lucidity. Still, Tucker wanted to try.

The door was opened by Juliana, not Evelyn.

"Tucker. This is a surprise."

"I came to see Evelyn. Is she here?"

"Where else would she be, Tucker? Shopping? Having her nails done? She's in mourning for her daughter. Why are you here?"

There was no mistaking Juliana's tone. With her hovering, he would probably get nothing from Evelyn. But he meant to try. If he could get inside.

"I need to talk to Evelyn," he said. "It won't take long. I know she's sad. I am, too. But—"

"Who's there, Ju-Ju?"

Taking advantage of Juliana's hesitation, he stepped around her and met Evelyn's gaze. "It's me, Evie. Can I talk to you for a minute?"

"Go back to the sunroom, Evie," Juliana said. "I'll take care of this."

Evelyn touched her head with a shaky hand. "No, no, it's all right, Ju-Ju. Let him in. I have things to say to him."

Ignoring Juliana's disapproving expression, he crossed the threshold before she could shut the door in his face. "What things, Evelyn?"

She waved a hand vaguely. "Come to the sunroom, Tucker," she said. "I need to sit down."

"She is taking strong medication, Tucker," Juliana whispered sternly. "You are out of line harassing her this way!"

"I'm not harassing her," he said. Brushing past her, he caught up with Evelyn and slipped a hand under her elbow. She was literally swaying under the influence of medication. He matched his steps to her shuffles and when they reached the sunroom, he helped her settle onto a chaise longue. She leaned back with a relieved sigh and closed her eyes.

"Evelyn, I was wondering if you could answer a few questions for me."

Eyes still closed, she said, "Only if you answer a question for me, Tucker."

"Okay . . ." Warily, he waited.

With visible effort, she managed to open her eyes. "Did you kill Margot?"

"No! Is that what you think?"

"I don't know what to think." She sighed. "There's the miscarriage, there's all the arguing and fighting over Kristy between you two, there's those newspaper articles . . . so much suspicion . . ." She trailed off.

"I didn't know anything about a miscarriage," he said. "And yes, we argued, but a lot of divorced couples argue over custody of children." Tucker sat down on the foot of the chaise and leaned forward, desperate. "Evelyn, I'm trying to trace Margot's steps the day she died. I'm trying to find the person who killed her. It wasn't me."

"The police believe it was you."

"Then why haven't they arrested me?"

"I don't know . . ."

"Who told you that?" But he knew. Juliana. He glanced at her standing in the door, arms crossed, glaring at him, looking like a drill sergeant.

"It doesn't matter," Evelyn said, closing her eyes.

He saw she was slipping into sleep. He touched her hand. "Evelyn, help me out here, please. Think. Did you talk to Margot that day?"

She blinked and managed to look at him with eyes dilated to black. He could tell she struggled to focus. "I . . . She called me. She wanted me to watch Kristy. You were . . ." She licked her lips. "Umm . . . she said you were late."

"What time was that?"

She sighed. "I don't know, Tucker."

"Don't go to sleep, Evelyn!" He squeezed her hand. "Did she say where she was going? Did she say who she was going with?"

Juliana moved to the chaise, giving him a fierce look. "Can't you see she isn't capable of saying anything that makes sense? She can't finish a sentence, for heaven's sake. You shouldn't try to make her think back to that horrible day." Moving between him and Evelyn, she pulled a knitted throw over her and tucked it gently up to her chin. "Don't worry about it now, Evie. Just close your eyes, darling."

"Wait—" Evelyn said weakly.

"I want you to leave, Tucker," Juliana said furiously. "Right now."

Lauren was right in thinking she would have to deal with Craig Rawls first thing Monday morning. She did manage to have time to take off her coat and get her coffee before he appeared. But then he was there, hovering, wringing his hands and sighing every few minutes.

"Have a seat, Craig," she said with a smile.

He did, although he looked as if he was too agitated to relax. "I won't beat around the bush, Lauren. The situation with your fiancé is becoming an embarrassment."

"I take it you've seen the morning paper."

"Yes, and so has the school board. We're shocked that your home was vandalized. Do you know who did it?"

"No. And the police are baffled as well." She paused, sipping her coffee, knowing that expressing his sympathy over what happened was not the reason for his visit.

"You're in danger, Lauren. What if you'd been in your house when he did this?"

"I appreciate your concern, Craig. In fact, I'm having a new security system installed today. Also, the police promised to increase their patrol of the neighborhood. I think I'll be okay."

"Well, be that as it may, we on the board have to think of the safety of the children. What if this . . . this stalker or whoever he is should decide to attack you here?"

"I must say I never thought of that," she said. "Security is a priority here. Nobody can get past the door without buzzing in. They must sign in at the front desk where they're given a name tag."

"And what if somebody had a gun hidden in their clothing?"

She sighed. "Craig. With all due respect, don't you think you're overreacting?"

"If I am, then so is the board. And I think you should keep that in mind."

She bristled at the implied threat, seeking a reply. "We can station a security person outside. Would that satisfy you? And the board, of course."

He paused for a beat or two. "The truth is, I . . . we don't like that your name is constantly showing up in connection with this . . . this whole incident, the murder. It's unseemly, Lauren. And I would think it's embarrassing to you." He paused again, as if trying to choose his words carefully. "This is a delicate matter. I'm not sure how to put it other than to say it outright. For the second time. Have you considered postponing your marriage plans? Just until this is resolved."

She sighed. "Actually, I have been giving that some thought, Craig. I love Tucker and want to be his wife. But for the sake of the school and my own career, I may need to change the date of the wedding." She paused, then added quickly, "I feel certain the police will find the person who killed Margot and Tucker will be exonerated."

"And I hope you're right," he said.

She stood up. "So until then, I plan to focus my attention on St. Paul Academy, on the students, and on implementing good changes that will keep us one of the flagship schools in the city."

Craig was on his feet, too. "Good, good. I'm glad to see that you're showing consideration for the school, Lauren. I don't mean any offense by that, but that's what we're about here, isn't it? The school and what's best for the students?"

"Yes, Craig."

"Then I'll let you get back to work," he said, clearly satisfied with the outcome of his visit.

• • •

Eileen appeared a few minutes later. "He's such a stinker," she said, wrinkling her nose. "And if I weren't a moral person, I'd use stronger language. I don't know how he can carry around such a load of righteous indignation so consistently and not get absolutely worn out."

Lauren managed to smile. "Thanks, Eileen. But I admit I'm troubled. He's right that it doesn't do the school any good to have my name showing up in those newspaper articles."

"You're such an asset to the school, Lauren. It's not your fault that Margot Kane was murdered. And it's not your fault that your home was vandalized." Eileen looked thoroughly disgusted. "First and foremost, this is a church. We're supposed to show Christian compassion, sympathy, support."

"And Craig sees everything as it relates to the school's financial situation," Lauren said dryly. "He'll let me stay on until something happens that affects the budget."

"Well, I'll be at your side at the board meeting," Eileen said. "And I hope they won't forget that Tucker is a member of this church. It's not as if he's some gigolo you met in a bar."

Lauren had to laugh. "If Craig heard you saying that, I can just imagine his reaction."

"If I get a chance, I will." She didn't even try to repress her sly smile. "And I'll say it to anybody else who suggests that your role at St. Paul Academy is in any way diminished because your fiancé's ex-wife is dead."

"Murdered, Eileen. She was murdered."

"Whatever. It's nothing to do with you."

9

After leaving Evelyn and Juliana, Tucker drove around aimlessly. He couldn't be sure that Evelyn knew anything. She was so drugged that whatever she said might or might not be true. He'd have to find another way.

The wood paneling, he thought. He needed to find the wood. It was his connection to the real killer. The only thing that could save him now. It had to have been taken sometime after four when he left that house and before eight when he got back and found Margot's body. It should have been easy. It was distinctive and rare, and he'd marked it when he'd taken it down. It was not an item any old thief would covet.

Who took it? Who, who, who?

He'd come up empty when he questioned his crews. The executor of the estate, which owned the property, offered nothing new either. The client who stood to get the newly paneled library knew nothing. The only other stone left unturned was the property itself, and it was cordoned off with crime scene tape.

Back at the office, he vented to Martin. "Juliana was determined not to let me get near her," he said.

"I'm not surprised that Juliana is playing the protector," Martin said. "They've been closer than sisters since college."

"She thinks I did it and she's got Evelyn believing it, too."

"Ju-Ju *suspects* you, Tuck," he said gently. "There's a difference."

"Not all that much. With her husband as DA, you can bet she's talking it up to him every chance she gets. I'm surprised I haven't been arrested already."

Martin leaned back in his chair, making it squeak with the shift of his bulk. "Evie will be reluctant to say anything that might reflect poorly on Margot. She certainly worried about her." He turned his gaze to the window, thinking. "Especially in the last few months. I had a feeling it was woman's stuff, you know? I wish I could help, but I was the last person Margot wanted to talk to."

Wrong, Tucker thought. He was the last person Margot wanted to talk to.

"Margot," Martin said, heaving a deep sigh. "I keep thinking of her, Tuck, wondering how it got so bad that I lost touch with my own daughter. Now that she's gone, I have a big hole in my heart, but I can't forget how much pain she caused Evie and me."

Tucker understood that and sympathized.

Martin's gaze strayed to the window. "When something like this happens, Tucker, you wonder if you could have done things differently. If I had tried harder, maybe I wouldn't have this feeling of failure . . . and I might be able to answer some of your questions."

"Don't worry about it," Tucker said. "I'll keep on looking." After a beat, he drove a frustrated hand through his hair. "I just need a lead, Martin, a clue—something that will put me on the right track. The killer is a twisted, sick puppy. Messing with Lauren to get to me proves that."

"Wait," Martin said, frowning. "You don't know it was the killer who did that."

"I do know. Not that I could convince Sherman. He thinks I planted the key in that trash basket. And until that happened, I was willing to let the cops move at their pace, but no more." He headed to the door. "I'm not sitting back and waiting for Sherman to decide it's not me. While he's focused on me, something else might happen to Lauren."

"What are you going to do?"

"I don't know." He shrugged into his jacket. "Yet."

Martin got up and walked with him to the door. "Whatever you do, son, be careful, you hear?"

Once in his truck, Tucker knew what he was going to do. He needed to find that wood. Or figure out what had happened to it. The logical place to start was the house in the Heights. He planned to check for himself, see what he could find. Maybe the police had overlooked something. The problem was that they had it taped off and crossing it was a crime. If he was caught, he'd be arrested. But at this point, he was willing to risk it.

He drove past it a couple of times looking for signs of activity. He was relieved to see that it was deserted. Still, he had to be careful. He circled the block once more before parking two streets over. He hoped to be able to get on the property from the rear without a curious neighbor spotting him or a passerby reporting him.

The adjoining property had been converted into a Mexican pottery shop. He had to get past the shop without being noticed to get into the backyard of the old house. Trying not to appear to be skulking, he strolled past the shop entrance and kept on going toward the rear, where he encountered a fence.

He groaned. Chain link. And at least five feet high. Luckily, he was in jeans and running shoes. Taking a deep breath, he found a toehold and got a good grip with his fingers and hoisted himself up and over. He landed on his feet with a jarring thud. He dusted himself off.

He was in.

Twenty minutes later, he stood in the room that had once been a library paneled with the missing rare mahogany. So far, he hadn't turned up anything to explain what happened to the wood, but it had been a long shot anyway. The cops had to have been over everything with a fine-tooth comb. If there had been anything, they would have found it. Not that they would have told him anyway. Since proof of how the wood had been taken would not be helpful to them, they had no incentive to investigate that aspect.

Disappointed, he headed out the back door to make a quick search of the grounds. The grass was ankle high. It could have been worse, he reminded himself, as he waded through. In summer, it might have reached his knees. And he would have been forced to watch out for snakes. As he moved farther away from the house, he slapped at a sting on the side of his neck. Mosquitoes were no respecters of season in Houston.

Eventually he had to search the front yard, which meant taking a chance on being exposed to street traffic. Like most old houses in that era, this one was raised so that the wraparound porch's deck was a good four feet off the ground.

He hesitated for a minute. He'd discovered a lot of interesting things under old houses he'd renovated. It wouldn't hurt to take a look, even though the police had probably searched the area. Squatting, he turned on his flashlight.

He couldn't see much. Grimacing, he crawled under the porch, swiping at spiderwebs while keeping an eye out for other critters. After a few minutes of searching, he reached the end of the porch. Disappointed, but not surprised, at finding nothing, he turned, still crouching to keep from banging his head. He was almost back to the point of entry when he saw it. His heart jumped.

His hammer!

For a moment, he couldn't believe his luck. It was lying in plain view on a brace that connected one of the two-by-twelve supports. How had the cops missed it? But thank God they had. If they'd found it, it would have sealed his fate. Breathing a fervent prayer, he grabbed it, scrambled out from under the house, and found himself face-to-face with a huge cop in uniform. And looking into the barrel of a gun.

10

He was in handcuffs when Sherman arrived. The hammer had been bagged as evidence by the arresting officer, a bull of a man named Ferguson. Meanwhile, a host of cops swarmed over the property, streaming in and out of the house, searching the thick shrubbery and wading through the grass the same way Tucker had earlier. He heard one of the officers grumbling that Sherman was going to be ticked off that the hammer had not been found in the initial search. Suddenly, as he was marched to the cruiser where Sherman waited, his heart sank. There sat a van, and emblazoned on the side a TV station logo. Someone on the inside at HPD had to be leaking every tidbit of this case. Otherwise they couldn't have gotten here so quickly. But who?

He'd always thought it ridiculous that people in police custody covered their faces from the TV cameras, as if doing so could preserve some vestige of anonymity. Now, he felt a similar urge, but with the handcuffs behind his back, he was helpless. And just when he thought it couldn't get any worse, Jordan Raines climbed out of an unmarked car. Tucker's pace faltered. With a sense of utter disaster, he knew he'd be on the front page of the *Chronicle* again tomorrow morning.

"Step lively, Kane." Ferguson prodded him onward with a sharp jab to Tucker's left kidney. "You don't want to keep the detective waiting."

"You must think HPD is made up of a bunch of nitwits, Kane," Sherman said when he was hauled in front of him. "You assume nobody's watching, so you can come out here and corrupt a crime scene?"

"I haven't corrupted anything," Tucker said. "I was looking for a clue to explain what happened to the wood."

"So you figured it would be stacked under that old house?"

When he didn't reply, Sherman shrugged and went on, "I think you were looking for something all right, and you found it." He wagged the evidence bag in Tucker's face. "What I can't figure is why it took you so long to come back out here to get it. Not that it mattered when you got around to it. I've had the place under twenty-four-hour surveillance from the get-go."

While Tucker considered how to answer—or even if he should answer—he became aware of movement behind him. Glancing over his shoulder, he saw Jordan Raines standing at the back of the vehicle holding a tape recorder, obviously listening.

"Can we have some privacy, Detective?" Tucker said through gritted teeth. "Raines is a reporter."

"Move on, Raines," Sherman said, but without heat. "We'll be taking him in. You can get a quote from him there." Ignoring Tucker's disgusted reaction to the idea of giving the reporter a quote, he referred back to his notes.

"Where were we? Oh, yeah. The reason you risked crossing that crime scene tape."

In spite of being trussed up like a Christmas turkey, Tucker was tired of being toyed with. "I wasn't looking for anything in particular, Detective. I'm as surprised as you are that the hammer was under the house."

"You mean the murder weapon." Sherman waited, but when Tucker didn't rise to the bait, he said, "You missing a hammer?"

Tucker was silent, fighting to hold a steady

gaze, yet inside he felt as though he stood on the edge of an abyss. Then, with sick apprehension, he watched Sherman pull out a card. Taking a pair of glasses from his pocket, he put them on and began reading. "You have the right to remain silent. Anything you say . . ."

Tucker tuned him out. Any hope he had of finding evidence linking someone else to Margot's murder seemed a distant one now.

"You understand what I'm saying, Mr. Kane?"

"Yes."

"Then let me describe the hammer we now have in evidence, thanks to you," he said, clearly enjoying himself. "Good quality, excellent brand, fine steel head, hard wood handle. Does that ring a bell?"

Tucker remained silent. He'd been read his rights, but he didn't intend to say another word until he had a lawyer by his side.

"Oh, I almost forgot." Sherman shook his head as if pained by his forgetfulness. "This one has your initials carved in the handle." He paused a long minute. "You have a hammer like that?"

Tucker said nothing.

Tiring of the game, Sherman snapped to Ferguson, "Take him in so we can book him for Murder One."

Ferguson hustled Tucker to the black-and-white cruiser. He hoped he'd get a chance to use his iPhone, but he wasn't counting on it. He wasn't sure he'd be able to make a call before he was booked. He wanted to alert Martin, otherwise he'd see it on TV. Sherman gave him a hefty shove, making him crack his elbow painfully on the doorframe of the car. Settling back, he resigned himself to going to jail.

The killer clicked off the phone with a triumphant feeling. Good news. Now the plan could really get going. It was out-and-out police incompetence that the hammer had not been found at the crime scene. It had been left in plain sight. But no surprise there. Sheer laziness that not one of the investigating officers had stirred himself enough to go under the house looking for the murder weapon. Infuriating to be forced to wait until Tucker decided to look for it. Or stumbled upon it. Obviously, he knew it was missing. He had to be stewing over that. But finally it was in evidence. His fate was sealed.

A small, satisfied smile. It had been almost too easy.

11

"I never knew how stubborn you could be," Martin complained as he climbed the steps at HPD with Lauren. "You'll probably be shocked by what you see and hear in this place. Don't say I didn't warn you."

"I'm all over being shocked," she said. "Being engaged to a murder suspect ended all my girlish illusions."

"I wish Tuck hadn't called while I was in your office," Martin said, still grouchy. "Any other time Evelyn would have been the one to pick up Kristy."

"What was he thinking, Martin? It's against the law to cross that yellow tape."

"He told me he was trying to find out what happened to that blasted wood." Martin opened the door and allowed her to enter ahead of him. "Jerry Blacklock said he'd meet us there."

"I hope he's good."

"The best defense lawyer in Houston," Martin said.

Suddenly she clutched his arm. "Oh, no. Don't look. Maybe he won't see us."

"What? Who?" Martin craned his neck and spotted Jordan Raines heading for them. Locking his fingers around Lauren's arm, he picked up his pace to the elevator. Which seemed, to Lauren, a mile away.

"Don't say a word," he told her in a low tone. "He can't quote you if you don't speak."

"Ms. Holloway," Raines said, approaching and showing a lot of teeth in his smile. "Are you still convinced of your fiancé's innocence?"

Lauren ignored him and looked straight ahead.

Unfazed, he turned to Martin. "Mr. Houseman,

Tucker Kane has been arrested for your daughter's murder. How far are you willing to go in support of your former son-in-law?"

Martin, stonily silent, punched the up button as if it were Jordan Raines's nose.

"Ms. Holloway, when you're with Kane, do you have any concern for your safety?"

Lauren struggled to hold her tongue. Martin was right. Better to ignore him than to say words that he would twist totally out of context.

"Mr. Houseman, did you know about Kane's violent past when you went into business with him?"

Mercifully, the elevator pinged and the door slid open. Lauren quickly ducked inside and Martin followed. But when Raines tried to enter, Martin blocked the entrance.

"Hey, this is a public elevator."

"So, sue me," Martin said, giving Raines a look so fierce that it would have stopped a freight train.

Lauren was trembling when the door closed. Martin put a comforting arm around her shoulders. "He's a jerk, Lauren. Don't give him the satisfaction of seeing that he upset you."

She felt her throat go tight. It was no wonder Tucker loved Martin like a father. Even without his formidable connections in Houston, it had been his lucky day to be in business with Martin Houseman. Maybe some of those connections would be helpful. His wife's best friend—albeit

Margot's godmother—was married to the district attorney. Would he offer Tucker leniency? Or was Tucker beyond help?

"Do you think Carter Brumfield will be willing to do something?"

"Not openly," Martin said. "We'll wait and see if he returns my call. He'll need to guard against doing anything to harm his political ambitions. Stuff like that can rear up and bite you when you least expect it."

"Crossing a crime scene tape is a misdemeanor!"

"He's arrested, Lauren. I'm not sure what the charge is. I didn't get much info from his phone call. As for Brumfield, I don't expect he'll show his face."

As they exited the elevator, Martin's cell rang. "Speak of the devil," he said, glancing at it. After greeting Brumfield, he spent a moment simply listening. "Yes. Yes. Thanks, Carter. I owe you one."

"Is he going to help?" she asked anxiously when he disconnected the call.

"Yeah."

Lauren breathed a sigh of relief as they left the elevator. But it was troubling that Tucker was even in a position to need the kind of help a DA could provide. She felt a sensation that was becoming more familiar by the day . . . that her world was on shifting sands. That all she knew and loved was in jeopardy.

Was God giving her a message?

"Here we are," Martin said, ushering her into an area that bustled with activity. Cops in uniform were in and out. Other people in dark suits roamed about freely. Chairs against the wall were occupied—by both men and women, looking down and out. She saw no sign of Tucker, but she felt sick thinking that he fell into that category.

As she stood with Martin looking about the room anxiously, Detective Sherman suddenly appeared, striding out of a room with a female officer following a few steps in his wake.

At first, Lauren didn't see Tucker. Her view was blocked by a huge prison guard with a shaved head and arms and legs the size of tree trunks. Sherman stopped when he reached Lauren and Martin. Then he nodded to the guard, who hauled Tucker from the room by his arm.

She'd convinced herself when she insisted on going with Martin that she was prepared for whatever happened, but she felt shocked to see Tucker handcuffed and his ankles shackled. It was impossible for him to walk normally, let alone to match the giant's pace. So he was forced to submit to the indignity of being dragged along like a dog on a leash. When he looked up and saw her, his face went as pale as paper.

"What are you doing here, Lauren?" Without waiting for her answer, he glared at Martin. "Take her out of here, Martin. Now."

"No." She backed away, out of Martin's reach. "I'm here because I insisted on coming. And I'm staying."

With his eyes burning, Tucker turned to Sherman. "Have one of your people escort her to a safe place downstairs, Sherman. She can wait there."

Sherman gave a shrug. "What'll it be, Ms. Holloway? It's up to you."

She met Tucker's dark eyes. She could see turmoil, misery, shame. "We're in this together, Tucker," she said softly. "If the tables were turned, wouldn't you want to stay with me?"

For a minute, Tucker seemed primed to argue. Both knew the chances of Lauren's ever being in such a situation were slim to none. Yet hadn't his chances been the same? He released a defeated sigh and nodded slowly. But he turned from her and refused to look at her again.

"You have yourself one fine woman there, Kane," Sherman said with a smirk that set Lauren's teeth on edge. "But you didn't need to make such a fuss. We've got what we want. For now." He signaled the mammoth guard, who began to remove Tucker's handcuffs and shackles.

"Crossing crime scene tape is a misdemeanor," Martin said with a look of disgust. "Were shackles and chains necessary?"

"Restraints are required when we detain a

155

murder suspect," Sherman said. "I had probable cause."

Martin frowned. "What probable cause?"

"We caught him coming out from under that old house with a bloody hammer. It fits the medical examiner's description of the murder weapon."

The murder weapon? Lauren thought, stunned. She shot a quick look at Tucker, but he was stone-faced.

Sherman's glance at Martin was apologetic. "Sorry, Mr. Houseman. I know this is real unpleasant for you."

Sherman waited a moment, then said, "We figure that's why Kane took a chance at crossing the tape. He was looking to remove his hammer from the premises. Lucky for us, I've had the house under surveillance since the murder, so we caught him."

"If all you say is true," Martin said, "I'm wondering why you're letting him go."

"If it was up to me, I wouldn't," Sherman said. "He's been charged with Murder One." He paused at Lauren's soft cry. "He'll still have to appear in court tomorrow morning. His lawyer just left." He glanced at his little notebook and then at Martin. "Jerry Blacklock. I'm guessing you had a hand in calling him. Hard to get hold of a high-powered guy like that on the spur of the moment."

Martin said nothing.

"Yeah. He's good, and frankly your boy is gonna need the best. Anyway, Blacklock was slick. He took care of the immediate situation . . . with a little help from friends in high places." He gave an elaborate shrug. "Works every time."

12

All three maintained a stony silence as they headed to the parking garage. Tucker's stomach was tight. He should have told her the hammer was missing. She'd be thinking it was one more unpleasant shock, one more secret he hadn't shared. When they got into the elevator, she started to speak, but he put a finger to his lips to stop her. She looked stunned at the implication that their conversation might somehow be overheard. He hated that she was getting an education in the underworld of crime. Hated having her witness his humiliation at HPD. He hated what was happening to them. He hated what was to come. And from the way things were going, he was certain there was more to come.

Once they were in Martin's car and heading down the exit ramp, he said, "Shall I drop you at the school, Lauren? I assume you'll want to pick up your car."

"Yes, thank you." Her eyes straight ahead.

"How about you, Tuck? I sent a man to get your truck and drive it back to the office. You want me to swing by so you can pick it up now?"

"I'll take him to get it," Lauren said coolly.

As if hearing the odd note in her voice, Martin sent her a quick glance. "You okay?"

"Yes."

"I wish you hadn't come," Martin said. "I warned you it wouldn't be pretty."

"You shouldn't have let her come with you," Tucker said, anger simmering inside him. "It's no place for a woman."

"I wouldn't have had to go if you hadn't taken it into your head to break the law by crossing that tape," she said coldly.

He knew he should shut up, but he kept remembering the shock and disgust on her face when Sherman hauled him out of lockup. "You want me to sit back and let them pin a murder rap on me? Because that's what they're doing."

She turned then, looking as fierce as a female tiger, and lit into him. "I want you to stay within the law! Why is that so hard for you, Tucker?"

Martin met Tucker's gaze in the rearview mirror. "We're all keyed up, which is understandable after what we just went through. But think how happy Sherman would be to know you two were going at each other over it."

Tucker muttered an apology and settled back in the seat, scowling. He knew Martin was right. If he kept this up, he would not be surprised if Lauren decided to wash her hands of him.

When he felt he had his emotions under control, he said to Martin, "Thanks for sending Jerry Blacklock. Good as he is, I bet he wasn't the person who managed to get me released. Who else did you call, Martin?"

"Brumfield."

He stared at his hands, shaking his head. "No telling what you'll have to do for his campaign as payback."

Martin's laugh was short and dry. "I thought of that." He braked at a traffic light and waited while two joggers crossed. "If he wants money, you can write the check."

Nobody said anything for the remainder of the trip. Tucker fixed his gaze out the side window, his thoughts as bleak as the Houston sky. It would be night soon, and by rights, he should be spending it in jail. But instead of feeling relief, he felt like a man waiting for the guillotine blade. Jerry Blacklock was good, but it would take a miracle worker to get him out of this.

Lauren's car was the lone vehicle in the school parking lot. As soon as Martin stopped, Tucker was out. But Lauren didn't wait to have the door opened for her. She thanked Martin and climbed in, not looking at Tucker.

The night had turned cold and windy. He shoved his hands into the pockets of his jacket, keeping a wary eye out for anything suspicious. Once they were both in the car, he studied her profile as she

159

backed out. He wanted to touch her, but knew better.

Eyes straight ahead, she asked, "Did you know your hammer was missing?"

"I have at least half a dozen hammers."

"I want a yes or no answer, Tucker. Did you know a hammer was missing?"

"Yes."

She made a small pained sound as if his words had pierced her heart.

"I didn't kill Margot, Lauren."

"Tucker." There was a sigh in her voice. "Damning information keeps coming out. You knew your hammer was missing and you went to get it back. That's very suspicious no matter how you look at it."

He desperately needed her to believe him. "I went there to try and figure out what happened to the wood," he told her. "I didn't know the hammer was there. My tools were in that old house because I'd left them there when I pulled off the paneling. The killer must have taken the hammer."

"Yes, but you never mentioned to me that your hammer was missing."

"I didn't want to worry you," he said, knowing it sounded lame.

Now at his office, she pulled up beside his truck. After a minute, she lifted a hand and pushed her hair back. It was a weary gesture. It told him how tired she was of all this. It scared him. Was this the moment? Was she going to tell him now that it was over?

"It sounds pretty dumb to wait so long to try to retrieve the murder weapon. Did you tell Sherman that if you'd known about that hammer you wouldn't have waited so long to get it?"

He'd been so certain about what she was thinking that it took him a moment to reply. "I told him. He dismissed it as a lie. He thinks every word out of my mouth is a lie."

"Yeah, well . . ." She turned to look at him then. "There's such a thing as a sin of omission, Tucker. You might want to spend some time thinking about that."

He studied her face in silence. She was so beautiful. He felt a rush of love for her and, on the heels of that, full-fledged panic that he might lose her.

She made a move gesturing for him to get out of the car. "They'll eventually find who killed Margot, Tucker. Until they do, you need to listen to your lawyer. Don't do anything else that makes you appear guilty."

"What if they don't find the killer?"

She sighed with impatience. "They will. If you don't trust the justice system, try putting your faith in God."

"Have you forgotten that I don't have an alibi, Lauren?"

She frowned. "What are you saying?"

"I'm trying to say that you can help me . . . if you're willing."

"Help you in what way?"

"This will all go away if you just say you were with me that night. Then we can get on with our lives. We can get Kristy back, buy a house . . ."

She stared at him in astonishment. "Are you serious?"

"You could tell them I was with you from . . . say from the time school was out, that you waited with me for the inspector . . . until I left and returned to get that wood." He saw she was shocked, but he plowed on desperately. "Do you remember if you came straight home from school that day?"

"Wait, wait. Stop. This is crazy. Sherman has already questioned me. Why wouldn't I have told him then that I was with you?"

"You can say I wanted to protect you. That I didn't want you dragged into something so . . . ugly."

"Can you hear yourself?" Her voice rose as she moved in her seat, looking at him as if he'd turned into a stranger. "Lying about where you were and where I was and at what time is just so . . . so . . . wrong, Tucker. Don't you see that?"

"There's no other way, I'm telling you."

"Telling the truth is the way."

"And getting myself convicted of a murder I didn't commit?"

She gazed at him wordlessly for a minute. "I can't believe you're asking me to lie."

"You don't understand! I need to get off their radar so I can have time to find who really killed her."

"That's the job of the police, don't you see that?"

"They aren't looking at anybody but me, especially now that they have the hammer! I don't need to wait to see if it's Margot's blood on it. I know it is. The killer planted it just so this would happen. You have to do this."

"Have to?" she repeated. "I have to lie?" She looked as if she was feeling sick. He felt sick himself, asking her to do something so . . . so . . . dishonest. So wrong.

"Have you already told Sherman this?" she asked suddenly. Suspiciously.

"No. I wouldn't do that."

She looked at him in silence for a long moment. "There was a time when I thought I would do anything for you, Tucker. I felt so blessed that I was to be your wife. I'm thirty-two years old. I had almost despaired of finding the right man to share my life with. Then there you were—a man of honor, a loving father, ethical and honest in your business, active in our church. You were everything I dreamed of in a man."

He felt rotten. Lower than a snake. And yet, still desperate.

She took in a deep breath. "I don't want you to be unjustly convicted, never that," she said in a quiet tone. "I know you didn't kill Margot. And what you're asking may seem harmless to you." She hesitated, then looked him in the eye and said softly, "But it goes against everything I believe in."

His face went crimson with shame. But another part of him was terrified at the thought of being jailed for life. Locked up behind bars. Everything he worked for, wanted for Lauren, for his daughter, for himself . . . over.

She shook her head slowly, sadly. "I can't lie for you, Tucker. I just can't. I'm sorry."

After a minute, when he knew there was nothing more to be said, he got out of the car. Then, before closing the door, he leaned down and said, "I'll call you tomorrow."

"Yes. I wish you would. We need to talk."

When he climbed into his truck, he felt chilled to the bone. He realized they hadn't kissed good-bye. Maybe they never would again.

13

His house was empty and cold. He tossed his keys on a table and went through to the backyard to let Buddy inside. The dog was all over Tucker, delighted to see him.

"*I'm* glad to see you, too, boy." He gave the

golden's ears a good rub and hugged him. For a minute he felt choked up.

As he made his way back to the living room, he saw Kristy's toys scattered about. He had a habit of buying things for her . . . lots of things. Falling into the trap of a lot of single fathers, he was always trying to make up for the time they couldn't spend together. He thought about driving over to see her now, even though she'd be sleeping. After what he'd just put Lauren through, he felt a desperate need to just look at his little girl, to touch her face, to soak in her innocence. Maybe it would help to cleanse himself of the shame of the last hour.

Feeling miserable, he shoved his hands deep into his pockets. What had he been thinking to ask Lauren to lie for him? And how was it that he expected Martin to intercede for him? To circumvent the system? What was happening to him? When Lauren listed all his honorable traits, she'd sounded so sad. As if he'd lost them. Had he? How had he lost touch with his principles? With his God?

He bent and picked up a pink bunny and held it against his face. It smelled like baby powder . . . like his baby . . . like Kristy. If it weren't so late . . . He glanced at his watch. But it was. The Housemans wouldn't appreciate his visiting at this hour. Maybe never again, if Evelyn had any say in it. If she'd been suspicious about him before, his arrest tonight would be the end. He had to hope that Martin would be able to persuade Evelyn, if not Juliana, to cut him some slack where Kristy was concerned.

Releasing a weary sigh, he trudged to the stairs and was halfway up when his telephone rang. Not his cell, but his landline. He'd thought about permanently disconnecting it, but never got around to it. For a moment, he was tempted to let it go. But one of the few people who knew the number was Lauren. Hoping against hope that she might be calling, that her mood when she left him had changed, he backtracked down the stairs and picked up the phone.

"Hello?"

"You ignored the message I left at Lauren's house. That was a mistake."

The hair on the back of his neck rose. The voice was indistinct as if filtered through a device to disguise it. Not male or female. "Who is this?"

"So I planted the hammer. You saved me the trouble of alerting Sherman when you found it."

"Who are you? What do you want from me?"

"Butt out. Or I'll take Lauren and Kristy."

14

Tucker sat down on the bottom stair, his heart beating like a jackhammer. Buddy whined and nudged his knee, but Tucker didn't respond. He was still in a state of shock. It had to be the killer.

He knew about the hammer. Tucker swallowed sickly, realizing the man was threatening Kristy . . . Lauren. Frantically, he tried to calm himself, but his thoughts were in chaos. It had been so quick and his reaction so visceral that the caller had broken the connection before he had a chance to try to keep him on the phone.

He tried to recall the voice. Was it a man? A woman? He couldn't tell, not the way it was scrambled. But man or woman, he got the message. It was an out-and-out threat to his baby and to Lauren, the two people he held most dear in the world.

What did he mean by "take"? Kidnap? Or that they'd meet the same fate as Margot? He got up and began pacing, Buddy trotting beside him. He was dealing with a madman. A monster. He should have recorded that call. Or what? And why? He got the gist of it. If Kristy and Lauren were to be safe, he had to "butt out."

But if he did that, how could he trust the word of a killer? He stopped, tried to gather his thoughts. What about the fact that he was due in court at eleven o'clock? If he left he'd be a fugitive. Where would he go?

He realized he still held the phone in his hand. Maybe he should call the police. But would they believe him? Not likely. He could just imagine Sherman's reaction, and it wouldn't be helpful. He might even be able to turn it around against him.

This was a nightmare. But no way could he afford to ignore the threat against Kristy and Lauren. He dropped his head in his hands.

Lord, help me. Guide me. Show me the way.

With a crushing sense of despair, he sank down on the stairs and wrapped his arms around Buddy. By morning, his dog would be the only creature on the planet that didn't hate him.

When Lauren left Tucker, she swung by her office, knowing a slew of things had probably stacked up while she was away. Glancing at her watch, she saw it was after six. She'd skipped dinner, but she had no appetite anyway, and she probably wouldn't be able to sleep tonight either. Not after what happened at the police department. She decided she might as well clear her desk so that when she got to her office tomorrow, she would be ahead of the game. And she wanted to be in court when Tucker appeared at eleven o'clock.

The school was empty and her office locked up tight. She had to use her master key. It was eerie inside the building. Spooky. But she squared her shoulders and kept on going. After what she'd been through today, she felt able to face anything.

She took out her phone and placed it within reach on the desk, then tossed her purse on a chair. After removing her coat, she began sorting through a stack of telephone messages. Nothing really pressing . . . if she didn't count three calls from Craig Rawls. The first two were marked urgent. The third she decided she couldn't ignore.

Call me ASAP when you get back from the police department.

She sighed. Holding the note in one hand, she rested her forehead in the other. He must have learned about Tucker's being arrested. Drumming her fingers on the desk, she debated calling him. It would not be pleasant. Might as well face the music now.

He picked up on the first ring. "Lauren. I've been waiting. Where are you? You're not still at the police department, are you?"

"No, Craig. I'm in the office. I thought I'd—"

"The office? At this hour?" There was shock in his voice. "There's no security after six o'clock. What are you thinking! I insist you lock up and go back to your car. I have something of vital importance to discuss with you. I will stay on the line while you leave."

"I appreciate your concern, Craig, but since I missed most of the afternoon, I need to catch up. The door is locked. I'm fine. What is it you need to discuss with me?"

"This is an order, Lauren. I'm not hanging up until you leave the school and are safely in your car. Otherwise, I will drive over and personally escort you out of the building."

Lauren felt a sudden wave of fury. She'd been subjected to enough indignities today. She did not have to tolerate Craig Rawls's high-handedness. Who did he think he was?

"I'm hanging up now, Craig."

"Don't—" She broke the connection.

For a minute or two, she sat trembling with rage. Or despair. She wasn't sure. She didn't care what Rawls wanted to discuss with her. He was too pompous to be taken seriously in her present frame of mind.

Dropping her head in her hands, she began to cry. Tears, scalding and copious, ran down her cheeks, through her fingers, dripping onto her desk calendar. Her world was shattered. *She* was shattered. The joy she'd rejoiced in only a few weeks ago was gone, vanished in the horror of Margot's murder.

She pulled a tissue from a box and blew her nose. She'd decided to postpone their wedding, and yet she hadn't been able to bring it up to Tucker. Yet even deeper in her heart was the fear that she might never be able to marry him at all. After tonight, she realized, she could no longer put off that decision.

She would tell him tomorrow.

At 5:00 A.M., after a sleepless night, she threw on a robe and went out to get the morning paper. She didn't look at it until she got back to her kitchen and poured herself a cup of coffee. Then, bracing herself, she unfolded it.

There, as she feared, beneath the fold on the front page, was another article, headlined EX-HUSBAND OF MURDERED SOCIALITE ARRESTED. Again, Jordan Raines's disgusting byline. And a bad mug shot of Tucker. He was unsmiling, even fearsome-looking. To someone who didn't know him, he looked as if he could be a killer. Sickened, she could only imagine how Tucker must feel.

She scanned it quickly, then picked up her iPhone and called him. It went at once to voice mail. Which meant his phone was turned off. Leaving a short message, she took her coffee and went upstairs to shower and dress. Her heart was heavy at the thought of telling him that she wanted to postpone their wedding. But now that he'd been arrested there was really no choice in the matter.

She'd tossed and turned most of the night. She was bitterly disappointed about canceling the wedding, but that paled beside her anger that Tucker hadn't told her about the missing hammer. Then, in the next minute, she worried that her reaction was unfair. That she'd been too quick to judge. He needed her to stand firm with him.

An hour later at school, Craig Rawls met her even before she got inside the building. "We have to talk, Lauren."

"Yes." She fell into step beside him. "I apologize for last night. I'd had a bad day."

He gave a grunt that could have been acceptance

or not. Consequently, she was dreading whatever he had to say to her as she unlocked the door of her office and took off her coat. "Would you like coffee? It'll probably be fresh at this hour."

"I never touch it. Gives me indigestion."

That made two of them, at least today. Her tummy was in a knot, too.

"Have a seat, Craig."

"No, thanks. This won't take long." He pulled a folded newspaper from inside his jacket and tossed it on her desk. "Have you seen this?"

Did he think she lived under a rock? "I'm not sure," she said, suddenly feeling reckless. "Hard to tell with it folded up like that."

Drawing a breath through his nose, he gave her a sternly disapproving frown. "Are you sure you want to take that attitude, Lauren?"

She sat down with a sigh. "I'm sorry," she said, rubbing her forehead. "Of course I've seen the paper." She saw his shocked face and hastily added, "Martin Houseman was able to find a lawyer for Tucker. He was released on his own recognizance. We'll be in court today at eleven."

He stared. "Do you think that's wise?"

"I'm engaged to marry Tucker, Craig. I need to show my support."

"This is bad, Lauren. Very bad. Unless you take some action to distance yourself from this individual, the fallout will reflect poorly on our school. Our parents are already questioning your judgment. Some of them are talking about pulling their children. I've tried to warn you, but you don't seem to realize the seriousness of the situation . . . as it relates to St. Paul Academy."

She stared at him in shock. She wanted to tell him that he was overreacting. She wanted to tell him that it was none of his business if she was engaged to Attila the Hun. She wanted to kick him out of her office and out of her life. But she wanted to keep her job.

"I hear you, Craig," she said. "If the board is meeting about this, you can tell them that I've decided to postpone my wedding. Or are you here to terminate me today?"

"Not today. Not yet."

The silence that followed his implication was awkward, to say the least.

"Out of courtesy, we felt we should give you a chance to . . . to . . ."

"Cut Tucker out of my life once and for all?"

"Basically," he said with an apologetic shrug. "They will be somewhat reassured that you are putting off your plans to marry him."

She stood up even though her knees were trembling. "Thank you. And I would appreciate it if you would keep me informed."

"I'm sorry about this, Lauren. But this man . . . he's in deep trouble. You may believe him when he says he's innocent, but the facts tell a different story. You're young yet. There are—"

"Other fish in the sea?" she said dryly. And before he had a chance to further advise her on how to live her life, she rounded her desk and walked him to the door. "Have a nice day, Craig."

She sat gazing into space after he left. Her job was important to her. She looked forward to being principal next year. But career ambitions paled beside what Tucker and Kristy brought to her life. She was to be a wife and mother. She had been convinced that she was on a life path that God willed with Tucker right there beside her.

Reaching for her iPhone, she called him again. It was her fourth attempt to reach him. She frowned when it went to voice mail again. Even with his phone off, he would have been checking his calls. Where was he? What was happening that he couldn't—or wouldn't—talk to her? Had the police picked him up again? She looked at her watch. Not yet nine. Two hours before he had to be in court.

Worried now, she decided to call his office. Janice Inman kept tabs on everybody. She would know where he was. Telling herself there was surely a logical explanation, she scrolled until she found the number.

"Janice," she said when the receptionist picked up. "Is Tucker there?"

"No. And I was just about to call and ask if you

knew where he was." Her voice lowered. "I read the paper."

"I'm worried. I've tried calling and he doesn't answer."

"Same here. Martin doesn't know where he is either." Janice paused. "This is so strange, Lauren. Tucker is very conscientious. He scheduled a job this morning in Montrose, but he didn't show up to give the crew instructions. It's not like him."

"I could drive to his house," Lauren said. "Maybe he isn't feeling well."

"If he's sick, he would have called the office."

"I have a key. I'm going over."

"Will you let us know what you find out?"

"Yes, of course."

A few minutes later, she went to the Panda Bears room to check on Kristy. Looking through the small glass window, she saw that the room was alive with three-year-olds in various stages of play. Kristy and two other small girls sat in tiny chairs at a table having "tea."

She backed away feeling relieved. Kristy must have been dropped off while Craig Rawls was in her office. She carefully cracked the door and caught the eye of the teacher, Jean Fellows, and beckoned her over.

"Sorry to interrupt, Jean," she whispered. "Who dropped Kristy off this morning?"

"Mr. Houseman." Jean looked concerned. "Why, is something wrong?"

"No, no. Everything's fine. Thanks, Jean."

Back in her office, she called Evelyn. "Did Tucker come by this morning to see Kristy before Martin brought her to school?"

"No," Evelyn said in a vague tone. "Juliana told me what happened last night. I knew . . ." She gave a broken sob. "I knew all along that he killed her."

Lauren felt a pang. It would hurt Tucker so much to hear Evelyn talk this way. "Martin was able to get a lawyer for Tucker, Evelyn. He was released last night. I just need to know if you've seen him. If he came by to see Kristy."

"I told you. No. And I don't want Martin to interfere in police business where Tucker is concerned. You should be having some very serious second thoughts about him, too, Lauren."

"Evelyn." She sighed. "You know Tucker. He did not kill Margot."

"What do we really know about him, Lauren?"

She could have ticked off ten or twenty things she knew about Tucker, but she knew that Evelyn was in no mood to listen. And she was in no mood to keep defending him. Bottom line was that he hadn't stopped by to see Kristy this morning as he always did.

She went back to her office to get her coat, feeling suddenly scared. Tucker wouldn't just ignore her phone calls. He wouldn't fail to contact his office when he had a work crew scheduled. Something was wrong.

On her way out, she ran into Eileen in the hall.

"I saw the paper," Eileen said. "I don't need to tell you the board will not be happy."

"Craig Rawls was waiting for me before I got to my office this morning. He basically said I have to decide between my job and Tucker."

"Oh, Lauren . . ." Eileen touched her arm. "I am so sorry. You'll choose Tucker, of course. You won't walk away from that precious little girl either."

"That's pretty much how I feel." She managed a weak smile. "But it's nice to hear someone who isn't urging me to cut him out of my life."

Eileen suddenly seemed to notice that she was wearing her coat. "You're not leaving now, are you?"

"I'm only leaving for a few minutes. I can't reach Tucker. I'm going to his house to see if I can find him."

Eileen gave her another sympathetic pat on her arm. "Take your time. And let me know what you find."

She found exactly nothing. Standing in the center of the great room in Tucker's house, she called his name. There was no answer. The house was empty. It *felt* empty. She let her gaze wander around, seeking some clue to what must have happened. But there was nothing.

She was on the point of heading upstairs when

she heard the refrigerator kick on. Out of curiosity she went into the kitchen and opened it. Empty. She stared in surprise. Tucker wasn't much of a cook, but he usually had a few things on hand—eggs, ketchup, cheese. The refrigerator shelves and drawers were bare. Totally cleaned out.

Why would he do that?

Feeling confused and now definitely worried, she decided to check upstairs. She first looked in Kristy's room. Tucker had made a big thing over getting her a youth bed. She had beamed at getting to sleep in a real bed. Now it was neatly made up and a pink bunny sat on top of the ruffled pillow. Somehow, Lauren felt chilled. Toys were usually scattered about, giving the place a general lived-in feeling. Today it was sterile and neat.

Worry was now full-fledged dread. She moved to Tucker's bedroom, not knowing what to expect. It, too, was neat and orderly. He wasn't particularly messy, but he wasn't this neat. Standing at the door looking in, something about the room felt . . . abandoned to Lauren. But she was overreacting, she told herself. Stiffening her spine, she walked to the closet and opened the door with a little more force than necessary.

For a minute, she tried to decide what was wrong. She'd seen the inside of his closet before. Now, studying the racks, she saw suits and dress shirts, but it seemed to her that a lot of things were missing—jackets, jeans, casual pullovers. The closet had a built-in chest where she knew he kept sweatshirts, T-shirts, socks, underwear. She pulled a drawer open. Then another. And another. All empty.

Everything . . . gone.

She backed out of the closet and sat down on the side of his bed. She was so stunned that she couldn't seem to think straight. He had left without telling her. Why? What about Kristy? What did this mean?

She stood up suddenly and went back to the closet to look for his luggage. The space was bare where he usually kept it. As crazy and inexplicable as it seemed, he had packed up and taken off!

She went slowly down the stairs, gazing at the silent, orderly living area with a stunned eye. He had given no sign last night that he was thinking of leaving. He was supposed to be in court at eleven. What had happened?

Buddy. It dawned on her that his golden retriever usually stayed outside on the screened porch. She quickly turned the lock and took a look. Buddy was nowhere in sight. Had he been anywhere near, he would have run up to greet her. For that matter, he would have barked when she came inside the house. Wherever Tucker had disappeared to, he'd taken Buddy with him.

Genuinely alarmed now, she took her iPhone out of her purse and called Martin. He picked up after the first ring.

"Lauren. Janice said you were going over to check. What's up? Where's Tucker?"

"I don't know. I was calling to ask if you've heard anything."

"No." He sounded mystified. "Evelyn says he didn't show up this morning to see Kristy. He always does that before coming to work."

"His things are gone, Martin." Her gaze took in the sterile, empty look of the room. "He's cleared his house of everything perishable . . ."

"What do you mean?"

"It looks . . . too neat, as if he's prepared the place for a long absence. He totally emptied his refrigerator. And his luggage is missing." Her voice dropped. "Do you think he could have been involved in an accident?"

"And he just happened to have his luggage along? I don't think so."

"Then what, Martin?"

There was a long pause. She imagined him frowning, thinking, worrying.

"Martin?"

"I think he's run away."

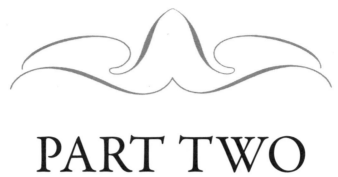

PART TWO

15

Rickey Armstrong again. Lauren hung up the phone after talking to Marian Perkins, his teacher, and prepared herself for yet another frustrating encounter with the boy. What had it been last week? Oh, yes. He had written a string of obscenities on a stall in the girls' bathroom. Her stern lecture had simply bored him. His mother had been in a dither over it, but she was more concerned with the cost of hiring a painter to cover the damage than with punishing Rickey. Then, only days later, he'd switched every student's belongings to different desks. That day, when Marian got ready to begin class, chaos ensued. Lauren didn't know what it was this time, but she vowed to take disciplinary action that would finally make an impression on the troubled teenager.

"Come," she said in response to Marian's light tap on her door. She looked especially distressed. "What is it this time?"

Without elaborating, Marian handed over a folded paper. "Take a look."

Lauren scanned a list of six names written in a barely legible scrawl. The first three were students in Rickey's class, two boys and one girl. The last was her name, as well as Marian and Carol Sanchez, whose class he'd been in last year. Rickey's note stated his disgust at being forced to put up with a bunch of stupid people every day in this crappy school. His plan, he wrote, would take care of that. Lauren blinked with shock at the last line.

Halloween will be really cool this year because everyone on this list will be dead. I'm the grim reaper.

She looked at Marian. "He says he plans to bring a gun to the school. You're sure Rickey wrote this?"

"He bragged about it in a text message, along with a chilling account of how he got the gun and the bullets." She handed over a cell phone.

Lauren quickly scanned the text. "Maybe I can understand his anger at us teachers, but why Talbot Ross and Jack Grantham? And Kelly Ridley, for heaven's sake. She's smart and pretty and popular. Everybody likes her."

"I do get that one," Marian said. "She's told him to his face that he's a bully. He doesn't like taking that from *anybody*."

"Who in particular does he bully?"

"Oh, Jack Grantham, of course. He despises him. Every chance he gets, he points out that Jack's here on scholarship. You remember when he accused Jack of cheating and planted test keys in Jack's backpack?"

"Yes, I remember." She sighed. "What about Talbot? What's Rickey's problem with him?"

"Talbot beat Rickey in the vote for class president."

Lauren shook her head in bewilderment. "And that's reason to kill him?"

"He's a troubled kid, Lauren."

Lauren nodded wearily. "I'll have to expel him," she said.

"Good," Marian said with feeling. "And maybe then we won't have to deal with him ever again."

She couldn't blame Marian for being fed up. They'd both grown more and more concerned that Rickey's behavior had crossed a line from annoying to outright dangerous pranks. She walked the teacher to the door. "I'll let you know what we need to do next."

Expulsion was a serious matter. She would surely get a headache from his parents . . . if they could be found. The Armstrongs were more difficult to reach than the governor.

She beckoned Rickey into her office. When he was standing before her, she held up the note. "Did you write this, Rickey?"

"I guess."

"What do you have to say about it?"

"It was a joke!" He made a sound of disgust and turned his face from her.

She studied his stony profile. How could a fourteen-year-old boy harbor such twisted emotion? What was going on in his head? What was going on in his home?

"Let's be crystal clear here, Rickey. Are you threatening to kill six people at St. Paul Academy?"

"Aw, I wasn't serious," he said.

"Really? Because that note sounds pretty serious," she said. Then, taking a plastic bag from her desk drawer, she held it up. "There are ten bullets here taken from your backpack."

He shrugged.

She waited, but he sat stubbornly silent. "If you won't talk to me, Rickey, I can't help you."

"I don't need help," he said sullenly.

"Then help me understand. What have these students done to you?"

Lauren waited a full minute. Most children began to fidget as the clock ticked. Not Rickey. He stood unmoving and stubbornly silent. "One more time, Rickey. Why did you write this note?"

" 'Cause I hate this school. It's a stupid place and so are the kids."

She settled back in her chair. "So everyone else is stupid and you think killing them is a good solution. Is that your story?"

"I told you—I wasn't serious," he said.

She resisted arguing further with the smart-mouthed brat. "Well, Rickey, here's my position and I'm sticking to it, too. What you've done is wrong. St. Paul Academy is a great school. We value our students. And since you don't, you won't be upset to know that I'm expelling you."

"You can try."

"Excuse me?"

Rickey gave her an insolent look. "Did you forget about those computers my dad bought for the school? The ones kids like *Jack* get to use? He's gonna be in here reminding you he pays big for me and my sisters to be here. So, no way that'll happen."

Without another word to him, she picked up the phone to call his parents . . . trusting that by some miracle she might catch one of them. As she waited, she glanced at her watch, rejoicing that the week was winding down. Four rings and counting.

Finally, on the fifth ring, someone answered.

"Armstrong residence."

She recognized the voice of Maxine, longtime, long-suffering housekeeper/nanny/chauffeur/ nurse and, most probably, chef. After several years of dealing with the family, she knew Maxine well.

"Maxine, this is Lauren Holloway at St. Paul Academy. May I speak with Cecile or John, please?"

"Nobody's here but me, Ms. Holloway. Is it about Rickey?"

She sighed. With no other option, she told Maxine what had happened and insisted that she pick Rickey up immediately. Next, she called

Craig Rawls. Her expulsion of Rickey would send him into a tizzy, but a boy in possession of real bullets issuing death threats required drastic action.

Again, she waited through several rings. Finally, on the fourth, she got Rawls's voice mail. Relieved that she wouldn't have to deal with what was certain to be a difficult conversation, she left a message. Then, rubbing a spot between her eyes, she took two aspirin. The weekend could not come soon enough.

The Round Top flea market was a smorgasbord of shops and vendors selling everything from housewares to farm equipment to live pets. She had agreed to join Eileen and her husband for the weekend in hill country. They were experienced flea-marketers, and Eileen had tried to interest Lauren in the quest for the little gem that might be nestled among tons of junk. Lauren remained lukewarm, though she had to admit she was having fun.

She'd bought several items she didn't really need, including eight etched crystal water goblets. They'd be handy when she next hosted her book club. As for the antique mantel clock, she probably shouldn't have, but when she heard its tinkling chime she couldn't resist. She had resisted adopting a darling golden retriever puppy that looked at her from a cardboard box near a table of odds and ends. His cute face brought thoughts of Buddy. In the nine months that Tucker had been gone, Lauren had wondered if he had taken the dog with him . . . or given him away.

Deep down, she still ached with pain over Tucker's abandonment. Countless days and nights she had waited—hoped—to hear from him. To no avail. Although she'd decided to postpone their wedding, she'd never gotten a chance to tell him. She'd teased him once about jilting her, which he'd vehemently said he'd never do. And then he'd done just that.

But worst of all, she'd had to live down the fact that she'd been engaged to marry a fugitive. Nobody believed his claim anymore that he was an innocent man and that somebody was setting him up for Margot's murder. Running away totally destroyed that argument. Now, she wondered if Tucker was behind all the incidents that had happened—trashing her kitchen, leaving the note, planting her keys. Killing Margot?

The day was almost over when Eileen dragged her into a shop that seemed to have everything and specialized in nothing. She was browsing in children's books when she had an eerie feeling that she was being watched. Looking around, she saw nothing suspicious in the faces of the other customers. Across from her, an older woman carefully examined a fragile tea set. A few feet away, a mother held tightly to her little boy's arm to keep him from breaking anything. Eileen was nearby scrutinizing the bottom of a piece of pottery. Other customers appeared to be shopping with no particular interest in her. It was only when she looked to the front of the shop that she discovered the source of her uneasiness.

A man stood framed in the door. With late afternoon sun at his back, his features were in deep shadow, but his gaze seemed fixed on her. She blinked, her eyes narrowing. Something about him . . .

Tucker!

She drew in a quick, shocked breath. She told herself it couldn't be Tucker. This man had a beard and his hair was much longer—rather what she could see of it under a baseball cap. And he was much too thin.

As she watched, he suddenly turned and, for a split second before he was gone, she saw his face. Her heart almost stopped. It was Tucker! Wasn't it? She froze, the books forgotten. No, she told herself, surely it was someone who resembled Tucker. Why would he be here?

But now her heart was pounding. She felt flushed and a little dazed. Her hands were shaking so that she almost dropped the books in her hands. She gave a distressed sound, unconsciously clutching them to her breast. It had been nine months since he'd disappeared without a trace. He wouldn't be at a flea market miles from home . . .

would he? Flea markets were not his thing. She must have been mistaken. Surely she was mistaken.

But that face. Oh, she did know that face.

She headed for the door anyway, hastily shoving the books into the hands of a startled clerk. She had to check. She had to be sure it really wasn't Tucker. Murmuring an apology, she made her way past other shoppers in a rush to get to the door. She had to know.

It was a gorgeous September day, and with dusk coming on, the crowd was down. She could see clearly both ways, but there was no sign of him anywhere. She decided she must have been mistaken. What was it, two, three seconds that she'd seen his face? Easy to make a mistake after only a quick glimpse.

"What's the matter?" Eileen came out of the shop looking at her curiously. "What happened?"

"You are not going to believe this, but I thought I saw Tucker."

"What? Where?" Eileen instantly turned, looking right and left. "Which way?"

"He was standing in the door. Right there. It was just a glance, and when I got out here, he'd disappeared."

"I wish you'd said something."

"Well, it happened so fast," Lauren said. "I mean, he looked like Tucker, but . . ." She trailed off, leaving the rest of her thought unspoken. "It was probably my imagination," she murmured, but her eyes were still searching . . . searching.

Eileen gave her a skeptical look. "You? Wouldn't you know the man you were once engaged to marry?"

"That's just it." She moved her sunglasses to the top of her head. "He wasn't much like the Tucker I knew."

"Why, what do you mean?"

"I don't know exactly. He was just . . . different, the beard, the long hair, the clothes . . ."

Eileen blinked. "Tucker Kane with a beard and long hair?"

"Not only that, but he seemed at least twenty pounds lighter and his clothes looked . . . well, shabby and too big."

"Maybe it was your imagination," Eileen said.

If he wanted to hide in plain sight, he'd have to look a lot different from the attractive, successful contractor he had been in Houston. "It's just that he looked so . . . so stern standing there. Sort of . . . frozen in place." Her gaze was troubled, moving beyond Eileen. "It was a shock," she said, ". . . after all these months."

Eileen touched her arm. "It's been . . . what, nine months, and you still get that look in your eyes when you say his name. I could just shoot him for the way he treated you."

"That look you see in my eyes is exhaustion," Lauren said, deliberately putting an edge in her voice. She shifted a shopping bag to her right hand and settled the strap of her purse on her shoulder. "Are you done shopping? I'm about ready to call it a day. I'm going to buy those books and then I'm heading to my motel."

"I bet they're for Kristy," Eileen said, smiling when Lauren nodded. "If you hadn't seen them first, I would have bought them myself." Falling into step with Lauren, who headed back into the shop, she said, "Aren't you glad you came?"

"Yes. After the dreadful week I had, I needed to get away."

"I hear you, honey." Eileen patted Lauren's hand sympathetically. "Have I ever told you how wonderful retirement is?"

"You don't have to tell me," Lauren said dryly. "You and Seth gallivanting all over in your RV, acting like lovebirds. I lose track of where you are." She headed for the checkout where she'd left the books. "It must be nice."

"It is. And speaking of lovebirds, what do you think of Jerry Blacklock? He's attractive, he's eligible, and he's very interested in you."

"He's boring, Eileen."

"He's a lawyer. He's supposed to be boring."

"Then let him find a woman who likes to be bored." She paused a beat. "Sorry, that was tacky."

She shouldn't talk so negatively about Jerry. Tucker's lawyer had been very helpful in

193

shielding her from Detective Sherman's harassment after Tucker disappeared. But she wasn't interested in him romantically.

Eileen propped her hands on her hips. "You won't give the time of day to any man who shows a smidgen of interest in you!"

"Can we change the subject?" She paid for the books and headed out of the shop. "I've been meaning to ask: How is it that handling discipline problems was in my former job description and yet when I was promoted to your job, I'm still handling it?"

Eileen grinned. "Maybe because you do it so well?"

They fell into step together and headed back the way they came. "I'm not sure there won't be some trouble over the latest incident."

"Don't tell me. Let me guess," Eileen said. "Rickey Armstrong."

"He wrote a note listing six people he planned to kill, Eileen."

Eileen made a startled sound. "Wow."

"Yes, so I expelled him."

"Which was definitely the right thing to do. You're responsible for the safety of the kids. I would have done the same thing."

"Yes. But as long as John Armstrong writes big, fat checks over and above tuition for his three kids, he feels he can throw his weight around. He paid for ten new computers."

Eileen winced and then laughed. "Well, the good news is he can't take them back."

Lauren managed a smile. "No, but trust me. I haven't heard the last of this. I'm sure I'll get a visit from Craig Rawls. He never quite forgave me for not immediately dumping Tucker." She made a face and sighed. "I'm so glad to get away for the weekend!"

Eileen paused, studying her. "But even now your eyes are busy searching for Tucker, Lauren. You really must think you saw him."

"Even if I did, I don't want to talk to him. I'm done with that relationship."

"Except for Kristy."

"Except for Kristy." Lauren couldn't hold back a smile. "She gives me so much joy, Eileen. I'm lucky Martin and Evelyn didn't cut me out of her life when Tucker left."

"She's lost both parents—it makes sense to keep you in her life, and let's be candid here," she said. "Leaving Kristy in your charge every day at the school suits Evelyn just fine."

"Eileen . . ."

"Yes?"

"Should I call the police and tell them I think I saw Tucker?"

"Oh, my, I don't know. That's entirely up to you."

"They'd be here in a flash. But I hate the thought of getting grilled by Detective Sherman again."

"He thought you knew where Tucker was."

"Well, I didn't."

"By the way, did you read in the *Chronicle* that Brumfield has formally announced his candidacy for governor?"

"Yes. But I'd already heard it from Evelyn. Juliana has been pushing her to throw a fundraiser for him."

"What does Martin say about that?"

Lauren put a finger to her cheek. "Let me see if I can recall exactly what he said." She smiled. "Something like . . . 'when pigs fly.'"

Lauren thought it strange that Martin could barely tolerate the husband of his wife's best friend.

"Brumfield definitely had strong incentive to see someone convicted of killing Margot," Eileen said. "Not only did the public expect it, but he had to've been pushed by Juliana. So he needed to solve that case." She smiled. "Now that Tucker is off the front page, Brumfield would probably like voters to forget the whole thing."

"I'd like to forget, too," Lauren said fervently.

"I know you would," Eileen said, placing a gentle hand on Lauren's shoulder. "I hope never to see you looking as fragile as you were when he left."

Sherman's tactics had been brutal right after Tucker disappeared. He couldn't believe Tucker would take off and not even tell his fiancée where he was going. *She* couldn't quite believe it.

Unless he really did kill Margot.

What Lauren had never told anybody was that Tucker had asked her to provide him with an alibi. She still felt uncomfortable about keeping that to herself. Had withholding that fact been, basically, a lie?

Eileen stopped at a bench under a shade tree. "I told Seth I'd meet him here," she said, setting her parcels down.

"I'm grateful to you for everything you've done for me," Lauren said. "You've been a good friend. I'll find a way to make it up to you, I promise."

"Oh, hush. What are friends for?" she said, studying her phone. "But you can make me happy right now by joining Seth and me tonight instead of going back to that ratty motel with only yourself for company." She punched in a number. "I told Seth we'd call when we were ready to leave. I wish you'd go to the concert in Austin with us. You'd love it. We could have dinner at that neat, new restaurant I was telling you about, then see the show. We'd have you back to your room by midnight. I don't know what you're going to do with yourself for the rest of the evening."

"Thanks, but I'd prefer to pick up something to eat here and go back to my motel. I'm sure I have a ton of emails stacked up since I left."

"So much for taking your mind off the school," Eileen said, with her phone at her ear. She held up a hand before Lauren could reply. "Seth. We're all

197

done. I'll meet you at the car in ten minutes." She ended the call and made one last plea. "Are you sure you won't change your mind?"

"I'm sure. Thanks anyway." After exchanging hugs, they parted, Eileen heading in one direction and Lauren in another. She bought a sandwich and bottled water from one of the many vendors, then made her way through the thinning crowd to the parking lot. But as she wove through the vehicles heading to her car, she caught herself scanning the area. As tall as Tucker was, he'd be visible even over the rooftops of trucks and SUVs. Realizing what she was doing disgusted her. Wherever Tucker was—if it really had been Tucker—he wouldn't hang around where he might encounter her again. He wouldn't take the chance that she might call the police.

Using her remote key, she unlocked her car and put her packages inside, taking care with the clock, placing its box on the floor. Then, settling behind the wheel, she headed out to the highway. It took a bit of self-control, but she managed to keep her eyes straight ahead.

In spite of September's heat, a trip to Texas hill country should have been a joy. On the way to Round Top, she'd seen the rolling hills and pastures dotted with cattle as charming, peaceful, calming. She felt none of that now. Even though she was convinced that she was immune to any emotion except relief where Tucker was concerned, just thinking she might have seen him again had shaken her. Why?

And what would he have been doing at Round Top? Where had he been for almost nine months? A thousand times she'd wondered how he could disappear without a word to her. Had he forgotten her? Did he ever think of her? Or Kristy?

Enough! With a frustrated sound, she shoved a CD into the changer hoping to let music put Tucker Kane out of her mind.

Her motel dated from the sixties, with parking in front of the rooms. She would have preferred a high-rise with an elevator for security, but none had been available in peak season. She'd found this place only because one of Eileen's friends had canceled. Now it didn't matter. After shopping for several hours, all she required was a clean bathroom and bed.

She decided to leave most of her purchases in the trunk of her car except the mantel clock. It had been pricey, and hearing its musical chime would be nice. Her house was too quiet. Too still. She'd considered adopting a cat. Maybe she would. She often had Kristy overnight on weekends and she would love a cat. But then, Kristy would prefer a dog. Like Buddy. Time had not dimmed her memory of the big golden or her daddy. If a child could be in denial, Kristy was. She talked about him as if he were her imaginary friend, always at her side.

She closed the car door with a bang. The child's lonely delusion was just one more reason to be furious with Tucker.

After punching the remote lock, she managed to carry the clock, sandwich, and water without dropping anything. But balancing the lot while unlocking the door was a trick. It was when she finally had it open that she became aware of someone approaching on the walkway from behind. Alarm drove her heart into her throat. As she rushed to get inside, she dropped the sandwich and water bottle, but the bag with the boxed clock caught in the door and she was trapped.

"It's only me, Lauren."

Tucker.

16

"What are you *doing?*" she cried. "You scared me half to death."

"Wait." He put his hand on the door when she would have closed it on him. "Please. I know I don't deserve it, but will you let me in? I need to talk to you."

For a moment, words failed her. But on some unconscious level, her eyes were taking him in—the beard, the weight loss that emphasized the line of his jaw, his sharp cheekbones, the sheer size of him. He'd always towered over her. Thin as he was now and with eyes that were guarded and watchful, he looked dark and dangerous. And older. Maybe most surprising was the smattering of gray at his temples. Had that happened in only nine months?

She finally found her voice. "Why talk to me now? You haven't bothered for . . . what, nine months?"

"Eight months, three weeks and"—he looked at his watch—"two days."

"Oh, please," she said, not bothering to hide her disgust.

"It's true," he said, his eyes roaming her face hungrily. "You recognized me today. I was afraid you'd tell someone and they'd come looking for me."

"Someone? Like the police?" Hands on her hips, she plowed on. "What if I did call? Are you going to hang around and wait for them? Or will you take off again?"

"That's not what I meant."

"Then I'm confused. Are you asking me to forget I saw you so you can go back to wherever you've been holed up and things will go along as they have been for all this time? Is that what you want?"

"What I want is to have my life back."

Fury flared in her eyes.

"You want your life back? You have some nerve, Tucker. You left a trail of broken lives behind you." Again she tried to slam the door on him and again he put out a hand to stop it.

"No, wait. Please. That came out wrong. It makes me sound like a selfish pig and—"

"At last, the truth," she said with heavy sarcasm.

"Look, I never meant for this to happen—running into you that way. When I saw you in that shop, I should have run like the devil, but—" He gave a short, humorless laugh. "It was like my feet were nailed to the floor."

She gave him a dubious look. "And you're here now because . . ."

He glanced over his shoulder, making a quick survey of the place. "It'll be easier to talk inside. I know you have no reason to trust me, but I need to—"

"Trust you? Trust you?" She looked at him in amazement. "Your ex-wife was murdered. You are the prime suspect. You abandoned me and your own daughter. Nobody hears from you until this minute, and you ask me to trust you?"

"If you'll just listen—"

"Why should I? Do you have a clue how you messed up my life, Tucker? You broke my heart. Not only was my job in jeopardy, I was publicly humiliated. It was a nightmare."

"I didn't kill Margot!" The words burst out of him, then he calmed himself. "I swear it, Lauren. You believed me once. Nothing's changed."

"Nothing's changed?" She stared at him. "Are you serious? Everything's changed. I believed you back then. We were in this together. But running the way you did made you look guilty. It sealed your fate with the police and everybody else. So what difference does it make whether I believe you or not?"

He looked at her in despair. "It means everything that you believe me, Lauren. Everything." When she simply turned her face away, he said, "Will you let me in the room? Please?"

After a minute, she relented, standing aside. "Come in, but don't close the door," she told him.

He took only a step, then bent and picked up the bagged sandwich lying on the floor and offered it to her. "I hope this isn't your dinner."

She tossed it in the trash. "I'm suddenly not hungry, go figure."

Now that he was inside, some of his nervousness seemed to fade. He looked around the shabby room. "Not exactly the Ritz-Carlton, is it?"

"It's fine."

"You shouldn't be alone here after dark. A lot of riffraff hangs around in peak season looking to fleece tourists."

She cocked her head giving him an incredulous look. "What is it with you? You muscle your way into my room and lecture me on safety precautions? That is just . . . ludicrous, Tucker."

"Are you going somewhere with Eileen and Seth?"

"That is none of your business! You lost the right to know anything about me a long time ago." She looked at her watch. "Are you going to talk, or not?"

He studied her face for a long moment. "Why didn't you call the cops when you saw me today?"

"I wasn't sure it really was you . . . after all this time," she added in an acid tone.

"I can believe that." He glanced down at his work shirt, faded jeans, and worn boots. "I don't get to the mall much anymore," he said dryly.

She realized she was still holding the bag with the boxed clock. Moving past him, she put it on the bed and sat down. "Now. I'm breathless to hear why you disappeared without a trace."

"Yeah, I figured that would be your first question." His gaze moved about the room. Spotting the bottled water that had rolled under the table, he scooped it up. Holding it in his hand, he studied the label as if it contained the wisdom of the ages. Stalling, she guessed. Trying to decide how much to tell her without telling her much of anything.

"Well?"

"Before I left I told you I was being set up," he said, talking in a low tone. "Someone was trying to pin Margot's murder on me. That's one reason I had to leave."

"Without telling me?" She stuck out her left hand suddenly, waggling the naked finger where she had once worn his engagement ring. "We were engaged, Tucker. Our wedding date was set. We were going to spend the rest of our lives together, trusting each other, loving each other. And then—poof!—you just disappeared. One day you're there and the next you're gone. No letter. No phone call. No text. No email."

"It was the hardest thing I ever did." His dark and tortured eyes clung to hers. "I figured nobody would be willing to help me."

"And too bad if it turned my life upside down? Is that what you thought? Once you disappeared, the police concentrated on me. Did you know that? They questioned me for days, Tucker. They tapped my phone, for heaven's sake! It was horrible."

"I'm sorry. How can I make you understand? I needed to find the real killer."

"And have you?"

"Found him? No."

"So skipping out to wherever you were was the best way to find him?"

"I was arrested. The whole world thought I was guilty. Sherman wasn't looking for anybody else. And before you tell me how stupid and selfish it was to leave, I had another reason . . ."

"I can't wait to hear this."

"I left because of you and Kristy."

She huffed out an irritated breath. "What does that mean?"

"It means the killer knew I was on to him. He called me that night . . ."

"What night?"

"The night I left." He faltered, his voice broke. "He was threatening to hurt you and Kristy . . . don't you see?" His eyes clung to hers. "I couldn't let that happen. Even if it meant I couldn't see you, I couldn't let him hurt you."

"Uh-huh," she said, one eyebrow lifting skeptically, obviously unconvinced.

"He told me to stop meddling. To butt out. And if I didn't, he told me, he'd get you first and then he'd get Kristy."

While she considered what he said and whether he could possibly be telling the truth, he added, "He's already proved he could get into your house. I couldn't take a chance with your life or Kristy's."

She spent a long moment studying him. And to his credit, he withstood the obvious doubt in her face, his gaze unflinching.

"Why should I believe this?" she said. "I have reason to be suspicious, don't I?"

"Ah, Lauren . . ." He was shaking his head sadly. "I'd do things differently if I could go back and relive that time." He dragged a hand through his hair, looking tired. "I feel rotten for leaving you. I would go to jail right now, today, if I thought it would make you believe in me again."

"Pretty words, Tucker, but we both know that

wouldn't solve anything, would it?" And yet if he was telling the truth, it almost made sense. "So do you have any idea who this mythical someone is?"

"None. No clue. I just knew I had to leave and I couldn't tell you where I was. I was afraid of what he would do to you if you knew."

"Like what, torturing me? Like plucking out my fingernails? Like waterboarding me? Is that it?"

"Or worse," he said.

She frowned, taken aback. "You're serious."

"Think about it. Would I abandon my daughter, throw away the chance to marry the woman I love, ditch my business, and ruin my reputation so I could live this life?" He spread his arms wide. "You should know me better than that."

"I don't know you, Tucker. And once you disappeared, I was convinced I never did."

"I've told you why. Other than saying I'm sorry to the bottom of my heart, I don't know what else I can do . . . at least, not right now. I'm trapped in a nightmare that doesn't ever end."

She reminded herself that she had closed her heart to his pain. "What about Kristy? She was heartbroken. Did you consider how devastated she would be when her daddy disappeared?"

He fixed his gaze on the floor so that she couldn't read his expression. "Kristy is on my mind every minute of every day. She's the first person I think of when I wake up and the last when I lie down at night."

"So much so that you haven't even asked about her," Lauren said.

"I know she's at your school," he said. "I know she loves you." He added, "I knew you wouldn't abandon her, too."

"Oh, really?"

"Yeah, really."

"Well, you might have walked away from her, but I couldn't. And it's thanks to Evelyn and Martin, not you, that I'm still in her life."

"And I'm grateful. Thank you."

"Don't thank me. Thank them. They've been very generous . . . considering."

"You mean considering they think I murdered their daughter so Kristy should be kept away from the woman I'd planned to marry?"

"It makes sense, doesn't it?"

He chose to pass on that. He drew in a long breath. "So . . . how is this affecting her? Kristy, I mean from your point of view as a professional. You see kids dealing with serious issues all the time. Is she okay?"

She studied his face, trying to resist a tug on her emotions. He might not love her anymore, but there was no doubt from the concern in his voice that he loved his daughter. "She wasn't okay at first. It was hard to explain what had happened to you. But she seems to be adjusting now."

"That's good," he said with relief in his voice.

"I put that down to a child's natural resilience,

Tucker. And God's grace. The Housemans have given her a sense of stability. And it helps that Sarah is back now."

"Sarah was always more of a mother to Kristy than Margot ever was," Tucker said bitterly.

"And Martin is more of a father than you proved to be."

He carefully set the water bottle in the center of the table. "I can't argue with that." He hesitated, then added, "As God is my witness, I never meant to hurt you or Kristy. Circumstances forced my hand."

"You mention God so casually, Tucker. Why couldn't you have trusted God to see you through? Where was your faith in all this?"

"I have faith that one day I'll be exonerated and you'll be able to forgive me."

"It's God's forgiveness you need to seek, not mine."

"And I'm working on it." He moved to the door. "I guess we're back to the reason I wanted to talk to you—please don't blow my cover. If you tell, I'll wind up in police custody or worse."

She gave him a confused look. "What's worse?"

"The killer wants me to stay hidden. I don't know why, but if I'm suddenly visible, he just might decide to carry through with his plan."

"As in, he might murder me, too?"

"I don't know what he might do, Lauren, but we can't afford to take any chances."

"I don't know whether to believe you." She gave him a sidelong look, eyes narrowed with suspicion. "Come to think of it, what were you doing here at Round Top? If what you say is true, wasn't being out in the open like that risky?"

"Yeah, but I—" He stopped abruptly as a woman suddenly appeared at the open door. Lauren recognized her as the desk clerk who'd checked her into the motel earlier.

"Is everything okay, Ms. Holloway?"

Tucker was startled. Lauren could see he was holding his breath . . . braced for her to blow his cover. She hesitated only a heartbeat. "Yes, everything's fine," she told the woman.

"I hope I didn't interrupt anything?" From the look she sent Tucker, Lauren guessed she'd picked up on the tension between them.

"Nothing that mattered," Lauren said. "But thank you for your concern."

"You can't be too careful nowadays," she said. Then, with one last look at Tucker as she turned to go, she added, "If you need anything, call. I'll be here until my shift ends at midnight."

Lauren decided she might have misjudged the quality of her lodging's security. "I appreciate that."

"We try," the woman said cheerfully. "Have a good evening now, you hear?"

"You, too."

Lauren stood without moving as the woman

headed back to the front of the motel. Beside her, Tucker was tense. Only when the woman disappeared into her office did he breathe out a relieved sigh.

"Thank you," he said quietly.

"I don't know why I did that," she told him. "It wasn't an outright lie, but it was close."

He said nothing for a beat or two, but just stood looking at her.

And she at him.

And then, taking her by surprise, he hauled her into his arms. Held close to his heart, she was suddenly awash in emotion too complicated to name. She felt warm and flushed. Her heart pounded with his. She was aware of desperation in him . . . and power. A voice inside warned that he could easily hurt her. He was a man used to physical labor, strong and in his prime. But it wasn't fear for her safety that she felt. It was something far different.

"I've missed you so much," he murmured in her ear.

With his words, sanity returned. She pushed hard against him and freed herself. "Stop! I don't want this, Tucker."

Muttering an apology, and not looking at her, he scrubbed a hand over his face and beard.

"Leave now," she told him coldly, refusing to be swayed by the emotional pull of her foolish heart. "And don't ask me to promise anything. Why should I make any commitment to you when you proved you don't know the meaning of the word?"

She sensed the war going on inside him. A part of her wanted to know the nature of that conflict, wanted to know if it could possibly be real. Were the reasons he gave for abandoning her and his child true? He was supposedly a loving fiancé and father keeping them from a murderer by his absence. What else would have driven a man who'd appeared to be the very soul of integrity and faith to abandon principle and responsibility?

"I mean it, Tucker," she said in a low, unsteady voice. "I want you to leave now, and don't ever come near me again. It's too late."

Only when she heard the door close quietly behind her did her composure fail and the tears come.

17

Lauren was shaken by her encounter with Tucker, but she got up the next morning—Sunday—and attended the early service at a small local church. Possibly because she was among strangers, people who didn't know that her ex-fiancé was the prime suspect in a murder, she was able to enjoy the familiar hymns and the minister's inspirational message.

So it was with a quieter heart that she drove back to Houston for a standing Sunday brunch date with Evelyn and Martin at the country club. After valet parking, she entered the ostentatious building and made her way to the dining room. Pausing at the entrance, she spotted the Housemans and Kristy at their usual table. As Lauren started toward them, Kristy's face lit up. With a squeal, she scrambled out of her booster seat and made a wild dash across the room.

Lauren scooped her up, laughing. "Hi, sugar bear. How's my favorite little girl in the whole wide world?"

"Guess what, Lolly! Guess what, guess what! I have the biggest surprise to tell you."

"Oh, really?" Lauren set her down, stroking a loving hand over her dark hair. "And what would that be?"

"I'm having swimming lessons and I can do it! I was scared at first, but now I'm not."

"That is incredible." Lauren took her hand and walked with her toward the table where the Housemans sat watching benignly. "But I'm not surprised. I knew you could do it."

Martin rose as they approached. A year or so ago, he'd had only a sprinkling of gray at his temples. Now there was no sign that his hair had once been coal-black. Like Tucker, he had been aged by Margot's murder and the terrible aftermath.

Martin greeted her with a kiss on her cheek, pulling out her chair for her after she'd turned to hug Evelyn. "You look fresh and lovely as always, doesn't she, Evelyn?"

"As always," Evelyn said. And although her smile was genuine, Lauren thought she seemed somehow . . . distracted. She'd worried lately that Evelyn might be too dependent on prescription drugs. She'd certainly had good reason to turn to antidepressants and tranquilizers after losing her daughter.

Three menus lay on the table along with filled water glasses and a basket of warm bread. "Am I late?" she asked after taking the proffered seat.

"Not at all," Martin told her.

"How are you, Evelyn?" Lauren said.

"She didn't get much sleep last night," Martin said before his wife spoke.

Lauren frowned. "Are you not feeling well?"

Evelyn gave Martin a stern look. "I'm fine, just fine. It was indigestion. I should never have eaten that rich food."

"She won't go to the doctor."

"Martin—" Evelyn looked meaningfully at Kristy, who was busy with crayons. "So how was Round Top?" she asked in a too-bright tone.

"Crowded. I bought a few things I probably didn't need." She paused and when Kristy looked up, she said in a teasing tone, "And some really neat books."

"Are they for kids?" Kristy asked.

"Hmm . . . yes."

Kristy's brown eyes sparkled. "Are you going to give them to me, Lolly?"

Lauren ruffled her curls. "I probably will . . . but I thought they could live in my house for now so when we have a sleepover, we can read them together."

"I love the drive to Round Top," Evelyn murmured somewhat wistfully, her gaze drifting to the window. She seemed lost in her own thoughts. "It's one of my favorite things to go in the spring when the wildflowers are so stunning. Especially the bluebonnets."

Martin reached for her hand. "No wildflowers right now, Evie, but we can go to the ranch . . . tomorrow. Just say the word."

"No, Kristy shouldn't miss school."

"Sarah can take her to school," Martin said. "Or we can take her with us. She's four years old. It isn't as if she's learning to read and do math."

Kristy lifted her head. "I can already read, Papa."

He smiled gently. "Really, punkin?"

"Uh-huh."

"Well then, you're one smart cookie."

Still gazing out the window, Evelyn seemed to have tuned them out. "Maybe next year."

Lauren felt genuinely concerned. Evelyn's behavior was almost gloomy. She gave Martin a questioning look, but his gaze slid off hers as he reached for a roll. "How about some of this wonderful bread, ladies? Better grab it while you can. It smells so good I could probably gobble all of it up myself."

"I know what bluebonnets are," Kristy announced suddenly. "It's flowers. I have a T-shirt with a lot of them all over the front. Daddy gave it to me."

Not for the first time, Lauren was struck by how Kristy often mentioned Tucker as naturally as if he was as present in her life as he'd been months ago. It had to be a child's wishful thinking, wanting something that was just a dream. Even so, her fantasies were sometimes so eerily realistic that her memories of Tucker must have been extraordinarily vivid.

"Has anybody else decided what to order?" Martin said, picking up his menu. "I think I'll have the fish tacos."

After ordering, Evelyn looked across the room and suddenly brightened. "Oh, look, it's Juliana and Carter." Raising a hand, she waved the approaching couple over.

Carter Brumfield. Lauren wished she could get up and leave. But she was trapped. Evelyn would be hurt if she didn't at least say hello to Juliana. Pasting on a polite smile, Lauren resigned herself to making nice.

Martin rose with a smile that looked no more sincere than Lauren's. While Juliana greeted Evelyn with an air kiss, the men shook hands.

"Martin, my man," Brumfield boomed. "Good to see you."

"Carter," he replied quietly, giving a brief nod. "How are you?"

"Couldn't be better. Up to my ears in campaigning." Brumfield smiled widely. "And it's looking good, really good."

"You know Lauren, of course." Not waiting for a reply, Martin said to her, "As of last Wednesday, Carter is officially in the race for governor."

"I'm just a glutton for punishment," Brumfield said, giving Lauren the benefit of his brilliant smile. "I bet that's what you're thinking, right?"

"Not at all," she said honestly. "Putting yourself at the mercy of the voters nowadays can be hazardous. It takes courage." Which was true, even if she didn't admire him. She still had nightmares over the way he'd allowed his staff to treat her after Tucker left.

"Yeah, it's a nasty job, as they say, but somebody's got to do it." Suddenly he snapped his fingers. "I've just figured out why you look so familiar, Ms. Holloway."

"Have you?" Considering that he was the DA, it struck her as strange that he said he didn't remember her. She wondered if it could be true. But why would he pretend otherwise?

"She was engaged to Tucker," Martin said quietly, heading him off. "Which is no excuse for the treatment she got from your man Sherman."

"Cops." Brumfield put on an apologetic expression. "As someone said, their methods are like making sausage. You wouldn't want to know the process."

"Especially if you're on the wrong side of an interrogation table," Martin said without a hint of a smile.

Brumfield slapped him on the back. "But that's in the past, eh? We didn't get that slick devil, but we will, we will."

"You have a lead?" Martin asked, his eyes narrowing. Beside him, Lauren held her breath. Tucker had taken a chance by coming to her motel room. Had someone recognized him? Reported it?

"Nothing concrete," Brumfield said. "But I want you to know and you have my word on this, Martin. We're going to get Kane. He can run, but he can't hide forever."

Lauren studied the words on the menu as if they were the Dead Sea Scrolls. Yet nothing registered. Her heart pounded. Her thoughts raced. Should she tell?

But as she hesitated, Brumfield veered away from the subject of Tucker Kane and launched into a pitch for campaign money. After a few minutes, his wife ended what had appeared to be an intense conversation with Evelyn and glanced pointedly at her watch. "Carter, you're scheduled for a photo op at the Galleria in fifteen minutes," she said.

Brumfield's practiced smile slipped for a

second. "I can tell time, Ju-Ju." But it was in place again when he turned back to Martin and Lauren. "I don't know who wants to be governor of Texas more, me or my wife." He laughed, but Lauren detected tension. "I'm telling you, she's got something lined up every moment of every day until the midterms. I hope I can hold up."

"That's what's required if you want to win, Carter," Juliana said quietly.

"I've been the DA for two terms, Ju-Ju," he snapped. "I think I know what's required to win a campaign."

Juliana's face tightened, but her reply was lost when her gaze went beyond her husband to a man who appeared at the entrance. She lifted a hand to get his attention. "Here's Jordan. We really must run."

When Brumfield ignored her. Martin said, "The reporter for the *Chronicle*?"

"Not anymore." Brumfield motioned Raines over. "He'll be working in the campaign videotaping, speechwriting, that sort of thing. According to Ju-Ju, I need someone to work on my image and polish my prose."

When Raines reached the table, Brumfield gave him a wry smile. "Got your work cut out for you, eh, Jordan?"

"It'll be a piece of cake, Carter."

"Yes, yes. Well . . ." He shot a look at his wife. "Ju-Ju is about to self-destruct, but first say hello to these good people, Jordan, so you can try to pry some money from Martin. You know Martin and Evelyn and their cute little granddaughter. And this is Lauren Holloway," he added. "Meet Jordan Raines, former reporter, and now an author when he isn't working for me."

"A starving author at the moment," Raines said, his gaze settling on Lauren. "We meet again, Ms. Holloway. And under much nicer circumstances today."

The best Lauren could do was a polite nod. After the scurrilous articles he'd written and his rudeness at the police department, how could he even look at her with a straight face?

Juliana gave Carter another pointed look and tapped her watch, to which he responded with a curt nod. But his politician's smile was in place when he said, "I'll be in touch, Martin. Policy's one thing, but money's the way to win. I'm counting on you to tap some of your contacts."

He moved off, glad-handing various people on his way out with Jordan Raines at his side, clearly in his element, and Juliana, the elegant, following.

"It'll be a cold day in you-know-where," Martin muttered.

"What?" Evelyn frowned at him.

"Nothing, nothing." Martin rose, looking at Kristy. "You want to go outside to the fountain while we wait for our food, punkin? You can make a wish if you have a penny."

Kristy was instantly on her feet. "I don't have any money, Papa," she said.

"Well, aren't you lucky, because I do." He took her hand. "Let's go."

As soon as they were out of sight, Evelyn turned to Lauren with a frown. "Lately, Martin seems determined to distance himself from Carter. We used to be so close . . . all of us. That makes it so awkward for Ju-Ju and me."

"She seems to be very involved in her husband's campaign."

"Carter was joking when he said she'd like to be governor, but the truth is, she would. And she'd be very good at it." She lifted a water glass and took a sip. "But that's enough about them. I wanted your opinion about the way Kristy fantasizes about Tucker."

"The T-shirt?"

"And a dozen other things. She talks about him as if he were actually in her life, Lauren."

She was echoing Lauren's own thoughts of minutes ago. "I think it's natural to wish for her daddy."

"But saying he gave her a T-shirt when he didn't isn't simply wishful thinking, it's delusional, isn't it?"

"No more so than other kids making up an imaginary friend," Lauren said gently, knowing the pain her friend carried in her heart.

"Martin bought that T-shirt for her, not Tucker."

221

Evelyn's tone was sharp speaking her ex-son-in-law's name.

Lauren felt a pang of conscience not telling her that she'd seen Tucker. Wasn't she essentially lying for him?

"I want to scream at her not to make him out to be a hero," Evelyn said. "He murdered her mother." She sighed as if the burst of temper exhausted her. "But of course I can't say anything like that to Kristy. It just infuriates me that she has this absolutely fictitious memory of that man."

Evelyn's hand was shaky as she carefully set her glass down. "I just pray I'll have a chance to see Tucker face-to-face before I die," she said bitterly. "I want him to know the pain and suffering he's caused Martin and me and Kristy. And you."

Lauren's mind flashed instantly to the look on Tucker's face as he'd talked about his daughter and his tormented life. It seemed Evelyn's prayer was already answered. Tucker was a man who lived in torment. She considered telling Evelyn about their encounter, but there were bound to be questions about why she hadn't reported him. She was still trying to figure that out herself.

She took the older woman's hand in hers. "I wish you wouldn't torture yourself by dwelling on Tucker, Evelyn. I sympathize with you, but I wish we could all find some measure of peace where he's concerned."

"Never." Evelyn's laugh was short and humorless. "And if Tucker isn't found and punished for murdering my daughter, I know I'll go to my grave wishing him in hell."

18

Tucker lay low for a couple of days after his encounter with Lauren. He figured if she called the police, it would trigger an all-out manhunt. And it would happen right away. But by late Monday all was quiet, so he breathed a little easier and headed back to Round Top to take care of business. Except for Luke Paxton, his contact at the flea market, only one other person knew where he was, and he needed to keep it that way.

It had been sheer luck that he'd spotted Lauren Saturday. And dumb to follow her. Dumber still to let her see him. He hadn't made that mistake before while keeping tabs on her and Kristy. But he'd reacted like a besotted teenager at the sight of her in that shop. And then, just looking at her hadn't been enough. He'd wanted to see her, touch her, hear her voice.

It might yet prove a fatal error.

He waited until it was almost closing time to slip into Luke Paxton's shop. Few people patronized the outdoor market at this hour—especially on a Monday—which meant less chance of anybody recognizing him. But still he pulled his baseball cap a little lower on his head and kept his sunglasses on as he made his way from his truck to the rear door of Paxton's shop. With a quick glance at his surroundings, he slipped inside. After a moment, satisfied that the place was empty, he let Paxton know he had company.

"Troy, just in time!" The shop owner's big voice boomed out. "I was just about to close."

"I know it's late—"

"No, no, come on in." Paxton studied his face with a shrewd eye. "But when you didn't show on Saturday, I figured something must have happened."

"I had a little complication," Tucker said, shaking his hand. "Sorry about that."

"Hey, no problem. I've got another nice order for you—custom cabinets. The lady liked the designs you sketched. Left a deposit. I told her it'd be three months before you could deliver."

"Four sounds better than three," Tucker said. "I need to finish the patio furniture for your builder buddy. And thanks, Luke." He put the money in his wallet without bothering to count it. He'd done business with Luke Paxton for about four months and knew him to be a straight shooter. Which made him feel ashamed for having to use a false name.

Ordinarily he might have stayed a few minutes to visit, but he didn't feel like pushing his luck. He turned down Luke's offer for coffee and was about to leave when Luke said, "Before you go, you'll want to hear what happened earlier today."

Tucker went still at hearing the serious note in his friend's voice.

"A guy dropped in, big talker. Claimed to be researching a book about the murder of a woman in Houston. Had clippings from the *Chronicle*." With his blue eyes fixed on Tucker, he added, "He wanted to know if I recognized the man in the photos."

"Did you?" Tucker braced for bad news.

"Maybe I did, and maybe I didn't." Luke reached under the counter and pulled out a gun. Tucker started, his eyes going wide as his pulse kicked into gear, but Luke waved a hand and chuckled. "Relax, I keep this for protection. It goes home with me at night when I close up." He tucked the gun in his belt and reached for a leather vest. After he put it on, he checked to see that the gun was concealed and continued, "About that guy . . . I told him I didn't know anybody who looked like that. And I don't."

Tucker felt a rush of relief along with an urgent need to escape. Luke liked to talk, but right now Tucker wanted to grab him by the throat and tell him to get on with it. "Did you get a name?" he said, keeping his tone as even as he could manage.

"Jordan Raines."

Tucker worked to keep his face straight, but his heart was tripping. How had Raines found him?

Or was he just fishing? When Tucker would have spoken, Luke raised a hand.

"You know I used to live in Houston. Too hot, too big, too crowded." He closed the lid of his cash box, checked to see that it was locked, and pulled a ring of keys out of his pocket. "It wasn't so much the size and the weather that motivated me to leave. It was the job. I needed to get away from the stress and corporate politics."

"You wouldn't be alone in thinking like that," Tucker said. While trying to appear unconcerned, inside, he was frantic. Was his cover blown?

"If it hadn't been for my pension, I wouldn't have stuck it out for nearly thirty years." Paxton tucked his cash box under his arm and clamped a fine-looking Stetson onto his head. "I remember that murder case the so-called writer mentioned. The woman's murder was all over the papers. I'd landed in the hospital with a bleeding ulcer, so I had a lot of time to read the papers and listen to the TV." Paxton gestured toward the door. "I need to close up now, Troy."

"Right." His thoughts racing, Tucker watched him lock the door and flip the OPEN sign to CLOSED.

"Yeah, soon as I was able, I put my papers in to retire," Paxton said, picking up where he left off. "Funny thing, I had a fishing buddy who was a cop at HPD. He was critical of the way that case was handled . . ." At the back door, he waited for

Tucker to go out ahead of him. "It wasn't the way he would have handled it. But at the time, all I could think about was getting out of town so I wouldn't reopen that hole in my gut."

Once outside, Tucker felt a lot less safe than when he arrived. Now that he knew Raines might be lurking, he couldn't linger. But he saw nothing and no one to give him cause for alarm. Still, knowing the reporter was liable to ambush him made him wary. As late as it was, most shops were closed and people were scarce, but now he urgently wanted to see Round Top in his rearview mirror.

"Red sky at night, sailor's delight," Paxton quoted, looking up at the western sky shot with brilliant color as the sun was setting. "Means it'll be a pretty day tomorrow. Good for business." He slapped Tucker on the back. "You let me know when you get that patio furniture done. I've got that builder breathing down my neck."

"Three weeks," Tucker said, thinking his pickup seemed farther away than when he'd parked it.

"Want a word of advice?" Paxton said.

Tucker gave a grunt that could have been yes or no.

"I've known who you are almost from day one. You aren't the man that reporter made you out to be."

Tucker gave him a quick look. With his heart racing, he tried to think. "What is it you're trying to tell me, Luke?"

"Just this, son. I'd stay out of sight for a while if I was you. That guy comes around again, I won't know any more than I told him today. But with him skulkin' about, it's up to you to keep your head down and your powder dry."

"I hear you."

"And you've got enough work to keep you busy, seems to me."

"I have, yeah." Tucker cleared his throat on a wave of emotion that almost choked him. Just when he'd convinced himself that God had deserted him, Luke Paxton befriended him.

"You have a source who can see that you get the materials you need?"

"Yeah." Tucker looked down at his boots and put out his hand. "Thanks, Luke. I owe you."

"No, you don't." Paxton's handshake was strong and steady . . . like the man himself. "You got a good supply of eats so you won't have to show yourself to do any shopping? I could take care of that for you."

Still battling emotion, Tucker looked him squarely in the face. "I'm okay. But I appreciate your advice." Muttering a quick good-bye, he escaped.

Half an hour later, he turned his pickup onto an overgrown trail. His hideaway was deep in the woods about a mile from the main road. It had been his home since he'd walked away from everything he valued in his life. Almost nine months of self-imposed exile. He was convinced he wouldn't feel more imprisoned if he were actually in a penitentiary.

He got out carrying his backpack, which he kept readily at hand. It was stocked with supplies for about five days' survival in the woods, if needed. As he closed the door of his pickup, a flash of gold hurled itself at him, barking joyously.

He reached down and gave the big golden's ears a good rub. If a dog could smile, Buddy did. He licked Tucker's hand and danced around him. But as Tucker straightened, he studied the landscape with keen eyes. Vigilance was a habit, and probably unnecessary, as Buddy would have alerted him had there been anything or anybody nearby. But his fragile sense of security had been shattered. Lauren knew where he was now, Luke Paxton recognized him, and Raines was probably closing in on him.

How had he been traced to Round Top?

He went directly to a shelf where he kept lumber he used for custom woodwork, mostly birch and cherry, and redwood for patio pieces. He stood looking about the shop that had become his life since Houston. It was fully outfitted with every piece of equipment necessary. Having a benefactor to set him up here, he knew his lot could have been much worse. But sometimes he felt so lonely, so forsaken that he wanted to throw his head back and scream out his rage.

But now his sanctuary was threatened. If the reporter was watching Luke Paxton's place, Tucker might have a problem getting completed pieces to him. He sensed he could trust Luke, but Raines wouldn't give up easily. He'd keep digging until he found him.

He reached for the specs from his latest project and took a minute to study them. Then, donning heavy leather gloves, he hefted a sheet of birch and carried it to a table to cut it. He marked the wood carefully, checked it a second time, then switched on the table saw and set to work. The whine of the machine was familiar and comforting, as was the scent of fresh-cut wood. It didn't take a psychologist to tell him that working with wood was pure escape for him as well as a source of income. He'd always been good with wood, good with his hands. The Lord knew he needed an escape after the stinking mess he'd made of his life.

He worked for the better part of an hour, concentrating intensely. Shavings flew from the saw blade, some falling to the floor, some sticking to his clothes, his exposed arms and face. It was only when he paused to wipe sweat from his brow and sawdust from his beard that he realized he'd forgotten to don safety glasses. He shrugged off his carelessness.

But the pause destroyed the rigid control he'd

had on his thoughts. Closing his eyes, he was back in that motel room with Lauren. No surprise that she threw him out. Who could blame her after the way he'd hurt and humiliated her? He peeled off his gloves and tossed them aside.

And he didn't need Lauren telling him how weak his faith was. He felt the void in his spiritual life almost as much as he missed her. Where once he'd felt joy and peace, now he felt mostly anger and frustration. He'd made some wrong decisions, what man hadn't? But he hadn't done anything bad enough to deserve the curve God had thrown him. He had not killed Margot, but he'd lost everything he valued anyway. What message from God was he meant to get out of that?

Suddenly his cell phone vibrated. It was a disposable and therefore untraceable. Still, it always unnerved him when it rang. Only one person knew he had it—or so he'd thought until today. But after the conversation with Paxton, he was braced for anything. He released it from the holder on his belt and checked the number. He recognized the caller, but he was still wary when he answered.

"Yeah?"

"It's me, Tuck. Everything go okay today?"

He relaxed, stroking Buddy, who'd sidled up. "Paxton took a new order for custom cabinets. I'll work up a list of materials in a day or so and get that to you."

"Great! Couple projects like that should keep you busy for several months."

"Yeah, if I don't have to run." Tucker moved to an ice chest and took out a bottle of water. "My cover may be blown."

"What happened?" The voice sharpened.

"Two things. I saw Lauren at the flea market." He heard a soft whistle. "She recognized me, of course."

"What did she say?"

"Nothing. At least, not then."

The caller was silent for a minute. "I saw her Sunday. She didn't mention anything. Do you think she'll tell?"

"I don't know. Maybe. I followed her to her motel to ask her not to."

"Wait, wait. You followed her to her motel? What were you thinking?"

That I wanted to see her. That I wanted to hear her voice. That I was so hungry for her that the risk of blowing my cover didn't matter.

"Tucker?"

He drained the water bottle. "Yeah."

"Do you realize what could happen if she goes to HPD?"

"I'll be toast."

A long pause. "Maybe I should talk to her."

Tucker tossed the empty bottle into a trash barrel a good twelve feet away. "That'd open a can of worms for sure."

"I think it's time, Tucker."

"Maybe." Leaning against the table saw, Tucker repeated the conversation with Paxton. "I'd like to know the cop's name—the one who criticized the investigation. I could ask Luke, but after today I'm leery that Raines is watching his place."

"Don't do it, Tuck." He paused as if thinking, then said, "I'm wondering if you need to consider making a new plan."

"Are you—"

"Asking you to leave the lodge? No. I just don't want to see you shanghaied by some yahoo when we don't have a clue what he's about."

"If I left, where would I go? Alaska? Canada? I can't leave. You know that. I'm not putting thousands of miles between me and my daughter."

There was a long pause. "So what can I do to help?"

"I don't know yet. Thanks to you, I haven't totally wasted these months, but every lead goes nowhere. Nobody admits to seeing Margot after I left her. But somebody did. I've got to figure out who and how the killer managed to frame me for it."

19

Lauren was still rattled by her encounter with Tucker over the weekend when she arrived at school Monday morning, but she vowed to concentrate on her job, not on her personal life.

She stopped at the lounge to get coffee, knowing her schedule was so packed she might not get a chance if she didn't grab it now. She poured it and paused to taste it, wishing for ten uninterrupted minutes, but duty called. She was heading to her office juggling the coffee with her briefcase, purse, and keys when she turned a corner and saw John Armstrong, Rickey's father, waiting for her, no doubt, to talk about Rickey's expulsion.

She sighed wearily. Judging by the look on his face as he paced outside her office, Lauren guessed she was in for a tongue lashing. She was careful to show no emotion as she greeted him.

"Mr. Armstrong. Good morning," she said. "How are you?"

He growled a greeting and nodded curtly. "Let's take this to your office, Ms. Holloway," he told her.

As opposed to standing out in the hall where kids and faculty would hear him rant and rave? Yes, indeed. "Do come in. Just give me a minute to unlock."

Seeing her hands full, he took her keys and opened the door.

"Thank you," she said. Flipping on the lights, she carried her coffee and briefcase to the desk and turned to face him. "Have a seat . . . please."

He refused and dropped her keys on her desk. "This won't take long," he said, glancing at his watch.

Lauren sighed inwardly and stayed on her feet, as well. She'd learned in past dealings with Armstrong that if she let him get the upper hand, things went downhill fast. "I assume you're here about Rickey's expulsion," she said, hoping to head him off. "I planned to call you first thing this morning. I tried to reach you and Cecile on Friday when this happened, but you were both out of town. I expect Maxine told you what happened."

"I want to hear it from you," he said.

"Of course." Lauren had to bend to unlock the top drawer of her desk where the file had been securely stored. "This is what we found in his backpack." She spilled ten bullets out onto her desk along with the list Rickey had written.

Armstrong released a harsh, humorless laugh. "And that's it? That's why you've expelled my son?"

"Yes. Absolutely. These are real bullets."

"And having them was a boyish prank, Ms. Holloway. I can understand you confiscating them, but I don't understand the expulsion."

She stared at him. "Are you serious?"

"He's a fourteen-year-old kid. He wrote a silly note and he definitely got a rise out of everybody here. Which was his intent, I'm sure. Kids pull stunts like that all the time."

"Not in this school, they don't," Lauren said.

"It's a way of trying to impress other kids. He said he was just fooling around," Armstrong said, his face growing red. "And I believe him. My son wouldn't hurt a fly."

She couldn't believe the man's attitude. "And what about the bullets?"

"What about them? Bullets are harmless without a gun."

"We don't know that he doesn't have a gun stashed away someplace, sir," Lauren said. "I have to think of the safety of the other students and my staff. Rickey's note says that he plans to kill six people!"

"It's just talk, for Pete's sake! You don't have squat to prove it's anything more than that. Talking big is a way of trying to impress other kids, Ms. Holloway. You're an educator. You know the psychology. Or at least you *should*."

She ignored the slight. "This is just one more in a string of troubling incidents with Rickey, Mr. Armstrong. You'll recall he was disciplined for planting a test key in another student's backpack and accusing him of cheating. Was that just a stunt to get attention, too?"

"He didn't do that. And you don't have squat to prove he did." He paused. "The other kid's on scholarship, right?"

"What does that have to do with anything?"

"Couldn't he have accused Rickey to get attention, too? Or do you think a scholarship kid's ethics are superior to a paying student's?"

"I don't think anything of the sort, sir," Lauren

said. "I believe Rickey's teacher. We have a text on his cell phone proving this latest incident." She took the phone from her desk drawer, found the text, and handed it to Armstrong. "I have expelled him for good cause. Nothing you've said convinces me to reconsider." She paused. "Or perhaps you'd rather deal with the police? I don't think they'd take an incident like this as lightly as you appear to."

His face had been flushed with temper before. Now he was absolutely livid. He thrust his neck out and almost snarled at her. "Is that a threat?"

"I have to think of my students, sir. Rickey is showing signs of dangerous behavior."

"My son will be back in school tomorrow morning or you'll be out of a job," he said, spacing the words between his teeth. And with that, he turned and stormed out of her office.

She was still fuming when Craig Rawls rapped on her door an hour later. Without waiting for an invitation, Rawls walked in and closed the door behind him.

"We're in a pickle, Lauren," he said. "John Armstrong just left my office in a rage. He wants his son back in class tomorrow." Looking frustrated, Rawls swiped a hand over his bald head. "I thought for a minute he was going to climb over my desk and punch me."

"Which is probably why Rickey thinks violence

is the way to settle problems," Lauren said. "I'm sorry Mr. Armstrong felt he had to go to you about my decision, Craig. But Marian Perkins and I are both extremely concerned about Rickey. If he isn't expelled we could have a tragedy on our hands."

"Do you think the problem is that serious?"

"Indeed I do."

He heaved a sigh. "We can't afford to offend John Armstrong for something that may or may not happen, Lauren. This year alone he's poured more than a hundred thousand bucks into the school."

"Surely you aren't caving to Armstrong's demands?"

He rubbed his neck. "Well . . ."

"Did you listen to my voice mail?" Lauren asked bluntly.

"I did. And I was troubled by it."

"But not enough to support me in expelling Rickey?"

"I agree he crossed a line, but—"

"There were ten live bullets in his backpack, Craig! You read the note. It said he had a gun."

"And John swears all the guns he owns are securely locked in a vault. There's no way the kid can get his hands on a weapon."

"He managed to get ammunition," she said. "I don't think we can afford to assume he can't get his hands on a gun, too." She leaned forward in her chair, desperately trying to make him see reason.

"A student told our computer science teacher that Rickey is posting threatening messages on his Facebook page, Craig. He claims his father allows him to practice shooting at their ranch in the hill country."

"Then we'll all be sure to stay away from there," Rawls said dryly.

She stared at him in silence.

"I've talked to a couple of board members," he said finally. "They agree with me, Lauren."

She took a deep breath. "Go back and tell them I refuse, Craig. Either I'm running the school or I'm a puppet to any board member or parent who has enough money."

"I think you're overreacting."

Lauren's fingers went to her temple and rubbed at the pain growing by the second. "His parents are out of touch with their own son, Craig." she said, looking up at him. "I've tried at least six times since school began this year to set up conferences with them. We've had one." She held up a finger. "One, Craig. They're too busy. They send Maxine, the nanny."

"Talk to Cecile. Maybe she'll be receptive."

Lauren suppressed the urge to grimace. Rickey's mother was as much a victim of John Armstrong's controlling personality as the rest of the family. "I've tried. She made a few vague statements about getting counseling for Rickey, but nothing ever materialized. If John Armstrong won't believe his son is capable of violence when he sees it in Rickey's handwriting, he certainly won't tolerate his wife contradicting him."

"We can't expel the kid, Lauren."

"And I can't be responsible for the education and welfare of all the other children here at St. Paul unless I'm allowed to discipline as I see fit, Craig. You're just going to have to trust my judgment on this."

She knew instantly she'd gone too far when he stood up. "Seems to me your judgment hasn't always been what it ought to be."

She gave him a tired look, knowing he meant her relationship with Tucker. "Are we back to that?"

"Your fiancé was arrested and charged with the murder of his ex-wife, Lauren. Some are still not convinced we did the right thing by promoting you to fill Eileen's job."

"Tucker was innocent, Craig."

"Then, instead of running, he should have allowed a jury to clear his name."

Since she'd spent a thousand hours thinking the same thing herself, she didn't have an answer. Instead, she said, "What does that have to do with my decision to suspend Rickey?"

"It's a judgment call. The Armstrongs are vital to this school. We wouldn't lose just Rickey, but his two daughters, as well." He shook his head impatiently, as if he was done arguing the point.

"I'll be frank. Your job might not survive if they pull their children out of St. Paul."

"You mean if they pull their *money* out of St. Paul, don't you?"

"With the economy in the shape it's in right now, we can't afford to lose a single student—let alone three." He stood up. "If that happens, the board will want your resignation immediately."

Her heart sank. She loved her job. She loved knowing she was contributing to the quality education of children.

She stood up. "May I have a few days to think this over, Craig?"

"I don't know why you'd need five minutes to think it over," he said, looking irritated. "John wants Rickey back in school tomorrow and I'm authorizing that. But yes, take until the end of the week if you must. But if you decide you can't abide by the reasonable expectations of the board, then I can only say it's your funeral."

20

Three days passed while Lauren agonized over the pickle she was in. Did she really want to remain at St. Paul Academy knowing Craig Rawls and the board were looking to get rid of her? And with John Armstrong's financial support at stake, it would only get worse. Maybe it was time for her to move on. It would be better to submit her resignation than to wait until they found some trumped-up excuse to terminate her, which would be a major negative on her resume as she looked for another job.

By Thursday, her decision was made. Rickey, of course, didn't miss a day. With Craig Rawls's edict, he'd shown up the next morning gleefully defiant. Fortunately, spring break began the following week. That would give the board a few days to find an interim principal. Besides, she felt sure Rawls had someone far less cantankerous than Lauren ready to step right in.

Rickey clearly had gotten the word that she was resigning within hours of her call to Rawls. She passed the boy in the hall at lunchtime on Friday, her last day. He shot her a triumphant look and actually gave her a thumbs-up sign. She should have felt resentment that he was pleased to be the catalyst that ousted her, but instead she worried that Rickey might do what he'd threatened to in the coming days and weeks at St. Paul. She was convinced it was a possibility.

One of these days, he'd find himself in a world of trouble. But it was not her problem now. Her problem was to find herself another job. She had sizable savings, enough to see her through several months, but she didn't want to sit around twiddling her thumbs. She would start sending out her resumes and trusting the Lord to see her through. Something would turn up.

It did that very night.

Martin Houseman called as she was doing her laundry. Her job might be kaput, but household chores were unchanged.

"I'm at the ER in Brenham, Lauren. It's Evelyn."

Lauren paused in the act of folding towels from the dryer. "What happened?"

"We were at the ranch. I woke from a nap after lunch and found her passed out on the bathroom floor."

"Oh, no. Is it a stroke?"

"I'm not sure. I couldn't revive her."

"A heart attack?" She held her breath.

"Maybe, but what do I know? And since an ambulance would take forever, I took her to the hospital myself."

Lauren heard the anxiety in his voice. "Have they told you anything yet?"

"Not yet. She regained consciousness as we arrived at the ER. That was an hour ago. I've been walking the floor ever since."

She glanced at a clock: 7:00 P.M. "So you haven't seen a doctor?"

"Not to talk to, no. It worries me that all her medical records are in Houston. I'm wondering if she'll be able to transfer to Houston."

"What about Kristy? Is she there with you?"

"No. And that's why I'm calling, Lauren. I left her with my ranch manager and his wife. Luckily, she was playing with our new kittens in the barn when this happened. She didn't see anything."

"I'm so glad. Seeing Evelyn that way would have frightened her."

"Yes, but it's a problem, as I don't know how long I'll need to be here."

When he hesitated, she said, "Do you need me to come and get Kristy?"

"Would you? Sarah's off on a cruise over spring break. This is so good of you, Lauren."

"I'm glad to do it." She got up and went to her closet. "I'll leave right away."

"You remember how to get to the ranch, don't you?"

"I do." Abandoning the laundry, she headed to her closet to get her luggage.

"You know, I wonder if you'll consider staying there instead of going back to Houston." He paused. "Kristy was enjoying country life so much, I'd hate to spoil it for her. You do have off for spring break, don't you?"

"I have no plans, Martin," she assured him, knowing he missed the note of irony in her voice. She had no plans for spring break or the foreseeable future.

"I can't tell you how much I appreciate it."

"It'll be great to have Kristy all to myself," Lauren said, transferring clothes from drawers to the suitcase. "I'll just pack a few things and get right on the road."

"Oh, my manager's name is Raphael Ruiz. His wife is Elena. I'll call him now to let him know you're coming and to let you through the gate. Nowadays it's always locked. And if you leave the ranch at any time, be sure to lock up and set the alarm behind you, okay?"

"I will," she said, understanding his concern. After Margot's murder, Evelyn had become obsessive about her need for security. An elaborate system was in place at their home in Houston and every door had multiple locks. Lauren suspected the ranch house was similarly secure.

"Oh, be sure to bring boots and jeans so you can ride. I'll have—" He paused, drowned out by an announcement coming over the hospital's public address system.

"Sorry about that," he said, picking up. "I was about to say that Raphael will help you choose a suitable mount. And don't feel as if you have to be with Kristy every minute. Elena is very willing to watch her during the day. She's getting older, so she likes to be at her place when it gets dark."

"That won't be a problem. Don't worry about us. We'll be fine." With the phone cradled between her shoulder and ear, she went to her bathroom. "Is there anything you or Evelyn need from the house? I can easily swing by."

"Maybe you could pack up a nightgown and robe, some of her underwear, that kind of thing,"

Martin said. "There's hardly anything at the ranch, since we were only going to be there for the weekend." He paused. "You're sure this isn't interrupting any plans you had for spring break?"

"I'm sure. In fact, I'll be glad to get away." If he only knew.

"I don't know how to thank you, Lauren."

"You don't need to." Still cradling the phone, she loaded her cosmetics bag with necessities and took it to the suitcase on the bed. "I'll be leaving in a few minutes. Be sure and call my cell when you know something more about Evelyn, will you?"

"Yes, of course. And before I hang up, there is something I need to tell—" He stopped abruptly. "Oh, here's the doctor. Gotta go."

With the connection broken, Lauren thought back to last Sunday when something about Evelyn had struck her as being off. Perhaps she'd been ill even then. Lauren breathed a prayer that it would not turn out to be anything serious. But she couldn't quite shake the bad feeling that was settling on her.

The bad feeling got worse later when she found Martin at the hospital and was told that Evelyn was having a CT scan. It should have been a relief that the doctors had ruled out both stroke and heart attack. Instead, it made her uneasy. There had to be a reason for her collapse. So after saying a prayer with Martin, she left the bag she'd packed for Evelyn and headed out to the ranch.

Because Martin had alerted Raphael that she was coming, he was waiting for her at the elaborate wrought-iron gate. An archway proclaimed the Houseman brand—a capital H topped with an inverted V. Lauren had been told during an earlier visit that the brand had been designed by Margot. According to Evelyn, Margot had dreamed of a life as an artist. She had lamented lately that whatever art her daughter might have created had died with her. Lauren thought it odd that she'd never seen a painting of Margot's in the Houseman home. Or anywhere else. Nor had Tucker ever mentioned Margot's dream to create art.

Once inside the large ranch house, Lauren discovered Kristy was still awake. Elena had no explanation for why the little girl was up more than two hours past her bedtime, though she suspected the housekeeper was simply comforting her. Although she perked up at the sight of Lauren, it was obvious that she was tired and cranky. Elena willingly turned her over to Lauren and was gone in minutes.

Kristy submitted to a quick bath, but she was so sleepy she seemed barely aware of it or of getting into her pj's. Once she was tucked in, she roused enough to say, "Don't forget to wake me up early because I want to show you the kittens."

"Okay," Lauren said. "But now, it's time for you to go to sleep, sweetie."

"I get to keep them all," she said drowsily. "Papa said so."

"Did he?" Lauren smiled down into sleepy dark eyes and felt a pang. Kristy's eyes were so like Tucker's. "G'night, sugar bear, sleep tight."

"Wait, Lolly," she said on a yawn.

"What?"

"Say prayers."

"Oh. Okay."

Kristy managed to bring her hands up to her chin. "Now I lay me down to sleep," she whispered, eyes closed. "Bless Grammy and Papa, bless Lolly and Sarah, and bless me when I ride Pickles tomorrow and don't let me fall off again like I did the first time I rode him. And bless Daddy most of all. Amen."

Lauren lingered even though Kristy was instantly asleep. It was something how she talked about Tucker as if he were in her life as much as the Housemans. It was no wonder Evelyn found it distressing, especially since Kristy never spoke of Margot at all. But was that proof, as Tucker claimed, that Margot had never been much interested in being Kristy's mother? It was true that he had been her rock. Which it so unforgivable that he had abandoned her.

And me.

She closed her eyes for a minute as the pain and

248

hurt washed over her anew. Tucker had been her rock, too. And when he was gone it had left a gaping hole in her heart and her life.

She stood up to leave. Abandoning her and Kristy was unforgivable . . . unless he was telling the truth. That they were in danger from a killer.

21

Next morning, after Lauren dutifully admired the kittens, Kristy raced to the paddock where Raphael had Pickles the pony saddled up and waiting. She literally vibrated with excitement as she was hoisted up, wearing a smile as wide as Texas. But after half an hour of monotonous circling, she begged to take a real ride. When Raphael brought out a gentle mare named Gracie and saddled her, Lauren took Kristy up in front of her.

"We won't go far," she told Raphael.

An hour or so later, they spotted a small, rocky creek and dismounted to let Gracie drink. Kristy wanted to wade in the creek. Unable to talk her out of it, Lauren helped her take off her shoes and socks. She was in the water and splashing when a vehicle appeared over the rise, heading their way.

Lauren shaded her eyes from the bright morning sun, but she still couldn't see much. Was Raphael out searching for them? She was only now noticing that they'd ranged farther than she realized and were out of sight of the barn and ranch house. As the vehicle materialized, she saw that the driver was not Raphael.

"Come out of the water, Kristy," she told the little girl quickly.

"No, Lolly, I want to find some pretty rocks."

"We can do that later," Lauren said firmly. She leaned forward and managed to catch Kristy's hand. "It's time for us to head back to the barn."

Kristy's instinct to argue faded when she spotted the ATV. "Who is that man?" she asked, pointing.

"I don't know." Lauren lifted her and settled her on one hip, then faced the stranger. But it wasn't a stranger. It was Jordan Raines.

He stopped the ATV and got out flashing a smile. He looked nothing like the sleek, well-dressed urbanite who'd chatted her up at Sunday brunch. Today, in boots and jeans with a flashy belt buckle, he could have stepped out of an old *Gunsmoke* episode. He pushed a classic Stetson back, revealing handsome features and perfect teeth. "Well, hello! Two beautiful ladies. This is my lucky day. Y'all catching any fish in that little creek?"

"This is the Houseman Ranch, Mr. Raines," Lauren said, thinking a formal introduction by Carter Brumfield didn't give him the right to trespass. "Were you aware that you're on private property?"

"Well, dang!" He moseyed toward them. "I took

250

off on this thing and I guess I covered more ground than I realized, you know?"

How had he gotten through the fence? Or wasn't there fencing around the entire ranch? She wasn't certain. What she did know for certain was that she wanted to get back to the ranch. "You'll have to turn around and go back the way you came. I'll notify the ranch foreman that there must be a break in the fence," she said. Reaching into her pocket for her cell phone, she realized to her dismay that she couldn't call because she didn't have the ranch number. But she hoped he wouldn't know that.

"Hey, not to worry," he said, his eyes on the phone in her hand. "These ranches are so huge I guess I just wandered off Blue Hills, which is where I'm supposed to be." With his palms stuck in the back pockets of his jeans—new jeans, she noted—he appeared boyishly chagrined. "We had to rush away Sunday, so I didn't get to chat with you." When she didn't respond, he added, "You're visiting the Housemans?"

"Lolly is staying with me because Grammy is sick," Kristy piped up.

"Aww, is that so? I'm sorry your Grammy is sick."

"Mr. Raines," Lauren said in a stern voice, "you're trespassing. I must ask you to—"

A shrill whinny from her horse startled her. As she turned to look, the animal reared on her hind legs, broke loose from her tether, and took off in a wild gallop. It happened so fast that Lauren didn't have a chance to do anything but watch in dismay as her only means of returning to the ranch house disappeared.

"Stay where you are," Raines said in a voice that had suddenly turned deadly serious. Lauren's heart lurched inside her. But when she turned to him, he was pointing to the ground beneath a cottonwood tree where Lauren had tethered Gracie. "It's a snake. That's what spooked your horse."

Lauren stared in horror at the coiled reptile. How had she not seen it when she tied up the horse? She must have been within a foot of it. With Kristy!

She drew an unsteady breath, her gaze fixed in horror at the snake. "Can you get rid of it?"

"I'll sure try." Keeping his eye on the snake, he bent down and slowly picked up a rock the size of his fist. The snake was now tightly coiled and vibrating its rattle. "Like I said, stay put. If we move," Raines said, "it might strike."

Kristy's arms were tight around Lauren's neck. "I'm scared, Lolly," she whimpered. "Let's go back to the barn."

"It's okay, baby." In spite of her efforts to control it, Lauren's voice quivered in terror. "He's probably more scared of us than we are of him," she whispered, not having a clue whether that was true.

"Here goes." Raines took aim with the rock and let fly. The snake slithered away and disappeared into nearby brush.

"Thank you," Lauren said with profound relief. "I really don't like snakes."

"Me neither," Kristy said fervently.

"Hey, it's not me you should be thanking," Raines said, his boyish grin once more in place. "It's my Little League coach. He taught me to pitch."

Lauren was still too shaken to laugh. Looking at the ground more closely, she set Kristy down. "Let's get your shoes and socks on, Kristy, and let this be a lesson to us. Next time we're out riding, we'll keep a sharper eye out for critters."

"What about Gracie?" Kristy asked, looking to where the horse had disappeared.

"Oh, you can bet she's back in the barn," Raines said. "Horses head straight for their stalls when they're spooked."

Kristy looked at Lauren, who was fitting pink sneakers on the little girl's feet. "Is that true, Lolly?"

"We'll soon know."

Kristy surveyed the vast landscape. "Are we going to walk all the way back?"

Raines spoke up before Lauren could. "You can ride back to the barn with me," he said. "That's the good thing about ATVs. They aren't spooked by pesky snakes."

"Thank you," Lauren said, "but we'll head on back."

"On foot?"

"We won't have to walk far. I'll just call Raphael," she said, remembering her earlier lie. "You should really be on your way, Mr. Raines." She hoped that if Raines's knowledge of horses was correct, when Gracie appeared at the barn without them, Raphael would soon come looking for them.

"This is a big ranch, Lauren. It could be quite a while before he finds you."

She frowned. "Speaking of finding us, was this truly a coincidence or did you know we were at the ranch?"

He cocked his hat at a rakish angle. "Oh, shoot, I confess. Ju-Ju told me."

"Juliana?"

"We're leasing the Blue Hills Ranch for the duration of the campaign. I'm here to plan strategy."

"The Brumfields are leasing the ranch next to this one?"

"Actually, it belongs to one of his strongest supporters, so we got a break in leasing it. It'll be great for entertaining, which is a plus for fund-raising," he said, winking at her.

She vowed right then to ask Raphael where the boundary lines were separating the two ranches so she could avoid getting anywhere near it. And this creepy man.

"How did Juliana know we were here?"

"Evelyn called her last night from the hospital. Seems they don't make a move without the other knowing it. As for me, I'm writing a book about a certain crime." He paused, giving a quick glance at Kristy. "I admit knowing your connection to that case, so I couldn't pass up the opportunity to talk to you about it."

"I thought you were working in the campaign."

"Day job," he said, making a face. "I grab time when I can to work on my book."

She was incredulous that he'd speak of Margot's murder in front of Kristy. "You seriously think I'd help you write a book about that crime after the dreadful lies you published?"

"Hey, you can help me set the record straight."

"Mr. Raines." Lauren pulled Kristy up close against her. "We need to get going. Thank you for getting rid of that snake. And good luck with the campaign."

"Jordan . . . please. Mr. Raines is my old man."

She took Kristy's hand and started walking.

"C'mon, Lauren," he said, falling into step beside her. "I'm a writer. You can't blame a guy for doing his job. And you could be an incredible research source."

"Absolutely not," she said, eyes straight ahead. But inside, she was alarmed. For Tucker's sake. What if Jordan Raines got wind that Tucker was nearby?

"Don't say no so fast," he said. "If you're worried I'd write something personally embarrassing to you, don't. I would never do that."

She stopped. "Oh, really? You didn't consider my feelings a few months ago when you wrote all those horrible things. Why would I believe you now?"

He raised both hands in a gesture of surrender. "I've changed."

"Pardon me if I find that hard to believe. The answer is still no."

He looked—again—boyishly chagrined. "Well, I'll keep hoping you'll change your mind. But for now, can I at least give you and Kristy a ride back to the ranch house."

She decided to be blunt. "Mr. Raines, please go back to your . . . whatever that thing is. We are walking back the way we came. Raphael will meet us." She stood her ground although she didn't know what she'd do if he kept pestering her.

Looking disappointed, he released a heavy sigh. "Okay, but it pains me to leave you out here alone. Anything could happen."

"What could happen, Lolly?" Kristy's eyes were big and worried.

Lauren gave Raines a fierce look. "Nothing will happen, sweetie. Raphael will find us, you'll see."

Without glancing at Raines again, she set off. It was a gorgeous day, but the sun was high now and beating down on them. After ten minutes, she was beginning to question her decision to refuse a ride. Maybe she'd overreacted, but the man was not to be trusted whether he'd faced down a snake on her behalf or not. She had Kristy to think of.

"Look, Lolly!" Kristy suddenly pointed to a pickup heading their way in a cloud of dust. "It's Raphael. He found us!"

"I knew he would, sweetie." Lauren injected more confidence into her voice than she felt. "I guess Gracie told him where we were."

"That's silly!" Kristy giggled. "Gracie can't talk."

While waiting for Raphael, Lauren turned, surveying the stretch of land behind them. There was no sign of Raines. But from the corner of her eye, she caught fleeting movement in the line of trees in the distance. She strained to bring whatever it was into focus. Had Raines gone in that direction instead of leaving? But the ATV would have been easy to spot. She stood gazing intently, but saw nothing more. She told herself it was probably a hawk zooming down on prey. Or some other animal. The ranch was big enough that there were probably many wild animals about, which was hardly a comforting thought. Raphael was almost upon them now, so she hurried to meet him.

The foreman stopped the pickup and got out. "You okay, Miss Lauren?"

"Yes, we're fine, Raphael," she said, as he opened the passenger door to let them climb into the pickup. "Gracie was spooked by a snake."

"Mr. Raines threw a rock and it went away!" Kristy informed him, eyes big with excitement. "He was going to give us a ride, but Lolly said no, but I didn't want to walk back to the barn. It's too long!"

"How did you find us, Raphael?" Lauren asked once they were under way.

"A minute after the mare got back to the barn without you, I received a call on my cell phone about someone in an ATV trespassing near the creek."

"Well, please thank him for me," she said. "I didn't have your number and it was either ride on Mr. Raines's ATV or start back to the barn on foot."

"No, he would not like you riding with a stranger," Raphael said.

"Who wouldn't?" She gave him a puzzled look.

"Do you know this Mr. Raines?" Raphael asked, frowning.

Yet she knew he hadn't been talking about Jordan Raines before.

"Yes. Barely," she answered. With a glance at Kristy, who was nestled beside her, she chose her words carefully, "I was surprised when he appeared. There must be a break in the fence somewhere."

"I will take care of that. And I think it is better for you to give this information to a person who will know how to proceed next," Raphael said, his Hispanic accent thickening.

"Who? What person?" Lauren asked again.

He glanced at Kristy before looking at Lauren. "You'll see."

22

By the end of the day, Lauren hadn't found an opportunity to break away from Kristy to ask Raphael to explain his cryptic remark. She didn't expect him to hang around the house, since he had chores to do, but it occurred to her that he might be avoiding her. So when she hadn't talked to him by nightfall, she was feeling impatient. She was hesitant about going to his home when he was done for the day, but he had to know she was curious.

At sundown, Elena left and still there was no sign of Raphael. Lauren made dinner for herself and Kristy, gave the little girl a bath, read her a story, heard her prayers, and tried her best to answer the child's anxious questions about Evelyn without going into too much detail. She then stayed with her until she fell asleep.

Back in the den, she found nothing she wanted to watch on TV, and the book she'd brought proved disappointing. It looked to be a long night . . . possibly a long week. If she got cabin fever after only one day at the ranch, she told herself, she might have to take Kristy back to the city, where they'd at least have a variety of things to do.

After making herself a cup of tea, she sat on the porch swing, taking her cell phone with her. She didn't want to miss a call from Martin. It had been several hours since he'd checked in with an update on Evelyn, and she couldn't think that was a good sign.

After a minute or two, she became aware of how dark it was. And quiet. In Houston, streetlights, security floods, homes with windows glowing, car headlights all combined to keep the world well lit. And noise was ever present—people talking, TVs blaring, car horns honking, ambulances wailing, dogs barking. But all she heard now was crickets chirping, owls hooting, and once, a few minutes ago, a coyote baying. Or did they howl? Did they prowl? Whatever they did, she hoped they kept their distance.

As she brought her mug up to her lips, she froze, thinking she heard something other than crickets. Or was it her imagination? No, she definitely heard something. Someone? She realized suddenly how vulnerable she was sitting alone in the dark with the door several feet away.

Footsteps.

Panicked, she lurched from the swing, making

for the door. Hot tea sloshed out and scalded her fingers.

"Oww!" She dropped the mug on the floor.

"Lauren, it's okay. It's me."

She turned, instantly knowing that voice. "Tucker?"

"Yeah." He materialized out of deep shadow and came up the porch steps. "I'm sorry. I scared you."

"What is it with you creeping up on me all the time?" she said, blowing on her burning fingers. "Can't you ever show up like a normal, ordinary person?"

"You're hurt," he said. Moving up close, he took her wrist. "I'm sorry. Let's go inside and put something on it."

For a second, as she felt the warmth of his hand, she was flooded with emotion. Would she always feel this delicious rush when Tucker touched her?

"It's okay," she said, freeing herself. "How did you find me? What are you doing here? Are you crazy? If Martin—"

"Where is Martin? Where's Evelyn?"

"They're at the hospital."

He looked shocked. "Is Kristy sick?"

"No, it's Evelyn. But if Martin knew you were within a mile of this ranch, Tucker, he'd get his gun."

"No, he wouldn't. And he does know I'm here." Wearily, he rubbed a hand over his face, heaving a sigh.

"You shaved your beard." She couldn't help reaching to touch his cheek.

"Yeah. It was time." When his eyes met hers she pulled her hand back.

"What do you mean Martin knows you're here?"

"It's a long story. Let's go inside where we can talk."

"You mean where you won't chance being seen by Raphael? Because he'll call the sheriff in a heartbeat."

"If you want to call Raphael, do it. He'll tell you it's okay."

She was shaking her head in total confusion. "This is so crazy. What is going on? I don't . . . I can't—"

"I saw Jordan Raines messing with you and Kristy at the creek this morning. When your horse bolted, I called Raphael on my cell and told him to pick you up."

She stared at him. "I thought I saw something. That was you?"

"I must not be that good at hiding if you saw me," he said ruefully. Reaching around her, he pushed the door open. "Go. Call Raphael. I'll wait out here. When you're done we can talk."

She hesitated, studying his face . . . or what she could see of his face in the dark. Now that he was clean-shaven, he looked more like the Tucker she knew. Give or take twenty pounds. But she closed those thoughts and focused on what he said. Everything was so astonishing that she didn't know what to think. And she wasn't letting him inside until she knew if he was telling the truth.

"Wait here."

She went into the house, turning the lock behind her. If he wanted to push inside, he could already have done it . . . easily. Her thoughts were reeling as well as her emotions. No surprise there. Everything regarding Tucker made her emotional.

In the kitchen, she found the Ruizes' number on a sticky note near the phone and dialed. It was picked up on the third ring.

"Raphael, Tucker Kane is outside on the porch. He tells me he has Martin's permission to be here. Is that true?"

"Yes, Miss Lauren. Mr. Houseman allows Mr. Kane to be at the ranch anytime."

"Was it Tucker who called you when Kristy and I were stranded at the creek this morning?"

"Yes. But you must say nothing of this to Mrs. Houseman. She is not to know that Mr. Kane is allowed on the ranch."

Lauren clicked off, now more troubled than confused. Why would Martin allow Tucker access to the ranch? Did he see him frequently? Did Kristy? If so, that explained why she continually spoke of Tucker as if she knew him, not from early memories, but because she actually saw him. And how could Evelyn know nothing about it? With a bewildered shake of her head, she made her way to the door.

Tucker was right. They needed to talk.

23

She found him waiting in the shadows. His eyes seemed anxious as they met hers. Somehow, that gave her a pang. She so wanted to believe him, to trust him again, but there was just too much hurt for that. Still, she beckoned him inside.

"Well, that was interesting," she said after closing the door. "Raphael verified your story."

"Why are Martin and Evelyn at the hospital?"

"Evelyn fainted and Martin took her to the ER. They're doing tests, but they haven't told Martin what the problem is yet. I'm watching Kristy."

"Lucky for them and Kristy," he said, looking as if he meant it.

She shrugged. "It's spring break." She decided not to tell him about resigning her job. It would only lead to questions she didn't want to deal with just now. "I didn't have any plans."

"Could we talk in the kitchen?" he asked. "I'm hungry. I haven't eaten anything since breakfast."

She hesitated a beat or two. What harm would there be in giving him something to eat? "There's ham in the fridge and bread in the pantry," she told him, leading the way to the kitchen. "I can make you a sandwich."

"Thanks, but I can make it."

He was clearly familiar with the house, but she reminded herself that, as Margot's former husband, he would be. She watched him move to the pantry and the bread box, taking mustard and ham from the fridge and opening the cabinet where plates and cups were stored. Soon he had everything assembled to make himself a sandwich. She didn't blink when he took a chef's knife from the wood block and sliced into the ham. It came to her with some surprise that she felt no fear of Tucker.

What she did feel she didn't care to examine. But there was no denying her foolish heart. Just looking at him stirred something she hadn't felt in a long time. She had to keep reminding herself how much he'd hurt her. How devastated she'd been when he left. How she'd longed to erase the memory of the awful event that had torn them apart . . . and its consequences.

She watched him bite into the huge sandwich. "Where have you been living?" she asked, glad he couldn't read her mind.

He chewed awhile and when he'd swallowed said, "Will you be mad at me if I don't tell you?"

"You're afraid I'll turn you in?"

"That's one reason."

"So I'm to trust you, but it doesn't work both

ways?" She took a quick, impatient breath. "Keeping my mouth shut about seeing you at all is the same as lying for you, Tucker. Don't you see that?"

He released a tired sigh. "I'm staying at Martin's hunting lodge. It's a couple of miles from here, but not on the ranch proper. He used to take friends there during hunting season, but he hasn't used it much in the last few years." He touched a paper napkin to his lips. "It's secluded."

She felt like Alice after falling down the rabbit hole. Starting with the encounter at the creek this morning until now, she was struggling to process the whole string of stunning events.

"I thought Martin and Evelyn were convinced you killed their daughter. Why would they help you?"

"Evelyn is convinced, but Martin knows I didn't do it." Tucker looked at his sandwich. "In spite of our differences, Margot was the mother of my child." He gave her a straight look. "Martin knows I'm not the kind of man who'd leave his daughter motherless, Lauren."

She ignored that. Tucker and Tucker alone had shaken her faith in him. It didn't matter what Martin did or didn't believe. "You're right about Evelyn," she said. "She's lost her daughter and, in her mind, you're responsible. She hates you, Tucker. She doesn't miss a chance to say it."

"I know." He laid the last of the sandwich on the plate, looking as if he had suddenly lost his appetite. "And nothing is going to change her mind until I flush out the real killer."

"How do you plan to do that?"

"I've been using the Internet and running down a few leads. That's why I'm here tonight. That's why I risked facing you directly. I need your help, Lauren. I can't show myself. I'd be arrested."

"I don't know what I could do," she said. *Even if I were willing.* She realized she had to constantly resist the urge to fall in with whatever he wanted. "Since you and Martin are so tight, why isn't he helping you?"

"He does help," Tucker said quietly, not reacting to the skepticism in her voice. "He's been a loyal friend to me through all this, and he's given me access to Kristy. She would have forgotten me if I hadn't been able to see her now and then."

Watching him drain the bottle of water, she thought of the long history between Tucker and Martin, as father- and son-in-law, building a successful business together . . . If anyone knew him, Martin did.

But enough to believe him when he said he didn't kill Margot? Enough to trust his granddaughter with him? "Now tell me why Martin can't do this?"

"Evelyn," he said, gazing at the remains of his sandwich. "If she learned that Martin had any dealings with me, she would confide in Juliana, who would go straight to Brumfield."

"I can't say I'll help you, too, Tucker. I need to talk to Martin first. And I need to think this through. I trusted you before. I believed in you, but you didn't trust me. If you had you wouldn't have taken off without a word. Heck, even Raphael knew where you were but you couldn't tell your fiancée!"

"I told you why I left. Someone was threatening you and Kristy. I couldn't chance putting you in danger. And I could see the strain the situation was putting on your career."

She had thought not to tell him, but now decided she might as well. "I don't have a career as of Friday. I resigned."

His mouth dropped open. "What?"

"Ever since Margot was murdered, Craig Rawls's mission has been to get rid of me. There was an incident last week with a student I chose to expel. Craig persuaded the board to issue an ultimatum. Rescind the expulsion or else." She shrugged. "I resigned."

"Who was it?" His face was tight with anger. "No, don't tell me. Rickey Armstrong, right? His dad got to Rawls."

"What does it matter, Tucker? If they didn't get me for that, they would have found something else sooner or later. I'll find another job."

He shook his head. "It's my fault. Everything was just fine before." He raised his eyes to hers. "Will they blacklist you?"

"I don't think they'll go that far. I think they just wanted me gone from St. Paul Academy." She reached for a towel and wiped up a few drops of water off the counter. "Enough about that. We were talking about why you left. I accept that you thought Kristy and I were in danger. But my feelings are unchanged. I still think your fear that you would have been framed bordered on paranoia. I still think—"

"That I could possibly be guilty?"

She did not want to go into that just yet. "Since you disappeared, nothing makes me think the justice system would have failed you. So, before I promise anything, I'll need to believe you don't have some hidden agenda."

She expected him to keep arguing, but he didn't. "If that's the way it has to be," he said quietly, "I'll have to accept it. I guess."

She leaned against the counter, her arms crossed. "You saw Jordan Raines on the ranch this morning. Did you know he's staying at Blue Hills?"

"No," he said. "But it figures. He's been asking about me at Round Top."

"Really?" She frowned. "I'm surprised. He told me that Carter Brumfield has leased Blue Hills Ranch, so he's there doing work for the campaign."

"Like what?"

"Planning publicity, writing speeches, being a general gofer." She shrugged. "Who knows?"

His reply was simply a disgusted snort.

She was still frowning. "He's also doing research for a book he's writing about Margot's murder."

"I'd think he had enough material in those articles he wrote. The book will be fiction anyway," he said bitterly.

"He wants me to talk to him about it."

He gave her a sharp look. "What did you tell him?"

"What do you think I told him, Tucker?"

"He's just trying to use you to get to me."

"Oh, stop! Please. I think I have sense enough to know when I'm being used."

"I guess you do," he said, chagrined. "It was a dumb thing to say."

She heaved a sigh. "I want you to go now. I'll get back to you after I have a chance to think this through. How can I reach you?"

"Tell Martin. He'll know."

She looked at him. "Are we going through this again? You're asking me to trust you, to help you in ways you aren't ready to talk about for some plan you won't share, but you won't tell me how to get in touch with you?"

He looked down at his feet, shaking his head ruefully. After a beat or two, he said, "I have a cell phone. Got a pen?"

"No, I'll store it in my phone."

"No, don't do that. If it should somehow get in the wrong hands, they'd find me."

270

The comment was a glimpse into his life lived in the shadows. While she'd faced the Craig Rawlses of the world, he'd been trapped in isolation. She felt an ache in her heart for how he'd suffered and tried to stifle it. Yet hadn't she suffered for the decision he'd made, too? He wasn't the only one. After writing the number on a scrap of paper and slipping it into the pocket of her jeans, she headed out of the kitchen.

When she realized he wasn't following, she looked back and found he hadn't moved. Instead, he was simply looking at her. She felt a familiar stirring, a quickening of her pulse. To stave it off, she spoke sharply, "What?"

He shrugged, his half smile crooked and wry. "I just like looking at you. I love looking at you."

"Don't—" Although he made no move to touch her, she put out a hand to hold him off. "You don't have the right to say things like that to me anymore, Tucker."

"I know." Nodding his head, his gaze darkened as it dropped to her mouth. "I know."

To her dismay, she felt tears well up in her eyes. "You don't know how much you hurt me, Tucker. Our plans, our wedding—" She broke off, unable to finish.

"I do know," he said, his voice going hoarse and unsteady. But there was nothing unsteady about the look on his face or the hunger in his eyes.

And she was tempted. If he simply asked, she

would be in his arms. She would know the joy of his kiss again. She would lose herself in sensation. All the ugliness and pain of the past months would be forgotten.

Momentarily.

Somehow she managed to find her voice. "You have to go now."

He stood without moving. Her vision was blurred with tears, but she could feel the conflict in him. He made a sound. A curse? She knew it was not directed toward her, but at their situation. At the unfairness of it all. After a moment, he simply reached for his plate, tossed his half-eaten sandwich in the trash, and turned back to her.

"One thing more before I go."

"What?"

"I want to see Kristy."

She frowned, ready to deny him.

"I won't wake her up. I just want to see her. I don't get many chances."

Lauren studied his face. "Okay. But I'm coming with you. Martin didn't say anything about giving you the run of the place."

"I won't be long."

At the door of the little girl's bedroom, Tucker moved quickly across the carpeted floor, pausing at the side of the bed. Lauren watched from the doorway. He seemed to be making a conscious effort to calm some inner turmoil, some powerful emotion, before dropping to one knee. He loved

Kristy. He had managed to overcome incredible odds to keep her in his life. Why couldn't he have kept her in his life, too? Did he simply love Kristy more than he loved her?

Kristy turned toward him, her little face angelic in sleep. Her hair was a curly tangle on her Dora the Explorer pillow, her cheek flushed and, as Lauren knew, silky-soft. While she watched, she saw Kristy's lips moving as if she might be dreaming.

Talking in her dreams, Lauren thought, her heart melting.

Tucker gently touched the nimbus of dark curls and whispered, "Hey, little girl. Daddy's here."

Lauren started forward to remind him of his promise not to wake her. And then, to her surprise, Kristy stirred, and as natural as if she were awake, her arms went around Tucker's neck. He took her fully into his arms and buried his face in her little-girl sweetness. For a few seconds as he held her close, rocking her back and forth, their dark hair blending, he and his small daughter seemed locked in a loving world of their own.

He again whispered in her ear. "Daddy loves you, baby."

Lauren's throat tightened. She swallowed hard and looked away. Of course he loved his daughter. She'd never doubted that. But that didn't mean she was ready to let him use her for whatever plan he had in mind. She needed to see far more change in him before she was willing to trust him again.

24

Lauren was watching a late-night movie when Martin returned to the ranch later that night. One look at his grave face and she stood up immediately. "What is it?"

"It's not good." He rubbed his hands over his face, looking bone tired.

"Martin, please. Tell me."

"They think it's colon cancer."

Lauren put a hand to her throat. "Oh, Martin. I'm so sorry." She hesitated. "But . . . are they sure? I mean, can they get an accurate diagnosis so soon?"

"I don't know, but they seemed pretty certain."

"How is Evelyn taking it? Is there anything I can do?"

"You're helping by just being here."

"This is so sudden," Lauren said, genuinely distressed. "How thorough are those tests? I think you should consider getting a second opinion. Maybe—"

"I'm thinking of taking her back to Houston as soon as we can get an appointment. No offense to these people here, but she'll be close to home there, close to her friends, the church." He paused with a sigh. "We're looking down a long and dark road here, Lauren."

"Yes, I can see that," Lauren said quietly. "So,

are you sure there's nothing more I can do?"

He gave her a look of profound gratitude. "I don't think I should beat around the bush, so I'll just say this straight out. You can take Kristy."

"Well, yes, of course. Didn't we settle that? I'll stay with her through spring break when Sarah returns."

"No, Lauren. Not just for spring break. I'm talking about taking her for the long haul, maybe permanently."

Permanently?

He must have seen her surprise because he went on, "At least for the duration of Evelyn's treatments, for however long that takes. It could be months." His voice thickened and he dropped his gaze. "I don't want to think beyond that."

Lauren sank onto the couch, wordless for a moment. Being Kristy's mother had once been her dream. But now . . .

"I see I've shocked you," Martin said, wearily lowering himself into a chair. "I'm pretty shocked myself. You'll have Sarah's help, of course—as soon as she gets back. I'll pay her salary. I . . . We wouldn't want to change that."

"No," Lauren said faintly. "Martin—"

He looked concerned, as if certain she was about to renege. "I'm counting on you, Lauren."

She smiled. "You can count on me . . . for however long it takes." She paused as she realized she had to tell him the rest of her news, though she hated burdening him. "I don't want you to worry over this, but maybe the time is right to tell you that I've resigned from St. Paul Academy." She saw his astonishment and quickly added, "Actually, they gave me a choice between resigning or being terminated."

"What possible reason did they have for doing such a stupid, ill-conceived thing as that?"

"Thank you for that vote of confidence," she said, touched. "I expelled Rickey Armstrong. He made some death threats . . . I refused to back down and the school board issued an ultimatum. Don't worry, I'll find another job."

"John Armstrong. That's the kid's father, isn't it?" Without waiting for her to say yes or no, he added, "So you picked the biggest dog to challenge?"

She gave a wry smile. "I guess so."

"Don't worry, dear. You won't miss a paycheck. You have a job at H & K Contractors as of this minute. Finish out spring break, then as soon as you get back to Houston, we'll do the paperwork."

She laughed. "What exactly do you see me doing at H & K Contractors, Martin? You don't need a schoolteacher, do you?"

"No, but since Tucker left, we sure need somebody who can organize and schedule. I'm also going to be out a lot with Evelyn's illness. So you see, you've just dropped into our hands like a ripe peach."

"A ripe peach, Martin?"

He laughed. "The pay is a lot better than you were getting at that school, too," he said.

She simply shook her head, knowing she was being rescued in the most generous and loving way.

Thank you, Lord.

Martin cleared his throat and said, "About Tucker—"

Lauren blinked. "What about him?"

"He told me you saw him."

For a minute, she was speechless. "You kept this from me, Martin? You saw the agony I went through when he left, and yet you said nothing?"

"I should have," he said, wincing.

"Yes, you should," she said, letting him see she was angry. She got up from the couch and paced a few steps before stopping and saying to him, "He came today."

"Tucker?" He appeared surprised. "And what do you think?"

She sighed, her anger fading. "I don't know what to think, Martin. Ever since he left, I thought I'd like to see him arrested and in jail, but when I had a chance to report him to the police . . ." She shrugged. "I didn't."

"I'm glad to hear you say that. I intended to prepare you for seeing him here at the ranch. I figured I'd have to persuade you to keep quiet. But in the . . . the shock of Evelyn's collapse, I never found the right moment. I'm sorry. Surprise is probably an understatement for what you felt when you saw him."

"Stunned is more like it," she said. "I assume it's true that he has your permission to be on the ranch whenever and however long he chooses."

"It's true."

"Why haven't we had this discussion before, Martin? Why did I have to learn everything this way?"

"Tucker was determined not to let you know. He was . . . is truly concerned about what might happen to you. He's unwilling to take that chance." He stood up and began pacing. "My wife's cancer changes everything, you realize that. She'll be very sick. We have to face facts. It will not be good for Kristy to see her while she's undergoing chemotherapy. And Kristy will want to see her daddy." He stopped and faced her directly. "She needs to be with someone who loves her, someone that Evelyn trusts. That's you, Lauren."

She was floored . . . and delighted. "Have you talked to Tucker about this?"

"No, but I have no doubt he'll agree. More than that, he'll be overjoyed."

"She's not a puppy to be adopted out to a good home, Martin," Lauren said in a chiding tone.

"Of course not. But of all people, it should be you." He paused a moment. "You may think it awkward to keep Kristy at St. Paul, considering. I'll leave it to you to decide."

"No, I think she should stay. It would not be wise to subject her to too much change."

"Then you'll do it?"

"Yes, if you're sure . . . but let's just consider it temporary. Things may look bleak right now, but Evelyn's cancer could be in remission or even healed in a few months."

"That might be true. I hope so. I pray it will be. Until then, I'm more than sure that your taking Kristy is the right thing. And tonight I can go back to the hospital and put Evelyn's mind at rest."

She wished the circumstances weren't so dire for Evelyn, but the chance to be Kristy's mother—even temporarily—was a gift she couldn't resist. Still, it wasn't without risk. "Martin, about Tucker . . ."

"Don't worry. If you think I'm happy about you taking Kristy, try multiplying it by a hundred and you'll have his reaction."

"It's not about Kristy. It's something else Tucker mentioned."

He gave her a puzzled look.

"He wants me to help him clear his name. He claims there are things he can't do from the lodge. He wants me to help."

"Is that so," Martin said slowly.

"From what you said a minute ago, I'm thinking you've been doing a lot in that regard already. And

Evelyn's needs must be your priority now." From the look on Martin's face, she could tell she was right. "So if I'm to believe his reason for leaving—that Kristy and I were in danger—where does that put us if I agree to take Kristy?"

"I don't know . . . except that I believe God's hand is in all this." He gave her a soft, quiet smile. "I think we should just leave it there—in His hands."

Lauren spent a restless night, and she wrestled with thoughts of telling the authorities about Tucker as well as helping to clear his name. Kristy, of course, hopped out of bed the next morning wanting to go to the barn and see the kittens. Knowing she would not give up, Lauren gave in.

Because it was so early, Raphael had not yet arrived. She tried to shake off the creepy feeling that she was being watched as she stood guard over Kristy in the shadowy barn. If Margot's killer had actually issued a threat against her and Kristy, and he somehow learned that Tucker was near, what was to prevent his making good on that threat? She decided not to come outside again unless Raphael was about.

To her surprise, Martin and Evelyn were in the kitchen when they got back a few minutes later. Martin must be making good on his promise to take her to Houston for a second opinion.

Kristy flew to her grandmother, threw her arms around her, and began chattering. Over their heads Lauren sent Martin a questioning look.

"Evelyn wanted to stop here before heading to Houston," he explained.

"I had a good reason," Evelyn said. "I wanted to see my baby." She ruffled Kristy's hair. "And I need to talk to you, Lauren." Although she was pale and seemed dangerously fragile, she looked determined.

Martin stood up. "Let's go out to the barn, Kristy. I need to check on my horses."

"Okay!" The little girl dashed to the door. "And I can show you the kittens! Lolly made me leave and I didn't want to."

The kitchen seemed overly quiet after they were gone. Evelyn released a weary sigh. "First, let me thank you for what you're doing, Lauren. It's a great relief for me not to have to worry about Kristy right now."

"No thanks necessary, Evelyn. I'm glad I can help." Lauren took a seat at the table. "You need to concentrate on getting well again."

Evelyn's smile was faint and fleeting. "I may not get well, Lauren. We need to talk about that."

Lauren shook her head vehemently. "No, we don't need to talk about that, Evelyn. First, take those tests, find out about your treatments, and until then, put negative thoughts out of your head." She stood up to put the coffee on. As she filled the pot, she added, "Once you're feeling better, you'll see. You'll be able to take care of Kristy yourself, just as you've done ever since . . . since—"

"Since Tucker murdered her mother?"

"Since her mother was murdered."

"Well, it's a great comfort that you'll be her mother if it comes to that."

"Please don't talk in terms of forever."

Evelyn raised a hand. "If you say so. But as you say, let's give it some time, see where all this is going. It's enough that you're willing to take her now."

Relieved, Lauren said, "Yes, and I'm thrilled to do it . . . for now." But she wondered whether Evelyn would be so willing to turn Kristy over to her if she knew Tucker was hovering in the shadows actively claiming his role as her father. But telling her was definitely Martin's job, not hers.

"So tell me, how are you feeling?" Lauren said.

"Like I've been run over by a truck," Evelyn said dryly. "Not so much because I'm in pain—actually, I'm not. Well, maybe a little. But the shock of it is . . . I guess I can't describe it. I knew something was wrong, and I suspected it was cancer."

"You've made an appointment in Houston?"

"We're working on it. I may have to wait a few days, but I'll want to go as soon as I can get in."

Evelyn suddenly pressed a trembling hand to her abdomen as if she felt pain. "I won't rest until Tucker's caught and punished for what he did."

Lauren was alarmed. A strip of white tape covered the site where she'd had an IV drip. Reaching out, she touched that frail hand. "Are you feeling faint? Shall I call Martin?"

"No," she whispered. Then, shaking her head, she lifted watery eyes to meet Lauren's gaze. "If he'd just waited he might have gone free," she said bitterly.

"What?" Lauren frowned in confusion.

"It hurts me to say this," Evelyn said, "but if you take Kristy, you need to know about Margot. Tucker must have told you that she never planned to have children."

"I know," Lauren murmured. She also knew how hard Tucker had fought to keep Margot from having an abortion when she found herself pregnant with Kristy.

"The pregnancy was an accident," Evelyn said. "And frankly, I'm surprised she didn't choose to abort, especially now that we know she'd already had one abortion."

"Not an abortion, Evelyn," Lauren said. "She miscarried. At least that was what you were told."

Evelyn waved a hand. "Maybe, but we don't know, do we? She simply didn't like the idea of being a mother, Lauren. She didn't want a child. She didn't want to change diapers or walk the floor with a colicky baby or keep to any schedule but her own. That's why a week before Kristy was born she hired Sarah."

Lauren knew that motherhood was not a priority to Margot. In that, Evelyn and Tucker were on the same page. But she was surprised to hear Evelyn confirm it . . . and in words that were not flattering to her daughter.

Thinking to offer some small comfort, Lauren said, "It's possible she suffered from post-partum depression, isn't it?"

"Maybe. But more likely she was simply self-centered." She gave Lauren a weary look. "You seem shocked."

"No, I—" Lauren waved a hand helplessly, then added, "Well, maybe . . . a little."

"You think I didn't know my own daughter?"

"Some parents don't seem to see beyond what they wish," Lauren said gently. "And I can't judge since I didn't know her well."

"You would have disliked her," Evelyn said flatly. "The truth is, you're ten times more suitable to be Kristy's mother than Margot was. Even as a teenager, she was a handful. Rebellious to a fault. She was smoking pot when she was thirteen. By the time she was fifteen, I never knew if she would be in her bedroom when I checked. She would sneak out and return at two, three, four in the morning." Evelyn's eyes clouded with painful memories. "After her high school graduation she was gone for five days. We didn't know if she was dead or alive. I should be ashamed to say it, but we were relieved to send her off to college. At last we could get a good night's sleep."

Feeling awkward at the painful admission, Lauren got up from her chair. "I'll see if the coffee is ready." But Evelyn was not to be deterred.

"We sent her to the best schools, but she didn't appreciate anything we did for her." She studied her shaky hands. "In your job you see students who're spoiled rotten. You look at their parents and you think the apple doesn't fall far from the tree, right?"

"Well—"

Evelyn smiled faintly. "It's understandable. But trust me, Martin and I did our best. We were simply baffled by Margot. Overwhelmed trying to control her."

"Being a parent isn't always easy," Lauren said. Glad for an excuse to be busy, she found napkins and spoons and put them on the table.

"We were happy and relieved when she married Tucker," Evelyn said, shaking out a napkin. "He was so solid we thought he'd be a good influence. She'd be grounded married to someone like him. And Martin loved him. I think he's always wished Tucker was his son. He certainly did everything in his power to encourage the match." She looked thoughtful for a moment. "And Tucker didn't have much family of his own."

Yes, Lauren knew. And she'd identified with his lonely childhood. With her mom and dad an ocean away, she'd sometimes felt she had no parents either. They'd hoped that their marriage would change all that.

Evelyn sat toying with a spoon. "Maybe Tucker was seduced by the idea of marrying into our family. Margot certainly managed to behave normally for the duration of their courtship. But they did get married . . . in a big way, of course," she said in a wry tone. "Naturally Margot had to have a lavish wedding."

She studied the pattern on a china cup. "However, it wasn't long before we sensed trouble in paradise. My, how they fought. And often. Tucker didn't have much patience, and his hot temper spilled over at work as well as at home. He was very demanding with his crews. They'd complain to Martin, but he always sided with Tucker." Her tone turned bitter. "He said it was okay with him that Tucker demanded quality work. Good for the reputation of the business."

The coffeepot signaled that brewing was done, but Lauren didn't rise. She was thinking about Tucker's reputation for being tough. He'd often complained to her how hard it was to get a full day's work out of this or that employee. But she'd never heard that his temper was out of control during his marriage to Margot.

"Margot was obviously unhappy," Evelyn said.

"Or maybe *frustrated* is a better word. At the time, I thought it was the pregnancy and that she'd get over it when the baby came. But Kristy's arrival just made it worse. When Margot said she wanted a divorce, we were not surprised. At least, I wasn't."

Listening, Lauren was troubled. She wanted to think that Evelyn's perspective was skewed. No doubt she'd gotten an earful of her daughter's dissatisfaction. But was she aware that, for Kristy's sake, Tucker had tried hard to save his marriage? And after the divorce, Tucker had been genuinely concerned about Margot's neglect of Kristy. He'd been openly critical of her about that. And frustrated.

But frustrated enough to kill her?

Apparently Evelyn thought so.

Lauren was silent, watching Evelyn stir sugar into her coffee with an unsteady hand, then carefully place the spoon aside. "I wanted you to know the truth about Margot. After I'm gone and Kristy asks, promise me you'll tell her good things about her mother, too, not her faults."

"Evelyn—" Such a fatalistic view was deeply distressing to Lauren. "You are going to respond well to treatment and have many more years with Kristy to tell her what you want her to know about Margot. Now stop it."

Unmoved, Evelyn looked at her sadly. "Promise me, Lauren. Please."

With no other choice, Lauren nodded.

25

Lauren spent another night tossing and turning. Contrary to what she'd told Evelyn, there really was a possibility the older woman might not survive. If so, both the Housemans seemed determined to leave Kristy in her hands. But Tucker was a major complication. He would never walk away from Kristy, meaning he would be a constant presence in their lives. And always on the sly as long as he was a murder suspect. So what kind of life would that be for Kristy? Or for her? Or, for that matter, for Tucker? There had to be a way to get out from under that dark cloud.

If he was innocent.

She turned and looked at the clock. Three-forty-five. Groaning, she flopped back onto the pillow, her thoughts still churning. Now that she'd had time to think over what Tucker said, she realized he couldn't do much as long as he was in hiding. He really did need help. Maybe for her own peace of mind, she should at least try to do something. Maybe she owed him that much.

If he was innocent.

By morning, she'd decided on a course of action. Starting with the police. She wanted to know what progress, if any, they'd made since their prime suspect disappeared. Considering how hard Detective Sherman had questioned her in his attempt to build a case against Tucker, she didn't know how receptive he'd be to telling her anything. And she definitely didn't look forward to talking to him. But it was the logical place to start. Fortunately, she could be back by midafternoon. Kristy would be okay with Elena for the day.

At the downtown headquarters of the police department, she submitted to a security check and, with her stomach in a knot, headed to the Homicide Division. Once there, she was relieved to see no one she recognized. They were a tough-looking bunch—mostly men—and obviously too busy to acknowledge her. Or maybe they were determined to ignore her. She headed directly to the lone woman seated at a desk at the far end of the room.

A desk nameplate read, "Isabel Pike." Unlike her male counterparts who wore street clothes, she was dressed in classic police uniform—mannish pants, a sharply creased shirt with a shiny name tag.

Clearing her throat, Lauren introduced herself and was rewarded with a practiced smile.

"So, what can I do for you, Ms. Holloway?"

"I'd like some information about an unsolved murder."

Eyebrows rose. "A murder . . . in Houston?"

"Yes. In the Heights. It was almost ten months ago. Margot Kane."

Because there was no reaction to Margot's name, Lauren assumed Officer Pike had not been around when Homicide investigated. Or maybe she hadn't even been in the city of Houston. Everybody who read or watched TV surely knew about the case.

"What kind of information are you looking for?"

"I wondered what progress has been made in the case."

"Are you a reporter?"

"No."

"Do you have some personal interest in the case?"

"I'm a friend of Margot's parents, the Housemans. Naturally they're anxious to know who killed their daughter." She conjured up a smile. "To find closure."

"Give me a minute to look it up," Pike said, turning to her computer. As Lauren watched, she tapped a few keys, read something on the monitor, and, when Lauren leaned over to see, Pike quickly blanked out the screen. "I can't allow you access to an ongoing investigation, Ms. Holloway." She smiled tightly. "Police policy."

"I understand," Lauren said. "I wasn't asking to look at the file. I was just hoping someone might give me the general status of the investigation. Maybe I could talk to Detective Sherman. Is he still the leading detective on the case?"

Pike consulted the computer again. "He is."

Lauren turned and scanned the room looking for the grizzled detective, but didn't see him. She turned back to Pike. "I'd like to talk to him. Is he here?"

"Not right now, but if you'll leave your number, I'll see that he gets your message."

She took a breath and tried not to look as frustrated as she felt. "Officer Pike, I'm confused. Rather than waiting for a phone call from Officer Sherman, how can I get information about the case today?"

"*Detective* Sherman."

"What?"

"It's Detective Sherman, not Officer Sherman."

"Oh. Okay. But my question still stands."

"Since it's an ongoing case, that's hard to say. But from time to time the press is notified of developments. If they're significant."

"But I'm not a journalist, so I would only know such information if the press chose to make it public, isn't that right?" She didn't wait for the obvious answer. "So since there has been nothing in the press, can I assume there haven't been any significant developments lately?"

She shrugged. "It looks that way."

"It's actually more than eight months. Almost nine. Do the police have any suspects?"

"That would be privileged information and—"

"I know. It's an ongoing investigation." Feeling more and more frustrated, Lauren tried again.

"How about this? Can you tell me if anybody has worked the case lately? Maybe Detective Sherman's caseload made it necessary to give it to someone else. You can check for that in the file, can't you?"

"I wouldn't be free to—"

"Reveal that? Really?" Her patience was hanging by a thread. "Officer Pike. Is there anything you can tell me about the case?"

"Only who the investigating officer is."

"Who isn't around." Lauren heaved a big sigh. "I guess I have no option but to leave my number."

Pike seemed to relent. "You need to understand, Ms. Holloway. Releasing information prematurely could jeopardize an investigation."

"I understand. I do." Lauren glanced around to find several of the officers watching, but nobody seemed about to step up. Annoyed, she settled her purse strap on her shoulder. "Maybe you don't recall—or you weren't here—but when Margot was murdered, it was all over the media. I'm sort of surprised at how difficult it is to get a simple update on the case."

"Any unsolved homicide is always open until we make an arrest," Pike said stiffly. As she spoke, her gaze moved from Lauren to fix on something—or someone—behind her.

"I'm glad to hear it," Lauren said, turning to see who the woman was looking at, but nobody in the room seemed to be aware of her. "Since it was such a high-profile case, I guess I assumed the Homicide Division wouldn't just give up."

As she spoke, Detective Sherman suddenly came through the door. When his gaze met Lauren's, his eyebrows rose in surprise. As he headed over, she remembered she'd often thought that Sherman could have been a character in a movie, given his physical appearance. He was a big man with a hard jaw and steel-gray hair cut close to his skull. Tiny bifocals seemed almost ludicrous perched on his pug nose.

He stuck out his hand. "We meet again, Ms. Holloway."

"Hello, Detective Sherman," she said, almost wincing when he squeezed her fingers a little too hard.

He was grinning as he spoke to Officer Pike. "You been making Ms. Holloway feel welcome, Izzy?"

"She's interested in a homicide case. Margot Kane."

"Is that right?" He gave Lauren a good, long look, clearly relishing the idea of having her in his clutches again.

"I looked it up and told her it was an ongoing investigation and police policy prevented—"

"You did good, Izzy," he interrupted as he rested a hip on Pike's desk. "Definitely my case. What's it been, Ms. Holloway? Six, seven months?"

"Almost nine."

"Nine. Go figure." He shook his head. "Ancient history around here."

"It's not ancient history to the Housemans," Lauren said coldly. "As the investigating officer, you should know how devastated they were over Margot's death."

"They sent you? Is that why you're here?"

"I'm here as an interested citizen trying to get information about an unsolved case, Detective."

"Uh-huh. As I recall, I had a heckuva time getting you in here for questioning when we were busting our butts to solve the case, Ms. Holloway. Big surprise to see you just walking in on your own . . . almost nine months later. Makes me wonder what's changed."

"Apparently nothing," she said tartly. She didn't know how much more she could put up with. She guessed it was as much for his own enjoyment as for the amusement of his buddies watching from across the room.

"We know who killed Margot, Ms. Holloway. You'd probably be married to him now if he hadn't skipped town." He scratched the side of his neck, pretending to be puzzled. "That would seem to put you in the opposing camp to Margot's folks. I'm trying to wrap my head around that."

"I'm no longer engaged to Tucker Kane, Detective."

"Then are you here to give us information on where he is?"

"No," she said, then wondered if he'd noticed her hesitation. She sighed inwardly. It seemed the more opportunities she had to lie for Tucker, the easier it became. Nevertheless, she managed to look the detective straight in the eye to say, "From the sound of things, the case has grown cold."

"No case of mine ever grows cold, Ms. Holloway. You watch too much TV. A woman was murdered. I don't just forget that."

"I'm glad to hear it. So, as the lead detective, will you take a few minutes to tell me anything?"

"Ms. Holloway. If we took time to tell everybody who asked where we were in an ongoing investigation, we wouldn't get anything done."

"So the answer is no?" Lauren waited, giving him a straight look, but his gaze never wavered. With a sigh, she made a show of finding her car keys deep in her purse. "Okay. So since you haven't reported any progress in the case since your prime suspect disappeared, maybe the media need to be reminded that there's still a killer out there somewhere." She turned to leave. "Maybe that should be my next stop."

"Well, now, hold on just a minute." Heaving a very deep sigh, he said, "I didn't mean you couldn't see anything in the file. Follow me." Scowling, he stalked off ahead of her.

Yes! She followed, trying not to look too pleased.

"We have good reason for trying to discourage folks from getting involved in homicide investigations," Sherman explained, as if conducting a guided tour. "Think about it. Murder is a nasty business. We cops learn to keep our emotions in check working a case. Private citizens don't have that ability. The victim is a loved one. So they're a distraction."

"I understand, Detective Sherman. I'll try to keep my emotions in check."

He gave her a sideways glance, to which she simply smiled.

His office was operating-room neat, as she recalled from the sessions she'd had to endure as he questioned her. Except for a stunning painting on the wall behind his desk. Abstract and wild and boldly colorful, she couldn't imagine Sherman choosing it. Squinting, she saw that it was signed, but the artist's name was impossible to read.

"That's a wonderful painting," she said, hoping to lessen the hostility emanating from the man.

"Yeah," he said, his head down as he rooted through a file drawer on the left side of his desk. "Guess who painted it?"

"I couldn't read the artist's name," she said.

"Margot Kane."

Her mouth fell open. "Really?"

"Yeah. It was in the DA's office. When she was murdered he said he didn't want to look at it anymore. Too sad. So I took it." He finally found what he was looking for and sat back in his chair. "Might be valuable someday."

So Margot had actually done some painting. It wasn't just Evelyn's wishful thinking.

"Okay, let's get to it." Sherman pointed her to a chair opposite his desk, a battleship-gray-painted example of bad institutional office furniture, just as she remembered it. The same two framed photos of his grandchildren, but nothing else on top except a yellow legal pad and a nameplate with "Sergeant Gus Sherman" engraved in brass. She didn't remember it being there on her last visit. She wondered now what his full name was. August? Gustave? Angus? She bet nobody in the unit knew. His computer rested on a small metal table beside his ugly desk, but other than the gorgeous painting and photos of his grandchildren, there was nothing to relieve the starkness of his office.

She took a notepad from her purse when he opened a three-ring binder. She noted the case number scrawled in black marker on the cover and the name KANE printed in large letters. She'd watched enough television and read enough mysteries to know this was the "murder book." Every fact recorded by the investigators in Margot's case was in that book. She'd love to look through it, but she knew that would never happen.

Without another word, Sherman opened it and took out a series of eight-by-ten color photographs. The last time she'd been in his office, he'd shown her only one shot of Margot in death. She was now more prepared for the ugly reality. And, she reminded herself, she was here looking for something—anything—that would be a clue, a lead to pursue in finding Margot's killer.

She braced herself. As she watched, he doled them out like playing cards so that they were upright and visible to her. Of course, it was Sherman's intention to shock her. To drive her away. She stiffened her spine and vowed not to be intimidated.

The first was a full-body shot, one she'd seen earlier. Margot's once beautiful face was pasty gray, her eyes open in death. Blood trickled from the corner of her mouth. Lauren felt queasy just looking. As Sherman said, murder was a nasty business.

She swallowed hard and turned her gaze to the second photo, this one a close-up of Margot's face. The photographer had to've been flat on the floor to get the shot. It gave Lauren an eerie feeling looking straight into the dead eyes of Tucker's ex-wife. She barely managed not to shudder with revulsion.

Next was a close-up of the fatal wound. Margot's mane of glossy black hair was spread out around her head on the floor where she'd fallen. The site of the blow that had killed her was matted with congealed blood.

The fourth was another view of the head wound.

She blinked at the next, a close-up of one hand, her left. A ring that was obviously a large diamond was still in place, as was a jewel-encrusted watch. Lauren couldn't see the brand, but it looked expensive. It would be, knowing Margot. And just barely visible beneath her was her evening bag.

The next was a photo of her right hand. Another ring—an emerald? A diamond tennis bracelet was on her wrist. Whoever murdered her wasn't a thief.

She looked through all the photos, but after that first shocking look at Margot's face, she managed to keep her emotions in check to the end. When she was done, she stacked the photos neatly before raising her gaze to find Sherman watching her. Still without a word, he tucked them back in the file and shoved a single page across his desk.

"I can let you see the original report from the responding officers at the scene," he said, handing it over.

She took her time reading it. The 911 call from Tucker was noted as well as his statement explaining why he was at a deserted house at that hour. The report listed names of the EMS individuals as well as other officials at the scene. She wrote their names on her notepad. She wasn't sure what she might learn from them, but it was worth a try.

"This tells me nothing new, Detective Sherman," she said, passing it back to him. "I know the date and time that Margot died and where Tucker found her. And that he immediately reported it. What I'm asking is whether there is any fresh evidence. What, if anything, is being done to find who killed her?"

"Didn't I say? Your ex-fiancé killed her, Ms. Holloway."

"But what if he didn't?"

He looked at her narrow-eyed. "You have new evidence?"

She ignored that. "I'd like to know if you've done anything on the case since Tucker left?"

"Like what? We know who killed her. We have the murder weapon. It belongs to Kane. His initials are on it. What's the point?"

"Well, think of it this way." She leaned forward in her chair. "If Tucker killed her, would he be stupid enough to leave the murder weapon at the scene?"

"He was stupid enough to go back to the murder scene to get it."

"He wasn't there to get it. He was looking for something—for anything—that might give him a clue to who the real killer is. He knew the police thought he did it. Put yourself in his shoes. Should he have just waited to be taken like a lamb to the slaughter? Doesn't that make sense?"

He shrugged, unimpressed. "Killers don't always make sense."

Frustration almost made her stand up and leave.

But she knew that was what Sherman wanted. She wondered how hard they'd tried to find Tucker. It wasn't as if he'd fled to Alaska or somewhere equally distant. He was living and working only two hours from Houston.

Why hadn't they found him?

She decided to take a new tack. "Did you look closely at Margot's life?"

Pretending surprise, he bumped the side of his head with the heel of his hand. "Gee, why didn't we think of that?"

She kept on grimly. "So you traced her steps on the day she was murdered? Where did she go that night before winding up dead at a deserted house in the Heights? Did you find a single individual who saw her between the time Tucker left her and the time she was murdered?"

"You know what? You're wasted as a schoolteacher," he said sarcastically. "You should be a detective."

"So where did she go, Detective?"

"Okay." Looking as if he'd like to toss her out on her ear, he opened the murder book and began paging through it, his head tilted to focus through his bifocals. He was obviously looking for something. While he made a big show of searching, she wondered about the crime scene.

"Was Margot actually murdered at that house?" she asked. "Or did it happen somewhere else and her body was planted there?"

301

He looked up at her over his bifocals. "Planted?"

"To implicate Tucker."

"Like I said, you watch too much TV, Ms. Holloway."

"This murder didn't only affect my life, Detective. A lot of other people were victims, too. I'm just trying to get a picture of how it could have happened."

"Why don't you put your questions to Kane?"

"I'm asking you."

"You know what?" He rested his massive arms on the top of his desk, his pale blue eyes cold with dislike. "It sounds like you're suggesting I don't know how to do my job, Ms. Holloway."

"No, I just—"

"Because everything you mention is basic homicide one-oh-one." He shook his head suddenly as if having to talk to her tried his patience sorely. "The facts we've got are what matters. She'd been with her ex—"

"Wait. You couldn't prove she was with Tucker, could you?"

"The nanny said he came and they argued."

"That was much earlier in the day, Sergeant. Around four o'clock. According to your own statement to the press, she was murdered at around six-thirty P.M."

"That doesn't mean he couldn't have lured Margot to the house in the Heights. They got in a fight over custody of the kid and he killed her in a fit of rage."

She could see why, in Sherman's mind, it could have happened that way. But so many things didn't fit. "That would mean Tucker would have lured her away, leaving Kristy alone, Detective. He wouldn't have done that . . . for any reason. He just wouldn't."

"He didn't have any problem leaving the kid nine months ago." Smugly confident, he leaned back in his chair. "Kane did it, lady, and once he had her there, he killed her."

"Can I see the medical examiner's report?"

"Now that is definitely information I am not free to—"

"Okay, okay. Ongoing investigation and all that." She studied him for a long moment. "You know what, Detective, I don't think you have a case at all. But I think it suits you—and others in the department—to let the public think Margot was murdered by Tucker Kane."

His heavy black eyebrows lowered. "You can think what you like, Ms. Holloway. You can stick by a killer if you want, but we have witnesses who put Kane at that house at the time of the murder. He is—"

"Witnesses?" She stared at him. "Who? How many?"

His smile showed a lot of teeth. "C'mon, Ms. Holloway. You know I can't answer that."

He stood up, signaling that he was done humoring her. "The way I see it, Tucker Kane is a killer . . . unless you can come up with evidence that clears him." He paused, giving her a smug look. "So is that what you're here for? You gonna supply him with an alibi at this late date? You gonna say those eyewitnesses are wrong? You gonna say he was with you?"

Lauren stood up, feeling intense dislike of this Neanderthal. "Thanks for your time, Detective."

He got to his feet. "What? You're taking your questions . . . ah, purse . . . and going home?"

She could hear him laughing all the way to the elevator.

26

She was frustrated, irritated, and disgusted as she waited for the elevator. Sherman was still just as awful as he'd been nine months ago. However, all things considered, she felt her efforts hadn't been a total waste. She'd learned that they had witnesses who could place Tucker at the crime scene. Now, she needed names. That might be difficult. She glanced at her watch, checking whether she had time to grab a bite to eat before heading back to the ranch.

"Lauren?"

She turned to see Eric Grantham, Jack's dad. She was aware that he was a policeman, but she hadn't expected to run into him today. And how would she explain why she was here?

"Hi, Eric."

"Hi, yourself," he said, smiling with warm surprise. "The principal is supposed to be on spring break, not at HPD. Tell me you're not here on official business about the school. Or Jack."

"No, nothing to do with the school." She smiled. "And certainly nothing about Jack." She was genuinely sorry that she wouldn't see Jack graduate one day. Of all the students at St. Paul, he was one of her favorites.

Obviously curious, Eric paused to let two uniformed officers pass. "Everything okay?"

"Are you assigned to Homicide now?"

"Yeah. I was finally promoted about a year ago."

"Congratulations."

"Thanks. It took a while, but . . ." He spread his arms wide, grinning. "Here I am."

Suddenly she was more hopeful. He was bound to be more helpful than Sherman. "Maybe you can help me, then. I came to ask about the investigation into Margot Kane's murder."

He frowned. "Do you mind me asking why you want to go there?"

"I guess it's a closure thing, Eric. Nothing was ever settled." Lauren paused when the elevator pinged and several people got off. She let it close without moving.

He eyed her narrowly. "You don't think Kane did it?"

"Not when it first happened, I didn't. I had doubts when he just disappeared." She gazed beyond him thoughtfully. "Now . . . well, I need to know. For myself. Not for the Housemans or for Kristy. Not even for justice for Margot."

Eric glanced around, as if checking to be sure they weren't overheard. "Who did you talk to?"

"Gus Sherman."

Eric gave a short laugh. "I can guess how helpful he was."

"Right. But, Eric, just putting my interest aside, the case shouldn't be ignored. Margot was murdered. She deserves justice."

Eric touched her elbow to move her out of the flow of traffic in the hall. "I've been meaning to come to the school and talk to you," he said. "I wanted to thank you for the way you stood by Jack over that cheating incident with Rickey Armstrong."

"Jack is a son to be proud of. He's an asset to St. Paul. I couldn't let him be victimized for something he would never do. I just did my job."

She didn't see any reason to tell him she didn't have that job anymore. He'd know soon enough . . . as would the whole school.

"I'll walk you to your car, but give me a minute to make a stop first," he said. "Are you parked in the garage?"

"Yes, but it's not necessary to do that." At least, she didn't think it was necessary to have an escort, but that parking garage could be mighty dark.

"No." He touched her arm. "Wait for me in the lobby. I insist. You won't be sorry."

It was an odd remark, but something in his expression convinced her. "Okay, I'll stop downstairs and get a snack to take with me. But I really need to beat rush-hour traffic."

He turned on his heel. "I'll be quick."

A man with a plan, Lauren thought. She was smiling faintly when the elevator opened, but her smile evaporated when she found herself facing Carter Brumfield and John Armstrong. It was an awkward moment, but she could hardly turn tail and run.

For a second, Armstrong seemed as startled as she was. "John. How are you?"

"Good, good. And yourself?"

"Fine, thanks." She nodded politely to Brumfield.

Armstrong's demeanor was sickeningly upbeat, but since he'd finally managed to oust her from her job, why wouldn't he smile, the snake? "I'm surprised to see you at the police department," he said. "What's happening? Did you discover one of our students packing heat?"

"As you know, I'm no longer responsible for St. Paul students," she said, ignoring the wicked glint in his eye.

"You remember Carter, don't you?" Armstrong said, still enjoying himself.

She nodded again at Brumfield. First, an interview with a surly homicide detective and now trapped in an elevator with two men she heartily disliked. To make matters worse, Armstrong reeked of alcohol. Lunch must have been liquid.

"Lauren is—actually was—the principal at my kids' school," Armstrong said to Carter.

Brumfield let that pass. "Nice to see you again, Ms. Holloway," he said, flashing a practiced smile.

"This woman knew how to run a tight ship," Armstrong said, warming to his subject. "She expelled Rickey last week."

To Lauren's relief, the elevator mercifully stopped. Maybe they'd get out. But they didn't. Instead, an elderly woman stepped in.

"Is it going up?" she asked them.

"Nope, down," Armstrong said.

"Oh, dear." She quickly backed out.

No sooner had the door closed than Armstrong was chatting her up again. "So, Lauren, how're you liking the hill country?" When she gave him a startled look, he added, "I understand you're the Housemans' guest this week."

Did the man know everything? She smiled tightly.

"Great place they have out there, don't you know?"

"It is."

He glanced at Brumfield. "A woman of few words is so rare, right, Carter?"

Brumfield, sensing toxic tension, wisely did not comment.

"My kids will be thrilled . . . or at least two of them will," Armstrong said. "It's going to ease my mind knowing you're nearby during their spring break."

His kids? Her confusion must have been obvious, at least to Brumfield.

"What John means," he said, "is that I've leased Blue Hills Ranch for the campaign. It borders Martin Houseman's land. So it's likely you'll see us there. But I promise you won't have to baby-sit his kids," he added dryly.

"I believe Jordan Raines mentioned that," she said, her eyes on the elevator buttons.

"It's a small world," Armstrong said, smirking.

"Indeed." Brumfield's tone was wary. Maybe he felt something going on between her and Armstrong and, like any prudent politician, he didn't intend to step in anything nasty. "It wasn't entirely coincidental that we were able to get Blue Hills," he said, obviously thinking he was on a safe topic. "Actually, Juliana heard about it through Evelyn."

"And it's perfect for the campaign," Armstrong said. "Course, that place you sold last month in La Grange would have been a great place for campaign events, too. But just a tad too small." Crossing his arms, weaving slightly, he leaned against the wall. "You should have seen it, Lauren. It was fabulous. Built in the late nineteenth century. Restored to perfection, gorgeous grounds. They featured it in a magazine . . . I forget which one. Last year, wasn't it, Carter?"

Brumfield smiled, said nothing.

Armstrong chuckled. "Juliana made that happen. Knew the right folks. But we needed something impressive for this campaign and Blue Hills fit the bill." He gave Brumfield a slap on the back. "After a couple terms as governor, we'll need to look for something even bigger, say in D.C. Right, Carter?"

Brumfield looked annoyed. "Those plans are very premature, John. Right now, I'm concentrating on this campaign."

"But you can't lose, my man." He winked at Lauren, who fought the urge to wave a hand in front of her face to combat the fumes. "Reminds me of a quote by a famous politician in Louisiana. I forget his name. He was so confident about winning that he said . . . let me see. I want to get this right." He glanced up at the ceiling, thinking. "The only way I can lose is to be caught in bed with a dead girl or a live boy." His raucous laugh shook the walls.

Lauren looked away in disgust.

"I apologize, Ms. Holloway," Brumfield said, shooting a glare at Armstrong. "Behave yourself, John."

"Sorry, sorry," Armstrong said, still chuckling. Not missing a beat, he went on. "Anyway, we chose well by leasing next door to Martin Houseman. When you think of movers and shakers in Houston, Houseman's name is one of the first to come up. And it doesn't hurt that Juliana and Houseman's wife are close. Hopefully he'll host a fund-raiser."

He paused, focusing on Lauren as if struck with a bright idea. "Hey, here's a thought. Why don't you see if you can talk him into it, Lauren? This woman has a straight line to the Housemans," he explained to Brumfield. "She's practically a surrogate mom to the Housemans' grandkid. I have that on good authority." He winked at her again. "St. Paul school board gossip."

Lauren glared at him. The man had his nerve! After what he'd done, he thought she would do him a favor? Maybe when pigs could fly. "Mr. Armstrong—"

"You know the kid's father is Tucker Kane," Armstrong said. "That would be the infamous Tucker Kane who was once Ms. Holloway's fiancé."

Brumfield's embarrassment was painfully obvious. "This is old news, John."

Armstrong, oblivious, wasn't done. "If Kane hadn't managed to slip the noose," he said to

Lauren, "you might have found yourself married to a killer, sweetie."

Sweetie. Lauren gritted her teeth and stared hard at the elevator board.

"But that was then and this is now," Armstrong said, waggling his eyebrows. "You know all about our little schoolmarm's shady past, don't you, Carter?"

Brumfield ignored him, clearly wishing the elevator would get to their destination as fervently as Lauren.

Finally the elevator stopped. It dawned on Lauren suddenly that she didn't have to concern herself anymore about John Armstrong and what he might think of her. He could no longer report her to the school board. She'd learned little from Sherman, but she was acquainted with Houston's DA, whether she liked him or not, and he might have information on Margot's death.

As she stepped out, she fell into step beside Brumfield. "By the way, I saw that stunning painting you gave to Detective Sherman when I was in his office a few minutes ago," she said, hoping to soften him up before asking for his help.

"What?" He seemed startled.

"The painting by Margot," she said, wondering at his reaction. "Evelyn mentioned that she was an artist, but I never saw anything she painted. She was very talented. Do you have others in your home?"

"No." His gaze was fixed straight ahead. "Juliana thought my office needed redecorating. She got hold of it somehow. I got rid of it because I didn't like to be reminded of Margot's murder."

"None of us do," she said, matching her steps to his. "So you can understand the Housemans' pain knowing there has been no justice for their daughter." When he did not comment, she took a deep breath. "I wonder if you'd be able to help me out, Carter," she said, assuming a familiarity with the man that as a politician, she knew, he wouldn't challenge. "I'm here at the police department for a reason. I was hoping to get some information about Margot's murder investigation."

Brumfield's eyebrows rose. She could see she'd surprised him.

"I don't have to tell you that Martin and Evelyn are still grieving over the death of their daughter. I know you're aware of that, Juliana being Margot's godmother."

"Yes. A real tragedy for everybody." He said the right words, but he was stone-faced. Not exactly the reaction she'd expected, but she plowed on.

"They want her killer brought to justice."

"And when we find Mr. Kane," he said, pausing at a door, "justice will be swift and sure."

Lauren suppressed a feeling of frustration. "Sir, I know the folks in the Homicide Division are experienced, and I wouldn't presume to tell them how to do their jobs, but they seem to have a blind spot about this case. They haven't bothered looking at anybody but Tucker."

Brumfield appeared amused by her naïveté. "Your loyalty is admirable, Ms. Holloway. But Kane is the killer. Evidence collected in the investigation points directly to him. He'd be on death row now if he hadn't gotten away."

"I don't agree," she said.

He looked at her with an expression that was almost gentle. "Based on what, Ms. Holloway? Your love for him?" He paused at a closed door. "You know what they say. Love is blind."

She was almost at the garage when she remembered she'd promised to see Eric Grantham before leaving. She glanced at her watch. She really needed to get going but he'd been so insistent. Sighing, she turned around just as Eric was coming down the steps of the building. He waved at her and in a minute was beside her.

"When you didn't show up at the coffee shop," he said, "I began to worry that you'd gotten yourself in trouble somehow."

"Actually, I ran into the district attorney in the elevator," she told him as they entered the garage. "Like everybody else, he's convinced that Tucker murdered Margot."

"That's the conventional thinking around here," Eric said.

"Which I've had drummed into me all day," she said as they reached the garage elevators. "What was it you wanted to see me about?"

"I wanted to give you something, but not here. Let's wait until we get inside the elevator. And don't look at it until you're away from here." Seeing her confusion, he was grinning as he punched the up button. When they stepped inside, he handed her a manila envelope. "Consider this payback."

She took it, frowning in confusion. "Payback? You don't owe me anything, Eric."

"Yeah, well . . . Jack could have been in big trouble but for you."

"Please. I just did my job." As he did not leave, she realized he was going to accompany her to the level where she'd parked. "You don't have to do this."

"Humor me. I'll walk you to your car. We get some shady characters around here."

"At the police department?"

"Yeah, some are behind bars, but you don't think everybody you saw in there is here to pay parking tickets, do you?"

She smiled. "In that case, thank you."

Once on the correct level, they walked to her car, chatting about school and Jack.

"Thanks, Eric," she said.

"My pleasure," he said, opening her door after she unlocked it with her remote. "I know I speak for a lot of parents when I say we appreciate the way you do your job."

Again, she thought she ought to tell him she was no longer at St. Paul, but with a glance at her watch, she decided she didn't have time to properly explain. He'd know soon enough.

"Take care driving home," he said. And with a smart salute, he left.

She drove all the way to the parking garage exit, keenly aware of the envelope on the seat beside her. No label, no markings, nothing. Plain manila like a million others. It was hard not to grab it to see what was inside, but Eric had been adamant about getting away from HPD to do that, which only stoked her curiosity.

But once she'd cleared most of the traffic heading northwest out of the city, curiosity got the best of her. Since she still hadn't eaten since breakfast, she exited and pulled into the drive-up lane of a fast-food restaurant. While waiting for her order, she tore the envelope open. Inside she found a number of copied documents clipped together. She read only a few lines on the first page before her mouth fell open in amazement. It was material from the Homicide Division. Material she'd never been meant to see from the case file of Margot Kane's murder.

Reading at lightning speed, she tripped at one of the entries. Sherman had somehow managed to find three eyewitnesses. She read their names . . .

and ages. And addresses. She stopped reading and clutched the file to her chest.

Thank you, God.

"Miss? Hello, miss."

Lauren turned a blank face to the person manning the order window. "Oh, sorry," she said, taking the bag he held out. She placed it on the seat beside her, pulled quickly into a parking space, and threw the gear into park. Ignoring the food, she concentrated on the file. A few pages after the document naming the witnesses she found an entry by Sherman listing the contents of Margot's evening bag. Lauren recalled getting a glimpse of it beneath her body in one of the crime scene photos. She scanned the items: lipstick, a thin leather case with her driver's license and a single credit card. A loose key, no label. Sherman's note: *Appears to be a house key, but does not fit doors in victim's house.*

So what house? She made a mental note to ask Martin if the evening bag and its contents had been returned to him or if it had been retained as evidence.

She almost forgot the key when she read the next entry. A receipt for two nights at a bed-and-breakfast in La Grange dated several months before the murder. Lauren looked up, thinking. La Grange? It was a charming Texas town, but hardly the kind of upscale tourist locale that Margot would typically frequent. And why keep the receipt? She glanced at it again. It had not been paid with a credit card, but with cash. Lauren was more puzzled than ever. Nobody paid a hotel bill with cash . . . unless someone had reason not to be identified. She studied the receipt again. The name was an illegible scrawl. She couldn't make Margot's name out of it or anybody else's.

Lauren sat looking at nothing in particular for a minute or two. Could the key fit a room at the bed-and-breakfast? But why keep it? And why keep the receipt? She reached idly for her drink and took a sip. One way she could get a few answers would be to go to La Grange and simply ask the proprietor of the B&B if she remembered Margot. Who had shared that room with her?

A thought struck her so that she almost dropped her drink. Was Margot having an affair?

Paging like mad, she searched for more entries, anything that might show if Detective Sherman had had the same thought and had followed up. But there was nothing more.

Had Sherman questioned Martin about this? Evelyn?

She slipped the papers back into the envelope and sat marveling over the incredible stroke of good fortune in running into Eric Grantham today.

27

Lauren left to go back to the ranch with daylight to spare. Tucker was in for a shock when she showed him the fruits of her visit to Houston. With Jordan Raines sneaking around, it was too risky to ask him to meet her somewhere. Maybe after dark he could manage another stealthy visit to the ranch house. By then, she would have scrutinized the file.

But now, with nothing to do but drive while questions teemed in her head, she decided to call Eric Grantham and ask about the three teenage witnesses. Fortunately, since his son was a student at St. Paul, she had a number for the Granthams in her iPhone, since Jack's mom had chaired the Fall Festival last year. Eric answered almost immediately.

"I have a question," she told him, going straight to the point. "Why didn't Sherman arrest Tucker after finding those three teenage witnesses who placed him at the scene?"

He paused and she thought he might be eating something. "No credibility," he said finally.

"Did I interrupt your dinner? I'm sorry."

"No, too early for dinner. It's junk food and I have to hide in the garage to eat it or Brenda will kill me."

"You can hold her off with your gun, Dad."

Lauren smiled, recognizing Jack's voice. "Shame on you, Dad."

"I know. I know."

"About those witnesses. How is it that they have no credibility?"

"The older kid is in a gang. He's been a runner for a drug dealer. The other two are brothers, not related to him, similar problems. When Sherman canvassed the neighborhood, the kid got wind of what they were looking for. He figured he could strike a deal with the prosecutor since he had his own legal problems. Wrong, as it happened."

Lauren came up behind a truck loaded with hay bales and slowed down to a crawl. "I didn't see that in the file," she said.

"And you never will." Eric laughed. "Yeah, Sherman let it stay in the file that he'd found witnesses . . . not mentioning whether they were legitimate or not. Shows he's working, right?"

"Thanks, Eric . . . again."

"My pleasure . . . again." She heard a smile in his voice as she ended the call.

Settling back, she refocused. So far, the most promising thing she'd gotten out of the file was Margot's receipt for a two-night stay in a B&B. If she had been there with a man, it could mean Margot was having an affair. Now all she had to do was to come up with a name.

• • •

It was still daylight when she got back to the ranch. First, she'd call Tucker, then see if she could find a phone number for the B&B on the Internet. She was deep in thought and juggling a sack of groceries she'd hurriedly picked up along with the envelope, the trash from McDonald's, and her purse when she glanced up at the porch.

Jordan Raines sat in the swing.

He stood up and spread his arms wide, smiling. "Don't shoot me. I'm here by invitation." He went down the steps and took the sack of groceries from her. "After John ran into you today, he called Mr. Houseman and—"

"Where is Kristy?" she asked abruptly.

"In the barn." He paused, as if expecting her to walk with him to the door, but when she didn't move, he added, "She's wowing Maya and Lainie with the kittens. Don't worry, Elena is with them."

She shouldn't be surprised. Now that Kristy knew the Armstrong kids were nearby, she would want them to come over every day. Or she'd want to go over there. Kristy and Lainie were fast friends. They were the same age and in the same class at St. Paul.

Jordan plucked a grape from inside the grocery sack and popped it in his mouth. "You should have seen Kristy's face when we got here and Lainie jumped out of the ATV. I never saw a kid so happy."

"Where is Rickey?" Lauren asked suddenly. She didn't want him anywhere near Kristy. "Is he in the barn, too?"

"Nah, he's too cool to be anywhere near his sisters. I left him zoned out playing on his laptop."

"Excuse me, Mr. Raines." Lauren started off in the direction of the barn, leaving him holding the bags. "Kristy needs to get ready for dinner. I'll get the kids, and you can take Lainie and Maya home. Wait here."

She might as well have saved her breath. He put the bag on the porch and fell into step beside her. "What's it going to take for you to call me Jordan? I'm starting to think you don't like me."

If her icy attitude hadn't convinced him, she didn't know what would. The man had an ego the size of Texas and skin as thick as an armadillo's.

"I thought we could enjoy happy hour without the kids," he went on in a chatty tone. "I brought a bottle of really good Cabernet. You would not believe how well stocked the wine cellar at Blue Hills is."

"I don't drink. Besides, I wouldn't make very good company. I've had a long day." There was no way she was letting him in the house.

"What if I told you I have information about Margot Kane's murder?"

Lauren stopped and looked at him. "What kind of information?"

He waggled his finger playfully in her face.

"Uh-uh. You have to invite me inside and make nice. Then we'll talk."

"Then we won't talk."

"Oh, come on," he wheedled. "You've got to know that case has all the ingredients of a blockbuster novel—she came from wealth, she was spoiled rotten, she was beautiful, narcissistic, socially active. She knew people." He paused to be sure she was listening. "Women hated her and men loved her."

She was suddenly alert. "Name one."

He blinked. "What?"

"Name a man who loved her. Or a woman who hated her." Lauren held her breath . . . hoping. He'd been rabid enough reporting on Margot's murder, maybe he had a name.

He laughed. "It was a throwaway line, Lauren."

With a huff, she began walking again. "So you don't know any women who hated her or men who loved her."

He shrugged, not denying it. "Just think how much better the book would be if I had some insight into Kane's personal life. Who better than his ex-fiancée?" He flashed a smile. "That would be you."

The look she sent him should have shut him up, but he went on, unfazed. "Margot was a rich study. This is just my opinion, but I think she was bipolar. She was probably hell to live with, too. Kane probably had provocation to kill her." He shot her a sideways look, shrugging. "Again, just my opinion."

"I don't know why you think this interests me. I'm no longer engaged to Tucker."

"Really? That's odd. 'Cause I know he's been sneaking around the ranch talking to you."

Shocked, she stumbled.

"Whoa!" He put out a hand, steadying her.

She shook him off, repulsed. Could he have seen Tucker? Or was he just taking a shot in the dark?

"I could call the cops on him, I guess . . ."

She gave him an angry glare. "And lose any chance to add juicy elements to your book?" Even though the thought of his calling the police thoroughly rattled her, she added coolly, "I don't think so."

"What would be even better," he said to her retreating back, "is if you could get him to talk to me directly. You don't think he killed Margot. Why not use the book to give his side of the story?"

She turned back again, facing him with her hands propped on her hips. "I don't know how to say this, Mr. Raines, except—"

"Jordan. Please."

"Mr. Raines. It offends me that you think I would be a party to a book that sensationalizes Margot's death. It's disgusting."

She wanted to scream at him. She wanted to slap

him . . . hard. He was a despicable human being. But if he'd truly seen Tucker, what would he do? She felt sick inside. Tucker was in deep trouble. How was she going to warn him?

28

Tucker was working at his table saw when he felt his cell phone vibrate on his hip. He glanced at the clock and frowned. Almost 9:00 P.M. Only two people knew his number—Martin and Raphael. Well, three, now that he'd given it to Lauren. But as much as he'd like it, he didn't expect her to call.

He stopped the saw and peeled off his work gloves before tilting the phone up from his belt to see the screen. And then he couldn't get the phone free fast enough.

"Lauren?"

"Yes, it's me. We can't talk on this phone, right?"

He frowned. "Depends."

"This is important."

"Why? What's happened? Is it Kristy?"

"No. She's fine. Can you come to the ranch house?"

"Now?"

"Yes, now."

"Yeah, sure." With the phone wedged between one ear and his shoulder, he began clearing the wood he'd cut from the table. "Are you alone at the house?"

"Except for Kristy, yes."

Tucker paused, digesting that. "Does this mean you've finally decided to trust me?"

"Raphael knows you'll be here."

"Oh."

"Go to the back porch, Tucker. I'll be waiting."

He took time only to brush wood shavings off his clothes and grab his rifle before jogging out behind his workshop to a shelter he'd built to keep a couple of Houseman horses, thanks to Martin. Tonight there was only one, a buckskin Kristy had named Buck. He quickly saddled up, seated the rifle in a leather sleeve, and mounted. Buddy, anticipating a nighttime run, danced around the horse's legs, eager to be included. Tucker opened his mouth to give the golden a command to stay, but hesitated when he saw the look on the dog's face.

"Okay, you can come, too, boy."

With a joyful yip, Buddy struck out ahead of man and horse. Tucker was careful leading Buck away from the camp through thick brush and low-hanging tree limbs. But once they were on the trail to the ranch, he gave the big horse his head. Buddy was in his element, easily keeping pace. Tucker liked riding just for the joy of it, but there was a practical reason for having a horse. He'd had to take to the woods on horseback a couple of times to avoid being seen since he'd holed up in the lodge.

His thoughts raced. Why would Lauren need to talk to him, especially at this time of night? What did it mean that she trusted him enough to be alone with him? Raphael was nearby, yes, but not close enough to rescue her if she felt truly threatened. He chose to consider that a positive step.

Suddenly, Buddy reversed and, with a sharp bark, circled back to Tucker. Tucker pulled Buck up hard, listening. He heard nothing, but Buddy was beside him now and growling low in his throat. The golden was in full alert, head up, body still, ready to charge at command.

And then Tucker heard it: the sound of an ATV.

Cursing himself for having been so engrossed in his thoughts that he'd let down his guard, he leaned forward and rubbed Buck's neck to calm the horse. Buck snorted and danced skittishly at being stopped abruptly. The intruder in the ATV probably couldn't hear it over the sound of the motor, but Tucker worried that he might have been seen.

With a soft command, he quietly backed the horse until they were in deep shadow in the trees where he could see the vehicle roaming around in no particular pattern. Squinting into the near-darkness, he tried to identify the driver. He could tell it was someone small. A woman? And then he grunted with surprise. It was a kid. A boy.

Although he was still a good fifty yards away,

Tucker could see fairly well. He wondered how the kid had managed to stray onto Houseman land. Besides that, it was getting too dark to be cruising on strange ground. Was he lost? And where had he come from? His next thought was more troubling. Had the kid spotted him somewhere on the trail?

Or was he riding into an ambush? Lauren knew if she called he'd come in a heartbeat. With his jaw clenched, he considered the possibility. And rejected it. She might be angry and hurt, but she wouldn't deliberately set a trap and watch him get caught in it. Then, as he watched, the ATV stopped and the motor idled. Reaching down, the kid lifted a rifle up from the floor. Tucker tensed, ready to move, thinking he might be shot at, but the kid pointed the rifle in the opposite direction. Suddenly, a deer bolted from the edge of the woods and the kid took a shot. The sound cracked in the night, startling the horse as the deer bolted into the trees. Buck danced skittishly, forcing Tucker to tighten the reins to stay in the saddle.

Shaking his head, he watched the kid shift the ATV into gear and ride off. Meanwhile, Tucker's heart was pounding. It might have been a kid, but a rifle of that caliber in the hands of a boy was a disaster waiting to happen. How he'd managed to get onto the ranch undetected was a mystery. And he was too close to the ranch house for comfort, too close to Lauren and Kristy.

By the time they'd reached the outlying grounds

at the ranch house, Buck was blowing hard and Buddy was panting. Keeping to the trees, Tucker dismounted and pulled his rifle from its sleeve. That done, he gave Buck a pat to his hindquarters. On familiar territory, the horse trotted directly to the water trough at the barn, and Buddy followed to get a drink, too.

Tucker stood unmoving for a minute or two. Nothing stirred to give him cause to be anxious. All was quiet except for the usual night sounds. The ATV was long gone. Still, he was careful to stay in the shadows as he made his way toward the rear of the ranch house. In a minute, Buddy appeared beside him and then the back door opened quietly and Lauren slipped out.

She was backlit from soft light streaming through the kitchen window. Just looking at her gave Tucker a sharp pang in his chest. She was so beautiful. She was everything a woman should be—intelligent, kindhearted, virtuous. And his worst fear now was that he'd lost his chance to share his life with her, but if there was a way under the sun to win her back, he planned to find it.

Beside him, Buddy quivered, sighting her. "Quiet, boy, it's okay," he said softly, touching the dog to keep him at his side. After assuring himself that the coast was clear, he released his hold on Buddy and went to meet Lauren.

He was several yards out when Buddy dashed

forward. Obviously not expecting a dog, Lauren gave a little squeal and scrambled back to the door. She fumbled with the latch in a frantic effort to go back in the house, but in one leap Buddy was on the porch and rushing up to her, tongue lolling, tail wagging.

"Buddy! Sit!" Tucker commanded, snapping his fingers.

The golden promptly sat. Head tilted, he was clearly puzzled over failing to get a warm welcome from someone he knew.

"I almost had a heart attack," Lauren said in a shaky voice. "I thought I was being charged by a coyote."

Tucker shook his head, repressing a smile. Lauren didn't look as if she'd welcome humor. "You think Buddy looks like a coyote?"

"They're the same shape in the dark," she said. Wrapping her arms around herself, she'd quickly regained her composure. "And they both have big teeth."

It was all Tucker could do to keep from hugging her. But he settled for saying, "I should have warned you I'd be bringing Buddy."

"It's okay. It's good to see him again." With a soft laugh, she reached down to pet the dog. "Hi, Buddy. I've missed you."

That done, she straightened and gave a shake of her head, an unconscious habit he had always found endearing. When she did it, her hair swung out, just enough so that he caught the scent of her—familiar and intoxicating. More than anything, he wanted to hold her, to bury his face in that long, honey-blond mass. He wanted to promise her that from this day forward she wouldn't need to fear anything . . . ever, that he would always be there for her, that he'd cherish her for the rest of their lives, that he longed for her to be mother to his daughter, wife to him, lover, and friend. But he said none of that. Instead, he asked, "Why am I here?"

"Do you want to go inside to talk . . . or stay out on the porch?"

"Not the porch. Somebody might take a potshot at us."

"Who?" She turned to look across the yard.

"Do you know any kid who might be tooling around in an ATV on Houseman land?"

"No . . ."

"I just watched a kid with a high-powered rifle shoot at a deer on Martin's game set-aside."

Lauren put a shocked hand to her chest. "Rickey. It has to be Rickey Armstrong. I've just learned that he's staying at the Blue Hills Ranch with his sisters. I'll have Raphael call the ranch tomorrow and tell them what you saw. But it probably won't do any good. He's spoiled rotten."

"Just keep him away from Kristy . . . if you can." Moving with her to the screen door, he said, "Am I here for bad news?"

331

"Partly, yes." She went in ahead of him. Buddy gave Tucker a questioning look. "No, boy. Stay."

Clearly disappointed, the dog dropped to the floor and, with a sad look at Tucker, rested his head on his paws.

"Now I feel bad," Lauren said.

"It's Buddy's job to be lookout," Tucker said, but he liked that she was softhearted about his dog. It was just one more thing about her that he loved.

"Let's talk in the kitchen," Lauren said, heading that way. At the table, she lifted a stack of papers and put it on a chair. "This has been a day to remember. I hardly know where to begin." She took a seat and he eased into a chair across from her.

She stood up suddenly. "Do you want something to drink? There's bottled tea in the fridge. I think it's peach."

"No, thanks," he said, watching her take it out of the refrigerator for herself. She was skittish, which worried him. "I'm okay." She set the bottled tea on the table.

Still standing, she said, "Jordan Raines knows you're sneaking around and seeing me at night. His words, not mine."

Tucker smothered a curse. "How do you know this?"

"I was gone most of the day. He was waiting when I got back, bringing Armstrong's girls to play with Kristy as an excuse to see me."

"You think he saw me or is he just fishing?"

"I don't know. I'm just passing on what he said."

"Well, if Rickey can ride around at night freely, so could Jordan Raines."

"Where's Raphael in all this?" Lauren said in a disgusted voice. "He's supposed to keep trespassers out."

"I'll talk to him." He looked up at her. "Is that it? Is that what you wanted to tell me?"

"No. And this is bad, Tucker. Evelyn has been diagnosed with colon cancer."

Cancer. The word struck fear in him. He looked away quickly, swallowing hard.

"They're going to M. D. Anderson for tests as soon as they can get in. That's the plan. I haven't heard from them today."

He couldn't stay in his seat. "Give me a minute," he said, getting up and moving to the screen door and gazing out at the darkness. He wasn't particularly close to Evelyn anymore, and yet hearing that she was in a battle for her life stunned him.

"It's a shock, I know," Lauren said softly. "Just the word *cancer* scares us all."

When he spoke, his voice was unsteady. "Is she . . . I mean, does she seem . . ."

"She's weak and pale, but if you're wondering if Kristy could tell anything, no, I doubt it."

Getting hold of himself, he turned and faced Lauren. "Cancer killed my grandmother," he said.

"Oh." It was a soft, sympathetic sound. "I didn't know."

How could she know? He'd never told her. There was too much he hadn't told her. He wasn't sure why he was hesitant about opening up about himself. So much of his life had been dark and filled with pain, and keeping it inside was easier. Maybe it was that he didn't want to bring that into their relationship. Was it wrong of him to want to keep Lauren on a pedestal?

"It doesn't have to be fatal," Lauren said, having no idea of his thoughts. "I'm praying hard. You should, too."

But would his prayers get any higher than the tops of trees? He'd been so bitter lately, blaming God for the unfairness of the mess he was in, that he was out of practice. Would God even listen to him?

He fixed his gaze on a full moon, feeling a deep sadness. Evelyn hated him now, but there had been a time when she had loved him. When he first met her—long before he married Margot— she had treated him like a son. It hurt to know she was stricken with cancer.

Without turning, he said to Lauren, "You said colon cancer, right? Is there a good chance she'll be cured?"

"If they've caught it soon enough, yes."

"Martin—" He stopped, got a grip on the ache in his chest. "I wish Martin had told me."

"He's in shock." She gave him a sympathetic look. "I'm sorry to be the one to tell you, Tucker."

He turned around. "You know one of the worst things I have to deal with?" He waited for her to lift her gaze to him. "It's hiding when I know I should be living life. Like now. You lose your job and I can't do anything about it. I can't be a proper dad to my little girl, and now that Evelyn's sick and Martin needs me at the business I can't show myself."

"I'm sorry," she said.

Tucker raked a frustrated hand through this hair. "Maybe I should just turn myself in."

"And disappear out of Kristy's life again? Besides, I don't think that's wise."

Tucker's brow furrowed, not sure what she meant.

"I went to HPD today . . ."

Tucker waited for her to go on.

"I wanted to see if I could find out more about the case, see if they'd made any progress, looked at any other suspects."

"And . . . ?" He leaned closer.

She looked up again, her gaze flitting between his eyes and his lips. "Well . . . I wonder if I was too quick to doubt you," she went on. "Sherman is hell-bent to get you, and there's just more evidence out there that doesn't line up."

He wanted to hug her, to pick her up and swing her about. What he settled for was a promise.

"Okay, I won't turn myself in, but just so you know, I'm not leaving Kristy again, no matter what. I don't expect you to put much stock in anything I say, but you can believe that."

"I'm going to hold you to that," she said.

Unable to stand still, he began pacing the confines of the kitchen. "What about Kristy? It won't be easy for Evelyn to care for a little kid while she's being treated for cancer, even with a nanny." He saw her shaking her head as she poured peach tea over ice. "What?"

"That's another thing I need to talk to you about." She took a napkin from a holder and blotted moisture off the table. "Evelyn and Martin want me to take Kristy. Not just for these few days at spring break, but . . . well, they're talking long term, Tucker. Until we see what happens with Evelyn."

He was stunned and, he realized in about two seconds, overjoyed. "Are you going to do it?"

"Would you be okay with it if I did?"

"Would I?" He couldn't help himself. He caught her hand and brought it to his cheek. "I couldn't ask for anything better. I don't know how to thank you." He resisted a longing to kiss her palm and settled for simply keeping her hand until she tugged gently and took it back.

"I'm doing it for Evelyn and Martin, not you. And Kristy, of course."

"But you are doing it?"

"I couldn't say no, could I? Under the circumstances."

"Whatever your reason, it's the best thing that could happen. It's almost too good to be true. Kristy loves you. She feels safe with you. She'll be almost as happy as I would be to live with you."

"It's temporary. I can't promise more than that. Oh, one more thing. I don't think we should pull her out of St. Paul. You agree?"

"Whatever you think, I'm good with it. She won't make job hunting harder? I mean, there'll be interviews. Some of them could be out of town." He almost broke out in a sweat at the thought of Lauren getting a job offer and leaving Houston.

She smiled. "Not to worry. I have a new job."

He stared at her. "Already? I mean, I'm not surprised. Well, yeah, I guess I am. But . . . are you kidding me?"

"Nope. I'm going to work for H & K Contractors."

"Now you are kidding."

"Martin claims he needs my organizational skills. I'm going to be picking up where you left off."

He was shaking his head. "That son of a gun. You've gotta give him credit. He knows a good thing when he sees it."

"I don't know about that, but I'm happy for his generosity. He promised to pay me more than I was making at the school. I jumped at it."

He studied the tabletop before looking up at her. "If all this hadn't happened, you wouldn't have needed a paycheck. We'd be married." He shrugged. "But you wouldn't have been fired either."

"Woulda, coulda, shoulda. Never works, Tucker."

He looked at her, hoping she saw how much he meant what he was about to say. "I'll make it up to you somehow, Lauren. I swear I will. I don't know how or when, but one day this will be over and we'll have our lives back. I hope to hear you say you love me again and that you don't regret the day you met me."

If he hoped to hear those words now, he would be disappointed. Instead, she pushed her drink aside and pushed an envelope across the table to him. "Do you know whether or not the Housemans were given Margot's personal effects? She was wearing gorgeous jewelry. There was an evening bag, too."

He scratched his forehead. "I think they got the jewelry. Evelyn told me she was going to put it in a safe-deposit box for Kristy when she was older."

"Do you remember the evening bag?"

He frowned. "No. And I don't recall her mentioning that. Why?"

"This report mentions that there was a key in it, but Sherman wasn't able to find what it fit. Margot had also kept a receipt for a weekend at a

B&B in La Grange. I thought that was odd—I mean, keeping a receipt dated several months earlier."

He thought about the note he'd found regarding drinks at seven on the night she died. Was there someone in her life nobody knew about? Somebody she did not mean for anybody to know about?

Lauren's hand was still on the envelope she'd given him. "I don't know how to say this except straight out, but—"

He said it for her. "Was she having an affair?"

"I think she could have been."

"She was such a liar. I wouldn't doubt it." He didn't realize he'd said it out loud until he looked up and saw Lauren's face.

"So it's true?"

"I don't know. I was suspicious when she said she wanted a divorce. It would explain a lot."

"So you never suspected who it might have been with?"

"I suspected everybody," he said with irony, "from the plumber to the accountant to the DA."

"Carter Brumfield?" Her eyes went round with surprise.

"That was a joke, Lauren."

He got to his feet, taking the envelope with him. He'd already searched Margot's house. All he'd found there was the note for drinks. Were the key and the receipt solid evidence that she'd been in a sordid relationship? If they could prove it, it could at least add enough doubt to the prosecution's story to make a jury set him free.

"Is that what this is?" He held up the envelope. "Proof of the affair?"

"Perhaps," Lauren said. "It's some of the evidence from the investigation."

Astonished, it took a minute before he began reading. With his eyes flying across the pages, he barely took time to digest what he read. When he was finally done, he looked up at Lauren. "How did you get this?" He tossed the pages on the table. "You must have charmed somebody."

"Actually, they were a gift," she said, a tiny smile playing at the corner of her mouth. Tucker felt an almost irresistible compulsion to kiss it. He cleared his throat. Not yet, he promised himself . . . but soon.

"I wanted to know what was happening," she said. "Too many people's lives are on hold, Tucker. We need to know who killed Margot."

We? She was linking them together in this whether she admitted it or not. "Are you saying you don't think it was me?"

She sighed. "No, I don't think it was you." She sent her gaze beyond him as if trying to find the right words. "There are just too many loose ends, Tucker. Something about this whole thing just doesn't pass the smell test." She looked at him, not quite smiling. "Is that a bad metaphor?"

"Bad or not, I'll take it, darlin'," he said, feeling a mix of relief and joy. Just going into the HPD building had to be hard for her. Gus Sherman was a ruthless cuss. The fact that she did it anyway gave him hope that he could win her back . . . someday.

"I take it you didn't get this from Gus Sherman?" He couldn't see that happening.

"No. And don't ask because I can't tell."

He considered pushing, but one look at her face told him it would be wasted effort. "But you've had a chance to look at everything?"

"Yes. Forget the entry about three witnesses placing you at the scene. They turned out to be useless to Sherman. Here's what I find interesting. Sherman finds the key and the receipt but he does nothing with that. I'm no detective, but it seems to me the thought of an affair should have entered his head. There's nothing in there stating that he talked to anyone at that B&B, or tried that key there."

"Maybe he did all that and didn't choose to report what he found."

"Or . . ." Lauren said, "he was told to bury it . . . since it would have taken the focus off you."

"If Margot was having an affair, maybe it was somebody Sherman needed to protect." He felt a rise of excitement. Hope. "Who would that be?"

"I was hoping you could make a guess."

"Well, I can't," Tucker said, sifting through the

pages again. Disgust filled him as he reread it. If Margot had left him for someone else, why hadn't another relationship developed after she was free?

Lauren got up and tossed her empty bottle in the trash. "You know what I think we should do?"

We. He couldn't hold back a smile. "No, what do you think we should do?"

"Actually, I'll do it before taking off to La Grange . . . in my car."

"Not without me, you won't," he said. "So, what's your plan?"

"You can't do anything until you can show yourself openly, Tucker."

"So I just sit back and wait for the woman I love to put herself at risk because I'm too chicken to stick my neck out? No, babe. It ain't gonna be that way."

She gave him a sidelong look as if trying to decide whether to argue. "We'll see. Meanwhile, listen to this. Evelyn told me some pretty unflattering things about Margot. Nothing about an affair, just other troubling behavior they'd coped with raising Margot." Seeing Tucker's look, she explained, "She was feeling pretty vulnerable about being diagnosed with cancer and said she wanted me to know the truth if I took Kristy. I don't think she would ever have been so . . . so starkly frank about her daughter otherwise."

All traces of Tucker's smile vanished. "Go on."

"So if Evelyn knew Margot that well, maybe she knows this, too."

"You think she'd tell her mother she was having an affair?" he said. "C'mon."

"In view of this . . ." Lauren crammed a sheaf of papers back into the envelope. "I think it's worth asking, but maybe not directly. Evelyn is fragile right now. I think it's best to let Martin ask her."

Tucker reached over and covered her hand. She paused from shuffling papers. "What?"

"I don't know how to tell you what this means to me . . . that instead of going somewhere that's relaxing and beautiful for spring break, you're up to your neck in this ugly business again."

"Texas hill country is relaxing and beautiful," she said. "People come from all over, especially this time of year."

"You know what I mean."

She sighed and, to his amazement, pulled her hand from beneath his and stretched up to touch his cheek. When she spoke, her voice was soft, wistful. "I can't help myself when it comes to you."

With his heart beating high and hard in his chest, he felt a surge of heat lancing all the way through him. It was all he could do not sweep her into his arms.

Lowering her hand, she cocked her head, considering his face, his eyes, his mouth. "You're . . . different now."

"I am different, Lauren. I struggle with a lot of rage that I'm in a sick situation when I haven't done anything to deserve it. No day goes by that I don't ask God why He's putting me through all this."

"Maybe to test your faith?"

"Faith." He managed a short laugh. "That's pretty much missing in my life now, like a lot of other good things." When she looked at him, he added, "But this one thing is unchanged—I still love you with all my heart."

It was too much, too soon. He knew it instantly. Her eyes fell and her breath caught in a tiny sound. A sob? Had the hurt been so great that she would never be able to forgive him?

29

Another restless night. Lauren swept the covers aside and got out of bed. It was the second night in a row that Tucker was responsible for keeping her awake. For a minute, when she'd touched his face, she had felt an almost overwhelming desire to step into his arms, to rest her head over his heart and forget all the reasons she should keep him at a distance . . . physically and emotionally.

She reminded herself that she was digging into this "ugly mess" to help Martin and Evelyn and Kristy and herself. Not Tucker. Yet she felt herself being drawn to him. She hated that she was putting her heart in jeopardy again, hated that Tucker still had the power to hurt her.

And yet . . . and yet . . . why was she so compelled to help him?

She moved through the house to the den and a desk where her laptop waited. So far, the possibility that Margot was having an affair was the best lead they had. She'd tried twice to call the B&B, but no one answered. Maybe there was something to be found on the Internet.

An hour later, her back ached and her vision blurred. It wasn't surprising to find a lot of material about Margot both before and after she was murdered. She'd been a popular Houston socialite and had often been featured in magazine articles, as well as the newspaper. She attended every black-tie affair and political fund-raiser that came to Houston. She'd partied with the city's movers and shakers at charity benefits. Margot truly lived life on a grand scale. But it would take hours to sift through everything that had popped up.

She opened a feature story in the style section of the newspaper that mentioned Margot's attendance at a fund-raiser for the Museum of Natural Science. As expected, there were frequent glimpses of Martin and Evelyn as well as the Brumfields. Also showing up were John and Cecile Armstrong. Seemed they all ran in the same circles. Jordan Raines showed up once or twice, too.

Lauren paused to consider the journalist. Could

he be the one? He certainly was interested in the investigation into her death. Was it possible that an ex-lover would act that way? Perhaps, but somehow, she just didn't think so. The real puzzler was how Margot could have kept her affair a secret when she was so visible.

Tucker was also very visible in her search once HPD detectives had singled him out as their prime suspect in an early interview. As she read, Lauren was reminded of the ferocious invasion of privacy he'd endured.

She remembered once being at a restaurant with Tucker and several of his business associates. A woman friend of Margot's had marched up to their table and savagely attacked Tucker, calling him an animal and a predator of helpless women. He hadn't responded, but had simply sat stone-faced while she ranted. Everyone in the restaurant was agog. From that day until he disappeared, he had not taken Lauren with him to a public place. She realized now that he had protected her as far as it was in his power to do so. But digging into it tonight was a hellish reminder of that dark time.

Before shutting down, she checked her email. Scanning it, she found a post from Martin saying Evelyn's treatment was to be delayed a week as tests showed she was anemic. Martin was surprised at how she'd perked up after a blood transfusion. So, tomorrow they were heading back to the ranch for a few days.

She would have closed her laptop down then, but an email with a strange subject line caught her eye. *Margot Kane: R.I.P.*

Frowning, Lauren opened the email. Reading it, her first reaction was utter shock. Followed by an insidious, sickening fear that settled in her stomach. With her hand at her throat, she read it again.

Stop meddling. Otherwise, what happened to Margot Kane will happen to you.

It was unsigned. And the email address originated from a public source. The library? Lauren wasn't computer savvy enough to know how to begin to trace it. Her first impulse was to call Tucker. But with his telephone use restricted, she decided against that. She couldn't go to him at this hour of the night either. Not only could she not leave Kristy alone, but she didn't know where to find him. She closed her laptop and went to the kitchen.

Rummaging in the pantry, she found a calming tea and set about brewing it. Her mind raced as she searched the list of people who knew she was asking questions about Margot's murder. It was a long list. The entire Homicide Department at HPD, for starters. Carter Brumfield and— probably—his wife. John Armstrong. Jordan Raines. Eric Grantham. And anyone else those people might have told. She poured scalding tea into a mug. She would have to wait until morning.

· · ·

Kristy was up at first light and eager to go to the barn for a pony ride. Lauren held her off, waiting for Martin and Evelyn. After the ominous email, she was leery of taking Kristy away from the ranch. Fortunately, the kittens were a happy distraction. And while she played with them in an empty stall, Lauren moved out of the child's earshot and called Tucker.

He answered after a single ring.

"We need to talk," she said.

"What's wrong?"

"I know it's risky, but is there a place you can meet me that won't—" She stopped, started again. "Just tell me if we can meet and where."

"Yes, if it won't wait till dark."

She chewed the inside of her cheek. Could it wait? Was she overreacting? But before she decided, Tucker spoke, "Come out to that creek where you and Kristy saw the snake. It'll have to be on horseback. You're more likely to be spotted in a vehicle."

"I don't want to see another snake."

"You won't." She could hear a smile in his voice. "Once you're there, you'll see a line of trees due west. I'll be waiting for you there."

"I'll have to wait for Martin and Evelyn."

"I thought Evelyn was in the hospital."

"She will be, but not until next week. I'll explain when I see you."

"Something's happened. Can't you—"

"Just wait for my call."

When Martin and Evelyn arrived, she decided not to add to their worries by telling them about the email. She put a pot of coffee on for them, but she felt as nervous as a cat on a hot rock wanting to leave to meet Tucker. As soon as she could, she told them she wanted to ride Gracie for a while. Martin gave her a shrewd look, obviously suspicious.

When Evelyn went to the bathroom, he pounced. "What's going on, Lauren? You only get on a horse when Kristy begs you to, so I know it must be something urgent. Is it Tucker?"

She hesitated and finally decided to be truthful. "Yes, but I didn't want to worry you. You have enough to deal with seeing to Evelyn."

"Have you and Tucker worked things out?"

She looked at him in surprise. "You mean . . . personally? No! I'm just going to meet him."

"Why?"

She sat down with a sigh, trying to decide how much to tell him. "I went to the police department yesterday and—long story short—I saw a file on the murder investigation."

Martin kept silent, though she saw the tension in his frown.

"Anyway, last night I got a threatening email. It said that if I didn't stop meddling, the same thing that happened to Margot would happen to me."

Shocked, he gave her a stern look. "For heaven's sake, Lauren! And you were going to keep this from me?"

"I didn't want to worry you," she said ruefully.

"What have you found out?"

She stood and moved to the coffeepot. "Would you like some coffee?"

He shook his head impatiently. "What I'd like is an answer to my question."

She filled a mug for herself, but she didn't sit down. "I don't want Evelyn to hear this, but . . . is there any possibility that Margot was having an affair?" She eyed him narrowly. "Can you think of anything she might have said . . . ?"

"No, of course not. I would have been all over something like that. And so would Tucker."

"It's just that there were some items mentioned . . . and that note Tucker found . . . that made me wonder."

"It is true."

Turning in surprise at Evelyn's voice, Lauren splashed coffee on the floor. "Oh, Evelyn! I thought you were in the bathroom."

"I was," she said dryly. "And don't worry, I'm not so fragile where Margot is concerned."

"What do you mean . . . it's true, Evelyn?" Martin asked.

"About the affair." She put a hand on Martin's shoulder, looking at him sadly. "Of course you didn't know, dear."

He looked at her in stunned disbelief.

"I didn't mean for you to ever know."

"Don't you know something like that could very well explain why Margot was murdered? You've watched an innocent man hounded out of his home and business and reputation when you had this information, Evelyn?"

"Tucker is not innocent!" she cried. "He killed her."

"Tucker isn't capable of murder. I know him."

"You always say that, but you don't have a scrap of evidence," Evelyn said bitterly. "You're so blind where Tucker is concerned."

He sighed heavily. "What hard evidence do you have that he did it?"

Evelyn sank into a chair. Burying her face in her hands, she began to weep. Lauren moved to go to her, intending to offer comfort.

"No, don't, Lauren," Martin said, wearily shoving his chair back. He moved beside his wife and laid a hand on her shoulder. "I'm sorry, Evie. You need peace and quiet right now. But I was just so shocked and—" He stopped midsentence.

"That's why I didn't want you to know." With her face in her hands, her words were muffled.

"Why?" Martin said, stroking her hair. "You don't think I'm strong enough to hear the truth about Margot? You think I don't know how messed up she was?"

Evelyn looked at him through tear-drenched eyes.

"I thought you wouldn't love her if you knew."

"I love her in spite of all she put us through," Martin said gently. "But I didn't know she was involved in an extramarital affair, and I can tell you without a shadow of a doubt that Tucker didn't know it either."

"Martin's right, Evelyn," Lauren said. "Tucker was suspicious, but he never knew for sure. He was shocked when he saw it in the file."

Evelyn raised a tear-drenched face. "What file?"

Too late, Lauren realized she'd let the cat out of the bag. She looked at Martin in dismay.

"You may as well know, Evelyn. Tucker has been in contact with Lauren and me."

She stared at him in shock, speechless for once.

"And I'm telling you," he said, "trusting that you will not tell Juliana the way you tell her every thought in your head."

Evelyn sniffed and plucked a tissue from a box Lauren offered, blowing her nose. "I don't tell her every thought in my head."

"Then promise me you'll stay mum about this."

She sat studying her husband for a long time. "How long has this been going on? How long have you known where he was?"

"What does it matter, Evie? Just give me your word. Because if you tell now, they'll arrest him. Kristy will be deprived of a father."

"Kristy? Have you let him see Kristy?" She was outraged.

"Yes, Evelyn. So, if you aren't willing to keep quiet for Tucker's sake, then do it for Kristy."

"Well," she huffed. "This explains why she's always going on about him." She turned in her chair and looked at Lauren. "I suppose you're in on it, too."

"Lauren had no idea," Martin said before she had a chance to defend herself. "Let's get back to the issue of Margot's affair," Martin said. "Tucker obviously hadn't known or he would have used the information in his case for custody." He gave Evelyn another admonishing look. "I can't believe you knew."

Her eyes were still red from weeping, but she straightened up in her chair and tilted her chin. "I was trying to protect my daughter's name."

Martin gave her a pitying look and spoke in a soft, sad voice. "I'm afraid it's too late for that, darling. But we can help her rest in peace by finding her killer."

"Do you know who it was, Evelyn?" Lauren asked.

Dabbing at her nose with a bedraggled tissue, she said, "No, but it was serious. For the first time in Margot's life she was really in love."

"Please say this was after she divorced Tucker," Martin said. "She did a lot of things that I disapproved of, but I hope infidelity wasn't one."

"Oh, Martin . . ." Voice quavering, Evelyn almost broke into tears again. "It did start while she was married to Tucker. And I don't think it ended with their divorce." She paused, then gave them both a defiant look. "Now you see why I think he killed her?"

Martin was shaking his head, trying to take it in. "It could also be motive for someone else to murder her, Evelyn. Don't you see that?"

"Was this man married?" Lauren asked.

"I don't know." Evelyn stared down morosely at her hands in her lap. "But I had the impression it was somebody we might know." She gave a weak shrug. "But that was just a feeling I had."

Lauren sat down at the table. "Do you think he's the one she was to meet for drinks the night she died?"

"I don't know. I told you the truth when you asked me that before."

But she omitted so much, Lauren thought. "Did this man live in Houston?"

"She was with him a lot, so I assume he lived here."

Lauren's mind whirled with possibilities. Her Internet search had come up blank. No one man seemed to stand out. She needed to talk to Tucker. Together maybe they could come up with who the man could have been. The B&B in La Grange was a place to start, but with the email threat, it might be dangerous to go on her own. Would it be too risky for Tucker to go? She was ready to head out to meet him when Evelyn spoke.

"Would you pour me a cup of coffee, please?"

"Yes, of course." She got up.

"Since we're revealing all of Margot's secrets, there is something else," Evelyn said. She watched Lauren take a cup from the cabinet. "It could explain why she fought so hard for custody of Kristy."

She paused as Lauren set a cup of coffee in front of her. "It's possible that Kristy isn't Tucker's child," Evelyn said.

Martin stared at her. "Are you serious?"

"I think it could be true."

"Evelyn," Lauren said gently, "Kristy looks like Tucker, dark hair, dark eyes."

"That other man could have dark hair and dark eyes," Evelyn said. "That would explain everything."

"No, it wouldn't. It's hogwash!" Martin was up and frowning ferociously at his wife. "Kristy is Tucker's daughter, Evelyn. Is this wishful thinking? Because you hate him?"

"I didn't say I believed it," Evelyn said weakly. "Just that it's a possibility."

"Well, it isn't." He took a few agitated steps around the kitchen, obviously rattled. But after a moment, he stopped by her chair and, shaking his head, said in a contrite voice, "I'm sorry, Evelyn."

She reached up and patted his hand. "It's all right, Martin. This has just been so hard for all of us."

Martin sighed heavily. "It has been a nightmare," he said, almost as if he were thinking out loud. "You rock along in your life, living as decently as you know how, then tragedy strikes. You deal with it as best you can, but then something else crops up. Where will it end?"

"I don't think it will ever end," Evelyn said in an unsteady voice.

"Why don't you go lie down for a while, Evie?" he suggested. "You look ready to drop. I'll keep an eye on Kristy, maybe take her for a pony ride."

His gaze was somber as he watched his wife shuffle out of the kitchen. He looked to the screen door where Kristy could be seen outside playing with the kittens. After a moment, he turned to Lauren. "Are you as shocked as I am?"

"About the affair?"

"Yes, and about Evelyn keeping such a secret?"

"Mothers will go to extraordinary lengths to protect their own."

"She wants to believe Tucker is a killer," he said in a tired voice. "It's blind obsession. Evelyn was always that way in anything pertaining to Margot." He shoved his hands deep in his pockets, his gaze again on his granddaughter. "And when you tell Tucker that she's known this all along, I won't blame him if he cuts us out of his life."

"There's very little chance of that," Lauren said dryly. "Evelyn's upset right now, but we need to find the right moment to talk to her about what else she may know." When he turned with a puzzled look, she explained. "Margot confided in her, Martin. She may have information she doesn't realize is important."

"I hope you're right. As for this email threat to you, I hope it puts to rest any doubts you might have about Tucker. Someone else murdered my daughter. And all our lives are turned upside down until he's found."

30

Raphael was obviously curious when Lauren told him she wanted to take Gracie out for a ride alone. "Do you have your cell phone, Miss Lauren?" he asked, holding the mare's bridle as she mounted. "That man might trespass again and I might not be able to rescue you."

"I have my phone. I'll be fine." She settled into the saddle and took the reins. "Thank you, Raphael."

He pushed his Stetson back so he could look up at her. "If you get in trouble you will call, yes?"

"I will call."

He released the bridle and she took off.

As she neared the creek, she was leery, worrying about snakes. But Gracie didn't seem skittish. That was comforting. Somewhat. Pulling Gracie up to a walk, she scanned the horizon in the distance looking for Tucker, but there was nothing but rolling hills and trees as far as she could see. She gave Gracie a little kick and, as Tucker had instructed, headed due west from the creek.

She worried that in meeting her he might be spotted by Jordan Raines. Or the person emailing threats. Anybody could be watching.

She was anxiously surveying the landscape when Gracie suddenly sprang forward, nearly unseating her. In seconds she was in a flat-out gallop. Lauren pulled frantically on the reins, but in vain. The mare seemed to know where she was going and was eager to get there. Then, up ahead, Lauren saw Tucker mounted on a horse at the edge of the tree line. With Gracie galloping, they'd reach him going at breakneck speed, but she didn't know how to stop. It was all she could do to stay in the saddle.

As they approached, Tucker yelled something, but it was lost as she sailed past him. He wheeled about and gave chase, easily catching up and keeping pace on his bigger and faster horse. While she concentrated on not being thrown, he reached over and grabbed the mare's bridle.

"Whoa, Gracie! Whoa!"

To Lauren's fervent relief, Gracie began to slow down. And in a few jarring yards, she came to a stop, rolling her eyes, snorting, and stamping. Reaching for Gracie's reins, Tucker got off his horse, all the while speaking in a low and gentling voice to the spooked horse. When she was calm, he moved around to help Lauren dismount. She almost tumbled out of the saddle, but Tucker caught and steadied her, both hands on her waist.

"Thanks," she said breathlessly. "I thought for a minute Gracie and I were heading for Houston."

"It was Buck she was heading for," he said, making no move to let her go.

"Buck?" She stepped back to free herself.

"My horse." He hiked his chin toward the two animals that were now both placidly chomping grass. "They're stall mates."

"She must have quite a crush on him," Lauren said, still shaken after the wild ride.

He smiled. "Maybe."

"Oh, you brought Buddy," she said as the dog bounded up to her. She put her hand out to let him sniff. "Hey, boy, we meet again."

"Watch out, he'll fall in love, too."

She smiled. "The feeling's mutual."

He laughed softly, then said in a low tone, "You keep saying things like that and I'm not going to be able to keep from kissing you." He tucked a strand of her hair behind her ear. When she glanced up at him, he said, "Don't worry, I know you're off-limits. But one day . . ."

She moved out of reach and kept walking. Her heart was beating hard and fast. When he talked like that, touched her like that, she wanted to forget their rocky past. She had to keep reminding herself to stay strong. To keep focused on finding

Margot's killer. Then she'd deal with her feelings about Tucker.

She noticed that he was scanning the area. "Are we okay here?"

"No, let's head into the woods. There's an abandoned sawmill not too far."

"Good," she said, and meant it. "You're not the only one who needs to keep a low profile."

He gave her a quick look. "What does that mean?"

"First let's get away from here." She gave Gracie a dubious look. "Do I have to get back on that horse?"

His smile was amused. "No, we can leave them here for a while. C'mon." He waited for her to fall into step beside him. She did, moving close. She felt exposed, as if someone might be watching. Seizing opportunity, Tucker slipped an arm around her waist. She didn't object.

"Do you think anybody can see us now?" she asked, looking about anxiously.

"No, these woods are thick. The sawmill is a little farther on. We'll stop there."

With Buddy bounding ahead, Tucker led her around a curve in the path through trees that had been replanted after the sawmill was abandoned. A large pile of sawdust was overgrown with vegetation. The few buildings that had once existed were long gone. All that remained was the main structure. Lauren looked around. The place was secluded. Her worry that they might be spotted eased a little.

Tucker led her over to a porch, all that was left of what had once been the sawmill. But it was a place to sit. He tested a couple of steps by bouncing his weight on them a time or two. "I think this is okay," he said.

As she stepped up on the lower plank, he noticed her sandals. "You need boots if you're going to be riding anywhere on the ranch like this. Or tramping around."

"I forgot to change. And I didn't intend to be tramping around," she said. "I prefer Starbucks."

"What's happened, Lauren? You're as skittish as a cat in a room full of rocking chairs."

"This, to start with." She pulled the printed email from her pocket. "It came last night."

"Is it another shocker?" he asked, unfolding it. "I'm starting to worry when you hand me paper."

She didn't answer, but watched his face as he read it. His jaw clenched and his mouth tightened. When he looked up, his gaze burned into hers. "Do you have any idea who sent this?"

"No."

"Has anyone else seen it?"

"If you mean did I call HPD to let them know, no. I only showed it to Martin. He was . . . upset."

She sprang up from the step. "What should I do, Tucker? Do you think whoever wrote that knows I've been in touch with you? This may not even be about me. It could be a way for someone to flush you out."

"Me?" He gave a short humorless laugh. "I don't give a damn about me. This is someone threatening the woman I love. And my daughter." He slapped the paper against his thigh. "I let him spook me once before. I won't let it happen again."

He began pacing back and forth, frustration and worry etched on his face. "We can't let him jack us around like this. We have to find him."

"Well, we may be a step closer . . . if Margot's affair is linked to her murder."

He stopped. "You know that for certain? Did you get a name?"

"Evelyn knew about the affair. Margot told her, but no name."

His brow creased as he concentrated. "Wait. You talked to Evelyn?"

"She overheard me asking Martin." Lauren's voice was gentle as she added the detail that was bound to hurt him. "It began while you were still married."

Tucker turned away. He was quiet for a minute, watching a hawk soaring overhead. Lauren had the feeling he was trying to control some deep emotion. And why wouldn't he?

"Evelyn didn't think it was important to let anyone know that my murdered ex-wife was having an affair?"

"She claims she was trying to protect her daughter's reputation."

"And what about Martin? He could have told me."

"I saw his face when she told us," she said earnestly. "He was as shocked as I was.

"Evelyn says she has the impression it's someone she—they—might know." She stopped, looking at the expression on his face. "When you've had time to digest all this, you could make a list of people you saw frequently in your life with Margot. I could do some checking—"

"Whoever it is wants to kill you, too," Tucker said, lifting worried eyes to hers. "You're done with this investigation. I don't know how I'll do it, but I have to take care of this myself, Lauren."

She could see from the stubborn set of his jaw that there was no point in arguing. "You do realize what this means?"

He seemed distracted, but he dragged his gaze back to hers. "Yeah. We have a new lead to follow. Thank God for that."

"He's managed to stay under the radar for over nine months," she said. "You just need to flush him out."

"Uh-huh. After we figure out who he is and how and when he met Margot and where he was at the time of her murder and whether he has an alibi. And doing all this long distance with no investigative tools except the Internet because I'm stuck here."

Meeting her gaze, his voice firmed. "I've had it,

Lauren. I've spent a thousand hours thinking about all this stuff, and look what it's got me. Exactly nothing. Zip. Zero. Nada."

"I understand it's hard to live your life like that, but—"

"So I'm done with skulking around hoping nobody recognizes me and blows the whistle." He slapped the paper with the email on it against his thigh. "What I need to do first is head to La Grange and check out that B&B." He shot her a defiant look. "You can go with me if you want, but whatever, I'm outta here."

"I hate to bring it up, but there's one more thing, Tucker."

Hearing something that boded ill in her voice, he braced warily. "What now?"

"Evelyn . . . I mean, well, she . . ." She reached down and picked a tiny wild violet that had pushed through the ground near a stump before looking up at him. "This is so hard."

"Spit it out. What could be worse than to hear that my wife was cheating on me and the woman I love is being threatened via email and my daughter is not safe?"

"Evelyn says this man—whoever he is—that he could be Kristy's real father."

He stood stock-still. For a long minute, she could see that he was unable to come up with a response. He finally muttered, "You did manage to say something worse."

"I'm sure it isn't true, Tucker," she said. "I flatly do not believe it and neither does Martin."

He looked at her. "How can you be sure?"

She frowned. "Well, aren't you?"

He didn't answer. He only shook his head, his mouth twisting bitterly.

She was surprised and shocked. "You can't seriously think that Kristy isn't your biological child," she said incredulously. "It's pure speculation on Evelyn's part. You know how prejudiced she is against you."

She waited but when he still said nothing, she gave a huff of impatience and, moving quickly, bent and adjusted the strap of her sandal. She straightened and spoke in a cool tone. "I need to get back to the ranch." She spun about and started off down the path.

"Wait. Wait a minute."

"No, I'm not waiting." She increased her pace. How could he think Kristy wasn't his daughter? It was beyond ridiculous. "I've told you what I came to say and now I'm going back to that . . . that horse, and I don't care what you think about me getting a threat from some crazed person, I'm going to find out who sent it and get to the bottom of this whole mess! For Kristy's sake!"

"Lauren, hold on a minute!" Tucker easily kept pace beside her, but she didn't stop. Up ahead, she could see the horses tethered to a low tree branch, but she knew not to dash up to Gracie. If she took off, Lauren would be right back where she'd been a few days ago, at the mercy of another man she didn't want to ask for help.

As she slowed, Tucker reached out and caught her arm. "Stop, doggone it! Just hear me out, Lauren."

She shook him off and moved to Gracie's side. "You can talk to me without grabbing me," she said, taking up the reins. "You can also help me get up on this . . . this excuse for a taxi."

"In a minute. Please."

She sighed and rested her head against the saddle. "So talk."

"Kristy is my daughter," he said in a low, intense voice. "Even if I found out that our DNA doesn't match, she's still my daughter. Whoever this guy is that Margot is supposed to have been sleeping with, he doesn't know Kristy and he isn't ever going to have a chance to know her. He certainly isn't going to steal her from me."

Lauren, on the verge of tears, turned her head to look at him. "Then why didn't you say that right away? When you got that awful look on your face and you were shaking your head, I thought . . . I thought—"

"That I could believe for a second that Kristy isn't mine?" He put out a finger and touched a tear trickling down her cheek. "Don't you know me better than that?"

She sniffed. "How many times are you going to say that to me?"

"As many as it takes for you to believe in me again. And no matter how—" He stopped abruptly, frowning. Going still, he looked beyond her to the open pasture. "Did you hear that?"

She calmed herself and listened. "No, I didn't hear anything."

"I thought I heard—Get down!" He gave her a hard shove that sent her tumbling to the ground.

She heard the sharp, unmistakable crack of rifle fire. High, frantic whinnies came from their frightened horses. Her heart beat wildly. Motionless now, she lay listening. After agonizingly long moments, she lifted her head, looking for Tucker. Her eyes went wide when she saw him lying on the ground. He was still. Too still. With a wild cry, she scrambled over, trying to keep her head down, frantic to get to him. And that was when she saw the blood.

Bright light. A long road. Tucker rose from the ground, his body weightless, his mind free. He strained to see, but clouds and mist obscured his vision. In spite of the brightness, no matter how he tried, he could not bring anything into focus. Still, he was flooded with a deep sense of peace. Profound and wondrous, it surpassed any pleasurable feeling he'd ever known.

"Tucker . . ."

Someone called his name. There was power and might in the voice. Then, somehow, his life and everything he'd ever thought or planned or done was revealed before him. He realized he could leave now with honor. All pain and doubt and humiliation would end. His long, agonizing exile could finally be over. He had fought the good fight. Just one step forward and he would be taken and he would know everlasting peace.

"Daddy!"

Kristy's voice, but far away . . . echoing down the long, white, bright road. He groaned with the agony of resisting the call of his daughter. The place beyond was so glorious. The temptation to let go and be taken there was almost irresistible.

And then another voice came out of the cloudy mist.

"Tucker . . ."

Lauren, bathed in white light, her face like an angel's. He realized he was in some strange suspended state while his body lay lifeless on the ground. He saw Lauren bent over him, frantic and fearful. As he watched, the compelling sense of peace faded. A part of him resisted, longing to hold on to it, to claim that everlasting joy and peace. He surrendered. It was not his time.

Fury boiled up in the killer. It was frustrating to have taken the heavy risk of getting out in broad daylight on the chance that Kane might show himself and then to have screwed up. He had to be hiding somewhere near. It was a given that Kane would not be able to resist trying to see Lauren. Well, today that had almost proved to be his undoing.

Patience, however, paid off. What was so irritating was that the first shot might not have killed him, and the second missed both of them. Another try might have done the job, but it was too risky to take the time. Still it was a thrill just to get the chance. Like it was almost meant to be. It would not be wise to let them keep on digging. Between the two of them, they'd figure it out . . . eventually. That must not happen. Not now. Not when the stakes were so high.

The killer lovingly stroked the rifle stock. A beautiful weapon. It would have to be cleaned to remove evidence that it had been fired. But not by the hired help. Couldn't take a chance on its being checked by Forensics. Not that that was likely. Stupidity reigned in most police departments.

An hour later it was done. Checking the sight now and taking no chance that it had been skewed during the cleaning and polishing. Accuracy was all-important. Next time it would not be a near miss. It would be fatal. To both.

One more chance. All that was needed was one more chance.

31

"Mr. Kane. Mr. Kane. Wake up."

A bright, energetic voice blasted in Tucker's ear. He tried to speak, to stop the noise, the voice, but nothing worked. The strange smells, the beeping electronic sound. Where was he? What was happening?

"Come on, Mr. Kane. I know you're in there."

No. Go away. Did he say it or just think it? Too much trouble. Too much pain. He worked to sink back into the soft, numb state, welcoming it.

"Tucker Kane! You need to wake up."

More noise in his ear. Irritating. He groaned, needing peace and quiet, needing deep, dark oblivion.

"That is his name, isn't it?" A pause, someone murmuring. "He doesn't go by a nickname, does he?"

"His name is Tucker."

Lauren's voice. Low, sweet. Anxious. It took enormous effort, but he blinked.

"Well, look at this," said the stranger. "Those eyelids work. I think he's finally decided to join the land of the living. We'll just check that BP and temp and by the time I'm done, he'll be wide awake."

"Could you wait a bit, please?" It was Lauren's voice again, whisper-soft. "I'll call you in a few minutes, okay?"

"Well, sure thing, honey. You just coax that big guy back to the real world and he'll be out of here by sundown tomorrow."

Blessed quiet. And Lauren. Tucker began to ease back into painless peace.

"Tucker." Lauren put her hand on his cheek and gently turned his face. Blinding pain flashed in his head. He groaned.

"You need to wake up, Tucker." She had his hand now. "Can you squeeze my fingers? Please . . . please try."

Try. She sounded so worried. He never wanted Lauren to be worried. He struggled to move his hand.

"Oh, thank heaven!"

She had kissed his hand, hadn't she? With a hot knife stabbing inside his head, he managed to open his eyes a crack. "Hurts," he croaked, needing to find that painless place.

"Stay with me, Tucker. Don't go away again. They want you to wake up."

"Pain . . ."

"I know. I'm sorry." Her voice was gentle with sympathy. "You can have pain medication. I'll call the nurse back."

It took almost superhuman effort, but hc brought his hand up and locked onto her wrist. Something played in the back of his mind, but he couldn't quite pin it down. "What . . . happened?"

"Don't think about that right now, Tucker. You need to rest."

He would have laughed, but the pain of it would have killed him. "Stay awake . . . or rest?" he said in a weak voice, eyes closed. "Make up . . . your mind."

Lauren gave a soft laugh, then stroked his face. "It was so awful." Her voice caught as she brought his hand up and cradled it to her cheek. "I thought you were going to die."

"Too tough," he murmured. "Too mean."

"No, you saved my life. If you hadn't shoved me—"

Trying to think was too much trouble. As long as Lauren was with him, touching him, he was content just to lie still with no talk, no thinking.

"We were both lucky," Lauren said, her voice as sweet as wine. "This is a safe place . . . for now."

And with her words, memory flooded back with a vengeance. The rifle shot. Abject fear for Lauren. His dive to protect her. "I have to get out of here." He clutched the sheet and tried to rise in spite of the fierce pain in his head. Didn't work. Hampered by a needle in his hand and steel rails on the bed. Defeated, he settled back with his head near to exploding. "You've got to help me, Lauren," he muttered.

"No. And even if I could, I wouldn't. You can't leave. The doctor said you need to stay twenty-four hours for observation after you wake. You were unconscious several hours, meaning there's some trauma to your brain. You could have a stroke."

"And if I stay, the cops will arrest me."

"What would you prefer? Being arrested or dying?"

He sighed and closed his eyes. No sense telling her that the minute he had a chance, he was leaving. "How long have I been out?"

"About seven hours. But it seems a lot longer. I was so scared, Tucker." Her voice was thick with tears. "I really thought . . . I mean . . . you were bleeding. I was trying to stop it and praying, asking God not to take you, but I couldn't feel a pulse. I was frantic. I didn't want you to die out there."

No pulse. He lay looking at the ceiling, trying to capture a memory. His forehead creased in a frown. But frowning hurt. He took a few deep breaths and waited for the pain to level out. "This will sound weird," he told her. "But when that bullet got me, I think I did die . . . for a few minutes."

She stroked his hand gently. "Well, you're here and alive now."

It felt good having her touch him. He let himself enjoy it for a few minutes.

Outside, the sun was setting, but clouds were gathering, dark clouds, heavy with rain. Nothing like the white, bright clouds in his dream. Or was it a dream?

"What are you thinking?" she said. "You look sad."

"When I was out, I thought I heard Kristy calling me. And then you." He managed a half-smile. "You looked like an angel."

"It must have been somebody else," she said. "I was in a state of utter panic, so you would have known I was no angel."

But he had seen her. And now that he was recalling it, he didn't want to let it go. "You were all in white . . . and there was a sort of radiance about you."

"No wings?" she said, smiling. "I think that's the pain meds talking."

The nurse bustled in. "Is our big guy awake now?"

"He sure is," Lauren said, backing to the door. "Hey—" She turned back to Tucker. "I'll be back in a few minutes, okay? Martin and Evelyn are waiting. They'll want to know you're awake."

"They didn't bring Kristy, did they?" Tucker winced as the nurse turned a light on overhead. "I don't want her to see me like this."

"She's at the ranch with Elena. She doesn't know you're here and we won't tell her."

"Good." He paused, settling back to let the nurse take his blood pressure. And to give his aching head a rest. "Because I'm out of here tomorrow morning," he said grimly.

"Not unless this number improves," the nurse said, stripping off the cuff.

"Don't worry about Kristy," Lauren said. "I'll take care of her."

Tucker wanted to thank her, but the mother of all headaches was raging inside his skull and Nurse Ratched was not done torturing him.

With his eyes still closed, he lifted his left hand, the one with the needle stuck in it. "Can you take this thing out?"

"Not yet, sugar. You need hydrating, plus it's where you get the good stuff."

He settled back, scowling.

Chuckling, she plucked a thermometer from her bag of tricks. "You have some real anxious people waiting to see you."

"So long as it's not my little girl," he said, closing his eyes against the light. "I don't want to scare her."

"Now open up." She shoved the thermometer in his mouth. "And that one lady out there looks like she belongs in this bed more than you do."

Evelyn. She was probably disappointed that the shooter's aim had been off.

"Okay, all done for now, sugar. But before anybody else is allowed in this room, there's one guy who's at the front of the line."

"Who?" he said, looking at her.

"The sheriff."

32

It was easy to spot Sheriff Benton Fox. He stood outside Tucker's room, six feet four inches of purebred Texas lawman. He wore street clothes, but with a western flair—a denim jacket and crisp jeans with a large belt buckle bearing a University of Texas logo, and boots that were truly impressive. Even without a huge ten-gallon hat, he would have seemed larger than life.

Lauren hesitated a second, then headed his way. She didn't want Tucker to be alone with a cop, especially if he was here to arrest him.

"Sheriff."

Fox's hand was on Tucker's door, but he paused as Lauren approached. "Yes, ma'am?"

She was prepared for the steely gaze of a seasoned lawman. Instead, she found herself looking at a man whose expression was oddly benign. He studied her from soft, brown eyes as closely as she studied him. Interest filled his gaze, but not suspicion. She stuck out her hand. "I'm Lauren Holloway. I'm assuming you want to ask me about the shooting?"

"Yes, ma'am," he said. "You were with Mr. Kane?"

"I was."

"Then let's get started. Between the two of you, maybe I can get a clear picture of what happened."

Holding the door, he ushered her into Tucker's room.

To her amazement, Tucker was sitting up. The head of the bed was raised to its limit and he was writing on a sheet of paper. "What are you doing?" she said.

He looked shocked to see the sheriff, his face paled and his body tensed. He gave Lauren an accusing look, as if she were responsible for letting Fox in.

"It's okay, Tucker," she said, seeking to reassure him. "This is Sheriff Benton Fox. He's here about the shooting . . ." She let her words trail off, hoping Tucker wouldn't say anything to alert the sheriff and thus wind up in handcuffs.

Fox reached around Lauren to shake Tucker's hand. "Looks like you're making a remarkable recovery."

"He's supposed to lie quietly," Lauren said, giving the paper in front of Tucker a sour look. "For twenty-four hours."

"Hard for some people to lie around and do nothing," the sheriff said with a sympathetic smile.

"I was making notes while things are still fresh in my mind," Tucker said, adding wryly, "What's left of my mind."

"A killer headache, huh?"

"Yeah."

"Well, if you're able to write out your

recollection of the shooting, I'm hoping you're able to answer a few questions."

Tucker carefully placed the paper with his notes on the wheeled hospital table so as not to snag his IV. When he turned to face Fox, he wore a wary look, as if expecting a trap.

Fox took a seat, balancing his big hat on his thigh. He pulled a tiny notebook out of his pocket and clicked his pen, ready to write.

"What can you tell me about the shooter?"

"Not much. He was on an ATV. I heard it coming over the rise in the east pasture. We'd just come out from a stand of cottonwoods."

"Any idea how he knew you were there?"

Tucker shook his head. "I can only guess."

The officer met his eye, waiting for him to go on.

"Lauren's horse took off earlier and I took off after them to stop him. The shooter could have spotted us then, but it would mean he'd been watching. I don't know how. We were on Houseman land."

"There's a hole in the fence," Lauren said. "Raphael was supposed to fix it."

Tucker leaned back against his pillow, as if he was in terrific pain, but he kept on, "We tethered the horses and went deeper into the woods to talk. He must have waited for us. He knew we'd have to get back to the horses."

"If you saw him on the ATV, how is it that he got off a shot at you?"

"Two shots. And I wasn't expecting to be dodging a bullet. If the sun hadn't flashed off the scope I probably wouldn't be talking to you right now."

"Quick thinking."

"It was instinct. Somebody points a rifle at me, I get out of the way." Tucker paused, looking thoughtful. Fox seemed relaxed, but his gaze was intent as he let him take his time. "It's hard to know which one of us was the shooter's target, me or Lauren. Did she tell you about the threatening email?" He nodded at Lauren.

"Martin mentioned it, but I'd like to know what it said."

"It was sent last night at eleven-forty-three," Lauren said. "I picked it up in the wee hours." She glanced at Tucker, surprised that he brought it up, then reached in her pocket for the printed copy she'd shown Tucker earlier. She handed it to the officer. "I couldn't sleep after I got it. See, it says, 'Stop meddling. Otherwise, what happened to Margot Kane will happen to you.'" She pointed to the line.

"That's a threat all right," the sheriff said. "What meddling is he referring to?"

"I've been doing some research," she said, "about a murder that happened last January. I must be making somebody nervous."

Fox glanced at Tucker. "You think that's why you were shot at?"

"I don't know. Could be the kid I saw shooting at deer yesterday on Houseman land," Tucker said.

The sheriff frowned. "You're saying you think a kid could have done this?"

Tucker looked at Lauren for confirmation. "He's not your ordinary kid. He's given her a lot of trouble at school. Tell him, Lauren."

"What's his name?"

She sighed. "Rickey Armstrong. But I can't believe he would do something like this. Especially since I won't be at the school any longer."

Fox paused, looking up. "What school is this?"

"I was principal at St. Paul Academy until Friday."

"She was forced to resign after Rickey brought bullets and a list of people he intended to kill to school," Tucker said grimly.

"Forced," Sheriff Fox said. "What does that mean?"

She shrugged. "Fired. More or less."

He was ready to write again. "His parents' names?"

"John and Cecile."

"Armstrong?" When she nodded, he said, "You never know about parents and kids these days."

But she'd seen Fox's eyebrows lift at the name. Whether Rickey was the guilty party or not, she knew she would hear from John Armstrong.

"Any other ideas, Mr. Kane?"

"Nothing you could sink your teeth into," Tucker said.

Fox gave Tucker a straight look. "I know you're agitating to get out of here, but you're in enough trouble as it is."

"When you came in," Tucker said, "I figured you were here to arrest me."

"I'll need to do a little checking, but the doctor won't release you for at least twenty-four hours anyway. Until then, I'll have a guard posted outside your door."

Tucker's reaction was a dark scowl.

Fox turned to Lauren. "Now, Ms. Holloway, what can you tell me about what happened?"

"All I know is that Tucker suddenly shoved me down to the ground as shots were fired. When everything was quiet I raised up and saw Tucker. He was bleeding. I thought . . ." Her voice caught. "I thought he was gone. I could not find a pulse."

"What about the shooter?"

"I never saw anything. I was in a panic. All I was thinking about was Tucker. And getting help."

"Well, after a while you may recall something." Fox closed his notebook and pocketed it. "If you do, here's my card. Call any time, day or night."

He rose, holding his hat by the brim. "I'll be moving on and letting you get some rest, Mr. Kane."

Lauren rose to follow him to the door.

"Wait," Tucker said when Fox left.

She turned back. "What?"

"We don't know who the shooter's target was, Lauren, so I don't want you going off anywhere on your own."

"I'm going to the waiting room, where Evelyn is very anxious to talk to you. Can I tell her she can come in?"

He groaned. "Do I have to?"

"She seems so determined. Maybe she knows something."

"Will you stay? And when she's done, tell Martin he needs to send Raphael out to get Buddy. Bring him back to the ranch. He has water, but he needs to be fed."

"Don't you remember? He was with us. Raphael's taking care of him."

"Oh."

"Yes, oh. Maybe the doctor's right about you not being ready to leave just yet."

He gave another groan, to which she rolled her eyes.

"Just tell me where they put my clothes."

She gave him a suspicious look. "Why? If you're thinking of escaping, you can't. You don't have your truck. You came in an ambulance. And Sheriff Fox will have stationed a guard outside this door."

In spite of a bandaged head and his weakened state, he managed to look stubbornly male. "I need my pants," he told her through gritted teeth. "This blasted gown gets all bunched up when I move."

"You shouldn't be moving," she said, unfazed. She picked up a couple of magazines she'd been reading while waiting for him to wake up and placed them within his reach. "Since you have to stay overnight, here's some reading material. They're old, but—"

"I don't want magazines. I want my clothes."

"I'll go get Evelyn now."

"Wait."

She stopped at the door again. "What?"

"Come over here . . . just for a minute. Please."

She went, but she was suspicious of the look in his eyes. White bandaging around his head made a stark contrast with his dark hair and tanned skin. And something about the way he was looking at her made her heart trip and her breath quicken. She felt a flush rise to her cheeks.

"A little closer," he said in a low tone. Before she knew it, his hand was at the nape of her neck tugging her down until she was only a whisper away.

"Tucker . . ."

"Shh, don't talk."

With a sigh, she let him touch his lips to hers. It was a soft, gentle melding, familiar and pleasurable. A sweet reminder of the way they once were. Of what they'd once had. And then, when she didn't stop him, Tucker took the kiss deeper, sealing her mouth to his. Closing her eyes, she went breathless and allowed herself the pleasure. She loved the taste of Tucker. She loved touching Tucker. She loved the rush that consumed her when they kissed.

She had missed this so much!

She was still swimming in sensation when sounds outside the room penetrated and, with a soft sigh, she pushed back from him. Reluctantly.

"Now go find Evelyn," he said, his voice a little rough. "I'm all better."

She didn't have to go far. Evelyn was pacing outside the room while Martin and Juliana stood by looking resigned and concerned at the same time. Flustered, her cheeks flaming, Lauren put a nervous hand to her hair, thinking it was probably a mess. She wondered if they'd be able to tell she'd just been well and truly kissed, with her lips still tingling and her knees a little weak.

Apparently not Evelyn. She seemed oblivious to anything except her mission. "May I go in now?" she asked anxiously.

"She won't leave without seeing Tucker," Martin said.

"It's okay," Lauren said.

Now that her chance had come, Evelyn seemed hesitant. Juliana touched her arm. "I'll go with you, Evie."

"No, I need to do this alone."

"Evie—" Martin looked concerned.

"No, Martin. I'm fine. Just a little nervous."

"Then make it fast," he said. "You need your rest and so does Tucker."

Lauren would have stayed out to give her the privacy she seemed to want, but Evelyn pulled her inside with her, closing the door on Martin and Juliana. Still, Lauren kept her distance as Evelyn took hesitant steps to Tucker's bedside. Eyeing him nervously, she clutched an oversized handbag to her chest as if for protection. But then, she seemed to gather herself, pasting a stoic look on her face.

"Tucker," she said, giving a curt nod. "How are you?"

"I'm okay, Evelyn . . ." he said, his eyes watchful.

"Good. I'm glad. First I need to tell you I truly mean that. I'm thankful. It was a close call, and I hope whoever shot you will soon be found and punished."

"Me, too," Tucker said, relaxing slightly and allowing a small smile to play at the edge of his mouth. "Thank you."

"This has been a terrible time for us all," Evelyn said. "First Margot and now someone shooting at you and Lauren. It's just beyond comprehension."

"I agree with you there." He couldn't recall ever having to make small talk with Evelyn. He wished she'd get to the point.

"You know I'm going into the hospital tomorrow?"

"Lauren told me . . . and why. I was real sorry to hear it."

"I wouldn't blame you if you were glad." Her lips trembled and she blinked rapidly, holding back tears.

"Aw, don't say that. I could never feel that way about you."

"Then you're a nicer person than I am." But when he opened his mouth to argue, she rushed on. "It's true, Tucker. I've treated you like a devil and now I'm paying the price. You may find this strange, but I don't believe my body will respond to any treatment as long as I have this darkness in my heart."

"Let it go, Evelyn. I have."

"No, not until I've said it all. I convinced myself that you killed Margot. Martin tried to reason with me, but I was stubborn. Margot's reputation was already in tatters and I didn't want to make it worse."

He gave her a puzzled look.

"I knew about the affair." She reached into her handbag and pulled out a book. "It's in here."

He frowned. "What's that?"

Evelyn tenderly caressed the leather cover. "It's actually a datebook. But it sometimes reads like a journal. You'll see. Margot had a habit of making notes—lots of them." She placed it on the bedside table. "You might find it helpful." She saw the look in his eye. "No, the name of the man isn't in it, but I do think he's the one she refers to with an initial."

"What initial?"

"D." When he reached to get the book, she handed it to him. "Before you ask, I don't know any man in her life with a first or last name starting with a *D,* but maybe you do."

"Did you show this to the police?" Tucker asked, paging through it.

"No, it was too personal," she said, shifting her gaze. "And once you'd disappeared, what was the point?"

Maybe to catch whoever really did murder her? Lauren thought. But she didn't have the heart to say it.

Tucker was quiet as she fixed the strap of her big handbag on her shoulder and turned to go. "I'm sorry about this, Tucker," she said in a shaky voice. "My concern was always for Margot and catching her killer. But after what happened today, I realize that person isn't you."

The door cracked and Martin looked in, his face grim. "Are you done yet, Evelyn?"

"In a minute, Martin."

She gave the datebook one last lingering look. "You can do with it . . . whatever, Tucker. I just want my daughter to rest in peace."

Lauren seemed barely able to contain herself as Martin ushered Evelyn and Juliana down the hall

387

and out of earshot. Seeing the look in her eye, Tucker held the datebook up out of her reach when she dove for it. "Let me see that!"

"Uh-uh, she gave it to me," he said, grinning. But suddenly he dropped the book with a groan. "Ouch. Headache."

And just as suddenly, Lauren was all concern. She tenderly cupped his face in her hands. "You want me to call the nurse to give you something for pain?"

"No," he said, eyes closed. "Just don't move. Except to kiss me."

"I'm not falling for that again." But she was smiling as she moved back to her chair, the datebook in her hand. "Lie still while I see what she wrote."

His only reply was a grunt.

"Okay, listen to this," she said, after scanning the first few pages. "She's meeting D at ten-thirty the night of January the fourth. Then again on January the ninth. Do those dates mean anything to you?"

"How long ago?"

"Two years?"

He opened one eye. "You're kidding."

"Hmm." She quickly paged through the next few weeks' entries. "Wow, Evelyn was right. She was definitely seeing someone . . . and often." She looked up at him. "This covers the six months before your divorce and six months after. But since you were still married during those first months, you'd have known where she was on those nights, wouldn't you?"

He didn't bother to open one eye. "You mean where she *said* she was going."

She sighed. ''I wonder if there was a datebook for that last year." She closed the book, but didn't give it back. ''I don't think you should keep this here. Anybody could come in and take it while you're sleeping."

"Well, that's comforting."

She dropped it into her handbag. "I really should get back to the ranch. I've been away from Kristy all day. I don't want her to be anxious."

When he didn't reply, she saw that he was almost asleep. Rising from the chair, she placed the magazines within reach, took the water pitcher to the sink, and refilled it with cold water. Everything done, she leaned over and gently kissed him. His eyelids fluttered and he made a soft, satisfied sound deep in his throat. But otherwise he didn't move. He was smiling in his sleep when she left.

33

Lauren was dressed to leave for the hospital the next morning when she heard a car arrive— speeding, actually, and stopping outside in a screech of brakes. In moments, the doorbell rang.

Twice. Elena would normally get it, but she was at the barn with Kristy. Hurrying down the stairs, Lauren glanced at her watch and made a face, hoping this wouldn't take long. Tucker had called at the crack of dawn saying he wanted to be gone as soon as she could get there.

"Tell Elena you'll be late getting back, that she needs to baby-sit Kristy," he'd told her. "We're taking a road trip to La Grange."

"Did you find out where the B&B is?"

"I don't want to stay on the phone. And don't tell anybody where we're going, okay? Just get here ASAP."

Which left her consumed with curiosity. Where had the security guard gone? Why wasn't he in police custody? As she reached the foyer, the doorbell rang for the third time, followed by loud pounding on the door. As she peered through the glass panels, she saw it was John Armstrong. With a sigh, she opened it.

"What in blazes have you done, woman? The sheriff just left Blue Hills after questioning my son about that fugitive Kane getting shot!"

She stepped back. "We can discuss this inside, John, but only if you calm down."

"Calm down!" He thrust his neck out at her, snarling. "I'm too freaking furious to calm down. Some redneck sheriff accuses my son of attempted murder and you want me to be calm?"

"If you want to talk rationally about it, yes."

"How about if I talk to Child Protective Services and fix it so you're denied access to Kane's kid? I know she practically lives with you half the time."

She gave him a blank stare for a beat or two. It wasn't enough that he'd orchestrated her ouster at St. Paul. Now his threats extended to Kristy?

She came out on the porch and closed the door behind her. "I'm going to overlook what you said, John, because I can see you're upset. So if you could manage to calm yourself long enough for me to ask a question, maybe we can talk."

He gave a snort. "I know you've got a grudge against Rickey. So Fox didn't just pull his name out of that overgrown hat he wears."

"I do not have a grudge against your son. I think he's troubled, yes. I think he has issues that jeopardize his future unless he gets help. And, yes, I told Sheriff Fox that Rickey was seen shooting deer on Houseman land."

"When? Who saw him?"

She glanced pointedly at her watch. "I need to run, John. Any other questions you have, you can ask Sheriff Fox directly."

"I know what this is all about," Armstrong said, speaking in a menacing tone. "It's revenge. You're ticked off because you're fired from St. Paul and you blame me. So you're taking it out on my son."

"I need to get going now, John," she said.

But he wasn't done. "You may not be at the school anymore, but you're supposed to look out for the welfare of children. I hold you responsible for this."

There was no point arguing. Turning her back on him, she went inside and closed the door in his face.

It took most of the drive to the hospital before she managed to have a thought that wasn't furious or frightful. She'd lost her job, been shot at, terrorized on her email, and threatened by a rude, obnoxious, overbearing cretin. She hoped she had seen the worst.

At the hospital, she headed for the elevator at a good clip. Armstrong had delayed her a good half hour from the time she told Tucker to expect her. She hoped he wasn't irritating the nursing staff. Patience wasn't one of his virtues.

But he had other virtues that were good and strong and true.

She was smiling as she passed the nurses' station on her way to his room. If she'd had doubts about what she felt for Tucker, they'd been laid to rest yesterday when she'd been bent over him on the ground praying that he would not die. She loved Tucker. Simple as that. She had never stopped loving him. Oh, she had tried, but closing her heart had not killed the powerful emotion that was her love for Tucker. It had simply pushed it down to a deep and lonely place.

She saw at once that there was no guard posted

at his room. Maybe he was inside, she thought. She tapped softly. Getting no response, she hesitantly pushed the door open enough to see inside. The bed was empty. Stripped. Moving in shock, she went to the cabinet where Tucker's belongings had been stored.

Empty.

Backing out, she rushed to the nurses' station. The nurse who'd taken Tucker's vitals the day before was seated at a computer entering data.

"Excuse me," Lauren said. "Where is Tucker Kane? The patient that was in room 214?"

"Oh, honey," she said, rising. "We've had a little excitement this morning. Sheriff Fox and a deputy came and took Mr. Kane away in handcuffs."

Lauren stared, stunned. "Handcuffs?"

"That's right. He was arrested." She rose, giving Lauren a sympathetic look. "I think he's in jail."

She stood frozen with shock for a long minute. "Are you okay, honey?"

"I need—" She stopped, caught her breath. "I need to go."

She turned and almost ran to the elevator, vibrating with impatience as she waited for it. What could she do?

The elevator opened and she stumbled inside, blanking for a second on choosing a floor. A mother and a teenage girl entered, looking at Lauren curiously before punching the button for the fourth floor. They were going up!

She dashed out just as the doors were closing. Flustered, she stabbed the elevator button again, then stood tapping her foot waiting for it to ping and signal to go down.

By the time she was outside, she was almost running to her car. Once in it, she realized she didn't know how to get to the sheriff's office. She didn't even know what county she was in. She had to calm down. She couldn't be any help to Tucker in a panic.

She sat for a minute as it dawned on her that there was a way to calm herself and to be helpful to Tucker. She closed her eyes and waited for the peace and calm that her faith promised . . . if she would simply ask in His name.

"Lord," she prayed, "please help me. Please guide me. Please show me how to do what needs to be done."

When she opened her eyes, she realized she held her iPhone in her hand. Of course.

Thank you, God.

She dialed the number for Information and got from the operator the number and address of the county courthouse. According to the GPS application, she was about fifteen minutes away. Once on the road, and with her emotions now under control, she thought of a dozen questions. She'd almost forgotten that they were supposed to go to La Grange. Why had he wanted to go there instead of simply calling the bed-and-breakfast?

And if he was arrested, had he been allowed a phone call? If so, he must have called someone else, not her. But who? Maybe his lawyer? But Jerry Blacklock was in Houston. Unless he was able to break away instantly, he wouldn't arrive for several hours. Her hands gripped the wheel, her thoughts racing as she tried to figure out what to do. What to do.

She found the courthouse without much trouble. As was the case in many small Texas towns, it was an impressive structure built in the center of a square. The sheriff's office and jail were inside. As she climbed the steps, she thought it looked like a movie set from an old Western. If somebody had appeared on horseback to tether his mount to a hitching post, she would not have been surprised.

When she was shown into Fox's office, he rose from behind a huge battle-scarred desk and greeted her with the same gentlemanly courtesy he'd shown the day before in Tucker's hospital room. "I thought I'd see you before long, Ms. Holloway. Have a seat."

"I'm too upset to sit, Sheriff. Why did you arrest Tucker?"

"If you won't sit, I can't either."

With a sigh, she perched herself on the edge of a hard chair. "Is he in jail?"

"He is. Houston faxed an arrest warrant."

"He has a serious head injury, Sheriff Fox," Lauren said, hoping he'd be sympathetic. "He should be resting . . . to avoid complications. Anything could happen if he's locked up in a cell."

"He was discharged by his doctors, ma'am," he said gently. "That means he gets to go to our little hotel."

Almost groaning in frustration, she put the important question to him, "What is the charge?"

"First degree murder."

She felt the oxygen rush out of her. Just when she thought that Tucker might be able to get beyond the nightmare it was worse. "First degree? How could that be?" she said, her voice rising.

"You probably need to talk to his lawyer about that, ma'am."

Of course. She took out her phone. "Excuse me, please, Sheriff."

"You're calling his lawyer?"

"Yes."

"Mr. Kane called him before we left the hospital." He glanced at a big clock on the wall. "I imagine he'll be here within the hour."

"Then could I see Tucker now?"

"I don't see why not." He moved around the corner of his desk and swept out his arm in a gentlemanly gesture, then proceeded to usher her down a hall to a steel door stamped with a sign printed in large letters: DO NOT ENTER.

"The holding cell is through this door," he said.

She was grateful for his courtesy. She felt on the verge of tears, and if he'd been harsh, she might have wilted. As she followed him, she thought of how horrendous the experience had been when Tucker was arrested by Sherman. Apparently they did things differently here than in Houston. It gave her hope that somehow Jerry Blacklock could get him out of jail. And soon.

They went through a couple of locked doors to an area of holding cells. It was not outfitted to house a large population of inmates, but several cells were occupied. Unlike the programs she'd seen on television, there wasn't a lot of noise. Nobody called out obscenities. She wondered if they were inhibited by Sheriff Fox's presence. In any case she was grateful. Finally, he stopped at the last cell.

Lauren took a deep breath, feeling a physical pain in her chest when she saw Tucker. He lay on the narrow cot in the dingy cell. Opposite the cot were a tiny sink and a toilet. The only window was high, far higher than anybody could see out. She could not imagine being confined in so dismal a place for any length of time.

Tucker appeared to be resting, probably because his head ached, she thought. But when Fox inserted a key in the lock, he quickly roused and sat up, although he paused for a moment as if he might be dizzy or in pain.

"Give me a minute," he said, getting to his feet slowly.

Lauren turned to Sheriff Fox and said fiercely, "I told you he wasn't well enough. He should still be in the hospital."

"And we'll send him back if necessary," Fox said in a calm voice. "I'll call the doc and have him looked over, but in the meantime, why don't you visit?"

Lauren simply looked at him.

With a hint of a smile, he pushed the door open. "Behave yourself, Mr. Kane. You're a lucky man to have this lady looking out for you."

Without a backward glance, Lauren went into the cell and walked directly into Tucker's arms. For a long minute, neither said a word. She simply wrapped her arms about him, letting him know with the warmth of her embrace that she loved him.

He kissed her temple and sighed. "I don't know what to say, Lauren. This is getting to be a habit, seeing me like this. I'm sorry."

"Don't be," she said, stroking his back. "I'm here same as last time. We're in this together. And we're going to see this through together. You know what we say in Texas when things get a little rough. It's just a little hitch in the gitalong."

He pulled back and looked in her eyes. "Are you for real?"

She chuckled. "You've got your arms around

me. If I'm not, there's something really strange going on here."

After a minute he relaxed, looking at her with an expression of wonder and love, then, shaking his head, he turned her loose and sat back on the cot. Resting against the wall, he closed his eyes. "I don't see how this can have a happy ending, darlin'. Houston has me in their sites again. They'll want me back there ASAP."

"You can't give up—" She stopped as the metal doors clanged and banged and Sheriff Fox appeared escorting Tucker's lawyer, Jerry Blacklock.

"You've got more company, Mr. Kane," Fox said, ushering the lawyer into the cell.

"Jerry!" Lauren hugged him, accepting a kiss on her cheek. "Thank heaven you're here. Tucker needs you."

Blacklock was tall, with red hair and penetrating blue eyes. He wore a button-down shirt, jeans, and gorgeous black leather boots. He shook hands with Tucker, who had risen to his feet gingerly. "Sit down, Tuck. You look like you've been rode hard and put up wet."

Tucker waved a weary hand and pulled Lauren down beside him. "Please, no more Texas sayings. And I may look beat, but I'm ready to hear you tell me how you can get me out of here."

"Right." Since there was no chair, Blacklock took a seat on the other side of Tucker and opened his laptop. "Here's the deal. Seems HPD has a witness putting him at the murder scene coinciding with Margot's time of death."

"I know about the witnesses," Lauren said, dismissively. "Detective Sherman's investigation turned them up months ago and discarded them as worthless to the case—teen drug addicts. Their testimony was discredited."

"Not teenagers, Lauren. It's a single witness." He looked at Tucker. "He's a former employee of H & K Contractors. He says on the day of the murder that you forgot a piece of equipment. Listen to this. He claims he took it upon himself to drop it off after he got off work that day. He was doing his boss a favor."

Blacklock's sarcasm was enough to tell Lauren he didn't buy the witness's story. "So, did he talk to Tucker?" she asked. "Did he see Margot?

"He claims he saw you, Tucker, when he got to the house. He makes no mention of seeing Margot."

Tucker pressed a spot between his eyes. Obviously in pain, but thinking, he said, "When was this?"

"He puts the time at around six-thirty." He paused. "That's convenient, eh?"

Obviously skeptical, Lauren couldn't stand still, not even in the confined space of the cell. She knew from reading the report of the medical examiner that the approximate time of death was

6:30 P.M. "If he saw Tucker, did he show himself? Or did he just drop off the tool or whatever it was and drive away?"

"That's pretty much the way he claims it happened."

"So a brand-new witness shows up just when Tucker happens to be in the hospital," Lauren said, "and is luckily within reach of HPD?"

Jerry smiled at her like a teacher approving the student's right answer. "That's one way to look at it."

Tucker was leaning against the wall again. "I bet I can guess this yahoo's name. Is it Will Ferguson?"

"You got it." Blacklock referred to his laptop notes. "He was terminated a few weeks after the murder, when you were long gone."

"He wanted a promotion to crew chief," Tucker said, "but I promoted his brother-in-law instead."

"That sounds like revenge," Lauren said.

Blacklock smiled as he closed his laptop and stood up. "It's a theory that I will definitely use in court," he said.

"Fine. But there's still a problem, Jerry. How can we get him out of here?"

"I will never call Jerry Blacklock boring again," Lauren said as she buckled her seat belt. "How he managed to get Sheriff Fox to release you on your own recognizance is a miracle."

401

"I don't think Jerry should get all the credit. I think you've dazzled Sheriff Fox."

"Come on," she said.

"It's true. But I'm not dissing a miracle. I'd pinch myself to check I wasn't dreaming, but I've got such a raging headache that I don't need any more pain."

How the sheriff would handle HPD detectives when they realized Tucker had flown the coop was a mystery. She could only assume that Fox's authority gave him power to do things differently than they were done in Houston. But now it seemed expedient to put as much distance as possible between Tucker and Benton Fox's jail.

She had assumed she would be driving, but Tucker had overruled her and climbed into the driver's seat. And once they were both buckled up, he roared off in a surge of horsepower. "I'd like to linger long enough to kiss you," he told her, throwing a quick look her way. "If you and Blacklock hadn't worked your magic on the sheriff, Sherman would have had me in cuffs and on my way back to Houston before sunset."

No magic, she thought. Just God opening doors as she'd prayed. The past months had put her faith to the test, and she didn't like to think of the times she'd felt doubt and frustration. But now she felt a deep sense of peace in handing it all over to God. Putting herself completely in His care.

For a few minutes, she surveyed the

landscape—rolling hills still baking in September sun under a huge, blindingly blue Texas sky. "Lately I've felt like I'm in a bad movie," she said. "As if I'm Bonnie to your Clyde. Do you get that feeling?"

"No. We haven't done anything wrong like those two. We're all about trying to right a wrong, Lauren." Hunched over the wheel, he covered another mile or so before adding grimly, "And I don't need to be reminded how lucky I am. I've known it from the start. From day one."

She smiled a little.

"I love you," he said gruffly.

She leaned over and touched his cheek. "I love you, too, Tucker."

"Good." He caught her hand and held it close for a minute. "That's good."

"So what about this company employee that Sherman just pulled out of a hat?" she asked, settling back. "Is that all it was? Just a grudge because you didn't promote him? Why would he say something like that?"

He shot her a quick look. "If it wasn't true?"

"Of course it isn't true," she said, not missing a beat. When he didn't say anything, she turned to look at him. He was clearly battling with some kind of emotion. "What?"

He slowed down, half-turned in his seat so he could look at her and still drive. "After all I've put you through, after all the stuff that keeps cropping up, it blows me away that you still believe me."

"I'm not as constant as all that," she said dryly. "Have you forgotten I spent a big part of a year hating you?"

"Because I left . . ." He sighed, regret in the sound. "We're not out of the woods yet, but if you'll just stick with me, darlin', we're going to have an incredible life together."

Laughing, she reached over and patted him on the thigh. "Hey, I'm taking that as a promise." For a minute or two, she simply enjoyed looking at him. Sensing it, he turned and gave her a slow, sexy smile before settling back to drive.

"Tell me more about this Ferguson character, Tucker."

"He was lazy and I suspected him of stealing company materials, but I was never able to catch him." He approached an intersection and turned onto a narrow county road. "After I left, I told Martin to be on the lookout, to watch him. He was bound to mess up. When he did Martin fired him."

She looked around suddenly, seeing nothing but rolling hills and grazing livestock. "Why are we going to La Grange? Couldn't we just call the B-and-B?"

"We're not going to the B-and-B."

"I don't get it—where are we going?"

He smiled slowly. "We're going to La Grange because that's where the wood is."

"The wood that disappeared?"

"Yep."

She gaped at him. "Are you serious?"

"As a heart attack."

"How did you—" She stopped, eyed him suspiciously. "Are you lying?"

"To you, darlin', never."

Her face went soft. Pressing her fingers to her lips, she threw him a kiss.

"I like the real thing better," he said.

But she was quickly refocused and peppering him with questions. "So how did you find it? Have you seen it? You couldn't have. You've either been in hiding, in the hospital, or in jail."

His mouth curved. He was clearly enjoying himself. "You know those magazines you left for me in the hospital? Well, last night when they brought my dinner tray, I tossed them to the foot of my bed. This particular issue landed open at a feature article about the restoration of nineteenth-century dwellings in Texas. What caught my eye was the title: 'Rare mahogany recreates bygone era.'"

"But what—"

"Rare mahogany, Lauren."

"You're thinking it's the missing wood?"

"I need to see it, but yeah, that's what I'm thinking. If it's from the Heights house, every piece will have a distinctive mark. No way to conceal it."

"Okay, but why assume it's from the Heights house?"

"Good question. When the article was written, the owners were . . ." He sent her a triumphant look. "Guess who?"

"I give up. Who?"

"Carter and Juliana Brumfield."

Her mouth fell open.

"Yeah, that was pretty much my reaction, too."

"Tucker!" She suddenly straightened in her seat, straining the seat belt to face him. "I know about that house! I just remembered." She screwed up her face, thinking. "I was in the elevator with Brumfield and John Armstrong. They talked about the house he'd sold in La Grange and how Juliana was so proud. She pulled off a coup by getting a magazine to do a feature article about it." She settled back, her voice going quietly thoughtful. "What irony."

"You know what this means."

"If you're thinking what I'm thinking, yes."

"The only person with opportunity to take it was the killer."

"I can't believe—"

"Listen. I had all night long to think about this. What if Carter Brumfield is the person Margot referred to as D? As in district attorney."

"The man she was having an affair with?" She was shaking her head. "That would be sick. Brumfield is . . . was her godfather."

"No, Juliana was her god*mother*."

He was still old enough to be her father. "So why would Carter kill her?"

"He's an ambitious politician. Once he's governor of Texas, the sky's the limit. Governor next, then who knows, maybe the White House. But if it came out that he was having an affair with his wife's godchild, his political future would be doomed."

With his gaze fixed on the road, his fingers were doing a restless tap dance on the wheel. "Now all we have to do is talk the present owners into letting us in their house to have a look at that paneling." He winked at Lauren. "That'll be your job."

"I don't know anything about paneling."

"Your job is getting us in the house. Since you've charmed Sherman and Sheriff Fox, the owners will just fall over themselves to let you in once you turn on that killer smile."

"Oh, please."

"And if that doesn't work," he said, seeing her rolling her eyes, "Benton Fox said I could use his name if we need it."

"Are you serious?"

"You keep saying that." He shrugged with boyish charm. "I'm just stating the facts, ma'am."

"Okay, in that case, I have to think of some way to thank the sheriff."

Tucker turned to her, looking over his

sunglasses with a slow smile. "We could name our firstborn Benton."

She couldn't help herself. She giggled. "You're acting pretty cocky for somebody who's probably got a Houston posse on his tail, buddy."

"No sweat!" he said with feeling. "I'm traveling with an angel. That'll keep the wind at my back."

Lauren turned her gaze to a stretch of pasture dotted with livestock. It looked so peaceful, cows placidly cropping grass, calves frolicking, birds soaring overhead. The sky a dazzling blue. "I can't believe Carter is so . . . evil, Tucker."

"Yeah."

In a minute, she released a deep sigh. "So let's go take a look at the paneling in that house."

34

The house was a gem of Texas architecture dating from the turn of the century. Lauren smiled, seeing Tucker's mouth almost watering as he stood taking it in. Set far back from the road, the front featured three dormers on the second story, a wide wraparound porch with long windows shining with wavy original glass, and a stunning lead-glass-paned front door.

"With or without a recommendation from Fox," Tucker said, removing his sunglasses, "I wouldn't let strangers inside if this was my house."

Lauren grabbed his hand and tugged him up the

steps with her. "What happened to my dazzling them simply with the power of my smile?"

He gave her a quick kiss on her temple. "I guess I lost faith there for a minute."

"Uh-huh. You need to work on that, mister." She turned the old-fashioned handle that rang a bell somewhere deep inside the house. As they waited, cows could be heard lowing in the distance. Overhead, a hawk screeched. "What a great place," she murmured. "Somehow I can't see Carter or Juliana Brumfield here. It's miles from a golf course. And shopping."

"It's one of the in places to have a second home, and Juliana has that kind of outlook." He shrugged. "Just a guess."

"Looks like nobody's home," Lauren said after a minute. She cupped her hands against the leaded glass to better see inside. "Oh, wrong. Somebody's coming. And she's carrying a baby." She stepped back, reaching for his hand, lacing their fingers. "Showtime."

After a bit of fumbling, the door was opened by an elderly Hispanic woman who was feeding a bottle to an infant in the crook of her arm.

"I'm sorry," Lauren said, genuinely dismayed. "Is this a bad time?"

Another smile. "No. Is okay. Baby good."

"Is Pat Wilson here?"

"Mommy shopping." Shaking her head. "Daddy riding. Back soon."

"Oh, dear." Lauren put on her best disappointed face. "We so wanted to visit."

"Is okay," the nanny said, stepping back. "Come. You wait inside."

"Thank you." Lauren poked Tucker in his ribs with an elbow, ignoring a smothered grunt as she followed the nanny into the house. "We can wait in the library," she said brightly. "Will that be okay?"

"Is okay." The baby's chubby hand bumped the empty bottle and sent it rolling across the floor. As Tucker bent to retrieve it, the nanny shifted the child to her shoulder. When Tucker handed over the bottle, she indicated by a gesture of her chin that the room was to the left of the foyer. "Sit. Wait. I go change baby."

"Thank you." Lauren stopped her with a hand on her arm. "What is your name?"

"Angelina."

Lauren smiled. "*Gracias*, Angelina."

Big smile. "*De nada.*"

As soon as she disappeared down the hall, Lauren turned to Tucker beaming. "Can you believe this!" she whispered ecstatically. "We walk right in and she takes us to the library."

"Yeah, but what if Mr. Wilson shows up and wants to know what the Sam Hill two strangers are doing in his house?"

"Good point. So let's get busy."

Tucker was already moving. Dropping to a

crouch, he ran his fingers along a strip of paneling above the baseboard. Lauren watched for some reaction, but she could tell nothing by the look on his face.

When he moved to a window and again used his fingers in a tactile search, she kept a nervous lookout.

He suddenly straightened, dusting his hands on his jeans. "Let's get going. If Wilson shows up with a shotgun, he probably won't wait to hear us drop Sheriff Fox's name."

"Did you find the mark?" She hurried to keep up with his long strides to the front door. "Is it the right wood?"

No need to hear his answer. The grin he flashed said it all.

The grin didn't last long. They made it to the porch as a man on a splendid palomino thundered up in a cloud of dust and pointed a rifle at them.

"Hold it! Take another step and I shoot."

"Hey, take it easy." Tucker instantly pushed Lauren behind him and raised both arms, palms out. Wilson dismounted, his rifle never wavering from his target: Tucker's midsection.

"Mr. Wilson, I'm Tucker Kane. I was just—"

"I don't give a crap who you are," he said, approaching the steps. "But you better have a damn good reason for busting into my house and terrorizing my housekeeper."

"Angelina was not terrified," Lauren said, trying to see around Tucker, who pushed her back. "She invited us in."

"Well, she had the good sense to call me," he said, the rifle still pointed at Tucker.

Heart pounding, Lauren decided that now seemed a good time to try her so-called womanly charm. She managed a wary smile. "We had a good reason for wanting to talk to you, Mr. Wilson. About your beautiful house, the library especially."

"I don't notice you waiting around for a tour," he said sarcastically. "Looks to me like you were both sneaking out."

Tucker shoved Lauren behind him again. "The library is paneled with stolen wood, sir," he said flatly. "That's why we're here."

Wilson didn't blink. "Take it up with the DA in Houston," he said. "He's the one who sold me the house."

"Mr. Wilson," Tucker tried again. "If you'll point that rifle someplace else, I think you'll be interested in hearing why we're here."

Eyeing him with suspicion, Wilson said, "Do you take me for an idiot, man?"

"This is ridiculous!" Lauren stepped out from behind Tucker with her cell phone in her hand. "Here. Call Sheriff Benton Fox—he knows we're here and why."

Wilson moved the rifle a scant inch away from

Tucker's belly. "I know Benton. How about you call him and put that thing on speaker. We'll hear what he has to say and then, if I'm satisfied, you can tell me what this is all about."

Lauren drove while Tucker made two phone calls, one to thank Sheriff Fox and the second to Martin Houseman. He figured it would be best for Fox to notify Sherman of a major development in the murder case. Better not to mention up front the connection between Carter Brumfield and the wood. Just locating the wood was enough for now. Sherman would stall anyway, if only for the sake of saving face. Eventually it would be identified as coming from the Heights house.

Then stuff would hit the fan.

"We have another problem," he said to Lauren. "I don't think it's a good idea to show myself at the ranch. I need to wait and see how Sherman reacts once Fox calls him. To be on the safe side, you need to drop me at the lodge."

"Does Brumfield know about the lodge?" Lauren asked. "Martin must have taken him to hunt there."

"No, Martin said he never invited him. He never warmed to Carter. But we have to be cautious. Once Brumfield gets wind of this, I don't know what he might do."

They were silent for a moment as Lauren thought through the events of the day. "What are the chances that Wilson would have papers authenticating the wood used in the restoration of that house?" she asked.

"He never thought we'd find it."

She smiled. "And we wouldn't have without help from above. I see God's hand in all this, Tucker."

Was she right? Could it be? Somehow, after he stopped dwelling on how unfair life was and how God had abandoned him, his life was suddenly turning around. "You'll need to remind me of that if I go off-track again," he said in a gruff voice.

She smiled. "I will. But for now, tell me how to get to the lodge."

It was deep in the woods near a creek about a mile down a rough trail overgrown with vegetation. Lauren was not surprised that Tucker had managed to live undetected here. When they finally reached it, she saw not a dilapidated shack, but a dwelling that was almost picturesque, a rambling structure that had a nineteenth-century look about it. To call it a cabin was a misnomer. Knowing Tucker's love for antiquities and his expertise in restoration, she thought living there might not have been all bad.

Except that he hadn't chosen to live there. It had been a prison.

"Kristy will be anxious if I'm away much longer," Lauren said. "I can't linger, but I'm curious to see inside. If it matches the outside, I can see it becoming a bed-and-breakfast one day."

"It was originally a hunting lodge," Tucker said, walking up the path with her to the front door. "Martin's friends hung out during deer and dove season. Frankly, it's surprising that nobody thought to look for me here."

"After Margot was murdered, they wouldn't expect her father to hide you," Lauren said.

"I guess." He reached around her to unlock the door, but was startled to find it ajar. He stepped back abruptly.

"Ouch, my toe!" Lauren said, scuttling backward.

"Sorry. The lock's busted." His gaze riveted to the door, he took her arm none too gently and nudged her to the steps. "Go to the car and wait for me."

"What—"

"Go! Somebody could be in there." Tucker reached up above his head to a porch rafter, then muttered a curse. "My rifle, it's gone," he said.

"Should we call nine-one-one?"

"Wait," he said, turning to the woods. "It's Buddy."

Barking joyously, Buddy suddenly bounded out from the woods, hurtling toward them like a golden tornado. Tucker saw he was going to launch himself at them and issued a sharp command. The dog stopped short, panting, tail swishing wildly.

"We're okay to go inside," Tucker said. "He

415

wouldn't act this way if anybody was still hanging around."

"How did you get here, Buddy-boy?" she crooned, rubbing the dog's ears. "You're supposed to be at the ranch."

"He's probably looking for me." With Buddy at his heels and Lauren following, Tucker headed to the door. "I need to check inside. If someone did break in they couldn't have found much of anything worth stealing."

"You think it was just a thief?"

"I don't have a clue." He pushed the door open and stepped over the threshold. "But it's suspicious considering—"

"What?" Her view was blocked, but she sensed his shock. The interior of the cabin was shadowy and still. It took her a minute to bring it in focus. When she did, she gasped in horror. A man lay sprawled on the floor in a pool of blood. Instinctively she clutched a handful of Tucker's shirt and turned from the grisly sight.

"Stay put, Lauren," he said grimly. "I need to check if he's . . ."

"Dead?"

"Stay back." Tucker gently pried her fingers loose from his shirt. Ignoring his order to stay put, Lauren followed close behind as he moved to the downed man. Now that her eyes had fully adjusted to the dimness, she braced herself to look at his face. Her breath caught.

"It's Jordan Raines," she said in a horrified whisper.

"Yeah." Now crouched beside the body, Tucker gingerly pressed Raines's carotid and held it a few seconds. "And he's definitely dead."

"I can see that." She realized nobody lying in such an awkward position—a leg twisted grotesquely and an arm beneath him—could be alive. Besides that, blood was everywhere. Raines's once white golf shirt was soaked, as was the floor. Behind him, a considerable area of the knotty pine paneling looked as if a mad artist had dipped his brush in red paint and slung it crazily. "Look at that wall, Tucker."

"Uh-huh." Tucker sat studying Raines's body and the area around it. "He must have been shot at point-blank range," he muttered almost to himself.

"We should call nine-one-one."

Tucker straightened and took out his cell phone. "Better yet, let's call Benton Fox."

35

They were told to keep out of the way while Fox's people worked the crime scene, so Lauren was sitting beside Tucker on the edge of the porch. Which was a good thing. Now that reaction was setting in, she wasn't sure her knees wouldn't buckle. Buddy lay with his head on his paws beside her.

417

"I thought you were gonna keep him out of trouble, Ms. Holloway," the sheriff said.

She gave him a wan smile. "I can provide an alibi for him this time," she said. "He's been with me every minute since you let him out of jail."

Fox chuckled. "Just teasing you, ma'am. Are you feelin' okay? You look faint."

"I guess finding a dead body left me a whiter shade of pale."

"She's had a bad shock," Tucker said grimly.

"Uh-huh." Fox gazed about, taking in the lodge and grounds. He pushed his big hat back a little so he could better see Tucker's face. "You sure found a nice place to hole up, Mr. Kane."

"Martin has been a good friend."

Fox watched his people moving about inside the cabin. "Got any ideas why Raines was killed?"

"He knew who killed Margot," Tucker said, adding with a shrug, "Just a guess."

"The man who knew too much, eh?"

"That's right," Lauren said, thinking to add her opinion to Tucker's.

"And you both think that's Carter Brumfield."

Tucker turned to look as a stretcher bearing Jordan Raines's body was wheeled out of the cabin. "The only person who could have removed that wood between the time I left and Margot's murder is the killer. Now it shows up in a room at Brumfield's former vacation house. You do the math."

418

Fox stroked his strong chin thoughtfully. "So why would he kill her?"

"Again, this is just another guess," Tucker said, "but say he was trying to break off their affair. What if—"

"They were having an affair?" Fox's eyebrows rose.

"We think so," Lauren said. "Her datebook mentions a man; we think it was Carter Brumfield."

Tucker looked weary with the sordidness of it. "Margot wouldn't like being dumped. I know her. She could be ruthless."

"A woman scorned?" Fox said.

"I think she'd look for a way to punish him, yes. Nothing better than to go public. His political career would be over."

"I dunno." Fox was shaking his head. "A man in his position, in the public eye. Hard to kill someone and get away with it."

"I agree," Lauren said. "So what if Brumfield had someone else do it for him?"

Fox was ahead of her. "He'd have to get rid of the only person to tie him to the murder."

"Jordan Raines," Lauren said.

"Your men haven't found the murder weapon?" Tucker asked.

"Not yet."

"When you do, it'll probably be my rifle. It's gone. It wasn't exactly hidden up in the porch rafters, and I kept it loaded. Whoever killed

Raines could have spotted it and decided to use it instead of his own."

"Pointing to you as the killer . . . again!" Lauren said with disgust. "Well, too bad, because we were together in La Grange and we can prove it!"

"An airtight alibi," Fox said, with a half smile.

"If you're done, Sheriff, we need to get back to the ranch." Tucker rose and, with his hands at Lauren's waist, lifted her off the porch. Buddy instantly scrambled up, eager to leave. "We need to check on my little girl."

"I'm done for now," Fox said, but he stopped them as they started toward the car. "You don't need me telling you what you should and shouldn't do now that you're on the scent and ready to hunt, Mr. Kane. But Carter Brumfield is a man with powerful connections, and not just in Houston. You'll want to be cautious." He tipped his hat as Tucker nodded. "Just my take on it."

As soon as they were in the car, Lauren said, "I've been thinking . . ."

"Me, too."

She glanced at him. "You first."

"How did Brumfield know we'd located the wood? We only told the sheriff and Martin."

"That was my question," Lauren said. "And I think we need to call Martin and ask if he told anybody else. He'll be at the hospital in

Houston with Evelyn. She was to check in today."

He nodded, trying to dodge potholes in the trail. "So do it."

Lauren already had her iPhone in hand. Martin answered on the first ring. "It's Lauren," she said to him. "How is Evelyn?"

"Nervous. She didn't sleep much last night. We checked in pretty early. They're getting ready to put her through a battery of tests." He paused. "What's up?"

Lauren decided a direct approach was best. "Martin, when we called and told you we'd located the wood, did you tell anybody else?"

"Well, now we know," Lauren said after ringing off. "Juliana."

Tucker nodded. "Has to be."

"If she overheard and if she told her husband," Lauren said, "that means she's known all along that she's married to a killer—worse yet, one who murdered her goddaughter." She tried, but failed to imagine a relationship so twisted. "All this time she's protected a killer while watching her best friend grieve without saying anything? That's dreadful, Tucker."

At the main road, Tucker turned toward the Houseman Ranch. "It's hard to tell which one is more ambitious," he said, "Carter so he can be governor of Texas or Juliana so she can shine as First Lady."

"I hope for Texas and the U.S.A. that they won't get to do either."

The first thing Lauren noticed once they were inside the house was how quiet it was. Too quiet. Even when Kristy played alone, there was never this absolute silence. The TV would be on the PBS Kids channel, sounds would be coming from the kitchen where Elena puttered about, Kristy would be talking or singing or laughing. Four-year-olds make noise. More ominous was the fact that Buddy didn't make a headlong dash to find Kristy.

"Kristy!" Standing in the foyer looking about, Lauren had a bad feeling. Chills down her spine. A flutter in her chest. "Kristy! Where are you?"

"Look in the bedrooms," Tucker told her. He was already striding toward the kitchen. "I'll check the rest of the house."

With rising alarm, Lauren made a hurried check of the bedrooms. All were empty. She met Tucker coming from the kitchen. "Any sign of Elena?"

"No. Let's go to the barn." He snapped his fingers to Buddy.

The barn was Raphael's territory, and ordinarily he would have emerged to meet anybody approaching long before they reached it. Today, he was nowhere to be seen. The area was as still and silent as the house. Lauren was beginning to feel real panic. "Maybe Kristy went home with Elena," she said, hoping. But it was not something the housekeeper had ever done, certainly not without letting them know. No, something was wrong.

"She usually leaves at five o'clock. Maybe there's an emergency. She told me her aging mother lives with her and Raphael."

"Taking Kristy with her?" Tucker said, his face grim. "And no note? I don't think so."

Now nearing the barn, Buddy picked up his pace, the hair on his back raised as he barked. "Something's up," Tucker said, shushing the golden with a sharp command. With her heart in her mouth, Lauren followed Tucker into the barn, praying hard.

Please don't let anything happen to Kristy.

It was then that they both heard sounds coming from the rear area of the barn. A keening voice. Someone banging on the walls and calling plaintively. Buddy rushed ahead to the tack room. The door was closed and a pitchfork was braced against it, trapping someone inside. With a muttered curse, Tucker tossed the tool toward a stall stacked with hay bales and wrenched the door open.

Elena almost fell into his arms, wailing and babbling a string of Spanish. Her face was flushed and her hair was in disarray. She was shaking and crying and trying to communicate something. The only word Lauren recognized was Kristy's name.

With fear in her heart, she put her arm around Elena, hoping—needing—to calm her. "It's okay,

Elena. You're safe now. Tell us. Where is Kristy?"

Tucker appeared with a cup of water. "Here, take a sip and tell us what happened," he ordered in a stern voice. "We need you to talk to us. Who took Kristy?"

With those words, Elena collapsed into another hysterical fit of weeping and wailing. As sympathetic as Lauren felt for the frightened housekeeper, she wanted to shake her out of her hysteria. Instead, she reached for Elena's hands, hoping to calm her down. When Elena winced, she realized the woman had injured herself pounding on the rough boards trying to get out.

"Oh, Elena. I'm so sorry this happened." She gently urged the woman down onto a bench. Tucker appeared with a clean washcloth and some water. He saturated it and wrung it out, handing it wordlessly to Lauren, who applied it first to Elena's face. That seemed to calm her somewhat. Next, she began to deal with her injured hands. "Now, Elena," she said, dabbing at bloody knuckles, trying to be as patient as she could be, "tell us what happened to Kristy."

"It is that b-boy, Miss Lauren," Elena said brokenly. "He push me in this room and leave me! He t-take Kristy. I hear her cry. Is bad. I say stop! Stop!" Shaking her head, tears streaming, she looked up at Tucker. "Sorry, Mr. Tucker, so sorry."

"Not your fault, Elena." The furrow in his brow was deep, his arms crossed over his chest.

"Where was Raphael when this was happening?"

She sniffed, using the washcloth to wipe her nose. "I don't know. We hear the gun and he go check." Tears welled up again. "Not come back."

Lauren looked at Tucker. "We need to call the police, don't we?"

"Yeah, but we can't wait. We'll tell the cops she's here. Let them handle it. We'll leave the ranch gate open."

"Wait here, Elena," Lauren said to the sobbing woman. "You will need to talk to the police. I'm sorry you were hurt."

"Is okay. I go to kitchen." She was already moving to the front of the barn.

Two seconds after she left, Tucker was hustling Lauren outside. "C'mon. We're going to Blue Hills to get my daughter. I'll drive. You call Benton Fox." He was striding along at a pace that Lauren struggled to match. His voice was grim with determination. "Kristy had better be there and he'd better not have harmed a hair on her head. When I get through with him, he'll think a few minutes' scolding in the principal's office is a walk in the park."

Behind his bravado, Lauren heard his bone-chilling fear for Kristy. She caught his arm and briefly hugged him.

Lauren didn't tell him what truly worried her. Rickey was capable of violence. Would he hurt Kristy?

Sheriff Benton Fox had his own way of doing his job. He made decisions that would be considered politically incorrect in Houston. He had a small staff of deputies who were fiercely loyal. He had a cell phone and no dispatcher to screen his calls. When his phone rang, he answered it personally. Lauren was counting on that as she dialed.

He listened without interrupting as she told him what happened to Elena and that they were on their way to Blue Hills Ranch. "I know what Mr. Kane's thinking with his little girl in jeopardy," Fox said, "but I wish you'd hold on until I get there. The Blue Hills Ranch was gonna be my next stop anyway."

"There's something else you should know, Sheriff Fox." She paused for a second. "Raphael Ruiz is missing."

"Houseman's foreman? I know Raphael."

"You might want to have some of your people check the area around Tucker's cabin. His wife said he heard a shot, probably the one that killed Jordan Raines. Raphael went to investigate and never returned."

"You don't say."

"Yes, sir. So how long do you think it will be before you can get to Blue Hills?"

"Twenty minutes."

She glanced up as Tucker turned on the road that

led to the main house at Blue Hills. "We'll see you there."

She rang off before he could issue more of his folksy directives.

Blue Hills was a sprawling stone, glass, and wood edifice that looked as if it could easily accommodate any size crowd that Carter Brumfield's campaign might host.

"Kiss that good-bye," she murmured.

Tucker threw her a quick glance. "What?"

"Just thinking about how disappointed John Armstrong will be when he finds out Carter has screwed up their plans to rule Texas."

Tucker didn't comment. He was looking at the collection of cars parked on the grounds. "Looks like they're already in campaign mode. There must be forty or fifty cars here."

Lauren leaned forward in her seat. "That means Carter is here."

"Very possible."

"They have to know Jordan Raines has been murdered. If this is a fund-raising event, would it go on anyway?"

He gave a short laugh. "If this is a fund-raiser, it was planned a while ago. Cancel it and lose those campaign contributions? I don't think so."

He parked, but Lauren stopped him from getting out of the car with a hand on his arm. "Maybe we'd better wait for Benton Fox," she said. "Brumfield might sic one of his goons on you. He'd like to make a show of arresting you in front of a bunch of people."

Tucker breathed a frustrated sigh, fixing his gaze on the house. Every window was lit, people milled about talking, laughing, drinking. "There's music," he said, shaking his head. "A live band. Didn't I tell you?"

Lauren was shocked. "Brumfield has to know we're on to him, yet he goes ahead with his campaign as if nothing's changed. What kind of man does that?"

"One who's arrogant and utterly confident that he can overcome whatever Benton Fox throws at him. He sees Fox as a redneck sheriff in a backwater county, while he's the district attorney in big town U.S.A." He shrugged. "Simple."

After a minute, Lauren said, "I have an idea."

He turned to look at her.

"Let me go inside by myself and try to find Kristy. You can wait here for the sheriff."

"No—"

"Tucker. We don't know what Rickey might be doing, but we can be sure Kristy is frightened."

She'd pressed the right button. Tucker released a pent-up breath. "Okay. Go." He watched as she pressed the handle and opened the door. "But if anything—*anything!*—happens, I want you to scream your head off. Don't even think about all those people in monkey suits. You yell and I'll come."

She smiled. "Thank you, my prince."

"And if Fox doesn't show up in a few minutes, I'm coming in anyway."

The security guard at the steps took one suspicious look at her jeans and T-shirt and moved to block the door. After asking to see her invitation, he said, "I'm sorry, ma'am, but if you don't have an invitation I can't let you in."

"I'm not an invited guest," she told him. "I'm here because a child has been kidnapped and I have reason to think she's inside this house."

"Whoa, good try," he said, not budging from the door. "I've heard some good stories before, ma'am, but that's the best one I've ever heard."

"Do you know Sheriff Benton Fox?"

"Ah, yeah. Doesn't everybody in Texas?"

She took her cell phone out of her pocket and scrolled to Fox's number. As it rang, she handed it over to the guard. "When he answers, tell him you need permission to let Lauren Holloway inside this house."

She waited impatiently while he did as told. A minute later, he clicked the phone off and handed it back to her. "You can go in," he said, looking at her with new respect.

"Thank you." Smiling, she walked quickly to the door. Just before entering, she turned and gave Tucker a thumbs-up.

Her smile slipped a bit once she was inside looking at a sea of glittering, sophisticated, moneyed people, many of whom she recognized as Houston's movers and shakers. She received curious glances at her inappropriate outfit, but she didn't care.

John Armstrong wasn't hard to spot. When their eyes locked, she felt the tangible fury in him. He began to make his way to her through the crowd. "What do you think you're doing!" Armstrong demanded in a tightly controlled voice. "This is an invitation-only event. How did you get in?"

"John, where is Rickey?"

Her question threw him. "Rickey? What does that have—"

"We can talk about it here in front of everyone," she said, giving a sweeping look at the crowd, "or we can talk about it privately. Either way, I mean to see Rickey. Now."

"This is outrageous!" He gripped her elbow painfully and began to march her toward the door. It was no easy feat finding a path through so many people who were vying for his attention. Armstrong ignored them all until a distinguished man stepped in front of them.

"John, we need you over here." Without acknowledging Lauren, the man added, "There's someone you should meet."

Armstrong managed a brief smile, a barely detectable crack in his stony face. "Frank. Give

430

me a minute, will you?" He flicked a look at Lauren that promised dire retribution. "Seems there's a problem with the hired help."

"Make it quick," Frank said. "I've primed this guy and he won't appreciate waiting. He's with Carter now."

Lauren barely registered that Brumfield was indeed present. Her only thought at the moment was to find Kristy. "Where is Rickey?" she demanded when they were finally out of the room.

"I don't know what this is all about, Lauren, but losing your job must have pushed you around the bend. You will not get away with this."

"Listen to me, John," she said, resisting the urge to grab his lapels and shout in his face. "Rickey came to the Houseman ranch today. He forced Elena into the tack room in the barn and locked it. Then he took Kristy away on his ATV. Now, one more time, where is your son?"

"That is slander. I can sue you for that kind of talk," he blustered. "It's ridiculous."

"Okay. That's it." She gave a huff of disgust and started back into the main room. "Maybe Cecile will listen."

"Wait." Clearly battling the urge to throttle her, he ushered her a safe distance away. "Are you serious? You think my son has your . . . has kidnapped the Kane kid? That he's holding her upstairs somewhere against her will?"

"I don't know where he's holding her, but

431

you're half right. I can assure you she didn't go with him willingly. We need to find out what he's done with her. And we're wasting time arguing about it."

"John, what's going on here?"

He turned swiftly. Seeing Juliana, he gave a sickly smile. "It's . . . it's just a little problem, Ju-Ju."

Ignoring Armstrong, Juliana addressed Lauren. "What problem?"

Lauren told her about finding Kristy missing and the housekeeper locked up. As she talked, Armstrong literally vibrated with rage. She knew when this was over he would not be satisfied that he'd ruined her at St. Paul Academy. He'd try everything in his power to destroy her personally.

When she was done, Juliana gave Armstrong a regal nod of dismissal. "I'll handle this, John. Go back to our guests. It is vital that nobody gets wind of this . . . situation. There has been enough drama today."

"I'm afraid not, Juliana," Lauren said. "I expect the sheriff to appear any minute."

She gave Lauren a cold look. "You called him about this . . . silly prank?"

"It's not a silly prank when a child is missing. Sheriff Fox is already on his way here to deal with the matter of Jordan Raines's murder. You have heard about that, haven't you?"

For a second, Juliana's careful facade was

shaken, but she rallied. "And we will handle it." She took a step, reaching out, but not quite touching Lauren. "John, one more thing. Where is the little demon?"

"Upstairs," he mumbled. "In the green room."

"Come with me, Lauren."

36

Lauren had to admire Juliana. She must know her husband was in deep trouble. She must know his political future was doomed. She knew the wood had been found and that it was a direct connection to her and Carter. So, probably most painful of all, she must know she would never be First Lady of Texas. And yet, as she climbed the stairs, she carried herself like a queen. Her backbone was ramrod straight. Her head was held high.

Once upstairs, Juliana threw open a door and surprised a sitter watching television with the two Armstrong girls. Both recognized Lauren and jumped up to greet her. Kristy was not in the room.

Lauren's heart sank as she approached the girls. Rickey must be holding Kristy somewhere else. But where?

"Hi, Maya. Hi, Lainie." She looked into their upturned faces. "Have you seen Kristy?"

Both looked at her solemnly. Neither spoke.

Maya was eight years old. Lainie was only four

and a half. Same as Kristy. Lauren touched Maya's hair, smoothing it back from her pretty face. "Maya, do you know where Kristy is?"

Maya dropped her eyes, unable to meet Lauren's gaze. Lauren guessed that Rickey had probably frightened them with who-knew-what threat to keep them from telling.

"Speak up, girl!" Juliana said sharply.

Maya flinched at the harsh order. Lauren slipped her arm around the child and gave Juliana a stern look meant to silence her. "Maya, you don't have to be afraid. You can tell me where Kristy is."

With a flick of her dark eyes at Juliana, Maya again tucked her head and said nothing.

"You can tell me this much. Does Rickey have her?"

She gave the tiniest bit of a nod.

"Where?"

"Barn."

It was barely a whisper. Lauren hugged her. "Thank you, Maya. You are a brave girl."

Almost sick with fear now, Lauren rushed to the door. If Rickey was holding her in the barn, Kristy's call for help would never be heard. She would be at his mercy. It didn't bear thinking about.

"We'll take the back stairs," Juliana said. "I'll just pop into my room and change my shoes. I'll catch up with you."

It took a second to process that Juliana intended

to go with her. In that dress? Of course. The consummate politician's partner, she would need to keep this unfortunate event under wraps.

But she found Juliana's behavior perplexing, almost bizarre. It was too late, wasn't it? Jordan Raines had been murdered today. The stolen wood from Margot's crime scene had been found and linked to the Brumfields. Any minute now the world would know Juliana's husband not as a candidate for governor, but as the prime suspect in a murder. So why was she acting as if it was just another day of unexpected complications in the campaign and thus something to be handled? Unless she had a far more sinister reason than damage control.

Lauren's thoughts raced. What reaction would a woman like Juliana have if she knew her husband—and her ticket to being Texas's First Lady—was jeopardized by her own goddaughter? Would she be crushed? Or would she be enraged?

Enraged enough to kill her?

The thought was so shocking, so evil that Lauren rejected it instantly. Carter was the killer, wasn't he?

Hurrying, she thought about calling Tucker, but she knew Benton Fox should be on the scene any minute. She could see the barn up ahead now. She couldn't tell if there was livestock inside, but the thought that Rickey might push Kristy into a stall with a horse almost paralyzed her with fear.

"I brought a flashlight," Juliana said, suddenly appearing from behind. She was winded from hurrying, but there was a determined look about her.

Lauren tensed, unsettled by her thought a minute ago as Juliana fell into step beside her.

"This kid had better have a good explanation for causing such a ruckus," she said grimly.

"Are there any horses in the barn?" Lauren asked.

"No. We leased this place for exactly what's happening now," Juliana said, adding bitterly, "It's proved to be a mistake. We should have confined all activities to Houston and Austin."

None of which was of interest to Lauren. "We need to find Kristy."

"Yes, of course." Juliana sent the flashlight beam in a wide arc. "There should be a switch to turn the lights on somewhere. I think we're on a wild-goose chase, Lauren. No kid would be here in the dark."

Maybe, Lauren thought. But she clearly didn't know Rickey.

Not waiting for Juliana to turn on the lights, she walked into the pitch-black interior of the barn and called out, "Rickey, are you in here?" She stood listening, but heard nothing. "Rickey, if you're here, please come out."

Juliana found the switch and the barn was suddenly flooded with light. Lauren blinked a second or two, adjusting to the brightness. As in most barns, stalls were on each side. She counted six. All were latched securely except one. She rushed to it and opened the door.

It was empty. Wheeling about, she began searching every stall. Fear made her fingers clumsy. The thought of Kristy hurt and needing her was terrifying.

"I'm going up to the hayloft," she said.

"I can't imagine that he's up there," Juliana said, unmoved by Lauren's panic.

Ignoring her, Lauren climbed the ladder. Once at the top, she saw nothing but stacks and stacks of baled hay. Then, as she was about to go back down, she heard a slight rustling sound. "Rickey, are you up here?"

Silence.

Fear for Kristy put steel in Lauren's spine. Stepping cautiously, she made her way around several haystacks. Toward the back of the loft, she stopped at a stack that seemed off balance. Peering around it, she found Rickey sitting with his knees tucked against his chest. He met her eyes warily.

"Where is Kristy, Rickey?"

"In that stall where you first looked."

"Come down. Right now." Without waiting to see if he obeyed, Lauren quickly made her way back to the ladder and was down on the floor in seconds. The first stall appeared empty, but as she moved farther inside, her gaze fell on the feeding trough. Approaching, she held her breath and looked down into it.

"Kristy!" she whispered.

The little girl was curled up in a nest of hay, snug as a bug, still wearing the tiny jeans Lauren had dressed her in that morning and her bluebonnet T-shirt.

"Is she all right?" Juliana asked, peering from the stall door.

"I don't know!" With deep dread, Lauren gently touched the child's cheek. And almost fainted with relief. She was fast asleep.

"I didn't hurt her."

Rickey still stood in the hayloft, looking young and defenseless in baggy jeans and a T-shirt with bits of hay clinging to it. His sneakers were untied, the strings dangling. The ears of his MP3 player hung on his neck. On his head was a Houston Astros baseball cap.

"Come down so we can talk, Rickey," Lauren said.

"That was not a request, young man," Juliana snapped. "That was an order."

"I want my dad," he said.

"It's too late to whine for your daddy," Juliana told him. "Get yourself down here. And don't make me tell you twice."

"Or what?" he said sarcastically, showing a flash of the familiar Rickey. "You'll shoot me?"

"Rickey," Lauren said, "you're in big trouble for taking Kristy and locking Elena up in that room. Come down and we'll all go up to the ranch house where you'll be with your parents."

"I'm not the one in big trouble," he said, throwing a hard look at Juliana. "She is."

Juliana propped her hands on her hips. "What is that supposed to mean?"

"I know what you did, Ju-Ju."

For a beat or two, Juliana seemed startled by the boy's sheer audacity. She turned on her heel, clearly intent on leaving. "Pick up that child, Lauren," she ordered, "and come with me. I'll send John out to handle this."

"No, wait, Miss Holloway. I want you to hear this." Rickey scooted down the ladder with the agility of a monkey and landed on his feet. When he turned, Lauren realized he was holding a rifle pointed at the ground.

"Rickey!" she said, shocked.

"I was at Mr. Kane's cabin," he said, giving Juliana a defiant look. "I saw everything."

Juliana glared at him. "Not another word, Rickey. Come, Lauren."

Spellbound and horrified at the drama unfolding before her eyes, Lauren didn't move. Couldn't move.

I know what you did, Ju-Ju.

Lauren wanted to stop him, but he went on, "I heard you and Mr. Raines coming to the cabin on

439

the ATV," Rickey said. "That's why you didn't hear me when I took off on mine. I hid in the woods." He looked at Lauren sheepishly. "Kristy was with me, Miss Holloway. I took her just to scare you and Mr. Kane for getting me in trouble. But she was okay. She didn't cry when I told her we were going to the cabin where her daddy lived and she could ride his horse."

"I think you should stop talking, Rickey," Juliana said, speaking with cool authority. She even managed a thin smile. "I'll send your father out. Don't worry, this can be fixed."

"I saw you take Mr. Kane's rifle out of the rafters," Rickey insisted. "I heard the shot. I told Kristy to stay in the ATV and I went to look. Mr. Raines was dead."

Juliana turned to Lauren and laughed. "See? The babblings of an emotionally disturbed boy," she said. "Haven't you thought so for some time now?"

Suddenly, he raised the rifle and pointed it at Juliana. "This is the rifle," he said. "I saw you put it back in the rafters and I took it. When they check it they'll know."

Lauren's heart stopped. "Rickey—"

"It's loaded. I found bullets in the cabin."

Lauren felt a rush of real horror. She and Kristy were trapped with a troubled boy wielding a loaded rifle and a desperate woman whose privileged life was crumbling.

"Give me the rifle, Rickey," Lauren said, speaking as calmly as she could manage. "Please?"

Juliana snorted with disgust. "Don't you see what he's doing, Lauren? He's trying to make you believe that preposterous story when he said himself he was at the cabin. He's been running wild on that ATV with a gun ever since he got here. He killed poor Jordan Raines and he almost killed Tucker. This kid has had a taste of killing and now it's caught up with him. Isn't that right, Rickey?"

He looked at Lauren. "That's not true! She's lying, Miss Holloway. I didn't do any of that."

"I know, Rickey," she said gently. "I believe you. But please give me the rifle. We'll go straight to the house and you can see your father."

He hesitated, keeping a wary eye on Juliana. Lauren prayed he wouldn't take too long to decide. But she could see that he was considering giving over. A tense moment passed, and then, to her profound relief, he moved to hand her the rifle. What happened next was so sudden that Lauren was taken utterly by surprise. Juliana lunged and with a hard jerk yanked the rifle out of Rickey's hands. Childlike, he turned to run, but Juliana was quicker. She caught the sleeve of his T-shirt and stopped him. Raising the rifle, she brought the barrel down hard on the boy's shoulder. He cried out and fell to the ground writhing with pain.

Shocked, Lauren moved to help him.

"Stay where you are!" Snarling, Juliana now pointed the rifle at Lauren. "Move away from him. Move!"

Lauren hastily rose, lifting her hands, palms out. "Juliana, think what you're doing. Let me help him. He's a child."

"He was ready to shoot us, Lauren." She spat out an angry curse. "And now we're all in a pickle."

Lauren's mind raced. "Juliana. Listen to me. Your husband is a killer. He murdered Margot. Sheriff Fox is probably at the house questioning him right now."

Juliana gave a contemptuous laugh. "Benton Fox is a backwoods hick. Carter will make mincemeat out of him if he tries to arrest him."

"And you'll want to be there for him. So let's go to the house, but first, please give me the rifle."

Juliana didn't move. With the rifle pointed at Lauren, she said, "You have been such a royal pain."

Taken aback, Lauren looked at her. "What?"

"Why didn't you heed my warnings?"

"Warnings?"

"I tried to stop you—"

"Stop me?"

"You and Tucker Kane," she said in disgust. "Between the two of you, I don't know which is more trouble. Now I've got to figure out what to do with you."

Lauren studied Juliana's face, trying to decide if there was a chance she'd listen to reason. She spoke quietly. "You could do the right thing, Juliana, and let me take these two children up to the house."

Juliana shook her head, hitching her chin toward Rickey. "Get him up."

"Think, Juliana. You were seen leaving the house. If something happens to us, how will you explain it?"

"I'll think of something," she said, unfazed. "We're going to the outbuilding where the ATVs are parked."

Lauren tried again. "You can't be thinking to get on one of those things now. It's dark. They're dangerous even in daylight."

"Don't argue. I said get him on his feet."

With no other option, Lauren bent and gently slipped an arm under Rickey to help him up. If the blow to his shoulder had broken a bone, moving him could cause more damage. As carefully as she knew how, she helped him stand. He cried out with pain. "Ow! My shoulder. It hurts." He began to cry. "I want my d-dad."

"Too bad," Juliana said cruelly, gesturing forward with the rifle. "Now, both of you. Out. And don't try anything. I know how to use this."

37

Tucker was pacing outside the ranch house when Benton Fox pulled up in an unmarked vehicle. He got out and, moving with his usual ambling gait, signaled the driver of a second fully outfitted cruiser where to park. Unlike Fox's wheels, the deputies' had the word SHERIFF printed large on the side. Blue lights on top flashed, throwing garish light into the night. Even after they got out, the deputies made no move to kill them. Which made a stir inside the house. Tucker saw people at the windows gawking. A fitting end to Brumfield's ambitions, he thought.

Fox pushed his big hat back and studied the house and the lay of the land. "Where is Ms. Holloway?"

"Somewhere inside," Tucker said, rubbing at pain throbbing in his temple. "She went in to get Kristy. We thought Brumfield might grandstand if he saw me."

Fox nodded. "And how long ago was that?"

"Fifteen, twenty minutes."

Fox started toward the front steps. "Let's see if we can find out what's happening."

Just then John Armstrong came out of the house, striding down the steps and making his way quickly to them. "Is this necessary, Sheriff? You can see we have an important campaign event going." He sent a quick, searing look at Tucker.

"Your daughter's in the barn. Lauren went to get her."

Tucker's gaze shifted to the barn. He could see lights, but no movement.

"I apologize for my son's behavior," Armstrong said. "It was reprehensible, what he did. You can be assured he will be punished." He stopped short as Benton Fox started toward the front door. "Sheriff! Wait. Don't—"

"Don't what?" Fox gave him a look that had sent lesser men to their knees.

Armstrong swallowed hard, wringing his hands in dismay. "Think of the impression it will make if you go inside, Sheriff. Carter had nothing to do with my son's actions. He needs this event to go well."

"I bet he does," Fox said without changing his pace. "A man has been murdered, Mr. Armstrong. He was a guest here at Blue Hills. I have a few questions for you people."

Shocked into speechlessness, Armstrong was left watching impotently as Fox and Tucker headed for the entrance of the ranch house.

"What's your plan, Sheriff?" Tucker asked. "I get it that you'd like to confront Brumfield about Raines's murder, but I'm here to get Kristy."

"My plan is to do both, Mr. Kane."

"Wait," Tucker said, reaching for the cell phone at his belt. "It's Lauren." He answered. "Yeah, where are you?"

"I have Kristy," she said in a dead calm voice. "She's okay. See you in a few minutes."

Tucker breathed a prayer, profoundly relieved. For two seconds. "What—" He stopped when he realized the call was ended. She'd hung up.

"That was quick," Fox said.

"Yeah. Kristy's okay. Lauren's bringing her up to the house now." It had to have been stress making her sound . . . unlike herself. Shaking it off, he decided he was looking for trouble in the wrong places. At least Kristy was safe.

As they climbed the front steps, the security guard Lauren had talked to earlier snapped to attention. Fox, recognizing him, gave a grunt of greeting. "How's it going, Archie?"

"Good, Sheriff Fox, good." His expression was a mix of fear and awe. He reached for the elaborate door handle and opened the door.

Stepping aside and standing ramrod straight, he let them in. Fox removed his hat and took a minute to survey the crowd from the foyer. There was no mistaking Fox was on a mission. Even without the star pinned on his shirt, he would have looked intimidating. An electric hush fell over the crowd. Brumfield, who'd been deep in conversation with a handsome couple, looked up. Frowning in annoyance, he began to thread his way across the room, ignoring whispers and curious looks.

By the time he reached Sheriff Fox, Brumfield

was openly outraged. "What is the meaning of this?" he demanded, ignoring Tucker. "Who are you? What do you want?"

"Sheriff Benton Fox, Mr. Brumfield," he said. "I'd like a word with you." He glanced beyond Brumfield's shoulder to the glittering crowd. "You might want to take this to a more private place."

Frustration aside, Brumfield knew better than to make a scene at a fund-raiser. He gave a brief nod. "This way," he snapped.

"Wait," Tucker said, causing Brumfield to check his stride. "Tell John Armstrong to come and get me when my daughter gets here."

Forced to acknowledge Tucker, he said coldly, "Your daughter? Kristy? What does she have to do with this?"

"Kristy has been kidnapped," he said. "By Armstrong's son. He brought her here to Blue Hills."

Brumfield gave a start of genuine bafflement. "Is that what this is about?"

"That and more," Sheriff Fox said. "We can talk here or . . ."

Huffing with aggravation, Brumfield stalked off toward a room that was closed off to the partying crowd. Once they were inside, he strode to an enormous desk and sat down. He shot a cuff back and made a big thing of looking at his watch. "You have three minutes."

"You were going to call John Armstrong," Tucker prompted.

Extremely irritated, Brumfield fished a cell phone out of his pocket and called a number. "John. When the Kane girl comes in, bring her to the office."

He broke the connection and released a frustrated sigh. "What next?"

Fox took a seat, crossed his long legs, and fixed his hat on one knee. "What can you tell me about Jordan Raines?"

Brumfield hesitated. "Other than that he was found murdered today? Very little. Jordan was a valued member of my team. We had a moment of respectful silence in his honor."

Fox nodded solemnly. "So where were you this morning, Mr. Brumfield?"

"Excuse me?"

Fox gave him a straight look. "I thought I was pretty plain. I want to know where you were when Jordan Raines was murdered."

"Are you insane? Can you seriously be thinking I had anything to do with murdering my own staff person?"

"I can, Mr. Brumfield. And while you're busy coming up with how I'm wrong, you might want to convince me you didn't kill Margot Kane, too."

Stunned into absolute speechlessness, Brumfield could only stare at him.

Tucker had not taken a seat. Now, standing with his back to a window, he said quietly, "I found the wood, Brumfield."

"Wood? What wood?" Looking confused, Brumfield tried visibly to gather his wits. He stood up. "I don't know what's happening here, but I don't have to put it up with it. I—"

"The paneling that you removed from the crime scene after you killed Margot," Tucker said. "The wood you claimed never existed so your flunkies at Homicide could frame me. The wood you used in your house in La Grange."

"This is absurd." He looked at Benton Fox. "Has Kane put you up to this? He's concocted a slick scheme to throw suspicion off himself. I don't know anything about any wood. And I certainly don't know anything about Margot's murder. Why, she was almost family. My wife was—"

"Family?" Tucker repeated angrily. "In what sense, Brumfield? You and Margot were having an affair. Kind of a sick family, isn't it?"

Brumfield was clearly shocked. His gaze fell when it met the accusation in Tucker's eyes. Now sickly pale, he dropped into his chair. Using both hands, he rubbed his face. "This is crazy. This can't be happening."

"You're denying it?" Putting his palms flat on the desk, Tucker leaned forward in Brumfield's face. "You weren't sleeping with my wife before we divorced? You didn't keep it going until it became inconvenient and a threat to your campaign? And when you realized you had to break it off and Margot got stubborn, you didn't kill her? Do I have it all wrong, Brumfield?"

"I can't believe this," Brumfield breathed weakly. He sat for a minute, head down, before finally raising his eyes to Tucker. "How long have you known? Do you realize what this means?"

"It means you won't be the next governor of Texas, Brumfield. It means you'll be in jail for murder."

Shaking his head, Brumfield said, "No, no, you have it all wrong. I admit I tried to break it off, but Margot—" He pulled a handkerchief from his pocket and wiped his forehead. "Well, you know how she was. She said she'd end it when she was ready, not before. But this—" He stopped, frowned. "You mentioned the wood. What was that about?"

Tucker straightened, puzzled by Brumfield's demeanor. If he was bluffing, he was a superb actor. Was it possible he wasn't the killer? "Given the time frame, the wood at the crime scene had to have been moved by the person who killed Margot," he said. "I found it in your former house in La Grange. It's a rare mahogany. It's traceable, Brumfield. The present owner has papers documenting its origin."

Brumfield waved a vague hand, still thinking. "Juliana would know about that. She was the one who renovated that house. She and Jordan got the wood." Suddenly he looked directly at Sheriff Fox. "You don't think—"

450

"Was Juliana aware of your affair?" Tucker asked.

"Yes. She found out. She was . . . upset. Mostly about the scandal and how it would affect the campaign."

"I bet." Tucker almost laughed. "So how upset was she?"

"What do you mean?"

"When Margot blackmailed you about ending the affair, was Juliana upset enough to kill her?"

Brumfield looked around as if he'd found himself in a strange place. He rose to his feet, a bit unsteady. "This conversation is over. I have guests."

But Tucker was on a roll. He shot Benton Fox a triumphant look. "She got Jordan Raines to help her. She'd need somebody strong to move the wood. That would explain why she killed him. He was the only person who knew she was the killer."

"She wouldn't do that," Brumfield said, now pleading earnestly. Needing them to understand. "Jordan is her nephew. She helped him with his career at the newspaper. She's the reason I hired him as PR man for the campaign. They were close. She wouldn't hurt Jordan."

"Like she wouldn't hurt her own godchild?"

Brumfield put his face in his hands. Benton Fox stood up. "Where is your wife now, Mr. Brumfield?"

"I . . . I'm not sure. Somewhere among the guests, I think."

"Let's go." Fox moved to the door. "You'll need to point her out to me." He paused, waiting. Brumfield rose slowly, moving from behind his desk as if he'd aged twenty years in the past twenty minutes.

Tucker followed, looking at his watch. "Lauren should be back with Kristy," he said. "What happened to Armstrong?"

"Here he comes," Fox said, pointing to Armstrong, who was heading toward them. Disheveled and breathing hard, his first words were for Tucker.

"I went out to the barn," he said, rushing his words. "Nobody's there. I even climbed up in the hayloft. There's no sign of them anywhere."

Before he was done, Tucker had his cell phone out calling Lauren's number. The call went instantly to voice mail. "Lauren, where are you? Call me. Now."

Hearing that, the sheriff turned and addressed Brumfield. "You're in a world of trouble, Mr. Brumfield. I'm not putting you in handcuffs, but one of my deputies will be watching you. If I come back and find you gone, Texas won't be big enough for you to hide."

Armstrong was beside himself, pacing. Sweat trickled down his brow. "I don't know what could have happened. Juliana knows she's needed here."

"Juliana?" Tucker gave him a stunned look.

"Yes, she went with Lauren to the barn. She should—"

Fear sliced through Tucker's belly like sharp ice. Seeing his face, Fox clapped a big hand on Tucker's shoulder. "Don't panic. They can't be too far."

Tucker was scowling as he looked up into the night sky, remembering a message that had sent him into hiding.

Butt out. Or I'll take Lauren and Kristy.

38

"Good girl. Now give me that phone. I don't want you sneaking any messages to Tucker."

With a loaded rifle pointed at her, Lauren had no choice but to hand over her cell phone. They'd left Kristy asleep in the barn. Her best hope now was that when she didn't show up with Kristy, Tucker would come looking for them.

But how long would that be? And how would he find them? Juliana had taken them to an outbuilding, a kind of garage for the ranch vehicles. Looking at her seated on a tractor cradling a rifle in her designer dress and wearing a small fortune in jewelry, Lauren had an odd feeling that she'd somehow landed in the Twilight Zone.

"Rickey is in pain, Juliana," Lauren said, hoping to distract her. "I need to make a sling for his arm. You're okay with that, aren't you?"

Juliana shrugged. "If it'll stop his sniveling so I can think, do it."

Lauren looked around for something—anything—to do the job. Various tools lay around. She made a pretense of searching. Maybe there was something she could use as a weapon. . . .

"This will work," she said, picking up a man's T-shirt that lay on the seat of a riding mower. Catching it at the neck, she ripped it all the way to the hem to give enough length to tie a knot. "Here, Rickey. Let's get that arm immobilized." He had stopped crying, but he was trembling, and he was still so pale that she worried that he was in shock. She arranged the shirt into a makeshift sling and slipped it over his head, then gently placed his arm in it. "There, that ought to do it. How does it feel?"

"It's a lot better," he said. "I'm sorry I got us in this mess, Miss Holloway."

"I know, Rickey." She gave him an encouraging hug. To her amazement, she felt a cell phone in his pocket! She looked him in the eye and saw that he knew she had found it. "But we're going to be okay, don't worry."

"Stop talking, you two. I'm thinking. And you, Lauren, sit on that stool where I can keep an eye on you."

"Mrs. Brumfield, if you'll let us go," Rickey said earnestly, "I won't tell anybody what I saw at the cabin."

454

"Oooh, I'm Mrs. Brumfield now, am I? What happened to Ju-Ju? A minute ago we were on a first-name basis."

"I'm sorry," he said. "That was rude. I won't ever do it again."

"Too late, kiddo. You were pretty cocky when you had the gun." She gave a cackle. "Now I have the gun so I give the orders." Her tone hardened. "Now shut up and let me think. I need to figure out what to do."

"I need to go to the bathroom," Rickey said suddenly. "Really bad."

Juliana huffed with irritation. She waved an imperious hand toward a dim corner of the garage. "Go over there and do it."

"On the floor?" he said, wide-eyed.

"It won't matter. And don't leave my sight."

"Can I turn around?"

"Please. I don't want to see it."

"Yes, ma'am. Thank you."

"So polite now," Juliana muttered sarcastically as he headed to the corner. "If I didn't know better, I'd think the kid had a personality transplant."

Lauren wondered if she could distract Juliana so that Rickey might be able to use his cell phone. "Juliana, please put the rifle down. Any minute the ranch will be crawling with people looking for us. If you're found holding us hostage, you will be in serious trouble."

"Don't you think I'm aware of that? I have to arrange it so that when they find you it'll be too late."

Too late? What did that mean? Feeling deep dread, she sent a fearful look at Rickey, his back to them in classic male stance. How was she going to protect him? But as she watched, her eyes narrowed. Something about him . . .

"Rickey!" Juliana called. "What's taking so long? Get over here."

"I'm hurrying, but I only got one hand, Mrs. Brumfield." Still he did not turn.

Juliana rolled her eyes and clicked her tongue. "That kid has messed up everything, but I think I've come up with a solution." Casually using the rifle as a pointer, she leveled it at Lauren. "He'll kill you with the rifle and when I struggle with him to save you, it will go off and . . . well, he was a troubled kid." She nodded as if having solved a difficult problem. "That'll work, I think."

Lauren stared at her in horror.

"What?" Juliana said impatiently. "You think nothing's changed and we'll just walk out of this place and go back to the party? You're the one reminding me about being in serious trouble. My plan fixes that."

The woman was certifiably insane. As panic clawed at her throat, Lauren struggled to calm herself enough to think. "Juliana," she said, using

456

a tone that worked with kindergartners, "you still have your life in front of you. It's Carter who messed up, not you."

"He messed up all right, when he got the hots for that little witch Margot," she said venomously.

Relieved that she'd hit on a subject that appeared to distract Juliana, she said, "You knew about Margot . . . when?"

"When she got pregnant." Her lips thinned with disgust.

Lauren's thoughts went racing around in her head, mixing with Evelyn's suspicions and Tucker's doubts. And finally everything settled into a single horrible possibility.

"Are you saying that Carter Brumfield is Kristy's father?"

"She *bragged* about it!"

But that didn't mean it was true, Lauren wanted to say. "What was Carter's reaction when you found out?"

"You mean when I reminded him that our plans were down the toilet if he didn't break it off with Margot? My goddaughter, of all people," she said bitterly. "Think of the scandal. Of course, like any man caught with his pants down, he promised to end it."

"And did he?"

"End it? No, not then. It was when she got pregnant again, the one that ended in a miscarriage."

Lauren was almost dizzy, putting it together. "So you tried to make Evelyn believe it was Tucker who hurt Margot when all along it was Carter? He was the one who threw her against the wall?"

"It was all an unholy mess. You just don't know what motivates men to do the crazy things they do, isn't that right?"

Lauren stared at her.

Juliana sighed deeply. "But when it got so complicated, I think Carter tried to end it. But she—" Her eyes narrowed with fresh rage. "Margot said she'd go public."

"Is that what Carter told you?"

"I know what you're thinking. Cheating husband tells wife he'll end the affair while he's making it with her every chance he gets. So I went to Margot myself and tried to persuade her to stop. Fat chance. She loved being in the catbird seat. I tried reasoning. I tried bargaining. I pleaded with her. Nothing worked. She didn't need money, she didn't need clothes or jewelry. She didn't need social cachet or the promise of a cushy position when Carter was governor. She didn't need anything. What she wanted was my husband."

Watching her flushed face and flashing eyes, it seemed to Lauren that her hatred of Margot might choke her. Almost holding her breath, she knew she had to ask the hard question. "So she had the baby and told Tucker it was his child?"

"Yes!" Juliana literally spat the word. "That's

why she wanted custody. It was like a sword she held over his head."

Lauren felt crushing disappointment. She hadn't wanted to believe Kristy wasn't Tucker's. But she was, a voice inside whispered. As he'd said when she first told him, Kristy was the child of his heart. Her DNA didn't matter. "You didn't find it difficult to pretend in front of Martin and Evelyn? Your best friend? You must have wanted to retaliate." Spellbound, Lauren tried to imagine the melodrama.

"If Carter's infidelity got out—not to mention his having fathered an illegitimate child," she said bitterly, "it would have been the end. No, there was only one answer. She had to die."

Chilling words. Shocking words. Lauren's thoughts raced madly. How had they not seen Juliana's motive in all of this? With her nerves screaming panic, she looked around wildly for a way for her and Rickey to escape as Juliana climbed down from the tractor.

"Yes, Margot had to die," she said, pointing the rifle at Lauren's heart. "And now so do you."

The crowd took one look at Carter Brumfield as he emerged from the room behind Benton Fox and began scurrying about like rats deserting a sinking ship. Benton Fox quickly ordered Archie to corral the crowd and stand guard to prevent anyone leaving.

"They've got plenty of food and drink in the party room," Fox said. "That ought to keep 'em happy until we find little Kristy and the ladies."

Fear was building inside Tucker. He thought again about Lauren's phone call and the strange way she'd spoken. She knew how worried he was, yet she hadn't taken a minute to put to rest his concerns about Kristy. Now he was afraid he knew why.

"We need to know the layout of the ranch, Sheriff," he said.

John Armstrong stepped forward, looking solemn and shaken. With his son missing, his arrogance had disappeared. "I have the ranch layout in these architectural plans. We got them from the Realtor when we negotiated the lease." He handed them to Tucker. "This is a big ranch. There's a lot of ground to search, especially in the dark."

Tucker quickly unrolled them. "We know they didn't leave in a car. That means they're either on foot or using one of the ATVs. We can check that easy enough. Where are the ATVs parked?"

"A good distance from the barn. I'll take you there."

"Does Rickey have a cell phone?" Tucker asked.

"Yes. I've tried to call him several times, but all I get is voice mail. That's got to be a first. He's constantly on it."

"Juliana probably took it from him," Tucker said.

Armstrong looked shaken, as if he hadn't thought of that.

Tucker turned to Benton Fox. "I'll need a weapon, Sheriff. I don't want to have to shoot anybody, but I'll do what I need to do when I find my girls."

"Hold up a minute," Armstrong said. "There're several guns in the house. I'll be right back."

"No, Mr. Armstrong," Fox said, stopping him. "Stay here. We have weapons. Your job is to lead us to that ATV shed." With his rifle resting on his shoulder, the sheriff adjusted his big Stetson. "No offense, but it just wouldn't look right for a man in a tux to be shootin' at anything."

Armstrong nodded. "Yes, whatever you say. But just so you know, there's extra ammo in the house. If we . . . if you need it."

"I appreciate that, Mr. Armstrong."

As they moved out of the vicinity of the house, Armstrong was in the lead.

"I hope you don't have to shoot anybody, but I'm sure mad enough to watch you and be glad. Eight years of hard work and planning ended in disaster tonight. Carter was going to be the next governor of Texas."

"Maybe you should have looked a little closer at his personal life," Tucker said grimly.

The sheriff cleared his throat. "I guess there's blame enough to go around when we start peeling off the layers of this onion. But right now our goal is to find Tucker's baby girl and Ms. Holloway."

"Let's get going," Tucker said. As much as he'd enjoy piling on Armstrong, there would be time enough to take his pound of flesh after he found Kristy and Lauren.

Please, God, don't let them be hurt.

They set out on foot, Armstrong still in the lead, since he knew the lay of the land. The barn was an easy two-minute walk. Knowing it had been searched, they passed it and veered off on a gravel road that ran alongside it. Tucker had a bad feeling. The night was pitch-black. They didn't have a clue where the two people he loved more than life itself were. Blue Hills Ranch was a huge spread. They would have to search every shed, every cabin, every outbuilding. And there was no guarantee his girls would be in any of them. For all he knew, they could be headed to Mexico.

"There's the garage," Armstrong said suddenly. "Up ahead."

They were still a way out when an electronic signal sounded from a cell phone. "It's mine," Armstrong said with annoyance, reaching into his jacket. "A text. It's probably campaign business. Word is spreading. I need to—" He stopped. "Wait. It's from Rickey." He scanned it quickly and, with a thin cry, stopped dead in his tracks, staring at the phone in his hands

"What?" Tucker took it from him and read it.

Dad help. Ju-Ju has gun 2 kill me & Ms H. We R N equip shed.

• • •

"Get over here, Rickey!" Juliana ordered. She held the rifle steady on Lauren as Rickey picked his way through several machines on his way back. His left arm was stabilized in the sling. His right hand was shoved deep in the pocket of his cargo pants. He should have appeared frightened, but instead he looked almost . . . cocky.

"Guess what?" he said.

Juliana laughed shortly, as if amused by his bravado. "Make it good, kiddo."

"I lied when I said the rifle was loaded. It isn't."

Lauren didn't know whether he was telling the truth or bluffing, and neither did Juliana, judging by the look on her face. It might have been funny if the circumstances hadn't been so unfunny. But as long as she focused on him, Lauren had a chance . . .

Snarling at the boy, Juliana said, "There's one way to see if you're lying, you little sack of spit." She pointed the rifle at him and released the safety.

"Okay, okay," Rickey said, holding up his good hand. "That was a lie. It is loaded. Don't shoot."

"That was very stupid, kid," Juliana said. "Now I see what your daddy means when he says you keep the whole house in turmoil. There probably won't be much crying at your funeral. They'll be relieved to get rid of you."

Lauren was appalled. "Juliana, he's only a boy. Please don't do this."

"You don't have to take up for me, Miss Holloway," Rickey said. "We're gonna get out of this."

Juliana smiled evilly. "Oh, really?"

"Yeah, because there's something else you need to know," he said, keeping a safe distance. He pulled his cell phone from his cargo pants and waggled it at her. "I didn't have to go to the bathroom. I was texting my dad. I bet he's outside right now and not alone. There'll be a bunch of people with him."

With a screech of rage, Juliana charged at Rickey, wielding the rifle as a club. It was the chance Lauren had waited for. She scooped up a heavy wrench she'd hidden at her feet and swung it with all her might. As she connected with a sickening crunch of bone on Juliana's shoulder, the rifle went off with a deafening blast. Rickey fell to the floor.

With a keening cry, Lauren tossed the tool aside and rushed to him, barely aware of the door being kicked in and Tucker bursting in wild-eyed. Benton Fox, behind him, bellowed, "Hold fire! Hold fire!"

"Rickcy, Rickey . . ." Moaning his name, Lauren was on her knees beside him, distraught. He lay curled in a fetal position, his uninjured arm protecting his head. As she began to move her hands over him searching for a wound, John Armstrong appeared and fell to his knees on the other side of his son.

"I'm okay, Dad," Rickey said, warily lowering his good arm to get a look at Juliana. "Is she dead?"

Grim-faced, Tucker checked her pulse. "She's out, but not dead."

Juliana lay on the floor, a pitiful heap in her designer gown and expensive jewelry, her right arm twisted at a grotesque angle. Her face was pale, her makeup giving her a macabre look.

"She must have hit her head when she fell," Lauren said.

Sheriff Fox studied Juliana, then looked up. "I've called for an ambulance," he said, then shifted his gaze to Rickey. "Looks like you need a doctor, too, son."

"He may have a broken collarbone," Lauren said. "Juliana hit him with the rifle."

"She was gonna shoot us," Rickey said, wincing a little as his father inspected his shoulder. "She planned to kill Miss Holloway first and say I did it and when she tried to get the gun away from me it accidentally went off and killed me. She was gonna blame me for killing Mr. Raines because I had the rifle. She is real crazy."

"I need to sit down," John Armstrong said weakly.

"Here, Dad." Using his foot, Rickey shoved a stool over.

"You were very brave, Rickey," Lauren said, still shaky. Her legs felt a bit unsteady and she wondered if she had any more color in her face than Juliana. "You should be proud of him, John."

"I was so scared that I wasn't thinking real good, Miss Holloway," Rickey said. "When you gave me that funny look I knew you wanted me to text my dad to get help. Only thing I could think of was to say I had to go to the bathroom so I could text."

"Smart thinking," she said, smiling at him.

Tucker drew Lauren into his arms. She could feel tremors in him and her heart melted. When he found his voice, it was rough, edgy with dread. "Where is my Kristy? I thought she would be with you."

"She's fine." Lauren framed his face in her hands. "She's in the barn asleep in a manger."

"I didn't hurt her, Mr. Kane."

The breath went out of Tucker in a rush of profound gladness. He closed his eyes. "Thank God."

39

"Come with me, Mrs. Kane. I have a surprise for you."

Lauren's heart melted hearing Tucker say her new name. Smiling, she gave him her hand and let him help her out of the car. They were supposed to be on their way to the airport for their honeymoon, but he had insisted on stopping here first.

"This had better be good, because our flight leaves at nine-fifty." Lauren glanced at her watch. "What if we get caught in traffic on the interstate?"

He shrugged, grinning. "I guess we'd have to go back to the condo and think of something to do until we can schedule another flight . . . tomorrow . . . or the next day. Or the next."

Lauren felt a warm flush at the memory of their first night as man and wife. It had been everything she'd dreamed it would be. She did not know there was so much happiness to be found in the world. She felt so *blessed!*

She gave him a soft punch on his arm. "You'd like that, wouldn't you?"

"Well, I've seen Hawaii."

"But I haven't. And I do not want to miss that flight."

He grabbed her hand and kissed it. "We won't miss it, darlin'. I'll get you to the airport on time. But there's something I want to show you before we take off."

Taking her hand, he helped her walk a series of planks leading from the street to what looked to be a house under construction. Lumber was stacked alongside a recently poured concrete foundation. Joists for the roof and walls were in place. Lauren took a breath, inhaling the smell of new wood as she looked up at him. He was smiling at her.

"What is this, Tucker?"

"Well, nothing much . . . right now. But in about three months, it'll be our new home." He waggled his eyebrows.

She put her hand over her heart. "Our home?"

"Uh-huh." He caught her hand and pulled her over to a makeshift table where a roll of architectural plans was spread out. "Take a look, darlin'."

Her heart aching with joy, she scanned an artist's rendition of the elevation. It was their original house plans, the plans she'd spent hours poring over before everything turned so dark. Seeing it now being built was a thrill. "It's perfect, Tucker. It's wonderful."

"You like it?"

She turned and threw her arms around his neck. "I love it!" She pulled his face down and kissed him. "Thank you, my darling."

They stood swaying a little, saying nothing, savoring the joy of having found each other, of having overcome incredible odds to be at this place . . . at this time.

"We are so incredibly blessed, Tucker," she said, resting her head on his heart.

"Yeah. It was dicey there for a while. A long while. When I was hiding in the lodge, sometimes I'd wake up in the middle of the night in a cold sweat. It wasn't from fear that I would be caught and arrested for a crime I didn't commit." He pulled back so he could see her face. "It was because I was afraid I would lose you."

"We were meant to be together, Tucker. You were the one person God meant to be my husband. I'm more convinced of that than ever now. I don't know why I had to experience long months of uncertainty when you disappeared. I don't understand why you had to suffer the injustice of being accused of murder. But bad or sad or tragic things do happen to people. God doesn't promise that won't happen. His promise is to help us get through it. I believe we're both better persons now because of it."

With his arms around her, his wife, Tucker felt an overwhelming gladness, a profound gratitude. "Do I think I'm a better man for going through this? Yeah, I do. I didn't feel that way when it was happening, but I am different. I feel God's presence in my life today in a way I never did before. I was a pretty lukewarm Christian before I got in trouble. And the worse it got, the further I drifted from my faith."

He leaned back so he could see her face. "But all that changed when I was unconscious out in that pasture. I know now that I was spared for a purpose."

She lovingly traced the line of his chin with her finger. "Do you know what that purpose is now?"

He was shaking his head before she was done. "No, but it's my plan to live my life finding it."

She said nothing, just smiled at him.

"Okay, let's go," he said. Turning, he caught her hand and they headed for the car. "We have a plane to catch."

Acknowledgments

I owe thanks to many people, without whom writing this book would have been a lot more difficult. To Jeanette Davenport, precious childhood friend, whose prayers and support encourage and amaze me. To friends in Special Topics Sunday School class: Donna Vanderweide, Alice Kagy, Karen Wimberley, Gayle Smith, and Maureen Bybee. Thank you for your loyalty and for understanding the agony of being on deadline. To Sergeant Cathy Richards of the Houston Police Department for technical advice. Any errors are my own. To my brainstorming group, Emilie, Jasmine, Connie, and Diane. You are the best! To Debbie Macomber, my eternal thanks. To Rachel Hauck, thank heaven you are so skilled at making notes on that laptop. To Polly Young, my sister-in-law, who is loving and helpful. To Alison, my incredible publicist. You do it so well, Ali. Thanks to Jen for taking charge of the mailing list. And finally, to Traci DePree. You are one incredible editor, and Becky Nesbitt was right on in thinking we'd click.

Lie for Me
Reader's Group Guide

1. Is it ever morally right to lie? Is there a difference between a big lie and the little white lies most everyone tells at some point? Can you think of instances in the Bible when people lied (with God's blessing)?

2. Did it diminish Tucker's character, in your opinion, that he asked Lauren to give him an alibi when it was a lie?

3. Lauren stayed fiercely loyal to Tucker through thick and thin. Most of us have not experienced a murder so close to home. How do you think you would have reacted if someone close to you were accused of murder?

4. Do you think Tucker did the right thing by disappearing without a trace and leaving Lauren to think he really was guilty? How do you react when people falsely accuse you?

5. From the start, the police concentrated on Tucker as the prime suspect. What could he have done to change that?

6. What strengths do you think you could call upon to help you cope with such a situation? Faith? Friends? Family support?

7. Have you observed behavior by the police or the media that gave you concern for a person you believed might be innocent?

8. What do you think about Lauren's belief in Tucker's innocence? Was she too naïve?

9. How did you feel about the circumstances of Tucker's divorce from Margot?

10. Have you experienced—or observed—anyone caught up in a bitter battle for custody of a child?

Lie for Me
Author Q & A

A CONVERSATION WITH KAREN YOUNG

1. **Did the plot for *Lie for Me* spring from any particular inspiration?**
   I usually come up with a plot from something I've read or seen in the media or something I've observed in my daily life. This plot, however, just came to me as a passing thought. Lying is so complex. Everybody does it, whether little white lies or big whopping lies. And sometimes we think, *I'll just do this because the end justifies the means.* But lying is such an immoral thing, and God found it so abhorrent that it is one of the Ten Commandments.

2. ***Lie for Me* is your third book published under the Howard imprint, and is categorized as Romantic Suspense/ Inspiration. Would you consider this new territory for you, or do you feel that there has always been a Christian element to your fiction?**
   Writing Christian fiction was/is new territory, but having good triumph over evil has always

been a message in my books. It has been joyfully satisfying to add the faith element to my plots. I work hard to make the message in my story resonate with nonbelievers in a way that doesn't turn them off from reading Christian fiction. Sometimes that is a very delicate dance.

3. How would you have reacted if you were in Lauren's shoes? Would you have lied for Tucker? Would you say that lying is *always* wrong?

I mention above that everybody lies at some time or another. When you reply to the question "How are you?" and say "I'm fine," when your head aches or you've had devastatingly tragic news, it's really a lie. I think Lauren's reaction to a question that elevated the act of lying (i.e., making it a criminal offense) was perfectly normal in light of her strong moral character. For someone not so strong morally, maybe the lie is justified, because it keeps an innocent man from being unjustly stigmatized.

4. Is the character of Lauren based on anyone that you have met or read about, or is she entirely fictional? Do you prefer to draw up your plots by channeling reality, or channelling your imagination?

Lauren isn't based on someone I know, but she's a composite of several people. My circle of friends and family is composed of truly moral, faith-based women (and men, of course). So Lauren took shape quite naturally out of my imagination. As for drawing my plots from my imagination, yes, to a certain degree. But I'm pretty well grounded in reality as an individual, so channeling my plots from real events, real emotion, real evil in the world is my strong suit.

5. **What messages or themes from *Lie for Me* do you hope readers will take away with them after they have finished the novel?**
I write popular fiction, and therefore I want my readers to take away a sense of enjoyment of the story. But I also want them to think about the consequences of making decisions on a daily basis and how a wrong decision (such as a lie) can take one's life in an entirely different direction . . . one that may not be desirable or in keeping with God's plan or purpose in one's life.

6. **In an essay on your Author page on SimonandSchuster.com, you mention how you frequently moved. What were some of the places that you lived in? How did**

moving so frequently influence you as a writer?

I'm almost embarrassed to tell how often I moved. I was raised in Mississippi on the Gulf Coast, married and moved to Japan. Next, to Georgia, back to Mississippi, then to Boston, MA, then New Orleans, then Lima, OH, then York, PA, then New Orleans again and Lake Charles, LA, then Wichita, KS, and back to New Orleans and finally to Jackson, MS, where my husband, whom I loved dearly, died. A year later, I moved to Houston, TX, a state in which I always wanted to live. So, yes, all that travel exposed me to different cultures. Culture is not an exaggeration. Just imagine the difference between Gulf Coast Mississippi and Boston, Massachusetts. But it was all grist for my mill, and I happen to be one of those people who can relocate from one state or neighborhood to another without much angst. Looking back, I'm thankful it didn't mark my three daughters in a negative way. But they seem to have been as resilient as I was. However . . . I notice none of them have moved much. ☺

7. **What's the most recent book you read?**
Cutting for Stone by Abraham Verghese. I belong to a book club at my church and, therefore, am compelled to read books I

might never choose if left to my own tastes. It has been enlightening and inspirational to read what my book club chooses.

8. **You are a much decorated author, having won a prestigious RITA award and *Romantic Times* magazine Career Achievement and Reviewer's Choice awards. Are there any accolades that you still covet as a writer?**
Not so much awards, but I would love to be more recognized among readers of Christian/inspirational fiction. I feel so blessed to be in this place at this time, career-wise. So, I hope that in time I will grow as an author so that my books will find a good place in the hearts of CBA readers.

9. **You have a strong presence and following on Facebook and Twitter. How has the popularity of the Internet and social media impacted you as a writer? What is most challenging to you about this new frontier?**
It is time-consuming to keep up with social media, but we authors are expected to "put ourselves out there" in a way that was unheard of just a few years ago. It is also time-consuming to write a book (as you might imagine), then to add the marketing/publicity efforts that are necessary, which

makes for a demanding schedule. Sometimes, I wish simply to hole up in my office with my computer and just write, write, write. That is no longer possible for us authors.

10. **Are you currently working on any projects that we can look forward to in the future?**
I am always working on "the next book." And since I usually have a book out a year, there should be something in 2012. The plot is extremely Southern in tone, but since I am "extremely Southern," too, that should come as no surprise. It is, of course, a mystery.

Center Point Publishing
600 Brooks Road ● PO Box 1
Thorndike ME 04986-0001 USA

(207) 568-3717

US & Canada:
1 800 929-9108
www.centerpointlargeprint.com